PORTRAIT
OF A THIEF

PORTRAIT OF A THIEF

A NOVEL

WITHDRAWN

GRACE D. LI

Tiny Reparations Books

An imprint of Penguin Random House LLC
penguinrandomhouse.com

Copyright © 2022 by Grace Li LLC
Penguin supports copyright. Copyright fuels creativity, encourages diverse voices, promotes free speech, and creates a vibrant culture. Thank you for buying an authorized edition of this book and for complying with copyright laws by not reproducing, scanning, or distributing any part of it in any form without permission. You are supporting writers and allowing Penguin to continue to publish books for every reader.

Tiny Reparations Books and the Tiny Rep Books logo are registered trademarks of Penguin Random House LLC.

LIBRARY OF CONGRESS CATALOGING-IN-PUBLICATION DATA
has been applied for.

ISBN 9780593184738 (hardcover)
ISBN 9780593186077 (ebook)

Printed in the United States of America
3rd Printing

BOOK DESIGN BY LAURA K. CORLESS

This is a work of fiction. Names, characters, places, and incidents either are the product of the author's imagination or are used fictitiously, and any resemblance to actual persons, living or dead, businesses, companies, events, or locales is entirely coincidental.

For my family, here and an ocean away

PORTRAIT
OF A *THIEF*

ACT ONE

Every work of art is an uncommitted crime.

—THEODOR W. ADORNO

1

WILL

"State your name for the record, please."

This was how things began: Boston on the cusp of fall, the Sackler Museum robbed of twenty-three pieces of priceless Chinese art. Even in the museum's back room, dust catching the slant of golden, late-afternoon light, Will could hear the sirens. They sounded like a promise.

"Will Chen."

"And what were you doing at the Sackler Museum, Mr. Chen?"

"I work here part-time. I'm an art history student at Harvard."

"Did you see anything unusual before the theft?"

"No."

"Describe what you saw during the incident. Any distinguishing features of the thieves, anything the security cameras might not have caught."

"It all happened very fast. I looked up from my essay and the alarms were going off. When I ran into the gallery, they were already leaving.

They had on ski masks, black clothes." He hesitated, just for a moment. "I think they were speaking Chinese."

For a moment, the only sound was the scratch of the detective's pen against his notepad. "I see. Do you speak Chinese, Mr. Chen?"

"Yes, I—does it matter? I couldn't really make out what they were saying. The alarms were going off at this point."

"Of course. And do you know what they stole?"

Will thought back to the empty room. If he closed his eyes, he could fit the pieces back where they were supposed to go—a pair of jade tigers, a dragon vase. A jade cup with three crested bronze birds, midflight. "Not really. I've been gone all summer."

The detective slid a sheet of paper across the table. "Can you read the title of this for me?"

It was a printout from the *Harvard Crimson*, from late August. Will swallowed hard. "'What Is Ours Is Not Ours: Chinese Art and Western Imperialism.'"

"Did you write this?"

"Yes."

The detective leaned forward, his fingertips touching. "Tell me if this sounds suspicious to you: A Chinese student writes an article about looted art, and a few weeks later, Harvard's largest collection of Asian art is robbed. All the priceless pieces mentioned in the article—gone."

Will leaned back in his chair. The golden light made everything feel like a painting, and he let his mind drift for a moment, thinking of the paper on Renaissance art that was due next week, the sculpture he still had to finish for his portfolio. "Not particularly."

"And why is that?"

"I was born in the US, Detective . . ." Will looked for a badge, a name.

"Meyers."

"Detective Meyers."

"What is your—"

"I'm Chinese American," Will said, lingering on the *American*. He adjusted the rolled-up cuff of his button-down, imagining how his sister would handle this situation. "You said I was Chinese. But I was born and raised in the US, just like you, and I work part-time at the Sackler, and three weeks ago the *Crimson* published a paper I wrote for an art history class at Harvard. Last time I checked, none of those are crimes. Now, if you'll excuse me, I have homework to do."

"This is procedure, Mr. Chen. I just have a few more questions, if you will—"

Will rose. It might have been a small thing, to be called Chinese instead of Chinese American, to have this detective who spoke in a Boston accent look at him as if this place, this museum, this *art* didn't belong to him, but—it didn't feel like a small thing. Not when he was at Harvard, this place of dreams, and he was so close to everything he had ever wanted.

It was his senior year, and the whole world felt on the verge of cracking open.

"I've told you everything I know," he said, "and I know my rights. Next time you want to accuse me of something, go through my lawyer."

In Eliot House, with his window open to the warm evening air and the distant sound of chatter in the courtyard, Will took a single jade tiger out of his pocket. The stone was cool, almost cold against his skin. It shone in the halfway light, the jade a pale, almost translucent green, with veins of reddish-brown at the tiger's head and tail. Despite the centuries, the edges of the carving were sharp enough to cut.

Jade Tiger (one of a pair), the placard had read. *Date: 3rd century BCE. Culture: Chinese.*

He had one tiger; the thieves had the other. It had been almost too easy to palm it, the glass between him and the art shattered in the theft. He traced a finger along the tiger's curved back, still a little in disbelief. He was sure it was worth hundreds of thousands, but that wasn't the important thing. The important thing was that it had been China's, and then it had been Harvard's, and now it was *his*.

He thought back to the paper he had written for class. *What is ours is not ours.* Who could determine what counted as theft when museums and countries and civilizations saw the spoils of conquest as rightfully earned?

From his coat pocket, a card fluttered to the floor.

Will reached for it, his breath catching in the stillness. For a moment, he was back at the Sackler, listening to the rapid, staccato Chinese of the thieves, their voices a counterpoint to the wail of the alarms. He had pressed himself against the wall, his heart pounding in his ears, and yet one of them had still brushed past him on the way out, so close it could almost be called deliberate.

The business card was a matte black, with the words *CHINA POLY* and an international phone number printed on the front in neat block letters. And below that, in a messy hand:

偷得不错。

Nice lift.

2

ALEX

When Alex Huang closed her eyes, she dreamed of Chinatown: the red lanterns strung along every storefront, the smell of fish markets, the rise and fall of Cantonese as buyers and sellers haggled. It had been three years since she had stood before the whole glazed ducks rotating in the restaurant's windows, flipped the sign from *CLOSED* to *OPEN* each morning at seven a.m. while her parents prepped the kitchen of Yi Hua Lou.

This was how things changed: slowly, and then all at once. An acceptance letter from MIT, a FAFSA form, a bus ride to Boston. Her younger siblings waving to her until she couldn't see them anymore. Holidays spent at school, in libraries or on friends' couches, summer internships on a different coast. A full-time offer from Google her junior fall. *Whenever you're ready*, the recruiter had said, but the sign-on bonus was more than her parents made in a year.

Within a month, Alex had moved to Silicon Valley.

The sun was setting in Mountain View, evening light pooling on her living room floor. Had it really been less than a year? She could still remember stepping off the plane that first day, how the sky had been wide in a way she wasn't used to after years of living in New York City and then in Boston. She had thought, *This is the beginning of the rest of my life.* It had been just a little terrifying. Everything she knew, everyone she loved, left behind on another coast.

And so there was just this: a Friday evening and an empty apartment, to-go containers scattered across the dining table. Her laptop was open, her work for the night still not done—never done, really—but despite its hum, her chewing felt too loud in the stillness. Alex reached for her phone, just for something to do, scrolled through all the tasks still left for tonight, the unread messages in her family WeChat group, and—a missed call from Will Chen.

That last one was the most interesting. *You called?* she texted him.

A moment later, her phone began to ring.

"You are the only person who would rather call than text," she said as a greeting.

"Hey, Alex. Good to hear from you too." Will's voice was low, liquid like honey, and she remembered briefly why she had thought, early on, that there was the possibility of *something.* "How long does it take to hack into a museum's security system?"

Alex cast a glance at her program; it was still running. "You know that being a software engineer isn't the same thing as being a hacker, right?"

"Alex Huang, I didn't think there was anything you couldn't do."

She couldn't help but laugh. Will was playing on her vanity, but—well, he wasn't wrong. Alex opened her personal laptop, sliding her work laptop to the side. There were so many questions she could have asked, but already this was the most interesting thing to happen to her in a long time. She would let it play out. "I suppose it depends on the museum."

"The Sackler? Let me send you the log-in info."

In a few quick keystrokes, she had pulled up the museum intranet. "Sounds familiar."

"Our first date," Will supplied.

Alex laughed. "I should've known we wouldn't work out the instant you suggested we go to an *art museum*." They had met on Tinder, during the brief period when they were both new to college and the dating scene, had gone to the Sackler and then for coffee on an overcast New England afternoon. There had been a couple of dates after that, but nothing else, and after seeing the heartbreak Will tended to leave in his wake, she was relieved neither one of them had wanted more. Still, they had kept in touch after she had moved to California, video chatting on late nights when Will's insomnia kept him up and Alex was afraid the loneliness would eat her alive, comparing younger siblings and the heavy weight of their parents' expectations, the specific traumas of their pasts laid bare as the hours passed. She knew him well enough to know that they would never date again.

The Sackler's video footage loaded on her screen. The museum was aglow, even though it was late on the East Coast, and on the cameras outside the museum, police lights spun red and blue over cobbled streets. She switched to another incognito tab and searched up *harvard sackler museum + news*.

All the headlines told the same story: smashed glass and black ski masks, twenty-three stolen pieces of Chinese art. There had been three eyewitnesses but no leads. She narrowed her eyes at her phone. "Why didn't you tell me there was a robbery?"

"Alex," Will began. There was a catch in his voice.

"Were you there?"

He was silent for a long moment. "That's why I'm calling."

Alex closed her eyes, thinking of the day she had withdrawn from MIT. It had been fall, the leaves just beginning to change color, and the Charles River twisted like silver wire through downtown Boston. It had felt like the beginning of something, like her whole life was unspooling. She had never described the feeling to Will, but she thought maybe he would recognize it. This evening, the Sackler's stolen art—what was this if not change?

A moment later, Alex had pulled up the footage from the night before. She shared her screen with him as she did, and together they watched the theft. Alex knew Will was watching the thieves, the elegance of their movements, the art that disappeared beneath their gloved hands, but she was watching Will. Will as he got up from his desk at the Sackler, as he ran into the other room. Will standing against the wall, his eyes wide behind his glasses and his dark hair tousled, looking for all the world like any other overwhelmed college kid save for the slight movement of his hand, the momentary glint of jade in his palm.

"Will Chen," Alex said, very quietly, "what have you done?"

His voice, too, was soft. "I know, I know. There's more."

So maybe she had been wrong. Maybe Will had been watching her, after all.

The theft was almost over. As they left, one masked figure brushed very close to Will. She zoomed in on the still, but she couldn't tell what the thief was doing, if anything. "A business card," Will said, and her phone lit up with an image. The words were in simplified Chinese, not traditional, but she could read it well enough. "And an invitation."

"Are you going to take it?" Alex rewound to the moment Will stole the artifact, that telltale shine. Her fingers hovered over the keys. It would take very little to erase this footage. A half-second jump between one frame and the next, chalked up to a minor glitch in the system, the fallibility of tech. It was also definitely illegal.

"If I did, would you join me?"

Her work computer chimed. Her program was done running, and there was more to do. There always was. Alex knew she should say no, return to a Friday night programming in her Mountain View apartment, the rest of her days, the rest of her life blurring together in the California sunshine. She had chosen this, after all. A steady paycheck and the slow upward climb to manager, lines of code in Java and Python and all the languages yet to come. It was the safe choice, the responsible one, the kind that she had spent her whole life making.

And yet—

In the cool, indifferent light of her apartment, Alex leaned back, thought of change. Three years ago, stepping onto MIT's campus for the first time. Leaving it behind before she was ready. And now—a museum of stolen art, security footage blinking on her computer.

Will's breathing was soft over the phone, and she remembered, too, that terrible first date, walking through the Sackler and then, afterward, the two of them drinking overpriced coffee and talking of dreams. They'd been freshmen then, still figuring out what it meant to go to the best universities in the country, to have so much possibility at their fingertips, but—it had all seemed within reach. His dreams. Hers. It had been so long since Alex had let herself think about what she wanted, separate from her family and her responsibilities, all that she owed the people in her life.

"Alex?" Will said, and it was a question, an offering, an open door.

In one swift, decisive motion, Alex pressed *delete*. "I'm in."

3

WILL

This late, Harvard was quiet, still, something out of a painting. Will would have done it in slow, sweeping brushstrokes, the sky curving around lamps that shone torch-bright. It was the kind of evening where the impossible felt close enough to touch, to taste. He took a deep, steadying breath.

What was real: the jade tiger in his palm, stolen from the Sackler just hours ago.

What was real: the future carved open.

He had made three calls tonight. The first, to the number on the back of the card, had taken him to an empty dial tone. Moments later, he had received a text message with a link to an Air China reservation under his name for five first-class tickets to Beijing.

The flight was a week from today.

The second call was to his sister. Irene had done all the things that he—skin humming, full of excitement and adrenaline and certainty that he would follow this adventure to its end—had not bothered to do. Over FaceTime, she had looked up the CEO of China Poly, its mission, all the ways it had its fingers in foreign trade. He was not used to uncertainty from her, and yet when she was done, her voice was low, hesitant as she asked, *Are you sure you know what you're getting yourself into?*

The third call had been to Alex. Irene would have warned him to wait, to think this through, but Will had always recognized in Alex all the parts of him he was afraid to look too closely at. She knew as well as he did—maybe better—what it was like to want more from the world than you were meant to have, to know that wanting wasn't always enough. They were both twenty-one by now, would turn twenty-two this year, and the future was so far from what either of them had once thought it would be. Still, with all that had happened today, he could almost believe they were eighteen again, young and ambitious and certain they could remake the world. He had never doubted that she would say yes.

Will cast a glance outside. The sun would rise in a few hours, turning the world harsh and brilliant and new. If it had been any other weekend, he would've been at a finals club party, searching for something, someone, to make him feel, but instead there was a rental car and the long drive ahead of him, Will packing his things as the rest of Harvard slept. He thought back to his sister, asking him for certainty.

I'm sure, he had said. It might have been a lie. Ahead of him loomed job applications, the threat of graduation on the horizon, all that he'd thought he would become by now. And yet—when the Sackler had been robbed today, when the museum's alarms had kept pace with the pounding of his heart, Will hadn't felt fear. Instead there had been a heavy sort of inevitability to it, as if his whole life had brought him here, to a museum of Chinese art and the thieves who took it back.

What was real, if not this?

The fall air felt like a beginning, and Will slung his backpack over his shoulder, slipped his phone in his pocket. His mind went once more to his sister, the sharp, pleased edge to her smile. *Then there's a driver at Duke I think you should meet.*

4

LILY

The night was dark as an oil spill. Lily Wu drummed her fingers along the curve of her steering wheel, waiting for the darkness to change, for her world to change. The air tasted of cigarette smoke and cheap beer, and even with her windows up she could hear the steady thrum of the bass from the speakers that jutted into the Durham night. College students lined both sides of Main Street. Their gazes raked over her red Mustang, the Audi R8 next to her that gleamed a sleek, hungry silver.

Five seconds.

The boy in the Audi rolled down his window. Lily kept her gaze on the light, red and fluorescent in the summer dark. Returning to Duke always felt like stepping into an unfamiliar world, bright and glittering and false. This—the harsh glow of the stoplight, the steady hum of her car beneath her palms—was the only thing that felt real.

Four seconds.

"Winner take all?" he called.

Three seconds.

Lily's foot never left the gas. The window was open, just a crack, and the night air was warm and expectant against her skin.

One second.

"Winner take all," Lily agreed, and then the light changed.

<hr />

It did not feel like it had been three years. Two, Lily supposed, since her junior year had barely begun, Durham cast in that late-summer haze of September. She still remembered the first time she had made the seventeen-hour drive from Galveston, Texas, to Durham, North Carolina. She had been in the driver's seat, as always, and her parents had taken rare time off work to make the trip with her. When they crossed the state line, out of Texas, out of this place she had spent her whole life, Lily had felt something in her open up. College, the future—for once, it did not feel so impossibly far away.

When they reached Durham at last, the sun was setting. The sky was a blur of red and orange and the deep, dark greens of those great Carolina trees. After she and her parents unloaded her suitcases in her new dorm room, they took the bus to West Campus to see the chapel for the first time. Her parents had lingered back, taking pictures of the chapel, the bus stop, their only daughter standing there with her head tilted up, but all Lily could see was the cotton candy sky and the sun against the stone, the way it cut into the sky like possibility.

No more, she had promised herself. No more street racing, no more near-death experiences. No more risk. Not when her parents were paying all they could and more for her education, when she would graduate over 100K in debt regardless. She'd be a good student, and an even better engineer.

It had seemed like an easy promise to make.

And then—a few days later, as she was walking out of Data Structures and Algorithms, she had overheard two white boys talking about the Durham races. *It's worth watching*, one told the other. When she grabbed her car keys, her blood singing, she told herself she was just going to watch.

Even then, it had tasted like a lie.

⸺

Behind her, the Audi was a distant memory. Lily eased up on the gas, just for a moment, letting the other car draw a little closer. Up ahead, the finish line was marked with clean white chalk. She gave him one foot, then two—she wanted this victory to feel *earned*—and then she flew across the finish line, the Audi just a breath behind her.

Two years, and still some things stayed the same. The crowd spilled from the sidewalk to the street, streetlights shining fluorescent against bare skin. This was summer at its best, engine exhaust and the lingering traces of smoke, and Lily tipped her head back and breathed it in, smiling. The other driver was slow to leave his car, slower still to drop his keys in Lily's palm. But he did, and her fingers curled around it, the jagged edges cool and unfamiliar against her thumb.

That night, when the races were over and Durham was quiet once more, Lily went to claim her Audi R8. It shone silver in the darkness, and she thought of midnights in Galveston and the reflection of the moon against the waves, the shimmer of Texas roads under a high sun. She would sell it back to its owner later, do the same thing she always did, but for now she left her Mustang in the parking lot, let herself enjoy the warm evening air, the easy calm of the empty streets.

A stranger was leaning against Lily's new car, his hands tucked into the pockets of his coat, just a little too heavy for early fall in the Carolinas. "Congratulations," he said. There was something familiar about the high arch of his cheekbones, the smile that flitted across his face like a promise. He was the kind of beautiful that made you want to look and keep looking. "I don't think we've met."

Lily tilted her head up to look at him, smiling despite herself. "Actually," she said, "I think we have."

⸺

It had been the easiest thing in the world to let Will Chen slide into the passenger seat of her new Audi, to press her foot on the gas until they were flying down an empty street, the trees casting long, hungry shadows against her sweeping headlights. Lily ran her fingers along the radio dials, the rearview mirror, getting acquainted with this car. Every year there were freshmen who'd learned of the races the same way she had, who'd heard her name and taken it as a challenge. The trick to it, then, was finding the one with the car she wanted most.

And then to wait.

Her own first year, it had been a surprise. Victory had been strange and sweet on her tongue. Two years later, it felt different. Home was that house in Galveston, the ocean air rough against her skin, but sometimes, when she closed her eyes, she dreamed not of the sea but of the lights in Brightleaf Square, strung up like unknown constellations, Durham at night shimmering with possibility.

She glanced at Irene's brother at the stoplight. His dark hair was tousled in a way that had to be deliberate, and the red, fluorescent light glanced off the angles of his face, the clean line of his jaw. He turned his glasses over in his hand, and she imagined the world as he saw it right now, a blur of green and black and flashing, silver lights.

They had met just once before, at orientation her freshman year at Duke. He had been starting his sophomore year at Harvard, had come down to help Irene move in, and Lily vaguely remembered not wanting her parents to meet him. Will, with his Harvard education and perfect, lilting Chinese, was every Asian parent's dream.

Was she so different from the girl she had been? It might have been the years at Duke, sharpening her against them like a knife. There was a time when she would have felt nervous to have him in the car with her, to know he had watched her race with bright eyes and that slow, slow smile. Lily turned the radio down, soft enough that it was just background music, the bass keeping time with her heart. "What brings you to Duke?"

He slid his glasses back on, one corner of his mouth lifting in a wry smile. "Irene thought I should pay her a visit."

"You know she's in New York, right?"

"I do now."

Lily laughed. "This is Irene's world," she said. "The rest of us are just living in it."

To her surprise, Will laughed too, the sound low and endearing. "I won't argue with that." The light changed, and the Audi leapt forward. "You know, when Irene told me her roommate was at the Durham races, I wasn't expecting"—he swept his hand in a vague, meaningless gesture—"this."

"What were you expecting?" Lily asked.

He didn't answer, but she knew it already. Lily was not the kind of girl who raced cars in the dark, who blew through lights, through life, so recklessly. She had spent her whole life trying not to be.

They pulled into Cook Out, the sign glowing fluorescent in the waiting dark, and Lily ordered for them both. Already this night felt like something out of a dream: dipping fries into an ice cream float at two a.m., the distant sound of laughter bubbling up like Cheerwine beneath a North Carolina sky. Lily leaned against the hood of the car, drinking in the starlight, the taste of vanilla on her tongue. Groups of other college students were scattered across the small parking lot, the curb next to the drive-thru line, and Lily tried to imagine what they saw when they looked over: Will, his coat discarded and the sleeves of his button-down rolled up; Lily in jean shorts and a battered T-shirt, her brown hair tangled from years of salt air. A new car between them. She didn't know Will, not really, and yet it was easy enough to be here with him, the Durham night soft and full of some yet-unknown promise. "So you're an artist," she said, and though she hadn't meant it as a question, it came out as one.

He hesitated for a moment. "I'm an art history student. There's a difference."

"It doesn't sound that different to me," she said. If it had been elsewhere, she would have made a joke about the humanities. But somehow, beneath the moon and the neon lights, Will's face cast in stark relief—it didn't feel quite right.

"I study history," he said. "I don't make it."

It sounded like a lie. There was something in the brightness of his eyes, the hint of a smile on his lips, that told her he knew it too. She thought for a moment of how many hours the drive would have taken from Boston to Durham. His sister was elsewhere, and yet Will had come anyway, waited for her in the shimmering night. "Why did you come here, really?" Lily asked. It was that strange halfway time between summer and fall, and Durham hummed with change. Irene was in New York still, interviewing with some consulting firm she hated, both of them playing their parts of what was expected of their junior year.

Will tilted his head up. "Tell me how it started," he said.

"The racing?" Lily asked.

"Everything."

He was changing the subject, she knew. She found she didn't quite mind. When was the last time she had been asked something like this? Had she ever? "I grew up in a small town by the sea," she began, and she was back home, the evening stretching slow as saltwater taffy, lights glancing off distant water. In the end, every child of immigrants had the same story. "At first, it felt like running away."

There was just one main bridge over the island, white and scalloped and open to the sea. Every time she had driven over it, she had dreamed of never turning back. What was at home? The weight of her parents' dreams, the judgment of that small town. The looming shape of her future, pressing down on her more with each passing year. Her parents never said that they expected more from her, but it was there in the air she breathed, the history held in her bones.

"And now?"

Even this late, the air was warm, and the metal of the car was cool against her bare skin. Lily crossed one leg over the other, her sneakers flashing white against the pavement. To everyone at Duke who had come from cities or the suburbs that spun out of them, Durham might have felt small, inconsequential. The world was vast and the town gleamed in miniature. But Lily looked up and saw the clouds, the way the Cook Out sign, neon, tinted the world red. It would be three a.m. soon, and the drive-thru line was empty. For a moment, she could imagine they were the only people in the world. "I'm not sure yet," she said. She was still running, after all this time. "I'm hoping it can be more."

The moonlight cast long, searching shadows against Will's skin. "Lily Wu," he said, and when he said her name there was a weight to it, "I came here for you."

5

DANIEL

D aniel Liang had always thought there were moments that, with the careful precision of a knife, could split your life in two. This was one of them: stepping on a plane to Beijing, his ticket and passport tucked carefully in the first pocket of his backpack, his final destination as nebulous as the San Francisco fog. *I'll see you there*, Irene Chen had said. After all these years, it had been enough.

She had called him one week ago, on a Saturday afternoon when he was in lab. The two of them saw each other just a few times a year now, on those rare occasions when their breaks lined up, but their shared childhood in Santa Clara Valley would always mean something. When Irene called, he answered. She had not told him much, if anything, but he knew her well enough to trust that she had her own reasons for it. Besides, he was not sure it would have mattered. He would not say no to Beijing, and he had never been able to say no to her.

Outside his seat window, clouds hung low and heavy over the airport. The plane was gradually filling up, the sounds of Chinese familiar and comforting as families made their way to their seats. Daniel had made this flight before—California to China, squeezed in a middle seat and kept awake by crying infants and the glow of seat-back TV screens, but never in first class. Never alone.

He swallowed a sleeping pill, leaned his head against the window. The glass was cool against his skin, and when he closed his eyes, he dreamed of Beijing. Not the city it was, smog and skyscrapers and an unfamiliar tongue, but the city it had once been, a red sun rising on the Summer Palace and the high, clear notes of the Beijing opera, a boy and his father walking through centuries-old artwork. The Beijing of his childhood had always felt too beautiful to be real.

When Daniel woke, the plane had landed.

The penthouse had high ceilings and a 360-degree view of the Beijing skyline, glittering and foreign in the early evening. Inside the foyer, cool light fell on bronze, on jade, on carefully carved stone. Each piece of art rested on its own marble pedestal, close enough to touch, the kind of indulgence that was only possible in a private collection—a *very secure* private collection. Daniel bent his head, examining a scene in glazed, glistening porcelain. The piece showed a boat on restless water, and as he leaned closer, he saw waves that reached grasping into the air, figures about to tumble into the tide.

He was not one for metaphors, but there seemed to be an obvious one here.

"Dehua porcelain, Ming dynasty," a voice said. "Thought to be lost during the destruction of the Old Summer Palace."

Daniel looked up. At UCLA, he would have mistaken her for a Chinese international student, fashionable in a not-quite-American way, another child of the mainland's nouveau riche, but here, high above

Beijing, in an apartment full of Chinese art—he wasn't sure. The world felt like it had shifted ever so slightly since Irene had called.

"I know," Daniel said. "Wasn't this stolen from a UK museum last spring?"

She looked at him the way she had looked at the stolen artwork, her gaze keen and calculating. "Wang Yuling," she said, holding out a hand. Her voice was crisp, with the trace of a British accent. "You know your art."

Daniel caught her other wrist, inches away from the phone in his jacket pocket. He recognized her now—China's youngest billionaire, CEO of its most secretive company. "I know my art *theft*," he corrected. His dad had spent two weeks in London after the break-in, working with Interpol to track down leads. The thieves had never been found.

Until now.

What had Irene gotten them into?

Yuling didn't look the least bit upset at getting caught trying to pick-pocket his phone. "As you should," she said. She crossed the foyer, toward a long, imposing hallway. "Come in, Daniel. Everyone else has already arrived."

He wasn't surprised she knew his name. China Poly knew every-thing. Still, he felt a shiver of unease. He trusted Irene, and yet—one did not attract the attention of the Chinese government without inviting trouble.

The living room was decorated the same way as the foyer, all gold edges and reflected light, the shine of new money. Will and Irene were already seated, and something in his chest unclenched when he saw them there. Whatever else this was, he had known them for ten years. Will was on the couch, and he caught Daniel's eye, smiled wide. Irene smiled too, and Daniel let himself linger for just a moment on the curve of her mouth, the light as it touched her face.

There were two other girls on the couch, both strangers to him, though

Daniel thought he recognized one from his flight, the other from Irene's Instagram Stories. Here for a reason, then, just like him. Daniel set his duffel bag down. He could have sat, but instead he leaned against one of the glass windows, crossed his arms. Beneath him, Beijing shone, and he thought of the stolen art in the foyer and Irene's voice on the phone, all that was vast and impossible.

Wang Yuling shut the door. "Welcome to China Poly," she said. "I'm assuming you know why you're here."

"Tell us again," Irene said.

Daniel raised a brow. *You told me nothing*, he mouthed at her. She smiled again, her lips flashing red. If it had been anyone else, he would have been upset.

Yuling laced her hands together. The Beijing sun glinted off the planes of her face, cast her into something of gold, of marble. She was only a few years older than Daniel, but family money and a searing, recognizable ambition meant that he looked at her and saw someone who might have been a distant cousin, who might have been as far away as the moon. "Then I'll start at the beginning. Do you all know the story of the 圆明园?"

Daniel recognized the Chinese name for the Old Summer Palace immediately. The Garden of Perfect Brightness, it had been known as once.

"Some of us do," Will said. Wang Yuling waited, expectant, and Will caught Daniel's gaze. "Daniel, will you tell it for us?"

Beijing was luminous at this hour, the summer sun burning off just enough of the perpetual smog that shrouded the city. In the distance, he could see the ruins of the Old Summer Palace, framed in red and gold in the dying light. For all his lack of knowledge of Chinese history, of art, of all the things his father prized, this story had lingered within him.

"It was built in the Qing dynasty," Daniel began, "as a gift from the Kangxi Emperor to his son." He told it how he had heard it the first time, the emperors and the treasures and the certainty of glory. It had been the imperial residences once, the jewel of a long-ago China: soaring pavilions and lush, sprawling gardens, a fountain carved with all twelve animals of the Chinese zodiac to mark the passing of the hours. But then, inevitably—the slow march of war toward the capital city, British and French forces burning the gardens to the ground. Not even two hundred years ago, and in this moment it felt closer.

Even now, the Old Summer Palace had never been rebuilt.

When he was done, he asked, "Is that right?"

Yuling's gaze lingered on the ruins. "It is," she said. "But there's more. All those looted pieces of art are still in Western museums. Of the twelve zodiac heads that made up the fountain, only seven are in China. The other five are scattered throughout the Western world. We have asked for them back over and over, only to be told they are no longer ours."

"I'm sorry." He didn't know what else to say.

"Don't be," she said. Her smile was slow, dangerous, as her gaze swept across the room. The five of them, with their carry-on bags and discarded boarding passes, looked so very out of place in this Beijing penthouse. "That's why all of you are here."

He swallowed hard. "What do you mean?" But even as he said the words, the pieces were clicking into place. He shook his head. "Don't say it," he said. "Don't tell me that—"

All of Beijing was reflected in the blaze of her eyes. "I want you to take back what the West stole."

⟞⟝

Daniel walked out.

What else could he do? He slung the strap of his duffel bag over his shoulder, crossed the living room too quickly for anyone to stop him, and then he was through a hallway and in that grand, polished foyer, waiting for the elevator with his hands clutched tight, tendons stretching taut under skin.

"Daniel," Will called. "Daniel, wait—"

It had been their senior year of high school. They were young enough that they felt invincible, the world split open like a fruit for the taking, and it was one of those fall mornings when fog hung heavy over the bay and all of San Francisco felt like a half-forgotten dream. In hindsight, Daniel might have blamed Will. It would have been easy to. Will, who had always loved art, who saw beauty and wanted it, to make or to consume or to just be around. But in the end, there had been no one to blame but himself.

That day, San Francisco's Asian Art Museum had been closed for some investigation or another. The Art Crime Team was used to having the two of them around by now—Daniel had spent too many weekends at his dad's office, and Will somehow found that *fun*—and so they'd walked through the museum as they waited for Daniel's dad to give them a ride home. Through the skylights, fog pressed down on them as they stepped over police tape, broken glass, the remnants of a theft the night before.

And then—why had he done it? Daniel still wasn't sure, only that it was his senior year of high school and he was so desperate for something to change—he had picked up a bronze coin from an open display, reaching his hand past jagged glass. The security cameras were shut off, the room empty save for the two of them.

Dare me to steal it, he had said.

Will had laughed until Daniel rolled the coin over in his hand, tossed it gleaming through the still museum air. So much of his life was a dare now.

Call it, he said.

Will's gaze didn't leave his. There was a question there, but the coin was spinning, spinning, spinning, and Daniel knew Will, knew that he would speak—

Heads, Will said.

Heads it was.

Daniel slipped it in his pocket, the bronze cool against his burning palm. The consequences would come later, but in that moment—he had felt only his racing heart, the feeling of being recklessly, terribly alive.

It had felt like *something*, at least.

In that Beijing penthouse, surrounded by marble and jade and falling light, Daniel met Will's gaze. It was almost as though they were there again, fog sweeping over water, a coin spinning end over end. Everything he was, undone in a moment. But it had been four years, and Daniel was not the same person he used to be, would not let himself be dragged backwards without a fight. He already knew how this story ended. "What the *hell*," he said, "are you thinking?"

Will reached into his pocket, tossed him an object that gleamed in the light. Daniel caught the jade tiger with one hand. If Daniel had not been his father's son, he would have assumed Will had bought it from a shop off the side of the street, one of many in Beijing that sold this kind of thing. But there was an unexpected weight to the carving, and when he examined it more closely, he found veins of darker green and gold. "What dynasty?" he asked.

"Qin," Will said, followed immediately with, "Does it matter?"

Daniel turned it over in his palm. It didn't, really, only that this was further proof it was *real*. Part of him wanted to know where the jade tiger had come from. The rest of him wanted to get as far from here as possible. "You could have told me," he said. If Will had called instead of Irene, if Daniel had known the truth of why they were here—

"Would you have come?" Will asked. He leaned against the wall, let out a soft sigh. "I didn't want to ask you, you know. But Irene thought—"

"That I'd say yes?" Daniel asked. He gestured at the foyer, the penthouse, everything that waited for them beyond it. His motion was an accusation. This was Beijing, somehow, impossibly, skin peeled back, bones glistening, and Daniel did not know if the city had changed or he had. "She knows me better than that."

Will held his gaze. He could have said something or another about Daniel wanting to be a surgeon, about *steady hands*. But they both knew it wasn't quite true. "That you might want to see Beijing again," he said at last.

"Is that it?" Daniel asked, raising a brow.

"China Poly booked us a flight back already," Will said. "For Sunday morning. Just—stay until then."

It was a Friday night. Two days. It might have been nothing. It might have been everything. "Why?"

Will hesitated. Daniel looked at his watch. In thirteen hours, he could be back in America. Beijing might be something out of a fever dream, half remembered when morning came. He had medical school interviews to prepare for, midterms in just a few weeks. The thought of walking away—it was a relief.

The elevator doors opened.

"Daniel," Will said, and Daniel turned. There was something soft in Will's voice, something unfamiliar. "Please. I don't think I can do this alone."

The jade tiger was still in his hand, the carving cool against his burning palm, and in that moment, Daniel could have sworn he saw the future: silver handcuffs snapping shut around Will's wrists, Daniel's father leaning over a smooth metal table, face contorted with a familiar grief. His dad had always seen something of himself in Will's ambition, his love for art. In another world, Daniel might have been resentful, but he had long accepted that he was never going to make his father proud. He knew he could have walked away—should have, perhaps—and yet Will was standing there, waiting for him, and Daniel thought not of the future but of the past, of ten years ago when his family had first come to America and he had been full of grief and rage and had nowhere to let it go. Will had been his first friend in a foreign country, and now they were back in Beijing, this place Daniel had always called home. He would not leave Will now.

The elevator doors closed.

Daniel tossed the jade tiger back to Will, let out a sigh of relief when Will caught it. He didn't want to think about where Will had got it from, how much it might be worth. "I'm not making any promises," Daniel said.

"I'm not asking you to," Will said. He was smiling, wide and almost relieved, though Daniel was sure he had to have known this, that Daniel would never leave Will behind. Between these two siblings, Daniel might have had his whole world.

Daniel picked up his duffel bag, turned back toward the penthouse. "Come on," he said. "Let's get this over with." Beijing was waiting for them.

He was not sure he wanted it to.

6

ALEX

Alex Huang had spent her whole life waiting. Years ago, it had been behind a restaurant cash register, homework spread out before her, waiting to hear the telltale bell at the door or a shout from the kitchen. As she grew older, she had waited for trains and test scores, all the ways her life might change. Bronx Science, MIT, Silicon Valley—to anyone else, her trajectory might have looked effortless, inevitable. *Our daughter*, her parents had said to anyone who would listen, customers and shopkeepers and neighbors, *is going to do great things.*

Once, Alex had been sure it was true. She had had plans, after all. College graduation, a start-up in the Bay, possibilities laid out before her. The kind of tech that did something real, something *good*, because tech had always been that for her—a new language, a new opportunity, everything in her world opening up. *Greatness*, her parents would have said, and Alex would have agreed.

Now, though, she wasn't so sure. She had been at Google for almost a year, one of countless interchangeable software engineers in Silicon

Valley, and sometimes she was afraid she would blink and the next five, ten, twenty years would pass like this, working a job she did not love in an apartment that had never felt like hers. What would she have to show for it? What else made up a life? She called home every week, sent home paychecks for her grandmother's medical bills and her family's ever-increasing rent, her siblings and their SAT prep classes, and each time it was a reminder of why she could not leave. But this heist, this weekend— Alex was tired of waiting for her life to change.

She would change it herself.

In the evening light, Beijing shone. Alex leaned forward, pressed her hands together, thought of the weight of her family's dreams, how it could drag her under. The CEO of China Poly had talked about China and what it had lost, what had been taken all those years ago, but Alex wasn't thinking of the past but of the future, the doors this might open. *I want you to take back what the West stole*, Yuling had said, but Alex had lived in the West her whole life, and New York City was more hers than Beijing had ever been.

"And what," Alex said, lifting her gaze, "will we get in exchange?"

Yuling examined them for a long moment. Will would have spoken of glory, of righteousness, called that enough. Alex knew how he felt about China and its lost art, the depths of his want. But she wanted a life, a future. Whatever else this meant to China, Alex knew that this was a *job*. "There are five missing sculptures," Yuling said. "Five museums across Europe and America. Return them to me, to our homeland, and China Poly will pay fifty million dollars."

Alex drew in a rapid breath. She had thought she knew wealth. She lived in Silicon Valley, after all, had grown up in New York City. She had seen the carelessness with which classmates and coworkers talked about trips to foreign countries, bought clothes and coffee without budgeting. But there was the kind of money that Alex dreamed of, that Alex made—the kind that, even now, did not feel like quite enough—and then there was *this*. Fifty million dollars. There were five of them here. Ten million dollars each could buy everything her family needed, more.

Yuling looked at them like she knew it.

"And if we say no?" a voice asked. Alex didn't move, just kept her gaze on the CEO of China Poly, on all that she wanted almost within reach. They wouldn't say no. Alex knew it. Yuling Wang must have too. But she laughed, pulled a thin white envelope out of her purse. "Your tickets home," she said. "Decide before then."

Yuling Wang swept out of the room, leaving behind the lingering scent of perfume, their tickets back to America, and for the first time Alex was able to look around the room, to take in marble and the shine of light off glass, the sun as it set over this unfamiliar country. There were four others there, and as they went through introductions, Alex tried to see it, how they could become a crew.

There was Will, of course, who had drawn them all together for this impossible job. He leaned against the wall, stance deliberately casual as his gaze swept over the rest of them. "Should we do an icebreaker?"

"Please, no." The girl who spoke was on the couch opposite Alex, positioned in the kind of way that made Alex think of magazine spreads, all elegant lines and an imperious red mouth, eyes that were dark and luminous. Her voice—she had been the one who asked Yuling Wang, so carelessly, about leaving this job behind.

"Fine," Will said. "Will you introduce yourself, at least?"

A slow, pleased smile. "My name is Irene Chen," she said, and of course this was Will's sister. *No one ever says no to her*, Will had told Alex once, when she had asked him to describe his younger sister. Looking at Irene now—Alex believed it. It was hard to hold her gaze. "I'm a junior at Duke, majoring in public policy. Lily?"

The girl next to her leaned forward. Her features were softer than Irene's, and there were the lingering traces of summer in the waves of her brown hair, the warmth of her skin. A set of keys flashed in her hands, quick and silver. "My name is Lily Wu. I'm Irene's roommate and a mechanical engineering major at Duke."

"And?" Will prompted.

Lily smiled. "Right. And—sometimes a street racer."

The only other guy in the room whistled low. He had dark hair, buzzed short on one side, the kind of jawline that could cut. The edge of a tattoo, black and curling, reached over his collarbone. "Are you any good?"

Lily smiled wider. "Better than you."

He laughed. "Daniel Liang." He said it the way it would have been pronounced in Mandarin, his accent crisp and perfect, at odds with the studied carelessness of the rest of him. "I'm a senior at UCLA, applying to medical school this fall. I'm here because my father works for FBI Art Crime, and"—he shrugged—"well, I suppose I'm not a very good son."

Alex examined him. It explained why he had walked out before, the hard set to his shoulders. The son of an FBI agent. It seemed—well, it could have been a good idea. It could also go very, very badly.

She had expected Will or Irene to correct him—they knew him, after all—but instead Irene said, easily, "We haven't broken any laws, you know."

"Yet," Will said.

"Ever," Irene said, and Alex did not have time to wonder what she meant before Irene turned her gaze on her. "And you are?"

"Alex Huang," Alex said. "I'm a software engineer." She supposed she should say more than that, but she wasn't sure what else there was. Everything that had brought her here, everything that she had left behind— if they could pull this off, what did it matter?

Irene raised one lovely brow. "Not a hacker?"

Alex hesitated. For all that she knew a heist crew's archetypes—leader, con artist, thief, getaway driver, hacker—she did not feel right calling herself one, not yet. "No," she said. She looked over at Will, illuminated in the Beijing sun. He had called her, one week ago, seen past everything that was ordinary about her life—about *her*—and offered something more. "Although I think that might change."

His smile was slow, pleased. "Let's get started." He set up a whiteboard, brandished a black dry-erase marker. *The Great Chinese Art Heist*, he wrote at the top, and Alex laughed.

Daniel crossed his arms, and Alex felt the mood of the room shift, turn more serious. "You're taking this joke a little too far, Will."

"Who says it's a joke?"

"Will," Daniel said.

"He's right," Irene said. She looked at her brother. "You know he's right. This is only going to end badly."

For a moment, silence hung low and heavy over the penthouse. Alex rose, taking the marker from Will's hands, and drew a line down the center of the board. She labeled one side *pros*, the other side *cons*. She had always made decisions like this. The day her full-time software engineering offer had come, the day she had decided to drop out of MIT—it had been a whiteboard and a list, all the reasons she should leave. All the reasons she wished she didn't have to. "Here," Alex said. "Maybe this will help."

"Pro," Will said, "making history."

"Con," Lily said, "getting kicked out of school."

"A felony conviction," Daniel added. "Any chance of med school gone."

Will leaned back on the couch, met Daniel's gaze with a warm smile. "Not all of us are smart enough to go to med school."

"Not all of us are in school right now," Alex reminded him.

"That doesn't matter," Irene said. She stretched her legs out, rested them in Daniel's lap. "We can all get felonies. And we all have futures to lose."

Alex thought of her parents, her family, all those people who were counting on her, and added everything to the list. The cons kept coming. A criminal record, jail time, the heavy weight of their parents' disappointment.

Alex looked at the pros. There were just three bullet points. *Making history*, it read. *China gets its art back. A shit ton of money.*

Those first two, they were Will's. "It doesn't seem like much of a choice, does it?" Will asked. He had been sitting before, but now he rose to stand next to her, and for a moment it was just the two of them facing a whiteboard, the Beijing night beyond. The skyscrapers, the stars, all of them glittered. "And yet . . ."

And yet, and yet, and yet. Alex could not walk away. "We're doing this, then?"

Will's gaze swept over the penthouse. He knew all of them, but to Alex they were still strangers. Still, she looked at Daniel, at Lily, at Irene, these people who might become her crew. Will would have to convince them, but she didn't doubt he could. He had brought them all here already. How could they turn back now?

At last, he looked at her, smiled. "Of course," he said, and his voice was all certainty. It might have been one week ago, her apartment washed in California light, code unfolding beneath Alex's open palms. It might have been one year ago, leaving MIT behind. This was how a life changed.

⁕

That night, as everyone else slept, Alex looked out at the city. The penthouse was large enough that they all had their own rooms, with king beds and heavy, plush carpet, windows that ran from wall to wall. She had stayed up late talking to Will, and though she should have been sleeping now, preparing for tomorrow and all that it would bring, she stood in front of her window, wondering. She didn't know Beijing, but she knew cities, skyscrapers and neon lights, the hum that always meant a place *alive*, and as she took it in, she thought of home. That Chinatown apartment, the paneling thin enough that she could hear the sounds of the kitchen below, the sound of oil sizzling and shouts in Cantonese. Her parents, shutting off the lights one by one, the tap of her grandmother's cane against the polished wooden floor. What could she do with ten million dollars? Everything. Anything.

Alex touched her hand to the window, felt the press of cool glass on against her fingertips. For a moment, she saw only her reflection—the sharp angle of her brows, the blunt edges of her short hair, all of it familiar and yet somehow not. If she let herself, she could understand why the others wanted to walk away. This was a grand, terrifying, impossible thing, and the consequences were larger than anything else she had ever done. China and unknown corporations, all that this country could promise them and take away. And yet Alex looked at the city spread out before her, reflected glass and brilliant, blinding light, everything that these coming weeks might hold. She had grown up in a run-down apartment in New York City, in a neighborhood that was always fighting to survive, had always known how much it took—how much you had to risk—to change a life. She had been the first in her family to go to college, the first in her family to dream of something more than this.

Alex had spent her whole life achieving the impossible.

What was one more time?

7

IRENE

Irene Chen had spent her whole life doing everything right. One week ago, she had been in New York City, the late-summer air warm against her skin, her heels clicking as she strode across the intersection of Broadway and Fulton, past yellow taxicabs and the rumble of the subway beneath her. She had taken an elevator up to the top floor of a building that was all glass and glinting light, leaned against the receptionist's desk as she waited for her interviewer to arrive. It had been easy then. A handshake and a wide, practiced smile, questions that she knew the answers to already. Her interviewer had leaned forward, pressed his hands together as he asked, *Where do you want to be in five years?*

Irene had looked past him, just for a moment, out the windows that spanned floor to ceiling. All of New York was spread out before her—the gray, gleaming waters of the East River, the skyscrapers of the Financial District, Brooklyn in the shimmering distance. She was almost tempted to tell the truth. Instead she looked at him, held his gaze.

Where you are, she had replied.

She had gotten the job offer that evening. She knew what would happen from there too. A consulting internship this summer, a return offer in her senior year. She would graduate Duke summa cum laude and work in finance for a few years—job experience, an impressive line or two on her résumé, networking—before going to law school, cutting a clean, linear trajectory toward the kind of career that other people only dreamed about.

She had not been expecting *this*.

This was the thing. Irene had spent all of college in the world of politics—summers in Beijing, in DC, learning about the players who caused the rise and fall of superpowers. And yet when Will had called her, at the end of her interview in New York, about a theft and an offer, she had not recognized China Poly's name.

She did now, of course. She had spent that evening in a hotel room that overlooked the Manhattan skyline, reading articles in Chinese about the rise of a corporation that no foreigner knew and a CEO with a background in art history. Then, now, it all had the feeling of a dream, pieces cobbled together in nonsensical ways. A week ago she had been interviewing for a summer internship, and now she was in a penthouse in Beijing, the skyline stark and silver against a hazy afternoon sky. She wanted to unravel this city, find her answers in the patterns it made in her outstretched hands. *Why us?* she would ask the rising sun. *Why now?*

Irene shut the door to her room, the sound loud in the stillness. When she had looked up Wang Yuling, that night in New York, she had gone through pictures where the CEO of China Poly smiled from European auction houses, her fingers curled around priceless art with something like possession, something like righteousness. The fierceness of her gaze, that *want*—it reminded Irene almost of her brother, though she would never tell him that.

She knew Will. She knew when he had called her, eyes bright, that he wanted this. This job, this crew. Everything and more. And she knew—because she knew her brother, because he had spent his whole life getting everything he wanted—that he would not be able to let this go. He had never been able to let go of any of his dreams.

But Irene was not her brother, and she had no interest in heists and their impossibilities, did not want to linger on what would happen if this all went wrong. She crossed the hallway, knocked twice on Daniel's door. It was a Saturday afternoon, the day before they would leave Beijing, and lingering jet lag meant that she was the first one up.

"Are you awake?" Irene said, pushing the door open. The room was saturated in golden light, but Daniel was still in bed, tangled up in his sheets. At her voice, he flung one arm over his face.

"No," he lied. The sheets were a bright, hotel-room white, and Irene yanked them off him, revealing bare skin, the curl of a dragon wrapped around his torso. He made some unintelligible noise through his arm.

"Let's get something to eat," she said. She could have asked Will or Lily, but she and Daniel had not yet spoken since they had arrived in Beijing, and she suspected they needed to. Besides, neither Will nor Lily would have said yes.

"It's so early," Daniel said, but he sat up in bed, ran a hand through his hair. "Let me get dressed."

Irene smiled.

They didn't go very far. Daniel led the way, navigating the Beijing streets with an easy familiarity, until they were at one of the many hutongs in the heart of the city, the narrow street crowded with vendors and the sounds of summertime. Daniel ordered two bowls of noodles, and they sat at one of the low plastic tables off the side of the street, steam rising between them. Irene picked up her chopsticks, took in pale sky and this familiar language, how everything around them was moving even as they remained. In China, time always felt soft, malleable, and Irene thought of the past few years, the two of them seeing each other only in passing. It still felt the same. Daniel, China, all of this had happened before.

Daniel took a long, deliberate sip of his tea, and Irene did too. It smelled like jasmine, soft and fragrant. "You know," he said, "I rescheduled a med school interview for this."

"Did you?" she asked.

"Well, I chose a different date. But I wanted this one."

"I'm sorry," she said.

He set his cup down, gave her a heavy look. "Are you?"

One week ago, she had been in a different city. She had looked out at Manhattan at night, thought of her brother and how much he wanted this, what Will might need to pull this off. What she would need, to do this with him. She had not hesitated when she called Daniel. Maybe she should have. Still, she looked up, met his gaze. All these years, and Irene had never lied to Daniel before. She wouldn't start now. "Thank you," she said instead. "For coming anyway."

He fell silent, his gaze on the city that rose around them. The last time they had been in Beijing together, it had been for a funeral. She wondered if he was thinking about it too. The fluorescent hospital lights, the beep of his mother's heart monitor. And then, weeks later, boarding a flight and kneeling before a plot of earth. It had been ten years, and yet like this, Beijing spilled out before them, it was as if no time had passed at all.

"Why are we here?" he said at last. "You and I both know that this isn't going to happen."

Irene ran her fingertip over the smooth edge of her chopsticks, thinking of time and how it moved, the future she had planned out so carefully. "Because Will asked," she said, and that was all the truth she had. Wasn't that what it always came down to? Her brother and his dreams. She let her mind drift for a moment, took in the faint blue sky, the distant, wavering sun. Five museums, five countries. There was the Met, of course, and the British Museum, and then three others: the KODE 1 in Norway, Drottningholm Palace in Sweden, and the Château de Fontainebleau in France. "Do you think we'd get away with it? If we did it."

"I thought you were the one who knew everything."

Irene smiled, just slightly. "Just tell me."

"Probably not," he said. "How could we?"

Irene tried to imagine it. Lifted security badges and lasers that shifted in the dark, the slow, complicated matter of peeling a museum apart. What could she not do if she wanted to?

"Are you tempted?" she asked.

"Why would I be?"

Irene raised a brow.

"I mean, yeah, it's millions of dollars," he said. "And I have all this useless knowledge about art crime. But my dad—" He sighed. "I don't know. I don't know if it makes me want to do it more or less."

Ten years, and she knew Daniel and his father, all the ways their relationship had fractured. "Both, maybe," she said.

"Probably," he said. The alley was hazy and almost dreamlike in the afternoon sun, the steam that curled into the air between them. "I've missed it here," he said, and it was a sigh.

Irene thought of these years as they passed. Visits to her grandparents in Yangzhou, the sticky summer heat and the whir of the fan in that small apartment. Her brother sketching those lush green trees through the open windows, Irene walking with her cousins along Wuting Bridge, thinking of everything that was passed down through generations. Irene was not Will, had never found herself prone to lingering on the past, but she had thought that there might be more to this. And so, later, classes in US-China relations, a semester in Beijing, all the ways to learn this country better. When she left, her friends had called it *abroad*, but Irene had known it wasn't. China was many things—traffic and mountains and the brush of ink over paper, emperors and innovation and the heavy hand of an authoritarian government—but she would never call it foreign.

Irene looked at Daniel, at Beijing in the afternoon light, this country they were always leaving and coming back to. "Me too," she said. She leaned back in her plastic chair, her mind on politics and moving pieces, all that might change in the years to come. The future, instead of the distant past. "Maybe the zodiac heads will be returned someday," she said, and she could almost convince herself of it, see how this could play out the way she wanted it to. "Geopolitics, the rise of a superpower, you know."

"Maybe," Daniel said. He set his chopsticks down, smiled at her. "Or maybe some real thieves will do what we won't."

Irene laughed. "And your dad?" she asked.

"Hopefully he won't catch them," he said. He rose, held out his arm. "Come on. Let's go back."

Irene rose. She thought of home, an ocean away, her parents getting ready for bed, Daniel's dad leaving work at last. She thought of the flight she had already booked for Daniel's graduation, for Will's, all the possibilities of her junior year. Classes and new challenges, a winter spent waiting for that first impossible snowfall, singing a cappella with beautiful girls beneath high, vaulted chapel ceilings.

He loves you, her brother had told her once.

Then that's his mistake, she had said.

She looped her arm through Daniel's. Even after all these months apart, she knew him—knew the steadiness of his voice, the tattooed dragon that curled possessively around his ribs and collarbone, those long, tapered hands, meant for taking things apart, putting them back together. "If nothing else," she said, "we got a free weekend in Beijing."

He laughed. She could feel it against her skin. "It's good to see you again, Irene."

⌒〜⌒

By the time they got back, everyone else was still waking up. Irene found Will in the foyer, his head bent over an art piece she didn't know. In the late-afternoon light, the room was washed in gold, and she leaned against a marble column, watched the careful movements of her brother's hands, thought back to years ago. A dimly lit art studio, she and her brother side by side. Their parents had signed them up for so many classes—art, music, more—in the endless quest to make them well-rounded individuals, to discover their *passions*. Irene had gotten bored of art class quickly— she had never liked anything she did not excel at—but Will had picked up a paintbrush and the hours had disappeared. For almost a year, she had kept going back with him, painted still life after still life of the same bowl of fruit. They had done everything together back then, but it had been more than that. The way he talked about art—it was like his whole world was remade. Irene had wanted so desperately to understand.

Will looked up at last, noticed her for the first time. "What?"

It should have been strange how comfortable her brother looked here, running his hands over art that was not his, in this penthouse they would leave so soon. And yet it didn't surprise her, not really. Sometimes she thought Will loved art more than she could ever love anything. "You know we leave tomorrow, right?"

Will was quiet for a moment. "I know."

The marble was cool against her skin. "Why do you want this so badly?" she asked, because she could not help herself, because after all these years she still did not understand.

"Why don't you?" he said.

When Wang Yuling talked about these heists—when Will talked about these heists—it was about what had been taken from China, all that had burned when the West came calling. There was truth to that, lingering and painful. But history was bigger than the West, and when Irene thought of what might become of the five of them, she thought of China and its own legacy of imperialism, how it could take and take and take.

Irene didn't hesitate. "What good would it do?" She had spent so long studying China and its rise, knew power did not change hands like this. For all that she had talked to Daniel about this earlier, let herself pretend, she knew what was real, what was not. She had her future waiting for her when she got back. "This is real life."

"I know that," he said. He hesitated. "Did you hear back from the consulting firm?"

Irene let herself smile. "Got the job."

"Of course," he said, his voice warm. "You should tell Mom and Dad."

He knew her better than that. "Already did," Irene said. "Called them before Lily and I stepped on the plane."

"I should've known," he said. He glanced at her. "You never told me your roommate was a *street racer*."

Irene raised a brow. She had met Will's exes before, knew what he called *temporary* they never did. It was hard to determine who was truly to blame—was it her brother, who liked nothing more than to surround himself with beautiful things, or the girls who thought they could change him?—but either way, she had not wanted the fault lines of his relationships to splinter anything else. "It never came up," she said.

He shook his head. "Do you really think so little of me?"

"Never," Irene said. That, at least, was always true. "How are the job apps going?"

Will looked down, turned the carving over in his hand. In a year, her brother would graduate. He would be in New York or London or anywhere else in the world, all his dreams come true at last. She wondered what it'd feel like.

"You really don't think this is possible?" he asked.

It wasn't quite an answer. Irene let out a long, slow breath, looked out at Beijing. The sky was a hazy orange, tipping toward sunset. "It's our last night," she said, and that wasn't an answer either. She didn't need to give one, not really. Will already knew what she would say. "What do you want to do with it?"

She had expected him to hesitate. Instead he rose, came to stand by her side. "Do you see that?" he asked, pointing to a building in the distance.

Irene had spent a semester in Beijing, knew the shapes of its skyline, but this one wasn't the CCTV tower, its geometric glass panes reflecting the setting sun, or the curving golden roofs of the Forbidden City. It looked almost like an office building. "What is it?" she asked.

"The New Poly Plaza, home to the Poly Art Museum. It's—" He hesitated, his gaze flickering away from her for just a moment.

The seven zodiac heads that had been returned to China were at the Poly Art Museum. Irene knew it as well as Will did. He could be doing it to convince her about this job—it was what she would've done, if she were him. He could be doing it because he was Will, and he had always loved art more than anything else in the world. Either way, Irene looked up at him, smiled. Tomorrow they would leave Beijing. Back to Harvard, back to Duke, back to everything that was ordinary. "Let's go," she said. "It can be a test run."

She saw the expression that flitted across his face, added, "I'm *joking*."

"I know," Will said, but something in his voice made her wonder. He looked at his watch, the face flashing in the red-orange light. It was a quarter till seven. "They're about to close."

"We'll make it," Irene said, and it was a promise. They had this last night in Beijing. She could give her brother this.

The rest happened very quickly. Lily was in the kitchen talking to Daniel, and Irene called both of them before looking for Alex Huang. Irene knocked on the open door of Alex's room, waited for her to look up. She was on her laptop, headphones on and her fingers quick and certain as they moved over the keys.

At last Alex looked up, slipping her headphones off when she saw Irene. "Oh, sorry," she said. "Did you need something?"

Of everyone here, Alex was the only one Irene didn't know. Looking at her now—for the first time, really, the light soft and red as it skimmed the high planes of her face, the brush of her dark hair against her jaw—Irene thought she could guess how Alex knew her brother. He was always like this, wasn't he?

Still, she wouldn't see Alex again after tonight, and Will's bad decisions were his own. She gave Alex an easy smile, savored the way Alex drew in a sharp, involuntary breath. "Come on," Irene said. "We're going out."

"Where?" Alex asked.

"Does it matter?" Irene asked.

Alex shut her computer.

Lily drove, of course. She made the streets look easy, effortless, and Irene adjusted the radio dials, turned it to a station she recognized from her semester in Beijing. It was warm out, the windows rolled down, and Irene sang along to a song she recognized, caught her brother's smile in the rearview mirror. Other than Alex, the three other people in the car were the people she loved most in the world. What else was there besides this?

Outside, the night air was warm, balmy, and Irene thought of the semester she had spent in this city, how it had felt to imagine that Beijing belonged to her. She had spent years studying Chinese politics, and if asked, she could give easy reasons, elegant ones, for the choice. There was the absoluteness of China's one-party system, the fierce, sudden rise of a country of over two billion people, power like a fist clenched tight around the Pacific. But sometimes there was just this. The evening air, Beijing great and terrible and hers, all that could be made anew.

The guard was reaching to lock the door when Irene caught it with her outstretched hand. She smiled at him. "Excuse me," she said, the words crisp and precise in Mandarin. "We're here to visit the Poly Art Museum."

It was just past seven. "I'm sorry," he began, "it's already—"

She thought of China's fuerdai, that second generation of China's newly rich, how it felt to be young and invincible. "We won't be long," she said, her hand still resting on the cool glass of the door. Irene had never cared for the bronze zodiac heads, but she knew how much Will did. She knew how much it meant to China, to have these pieces. Art and power. They were always one and the same. "We just want to see the zodiac heads. It will be quick."

"I'm sorry, but—"

She turned to Will. In English, she said, "Give me a minute."

If she hadn't known him so well, she would have missed the smile that flitted across his face. "Are you sure?" he asked.

The guard was looking at her, his expression wavering into uncertainty, curiosity. After all these years, her accent was good enough that no one thought she was American unless she wanted them to. She wanted him to now. "You . . ." he began.

"I'm American," she said. There was a word for the diaspora, something of bridges, of distant lands, but she didn't use it. Instead she chose 美国人, *American*, the consonants bright and jangling against her tongue. All these countries that she could call hers.

"Your parents are Chinese?" he asked.

"Of course," she said. "But this is my first time here." It was the first lie she had told. Easier to have everything almost true, to be close enough to feel like it. Her hand was still on the door, and though he could have pushed her away, he hadn't. She let her voice soften, grow wistful in the way that Will's always did when he talked about art, what was lost and what was found. "I grew up hearing about the Old Summer Palace and the missing zodiac heads. I just—I wanted to see them once before leaving. I don't know the next time I'll be back."

Put like that, she could almost believe it herself. This summer, she would be working in New York. Next summer, she would graduate. It would be the beginning of the rest of her life. When would she be here again? She did not let herself linger on the thought. China, her future. It would be here when she wanted it to be.

He opened the door. "Fifteen minutes."

She looked at her brother, her smile slow and full of easy confidence. She had never doubted he would say yes. "I told you so," she said to Will, and then Irene was stepping through the glass doors, into the New Poly Plaza and all that it held.

8

WILL

The elevators opened to dim light and heavy, muted carpet, glass plinths so thin and translucent that sculptures looked suspended in midair. Inside the museum, awe pressed down on Will with the darkness, broken only by the spotlights that glinted against bronze.

He leaned forward, his glasses almost bumping the glass case. The statue before him was a polished bronze, carved to resemble the first of the twelve animals of the Chinese zodiac. The rat's clever eyes seemed to almost wink at him, and Will thought of centuries ago, a sculptor pouring bronze into a stone mold, light that moved like water. He had not sculpted that way before, but he knew how the bronze would feel under his palms, slippery and changeable and cool to the touch. When he had first told his parents he wanted to study art, their silence had been long, excruciating. And how to explain this—the ache he felt when looking at the lines of a sculpture, how history could be found, made, left behind by an artist's deft hand?

"So?" Irene asked, and Will came back to the museum, its glass cases and the watchful eye of the overhead cameras, the five of them the lone visitors on this quiet evening. "Is this everything you wanted?"

What did he want? So much he felt like it might pull him under. He touched his fingers to the case, let himself imagine. Alex and an empty security office, her hands moving over the keys; Daniel kneeling before a glass case. Possibilities, unfolding. Everything felt real, urgent, alive. Will had known since the first day that he could not leave this behind.

He took a breath in.

A breath out.

The lights shut off.

They were in sudden, plunging darkness for a moment before the emergency light flickered on, illuminating just the four of them, the long shadows cast by the museum cases. The red light of the CCTV camera had gone dark.

Daniel's voice cut through the still museum air. "What the hell is going on?"

It had been last night. Will had caught Wang Yuling as she left the penthouse, the Beijing light falling fast. This was what he knew: He would have to convince the rest of his crew that they could break into a museum, and to do that—well, they would have to break into a museum. Ideally, the Poly Art Museum itself.

We won't actually break *anything,* Will had promised, and he hoped it was true.

Wang Yuling had almost laughed. *Just make sure you put my art back,* she said.

"Welcome," Will said, "to our first heist."

"You're joking," Daniel said.

"Only a little," Will said. He caught Alex's eye as she returned; her smile was quick and pleased in the darkness. "How long do we have?" he asked.

"Ten minutes before the system resets," she said. "Daniel, you're up."

Daniel raised a brow. "Am I?" he said. His gaze swept across the museum, lingering not on the art but on the glass cases, the locks that flashed silver. "I'm guessing Wang Yuling knows that we're here."

"Of course," Will said. Yuling had agreed so easily that Will suspected this was not just an opportunity but a *test*. Whether they wanted this as much as she did. Whether they could pull this off. "Can you do it?"

"You know I can," Daniel said. He looked from Will to the glass case, flexed his hands. "How many times do I have to say that this is a bad idea?"

"More than you have, apparently," Irene said, but she was smiling too. Whatever Will said, whatever he felt—this was not a real robbery. This was just the five of them, a museum laid open in the low light, and it was easy to pretend. Daniel knelt at the base of the glass case, running his fingers over the keyhole, and Irene—one step ahead, as always—began pulling out the bobby pins from her braided hair. Less than a minute later, there was a soft, careful click, and the case opened beneath Daniel's hands.

He rose, tilted his head at Will. "Your turn." He was smiling, just a little, and Will thought of the evening before, how close Daniel had been to walking away. And yet—he was here. They all were. It had to mean something.

Will stepped forward, picked up the bronze sculpture with bated breath. It was heavier than he'd expected, and he turned it over in his hands, careful. He knew he ought to be thinking of gloves, of ski masks, of backpacks strong enough to hold this weight, but instead he closed his eyes and saw a palace that cut into the Beijing air and a fountain shimmering beneath a high sun, water that was clear and blue and endless. History, close enough to touch. Wang Yuling had promised them fifty million dollars for the five missing zodiac heads.

Will would have done it for free.

The rest of his crew were waiting for him. He passed the sculpture around, took in how gentle Alex's hands were as they ran over the bronze, how Lily tested the weight of it in her palms. Daniel was the last one to hold the zodiac head, and when he set it back, he lifted his gaze to meet Will's. "This doesn't change anything, Will."

"Why not?"

"This was the easy part."

"Then tell me," Will said. "Where does it go wrong?"

Daniel ticked it off with his fingers. "The license plate. The car registration caught by CCTV cameras. IP addresses tracing where the blackout came from. Irene's face sketched by an artist based on the guard's description. Your prints on the plinth. Mine on the lock. My father recognizing either of us. Do you want me to keep going?"

"We'll plan for it."

"You really believe that?" Daniel asked.

Will held Daniel's gaze. Ten years of friendship, of shared classes and late nights studying and talk of dreams, of who they would become when they graduated high school, college, all the ways to measure a life. Even after four years apart, he looked at Daniel and saw his brother, his best friend. "I do," he said. He looked at the rest of his crew, illuminated in the thin, fluorescent light. "Listen," he said. "I know this seems ridiculous. But we're here, in Beijing, surrounded by history. How much more real can this get? How much could we do with this kind of money?"

"Are you sure that's the only reason you want to do this?" Irene said.

He had never been able to lie to his sister. "You know it isn't," he said. "But what does that matter, now that we're here?"

He looked at the four of them. Alex, her family, the weight of their expectations. Lily and her dreams, how she had talked of running away. Daniel and the cost of a medical education, how much he still longed for Beijing. Irene—well, he had never known what his sister wanted. But he knew she wouldn't leave him, not like this. And she had never failed at anything before. "I know we've already listed the reasons we should walk away. But I think we can do this. I really do. We'll do our research and take our time, and if at any point anyone changes their mind, we'll stop. Besides"—he swept his hand across the museum, at the city that lay beyond them—"how can you see this, know what we could do, and walk away now?"

"Fifty million dollars," Lily said. Her voice was wondering. "Let's do it."

"I'm in," Alex said. "I always was."

He looked at Daniel, at Irene. These were the two people who knew him best in the world, who knew all his flaws, his wants, his fears. "Fine," Daniel said at last. "Because we're in Beijing, and because I don't think you can do this without me. But if anything goes wrong—"

"It won't," Irene said.

Will held his sister's gaze. "Is that a yes?"

"For now," she said, but she was smiling. "You want too much, Will."

These thefts, this art. A future unfolding. "What's wrong with wanting everything?" he asked.

The lights flickered on. If anyone had walked into the museum now, all they would see were these two siblings, faces turned not toward each other but to the art surrounding them. "Nothing," Irene said, but her voice was soft as a warning, "as long as you know how to get it."

The last time Will had seen the Old Summer Palace, it had been just before his freshman year of college. The word *Harvard* had been like a banner or a brand against him, and he'd traced his fingers over the inscription at the mouth of the palace, letting the words sear themselves into his skin. *A reminder of what we have lost*, it said, characters carved unforgiving into pale gray stone.

Will had felt that loss, had recognized in it something of himself. Going to China, those few summers that he did, was the only time he felt found. Loss was the hesitation in his voice when he spoke his mother tongue, the myths he did not know, a childhood that felt so vast and alien from his parents' that he did not know how to cross it.

Will Chen, twenty-one years old now, tilted his head up toward an early-morning sky. The crescent moon shone silver as a scythe, and he might have been in the past, the present, the future, every version of himself standing before the ruins of the Old Summer Palace, hands open and asking as they touched an archway that curved into empty air.

Four years at Harvard, almost, and had he changed so much? He still longed for moments in oil paints and motion done in charcoal, would have painted this morning like an Impressionist scene, clear from a distance but incomprehensible up close. He had spent these years searching for what it meant, to be the eldest son of an eldest son, to go to a school that flung open doors, but now it was his senior year and he had not yet figured out who he was supposed to be, how to *become*.

His life for so long had been a question. And though he knew he could not make this heist everything, just being here—beneath a Beijing sky unfolding, the Old Summer Palace close enough to touch—felt like an answer.

"A bit early for a morning run, isn't it?" a voice called.

He turned. Lily Wu pulled off her helmet, her brown hair tumbling over her shoulders and an easy smile on her lips. In one smooth motion, she swung off her motorcycle and kicked it into park. He thought of one week ago and the shine of her eyes in the dark, her hands as they spun a set of keys in endless, constant motion. *Lily Wu*, he had said, *I came here for you.* She had laughed, but they both knew it was true. They had leaned against her car as the moon rose, their milkshakes melting in their

Styrofoam cups, and when morning came, Will knew he wanted her on this impossible job. "And yet you're up too," he observed.

"I was feeling restless," she said, and it was exactly the right word for how he was feeling too, just a few hours away from their flight back. "I figured I would do a bit of exploring."

"And the motorcycle?"

"There's a key rack by the foyer," Lily said. Her voice was light, teasing. "Maybe you were too distracted by the art to notice."

Will laughed. "Come on," he said. The sky was purple and dreamlike, starless, though the moon shone bright and unwavering above the remains of the Old Summer Palace. "Let me show you what this used to be."

They walked through the ruins, past fallen arches and chunks of stone, and as they did, Will built the palace for her: the gates that rose white and radiant, staircases that climbed and climbed, balconies with clean lines and a hint of Western design. And everywhere the gardens that remained, green and alive even now, wildflowers blooming between cracks in the stone.

"I can't believe I've never been here before." Lily's voice was filled with soft wonder.

The flowers here were a bright, cadmium yellow. Will knelt to pick one, spinning its stem between his thumb and forefinger, and thought of colors on the tip of a paintbrush, a canvas that stretched wide and waiting. "The Old Summer Palace?"

She hesitated. "China."

He didn't know what to say. After all these years, his parents still called it *going back*, as if anywhere else could not be home. He had spent his whole life trying to make China love him back. "Lily . . ." he began.

"My parents came to America and never looked back," Lily continued, her voice soft. "And I always thought it was because there was nothing here worth holding on to, you know? I wasn't—I wasn't expecting *this*."

"This?" he asked, though he knew what she meant. All the colors here felt more real. Or maybe it was just that he did.

She gestured at the palace, at Beijing. "It feels familiar, kind of, but also new, and I expected to feel displacement, maybe, or anger, and I *do*, really—but I'm also wondering, I guess. About everything that I grew up without."

At last, he looked at her. The sun was just beginning to rise, and it touched her hair with a fierce, pure red, silhouetted her against the ruins. If they had met at Harvard, he would have asked to paint her just for the sake of running his hand along her jaw, his fingertips tilting her head to the light. He had done this so many times before, after all.

She caught his gaze, held it.

What's wrong with wanting everything?

Nothing, as long as you know how to get it.

Will looked away first. The future—it was museums broken open, the wail of sirens in the dark, Lily's hands on the wheel of a getaway car. He would not mess it up, not like this. "Look," he said. They had walked through the whole of the palace, somehow, were now back at its entrance. The ground was carved open, jagged rocks all that remained of the fountain that had once been, the statues waiting to come home. "This was where it began."

Lily walked forward, stopped at the inscription just as he had so many years ago. Her fingertips traced the name of the Old Summer Palace, forming the strokes slowly and carefully. "Can you read this to me?" she asked.

If he closed his eyes, he could pretend that they had walked into the past, that the palace and its gates were open and waiting. China and its art, its history, would always be a story of greatness. It would always be a story of loss.

The inscription had not changed, but this time, he translated it differently. Light glinted off the characters, turned stone to lustrous gold.

Will thought of years and centuries ago, a palace on fire and the rise and fall and rise again of an empire. Art could change hands so easily, with checks or museum loans or the shattering of glass in the quiet dark. "A reminder," Will said, and his voice was low and almost reverent, "of what must be reclaimed."

Lily looked up at him, the sunrise warm against her skin. "Well, let's go," she said, smiling. "History isn't going to make itself." She spun her keys, silver flashing quick and sure in her open hand, before turning toward the street. Cars honked, loudly and often, and pedestrians cut through the edge of the palace while talking into their phones. China was always like this, the new and the old pressed up against each other, the past constant as the smoke, as the fog. In a month, they might be touching down in a foreign country, dreaming of a museum unlit in the darkness, the first of the five missing zodiac statues waiting to be brought back. Will cast a final glance at the ruins of the Old Summer Palace, and then Lily's motorcycle roared to life and they were flying through Beijing, toward a future that gleamed bright and impossible in the distance.

9

IRENE

rene Chen was familiar with the commotion of the Beijing airport—
the sounds of Mandarin over the loudspeaker, the sunlight as it
skimmed over duty-free shops and automatic glass doors, travelers as
they hurried across the sprawling terminals—but here in the first-class
lounge, the world was quiet. She could hear the soft sound of Chinese
traditional music playing over the speakers, the tinkling of glass at the
open bar. She swept her gaze across the lounge, its low light, and thought
of the night before, the Poly Art Museum and that moment of brief, absolute darkness. Part of her had known that this would happen. How
could she not? Her brother, his dreams. China and everything it meant
to them both. She could still remember a year ago, telling her father she
was going to spend a semester in Beijing. She had expected him to be
proud—a child at Beida, even for just a semester, was that not every
Chinese parent's dream?—and yet he had looked out at the line of
trees, the laundry strung up outside her grandparents' apartment. For
the first time, Irene had noticed the gray in his hair, the careful lines

around his eyes. *Every time I come back*, he said, *I recognize this country a little less.*

Change, swift and inevitable. The country of so much of her childhood, of her father's stories, was not the same one she was in now. And yet she studied Chinese politics and Will studied Chinese art, both of them reaching for the country their parents had left behind.

What was the difference, then? If it had been her, if Wang Yuling had asked Irene instead of Will, she would have said no. It had been almost thirty years since her parents had moved to America. Her future—it was worth more than the past.

She wished her brother felt the same way.

Irene rose, stretched. She had been sitting for too long. They were on different flights, leaving within the next few hours, and she and Lily would fly twelve hours to JFK before transferring domestically.

Across from her, Alex slipped off her headphones. "Where are you going?" she asked. Irene had thought she'd been asleep, or almost there, but her eyes were bright. The only makeup she wore was a sweep of eyeliner.

"Just for something to eat," Irene said.

Alex unfolded herself from her leather recliner. "I'll come with you."

They walked to the dining area, and Irene examined Alex. She was dressed comfortably, casually, but still there was the severe beauty of her features, the dark hair that just barely brushed her jaw. When she tilted her head, three silver studs glinted in one ear.

"Tell me about yourself," Irene said as they reached the tables with their polished silver platters, the rows of fluffy white buns. Condensation glistened off pitchers of fresh fruit juice. Irene had flown first class before, for interviews and formal events. Still, each time it was a luxury.

"What do you want to know?" Alex asked. She reached for two cups, poured watermelon juice for them both.

Irene had looked Alex up already. It had been about what she had expected—a girl from New York, Boston and then Silicon Valley, every-thing in her life falling into place. "You said you're a software engineer?" Irene asked.

"I am," Alex said. "I've been working at Google for the past year. Before that I was at MIT."

Irene reached for a ladle, spooned congee into her bowl. "And how do you know my brother?" she said, though she knew the answer already. Alex Huang was exactly Will's type—the kind of beautiful that looked like art. Still, she wanted to believe that her brother knew better than to ask his latest fling to join a *heist*. Beijing and its promises were uncertain enough already.

"It's a funny story," Alex said, and Irene thought, *It always is.* "We actually met on Tinder a couple years ago. It was freshmen year, and—"

Irene added toppings to her congee, only half listening. She spooned in a sliver of century egg, its insides glistening, several heaps of pork floss that came apart in her bowl, pickled cucumbers sliced into small, delicate pieces. This was the thing. Irene was never wrong. She was also incredibly, supremely uninterested in hearing how her brother's rela-tionships went. She knew them all already. "I see," she said. And then, lightly, "So you're his ex." She couldn't tell if that was better or worse.

"I wouldn't call it that."

"Why not?"

"It was two dates," Alex said. "And I'm not here for your brother."

Irene looked at her. This, she hadn't been expecting. "Then why are you here?"

"Do I need to answer that?"

Irene shrugged, looked away. "You can do whatever you'd like," she said. It didn't matter, really. Irene had classmates who had left Duke for the same reasons Alex had left MIT, the shine of tech and new money, all of them young and ambitious enough to think the sun rose and fell in Silicon Valley. Alex was no different from every other software engineer who dreamed of being something more.

"And you?" Alex asked. "Why are you here?"

Irene knew how this should have gone. *The same reason you are*, she should have said, because Irene had spent her whole life learning how to be liked, the effect of a carefully chosen word or a smile shared like a secret. She had learned it from Will first, who did not even notice he was doing it, how easily the world gave way for him, and then the rest had been all her own. Twenty years, and Irene knew the truth was whatever she wanted to make of it.

And yet—

Irene looked at Alex, took in the sweep of her hair, the sharp line of her jaw. Her brother had asked Alex on this heist as if it were a date, hadn't even told Irene how he knew her. *A hacker*, he'd called her. Irene wondered if he'd known, even then, that it was a lie. In another world, Irene might have admired a girl who could change her life so easily, who could leave everything behind for something like this. If this had been a New York bar, the light low and the taste of possibility in the air, she would have found Alex Huang the kind of beautiful that made her want to tip her head back, to drink her in like a shot. But Irene was not as foolish as her brother, and Alex was an unknown in a job that already had too many.

"Because this crew needs me," Irene said. She smiled at Alex, quick and almost vicious. Why should she care about what this stranger thought of her? "But I'm not sure we need you."

Alex's hand faltered as she reached for a red bean bun. "Excuse me?"

Another time, another place, Irene would have held her tongue. She did not know Alex, and even if she had, she did not do this kind of thing. But it had always been like this. High school, the years before, her friends falling for Will as if they could not help themselves. It always ended the same way. Her brother—ambitious, dreaming, who loved art more than anything or anyone—had never known how to be happy with what he had, and sometimes she wondered if he knew how hard other people had to work for the love that came to him so easily. It didn't matter. She would not let his bad judgment get in the way of this heist.

"You shouldn't be here," Irene said, and she thought that Alex must have known it too. Alex did not know any of them besides Will, and if they were going to pull this off, they would need more than just a software engineer, more than whatever her brother thought Alex could be. "You aren't a hacker, and you aren't a thief. What can you do that the rest of us can't?"

Alex's gaze was steady as it met Irene's. Irene had been hoping for that to be enough—for Alex to leave, to change her mind, but instead Alex just said, softly, "You don't know me."

I don't need to, Irene could have said. She knew her brother, knew that however much she loved him this was the one thing he had never been able to get right. But she had said too much already. In the distance, she could hear the loudspeakers announce her flight. She was going home. "I don't," Irene said, and it was almost agreement. She let her voice soften, just a touch. "I hope you'll prove me wrong."

Beyond her window, the sky was a deep, unyielding blue, the clouds curving over the edge of the distant horizon. The first-class cabin was washed in artificial light, and everyone around them was sleeping. On any other flight, Irene would be too, but first class meant endless cocktails and meals served with real silverware, flight attendants who smiled and passed Irene phone numbers on folded napkins. Next to her, Lily was looking out the window too, watching China disappear beneath them. "So?" Irene asked. "What do you think?"

Lily's expression was soft, contemplative. "I don't know yet," she

said. She finished her cocktail—something the pale pink of a sunrise—
and another came. "I think it'll feel different when we're back. You?"

Irene spun her wineglass between her fingers. The liquid was red,
dark. In truth, she didn't want to think about this at all. This job and
what it might mean, all that she had to still plan out. Wang Yuling and
how she spoke of what was owed, her brother and all the ways his rela-
tionships came apart.

What was she afraid of? If anyone had asked her, she would have lied.
She thought Lily might too. They understood that about each other, how
hard it was to peel yourself open, to lay yourself bare. But Irene stared
out at the sky, the tumultuous blue of the clouds and the distant, glittering stars, and thought of the future. Perhaps there was just this. The
curved, sickle moon. The emptiness of the sky. Her parents, both their
children gone for college, a house in Santa Clara that was too big for the
two of them. All that Irene had to be. Alex Huang and everything Irene
did not know. One month, and they would be elsewhere. Irene was used
to certainty, and this job was anything but.

The hum of the plane was soft, muted. "That this will change everything," Irene said, and it was the only truth she had.

Lily was silent for a long moment. Three years, and Lily knew Irene,
knew her fears and her dreams, had never asked her to share more of
herself than she could bear. "Maybe that's a good thing," she said. "Don't
you wonder, sometimes? If all the late nights and the studying and the
summer internships—" She hesitated.

"What?" Irene said.

"I don't know," Lily said. "Is this all there is?"

Irene didn't know what to say. This wasn't about jobs, really, or even
the future. It was about themselves, the fact that they were hurtling
toward the end of college and the beginning of the rest of their lives,
that they were doing everything right and yet—sometimes Irene was
not sure she recognized herself.

"What else could there be?" she asked. Irene was not her brother, had never wasted her time with impossible dreams. There was just *her*, her limits and her capabilities, everything that she willed to be so. Still, on this flight back to America, to all that she used to be so certain about— she wasn't sure. Change. It was a little terrifying.

Lily looked over at her, smiled. "I guess we'll find out."

And so the plane soared on. Whatever else had happened this weekend, whatever else might change, in this moment they were just college students on a flight, soft light and pressurized cabin air and the world spread out before them. Lily ordered them another round of drinks, and Irene turned once more to look out the window, took in the vast, infinite dark, the reflection of the plane in the layered glass. She had spent her whole life doing everything right.

This heist, reckless as it was, would go the same way.

10

LILY

It was a warm fall evening, and Lily Wu was in Perkins Library, working on a problem set for fluid mechanics. Time moved slowly, lazily around her. The library was almost full, even at this hour, with students working on papers or psets or just procrastinating on Netflix. Her laptop battery icon began to blink at her, and she snaked her charger beneath the table, fingers running over the smooth black plastic of an empty outlet. It was all so *ordinary*. This evening, the work before her, the soft murmurs of shuffling papers and distant, indistinct conversation.

She might have dreamed the weekend before. But it had been two days, and Lily could still remember the rumble of Beijing's highways, how the city moved like it was a living, breathing thing. She was used to small towns, the kind you could fly through in a minute, foot pressed down on the gas, stopping only for the fluorescent red of a stoplight, the shine of a distant cop car. Beijing had felt like it could swallow her alive. She had wanted to spread her hands out, let herself be consumed. She had wanted to leave and never look back.

She was still jet-lagged, Beijing lingering in ways she had not known to expect. The air had smelled of smoke, of sizzling oil, of everything that shone too bright, and Lily thought of museums and getaway cars and history she didn't know. She wasn't sure what to make of this country that her parents had once called home. She never had. A penthouse with vaulted ceilings and white-veined marble. The CEO of China Poly. The story of the Old Summer Palace, Will Chen standing next to her as the sun rose. And Irene, her best friend, how she moved through this foreign country as if it were hers.

Lily shut her laptop. She couldn't concentrate. Across from her, Irene glanced up from the paper she was working on, slipped her headphones off. "What is it?" she asked, her voice soft enough that they wouldn't disturb the people studying around them.

Lily shook her head. She wasn't sure she had an answer. "Let's head back," she said. "I'm not getting anything done here." They had their first heist meeting soon anyway. *Project* meeting, she corrected herself, because they would not call it a heist, would not be careless in this or anything else. When one of their friends had asked what kind of project, Irene had looked up and said, unblinking, *An exploration of pre-revolutionary Chinese history.* It had sounded *incredibly* boring, even to Lily, which had definitely been the point.

The two of them packed up their things. They had been roommates for three years, had done this often enough. Studied together in libraries, in coffee shops, in the spire on top of Few Quad when the weather was warm and the windows thrown open. Duke might have been a dream too. Lily swept her things into her backpack, waited for Irene, and then the two of them walked back to their dorm. It was still warm outside, though September was almost over, and as Lily swiped them into Few, pulled open the dorm's heavy wooden door, she was suddenly, abruptly aware of how this job would change everything. She should have been afraid. But she took one last breath of the evening air, thinking back to their plane touching down in Beijing, doors that opened to summer air, to humidity. It had felt like Galveston, almost, like home, and Lily had looked around at this strange, unfamiliar place and thought, *Finally.*

⌒

It began like this: the five of them on a Zoom call, *Ocean's Eleven* pulled up on Netflix. They had a list of movies to watch, books to read, some fiction and some not, all of them about art or thefts or both. Despite the differences in time zones, they all stayed up. Lily had seen this movie before, but it felt different to watch it now, knowing that in a month they would be in Europe, attempting a heist of their own.

"So," Irene said, as the credits played, "you expect *us* to do *that*?"

Daniel laughed.

Through the screen, Will took off his glasses, polished them against his sweater. Behind him, Boston was lit up in the darkness. "Maybe not exactly that," he said.

"Then what?" Irene asked.

No one seemed to have an answer, and Lily tried to imagine pulling this off. It had been just two days since they had all been in Beijing, in a penthouse that was all light and burning gold, and yet—in the quiet of her dorm room, she could not be completely sure it had happened the way she remembered, that it had even happened at all.

"I don't know yet," Will said. "But we'll make it work."

Irene looked from the screen to Lily, raised a brow as if to prove a point. She was likely right. They didn't know anything about museum break-ins, about art theft, about the kind of crime that this entailed. And yet—two days ago Lily had seen the sun rise on an unfamiliar country, had driven on foreign roads.

"This is impossible," Irene said.

Lily said, slowly, "I don't think it is."

Irene looked at her, curious. "You really believe that?"

Did she? Lily was a street racer. She'd seen all the *Fast & Furious* movies, the way they lingered on the smoke and the flash of headlights in the dark, all the moments when you could not look away. In real life, it was not quite the same. It had unfolded carefully, quietly, in the summers spent working at her neighbor's auto shop, saving up for something that would let her leave, all those evenings when her parents were working late and she looked outside at the wavering sea, the bridge that stretched toward the mainland. She had believed in something more then. She believed in it now. "All this means," she said, "is that there's more left to do."

Will smiled.

And so the night went on. The five of them talking over video chat, pulling together pieces of heist movies and the books they'd read so far, trying to make this into something that was *possible*. On a new computer, Alex set up remote access for them, and they began to populate encrypted folders, breaking this heist down into its components. How to enter a museum, to navigate around guards, security systems, everything that was designed to keep them out. How to retrieve the sculpture waiting for them in a glass case and beneath the sharp eye of a camera. How to leave a museum and a country without getting caught. How to build alibis, how to lie, how to do all the things that turn them into criminals.

How to live with themselves if this all went wrong.

⁓

"Are you still up?" Lily asked. Even with her eyes open, she could barely make out the shape of their dorm room. It was all darkness and the scratch of her sheets, Irene's steady breathing from the other side of the room.

"Yeah," Irene said. "What is it?"

"I don't know," Lily said. In bed, she ran her fingers over her knuckles, thinking of China, of cars in the dark, of art that was waiting to come home. For all her confidence earlier, these past few days had felt almost like make-believe. "This just—it doesn't feel *real.*"

Lily could hear Irene smile. "I know what you mean," she said, and Lily remembered their flight back from Beijing, ten hours in a first-class cabin. The two of them had gotten drunk off free cocktails, talked about everything but this impossible job.

It had been three years since they had first met each other in a freshman dorm on a sticky August afternoon. Lily hadn't been sure about Irene in the beginning. Irene had been everything Lily wasn't, confident in herself and who she was meant to be, and Lily was just a girl from a small town in Texas, trying to find a place she might call hers. But Irene had been there for Lily's first Durham race, had dumped a beer on a stranger who acted a little too surprised that a Chinese American girl could drive like *that,* and when Irene's ex-girlfriend broke up with her, Lily had stayed with her in that bathroom stall until Irene's hands were steady enough to redo her eyeliner. Irene was her best friend, the closest thing to a sister she would ever have.

"Why do you think China Poly chose us?" Lily asked at last. A foreign country, looted art from centuries ago. It had all the qualities of a dream.

In the dark, Irene's answer came easily. "Because if we get caught, China won't be held responsible."

It was a very Irene answer, immensely practical. If it'd been another time, Lily would have asked if Irene thought they would get caught. She wasn't sure she wanted to know the answer. "True enough."

"You think there's more to it?"

"I don't know," Lily said. Twenty years, and she had never called China hers. How could she when she had never been? She did not know its songs, its roads, its rivers. She did not know the terms of address for kin, the names of provinces, anything that she ought. All she knew was that her parents had left, and that they did not speak of what they had left behind.

She had never minded until now. Her parents had lived through the Cultural Revolution, had come to America looking to start anew. Their parents—her grandparents—had died before she was born, to famine or persecution or any of the countless tragedies that happened in a country in upheaval. Without family in China, with all their friends lost to time—Lily had never needed to ask her parents about why they hadn't taught her Chinese, why there were no summer trips to unknown provinces. Twenty years, and she was used to being asked where she was from, to giving an answer that felt like a lie. She could never be Chinese enough for China. She could never be American enough for here.

"Do you miss it?" Lily asked. "China?"

"Always," Irene said. "How can I not?"

Lily had expected that answer. Still, she kept her gaze on the ceiling, the heavy dark. "Even though it's not yours?" she said.

"It is," Irene said. In the darkness, her voice softened. "And it's yours too, whenever you want to claim it."

Lily didn't know if she would ever feel Chinese enough to call China hers. But if they could pull this off, if they could bring China back its art—she didn't know. It meant something, that Will had asked her for this, that in these heists she might be enough.

Irene's breathing was so even, so steady, she might have been asleep. Tomorrow they had more to do, the first of these five thefts to plan. Lily closed her eyes, tried to slow her breathing too.

"Lily?" Irene asked. "Are you still there?"

"Yeah," Lily said.

Irene did not often hesitate. She did now, just for a moment. "What did you think about my brother?"

Her voice was so casual, so deliberately light, that Lily could almost believe it didn't matter. But they had lived together these three years, and for all that Lily knew Irene loved her brother, admired him, she did not mention Will unless someone else brought him up. The oldest son, the one to carry their family's legacy. Lily thought she might understand what it felt like to live with that weight. He had taken notes as they watched *Ocean's Eleven*, his gaze never leaving the screen.

"Every bit as pretentious as I knew he would be," Lily said to the dark, and it was true.

Irene laughed. "You know," she said, "he doesn't even really need glasses. His prescription is so light that it's mostly for the aesthetic."

"You're joking."

"If only." Irene was quiet for a moment. "Thanks," she said. "For getting it."

Lily smiled at the ceiling. "Always."

Another laugh, softer this time. "Can we sleep now? Is there more?"

"No," Lily said. "Let's go to sleep." She wasn't sure she could. Still, she closed her eyes, pretended. The dark was soft against her skin. What was real, what was not. This job. Strangers and new cars and shifting plans that felt like something out of a movie. In the end, though, her thoughts drifted to home. They always did. Galveston and its beaches, sunlight that scored red against gray water. The cry of the gulls and the sting of the salt wind, shrimp po'boys eaten on a wooden pier. For all that she loved it, she had wanted nothing more than to leave. Perhaps her parents had felt the same way about China. She had never let herself ask. She would never know.

As sleep reached for her, Lily was still thinking of Galveston, those years she spent racing—or was it dreaming?—hoping to go somewhere, anywhere else. The stories her parents had never told her about China, the empty space it had carved within her. How it felt to search and never find. All these years, and Lily had never known how to love a place and not leave it behind.

11

WILL

This was how it'd happen: Will Chen and an open skylight, gray morning air washing over him as he knelt on the museum roof, as he strung a fishing line down empty space, past motion detectors and the shimmering red light of laser beams. He hooked the line carefully, deliberately—

The sculpture was too heavy to bring back up. He couldn't get through the glass case. He knew that already.

Will crossed out *Galleria d'Arte Moderna Ricci Oddi heist, 1997, Klimt's Portrait of a Lady* in his notebook.

This was how it'd happen: Night that fell soft and velvet blue, his hands steady as he lifted the sculpture from its glass plinth, as he replaced it with a flawless forgery. He could imagine it, Daniel picking the lock, the shine of bronze in the dark, a swap that would take just moments.

Only—how would they get into the museum without the alarms going off, without the guards noticing something was wrong? Even if they could, how could he sculpt a piece so perfect no one would notice the change?

He crossed out *Caracas Museum of Contemporary Art heist, 2000, three Matisse paintings.*

This was how it'd happen: It was the most famous art heist in history. He'd knock on the museum entrance, tip his hat at the night watch. *Police*, he'd say, with the kind of certainty that did not permit questions. *We've gotten word of a disturbance.* When they opened the door, he'd pull out his—

Will crossed out *Gardner Museum heist, 1990, 13 works.* In real life, it had gone like this. The thief, dressed as a police officer, had raised his weapon, said in a clear, steady voice, *Don't give us any problems and you won't get hurt.*

The guard had responded, *Don't worry, they don't pay me enough.*

The thieves had spent over an hour in the Gardner, time stretching long and luxurious as they strolled through empty rooms, chose the art they wanted to steal. A Rembrandt seascape, five drawings by Degas, more. Will had visited the Gardner before, seen the empty frames hanging on the wall, the space left behind by a stolen Shang dynasty gu. It was in Boston, not far from Harvard's campus, and the thieves had never been caught. Still, this could not be *their* heist. They would have to find something else.

Will looked at his notebook again, all the art thefts that had occurred throughout history. Despite what he had expected, most of them did not happen the way they did in movies, in books. He ran through a series of smash-and-grab jobs next, quick and bloodless. The Zimbabwe National Gallery, a lone visitor pulling six pieces of art off the walls and running out the front entrance. The Louvre on a busy Sunday afternoon, a Corot sliced from its frame and carried out the door. He took notes on each one, marking down the minutes required, how the thieves had gotten caught. What went right and what went wrong. The sun rose outside his window, the Charles River glittering in the distance, and Will began to put together a plan. He was not a thief—none of them were, not even close—but he had always been an excellent student.

———

It felt, strangely, like a group project. Will waved at his suitemates as they left for a late, midday brunch, sunlight streaming through the suite's bay windows. It was almost afternoon, and if this had been another time, another year, he would have just woken up too. This place could have been his whole world. Harvard in the fall, sunlight and rustling, red-gold leaves, papers and deadlines on the horizon, training for the start of track season. Instead Will ran a finger along the spines of the books on his desk, nonfiction checked out from the library on art crime, on museum thefts throughout history. All of it, compiled into a notebook and a list, a series of crimes crossed out and put back together.

It had been just under a week since they had returned from Beijing, days of reading and research and movies that were more than a little improbable, and Will turned his gaze to his laptop, the four other members of his crew. A map of Sweden's Drottningholm Palace was pulled up on his screen. There were five museums, five missing zodiac heads. This one would be the first. Stockholm had had the cheapest flights, and despite the cash Wang Yuling had given them for this job—stacks of crisp hundreds tucked into unmarked envelopes like something out of a spy movie—Stockholm had seemed as good a place to begin as any. Thousands of miles away, the whistle of the Baltic Sea on a cloudless night. It was so far from this quiet, sunlit afternoon.

Will laced his hands together. "Let's get started," he said, and hoped he sounded more certain than he was. "Alex, you're on museum security. Find us a way into the museum without getting caught. Can you do that?"

If he didn't know her so well, he wouldn't have noticed her hesitate. It could have been the camera, lagging for just a moment. "Easily," she said, and he hoped it was true.

"Good," he said. "Daniel, once we're in the museum, it's on you. You'll be in charge of taking the zodiac head from its case."

Daniel nodded, just barely. Will couldn't help but think of all the thefts he had read about, the movies they had watched. It was never as easy as it sounded.

He looked at Lily. "Lily, you'll plan our escape route. Get us out of there safely," he said.

There were four paths out of the museum. The first led back to the main road. The second led deeper into the palace. The third led into the surrounding forest. The last opened to a nearby lake. "Done," Lily said. She didn't hesitate, and Will remembered Beijing, this girl on a motorcycle and the fierceness of her gaze. Possibilities, unfolding.

"And me?" Irene asked.

Will hesitated.

He wanted to believe they wouldn't get caught. And yet—they were students, not thieves. Will swallowed hard, thought of the future and all the ways this could go wrong. "Make us a plan," Will said, "for when the authorities start to investigate."

And so they got to work. In just over three weeks, they would be in Sweden, Drottningholm Palace waiting for them in the darkness. All this planning, and it would still be over in minutes. He was afraid, just a little. There was so much he loved about Harvard, so much he could not bear to lose. But as the light changed outside his window, fall swirling soft and golden around him, Will thought—as he always did—of history.

It was made in moments like this.

12

ALEX

For all of Alex's confidence, all her certainty, she did not quite know where to begin. It was an early morning in California, and pale blue light fell on distant mountains, on empty streets, on her apartment with its marble countertops and carefully chosen furniture. She opened her laptop, stared at the blinking cursor.

It had felt different in Beijing. She had been so sure of herself, of what she could do. But it had been a week since they had returned, and she could not find a way into Drottningholm Palace. Museum alarm systems, police radars, all the technology that might get them caught.

There was so much she didn't know.

Alex closed her eyes for a long moment and then called home. The phone rang once, and then twice. Alex was about to hang up when her grandma picked up. "Hello, Yi Hua Lou Restaurant, how may I help you?"

"Popo," Alex said, and it was strange and familiar and wonderful to slip back into Cantonese, to pretend she might be home again. She looked out the window, thought of New York in early fall. Columbus

Park and the trees changing colors, the roar of the subway beneath her feet. It had been so long since she had been back. "I just wanted to say hi."

Her grandma would be leaning against the counter, her cane set aside, one hand wrapped around the corded landline they still hadn't gotten rid of. Alex could see it, even now. All these years, and she had memorized her grandma's voice, the way she moved, all the slight, gradual changes that came with age. Change came faster now that Alex was gone, now that she could no longer watch so carefully. "How is work?"

"It's good," Alex said, just as she always did. "Busy," she added, because it was truer now than ever. She ran her finger along the sleeve of her *Made in Chinatown* hoodie, let out a soft sigh. There was work and then there was this theft, and her days could blur together into lines of unfamiliar code. Will had called it a group project. Alex had never been very good at those.

In the background, Alex could hear servers shouting in Cantonese, her father's voice from the kitchen. "You can do it. We're all—" More background noise. Alex imagined her grandma covering the phone, yelling for whoever it was to keep it down. Anyway, she had not changed so much.

"I'll call back later," Alex offered. "I know it's the middle of the day."

"Call anytime," her grandma said. "We miss you, Alex. You are all of our dreams."

Alex tried to smile. Her parents, her grandma, they were so easy with their love. They made it easy for her too. And yet—as she said her goodbye, as she promised to call back soon, she couldn't help but feel a little afraid, a little overwhelmed. Her whole family—so many of their hopes rested on Alex's shoulders.

So much of this heist did too.

Alex hung up the phone and got back to work.

The weekend slipped away too soon. There were security company records, museum blueprints, guard schedules, all of it in different places, all of it in Swedish. She had not yet tried to access the museum's internal server. She didn't even know how to start. For all that Alex knew Java, C++, all the languages that went into software, this kind of code—taking a museum apart, putting it back together—was strange, unfamiliar territory.

When Sunday evening came, Alex took a long, slow breath, opened Zoom. Her windows were open, the fall air cool against her skin. Had it really been just a week since she'd been in Beijing? The other four members of this crew were online already, going through updates, and when it came to Alex, she hesitated. "I'm still working on it," she said.

They had three weeks left.

"What do you know so far?" Will said.

Alex opened her folder. *Not enough*, she wanted to say. But how could she? None of them knew anything about tech, and she had to believe it would come together in the end.

"The guards rotate every two hours," Irene said, crisp and certain, and Alex looked up. One week ago, Irene and her cool disregard. *You shouldn't be here*, she had said, and a part of Alex had believed her. "And there's a silent alarm system that routes straight to the police station. Plus everything else you'd expect—motion detectors, heat sensors, lasers, CCTV, the like."

That was my job, Alex wanted to say. *Not yours*. But that was pride, nothing more. "How did you find out?" she said instead. On another screen, she opened up the Drottningholm website again. She might have missed something, and yet—she didn't think she had.

Irene lifted a shoulder, the motion swift, elegant, arrogant. "I asked."

"What?" Alex said.

"A friend of a friend from study abroad has contacts in European security. I got a phone number and then called the firm that does security for all the Scandinavian museums, told them I was a student writing a paper. It was . . . true enough."

Against her better judgment, Alex was impressed. "Did you tell them your name? Your school? Identifying information?"

Irene held Alex's gaze. "What do you think?"

Alex looked away first. Hadn't Will told her already? His sister was always like this, perfect to a fault. It would have been easier if Irene were—Alex wasn't sure. *Less*, maybe.

The rest of the call went like this. Lily talked about transportation, about police radars, and Daniel and Will discussed similar thefts, what this crew could learn from history. Alex wasn't particularly paying attention. When the call was over, she reached for her phone. She hesitated for several seconds before calling Irene.

"Hello?" Irene said.

"Hey," Alex said. "I wanted to say—" She took in a breath, let it out slowly. "I wanted to say thanks."

Silence, brief and almost surprised. "For?"

Alex leaned back against her chair, closed her eyes. The Beijing airport, Irene's voice in all its polished, terrible precision. Alex could almost convince herself she had imagined it. "Looking into the security system," she said. "I—you did it faster than I could have." Whatever else, she had been raised to thank others when they did something for her, and Irene had. Still, the words were hard to say.

"No need," Irene said. "I didn't do it for you, anyway."

She could imagine Irene in a dorm room, the light tracing the high planes of her face, the arch of a brow. When Alex had returned to California, she had looked all of them up. Irene might have known everyone in this crew, but Alex didn't, and she had wanted to know what she was getting herself into. She had looked up Daniel, read about his mother's death, his father working in FBI Art Crime, thought about grief and all the shapes it took. She had looked up Lily, pulled up a map of a small Texas town. She had traced the routes on it, imagined a car and a long road, how this girl could be their getaway driver. And, of course, she had looked up Irene. Irene, who had been the valedictorian of her high school class, who was at Duke on a full-ride scholarship, who had never known what it felt like to not have enough. The world would carve itself open for Irene Chen.

"I know," Alex said. She wanted to say more. They could be friends, she thought. If Irene wanted to. But she remembered Beijing, the judgment in Irene's voice as she called Alex Will's ex, as if that was all she was, as if that was all she could ever be.

Through her open window, the evening air was cool against her skin. Irene was waiting for her to say something. "Well," Alex said, uncertain, "thanks for your help." They were in this thing together, weren't they? They were on the same side.

Irene didn't even hesitate. "Next time, don't need it," she said. Before Alex could respond, before she could even figure out how to, there was a click and then empty air. Irene had hung up.

Alex looked at her phone for a long moment, and then at her window. Evening light, dark and blue, fell over her empty apartment, and Alex swallowed hard. This conversation—it had not gone how she had wanted it to. Irene Chen, with the practiced knife of her smile, the beauty she wore like a weapon, could have been every Asian girl at Bronx Science, at MIT, who had looked at Alex and found her wanting. Once, it would have hurt. But Alex took a slow, careful breath, thought of her family, what they dreamed of, what they wanted. She thought of her own future, all branching possibilities. She could not fail. She opened a new window and began to code.

13

DANIEL

It was one of those rare overcast afternoons, fall leaves turning the UCLA campus gold and melancholy colors. Daniel Liang badged into lab. He could have gone to his dorm or the library, all the different ways to fill his hours, but he spent so many weekends away, interviewing for med schools, and he had missed this—the familiar sterility of his bench, the quiet hum of the PCR machine in the background. He pulled on a lab coat, gloves, began to section mouse brains for staining. Like this, it was easy to let his mind drift, to let the past ten years fold in on themselves.

Two weeks ago, he had been in Beijing. It had felt like something out of a distant dream, walking those streets with Irene, remembering everything as it once was. Museums with his father, a life that he had taken for granted. He hadn't thought of it in a long time, but now, beneath the lab's steady fluorescent lights, surrounded by the steady hum of the industrial-size freezer, he did. He did not think of his mother, the loss like a wound still open. Instead his mind went to Beijing and his father talking about art, the wonder in his voice, all the afternoons they had spent pulling apart the intricacies of art theft. Not breaking in—that part was easy, graceless—but everything after. Museums were meant for this, after all, the opening up. The difference between thieves who were caught and thieves who were not always came later.

Like this, it was easy to see where their own heist would go wrong. What did they know of breaking in, of getting out? Only what Daniel could remember, what he could hold on to after all these years. He stayed in lab for a while longer, finishing up the work he needed to do, still thinking of distant palaces, of impossibilities. It was easier to think about the future than the past. It had always cut him open. Ten years, and his father called this country *his*, worked so hard to be American. He had consulted for the FBI first, a few cases here and there between his work as an adjunct professor, and then, somehow, that had become a full-time offer and a business card that read *Investigator, Chinese Art Specialist*. The first, the only. But Daniel—he still did not know how to make this place his own. All these years, and he still dreamed in Chinese, closed his eyes and saw Beijing. Even if he wanted to, he could not let go of the past.

It was dark by the time he left lab. He picked up a sandwich on the way back, his mind elsewhere, and when he got to his dorm room, he called Will. The phone rang once, twice, three times before he picked up.

"This isn't going to work," Daniel said. He sat on his bed, the gibbous moon cool and silver against the darkness of the sky, thought of a Chinese poem from centuries ago. The fall of moonlight like frost, home and all that had been lost to time. Had it really been so many years?

Will's voice was groggy, and Daniel remembered that it was later on the East Coast. "What do you mean?" he asked.

The future, not the past. Daniel took a breath in, let it out. "It doesn't matter how we go in," he said, and he could imagine it, the empty museum, how the quiet would feel almost like this. "We're going to mess up somewhere. We'll set off an alarm on accident. We'll get spotted by a security camera."

"Alex can shut the place down."

Daniel rested his head against the wall. In two weeks, they would be in Sweden. Time had always moved too fast. "Even if she can, should she? The authorities will trace us, and we'll get found out."

"You think we should back out," Will said. It wasn't a question, and Daniel knew he was sitting up in bed now, that he had put his glasses on. His voice was low, serious, and Daniel wondered if Will would leave this behind, if he asked. If Will could.

"No," Daniel said. He had had long enough to think about this. Ten million dollars was his medical education, his future. But it was not just that. If they could do this—if he could do this—he might be able to leave the past behind. It had been a decade in America, of that house in the suburbs that always felt too big, his dad looking not at him but *through*, as if Daniel could not be bone or blood, enough to hold on to, enough to keep.

He had always known that he was not enough for his father.

What was the point in trying?

"Then what?" Will asked.

Daniel closed his eyes, thought of Beijing and childhood, all that he had learned about art theft without even meaning to. His father's hand in his, a museum in the rising sun. Whatever else he was, whatever else he wanted—he was his father's son. He knew how this had to go. "The way in doesn't matter," he said. "What we need is a way *out*."

14

WILL

It would go like this: Moonlight that fell bright and silver, the sound of glass smashing in the dark. The three of them running through the winding, empty hallways of a foreign museum. The sirens would be going off by then, but Will knew how this went, didn't he? This had started with the Sackler, after all, a robbery in broad daylight and a crew that moved too quickly to be caught. It seemed only right that they would do the same thing.

Irene's smile was slow, pleased. "You're saying we can't get in without getting caught?"

"That doesn't sound like a good thing," Lily observed.

"It is," Irene said, and Will was smiling too. He loved seeing Irene like this, brilliant as she always was, one step ahead of him and everyone else. "If we can't get in unseen, then why bother?"

"Exactly," Daniel said. He walked them through the rest of the plan. It was clean, simple, easier than anything they had come up with in the past two weeks. The three of them and shattered glass, a getaway that couldn't be traced. Police radar monitored and accounted for. It was not a heist from a movie, the glamour of *Ocean's Eight* or the high-speed car chases from *Fast Five*, but it was something real, something possible.

Will looked out his window, at the distant sheen of the Charles River, the lights that shone along the bridge, remembering the Sackler on a late August afternoon, sunlight as it spilled through glass and open air. Had he known then what his life would become? He must have. He turned back to his screen, wondering. Against all odds, despite all that was practical or realistic, this was a *crew*.

A leader. Will had spent so many years studying art and how it changed hands. His whole life—it had brought him here. Of course it had. He would be the one to sort through the art at Drottningholm Palace, determine what they would take and what they would leave behind.

A con artist. His sister, her smile in the dark. Irene was a public policy major, had always understood people and what they wanted. She could shape the world to her will.

A thief. Daniel in a faraway palace, his hands as they skimmed over the stolen art. He would be a surgeon someday, had always known how to break things open, put them back together exactly as they were.

A hacker. Alex, who had left MIT for Silicon Valley, who had never found a problem she couldn't solve. When they got to Sweden, she would manage their police radar, their burner phones, construct alibis for them based on location sharing and GPS.

And, finally, a getaway driver. Will thought of seeing Lily for the first time, headlights sweeping over an empty road. Beijing, the two of them on a motorcycle beneath the rising sun. When Lily drove, nothing could touch her if she did not want it to.

Irene's voice cut through his headphones. "Explain this to me one more time," she said. "We're going to distract the Swedish police *how*?"

Alex shrugged lightly. "I'll figure it out."

Irene raised a brow. "And why you?"

"Well, it can't be any of us," Daniel said evenly. "We'll be in the museum."

"Then Lily," Irene said.

"I'm *driving*," Lily said. She was smiling, just a little.

"Multitask," Irene suggested.

Will laughed. Some days, this felt like his future, unfolding. Others, it was just another group project, college kids and changing responsibilities, all the ways they could disagree with each other. "Come on," Will said. "We have more to do."

They had two weeks left.

When the call ended, Will reached for his backpack, headed to studio. Harvard in the fall was fiercely, improbably beautiful, all colonial brick and trees that reached for a cloudless blue sky, leaves that crunched beneath his feet as he crossed the Yard. Will pushed the glass door open, took in sunlight as it fell through open skylights and the sculptures that lay unfinished on empty work benches, the way the air smelled of oil paint. He didn't have class today, but there was something comforting about being here all the same. He should have been working on job applications, but he didn't want to think about that now, two weeks away from their first heist, when all of this might not matter if everything worked out like it should. And yet, as he set up his workstation, his mind went to the columns of the Met, those red banners and high arches, the cover letter he had spent hours on in the depths of night, when no one was around to see how much he *wanted*.

What's wrong with wanting everything? he had asked Irene. These thefts, his future. Art was the only thing that could ever last, and even then—he would graduate in only a handful of months. He was so afraid of leaving Harvard behind. He did not know what would come next. He closed his eyes, let out a long, slow breath. What did it matter? It was a fall afternoon, and outside the leaves were falling, and he did not have to let go of this just yet. The world felt like it could crack open with a touch, spill yolk and careful possibility. Will pulled on his gloves and reached for a chisel. Two weeks, and they would be in Sweden. He thought of Chinese art, lost and found, the gleam of a bronze zodiac head in the dark.

If they could do this, if they could pull it off—

What else mattered, except for this?

15

DANIEL

A nd then, somehow, it was late October. Daniel Liang stepped out of his Uber, tilting his head up to breathe in the cool air. It was still warm in LA, but here in Northern California the evening was a dark, venous blue, the wind lifting leaves down empty sidewalks, past suburban houses spaced even as a metronome. His house was the only one with its lights still on, and he rang the doorbell, waited to hear his father's steps inside that wide, empty house.

The door clicked open. Liang Yaoxian and his son had the same build, tall and broad-shouldered, the same dark eyes and clean jawline, but Daniel was taller than his father now, and it was strange to look down at him, to see reading glasses and new lines around his mouth, hair that was more silver than black. "Ba," Daniel said.

"Son," his dad said in Chinese, that Beijing accent unchanged. Daniel had friends who spoke to their parents only in English now, years in America forming a hard-broken habit, but he could not imagine either of them ever leaving this language behind.

Daniel took off his shoes at the door, set his duffel bag down next to them. The house smelled like just-steamed rice, and dinner was on the kitchen table despite the lateness of the hour, wrapped in plastic to keep the warmth in. "You didn't have to wait for me."

"I had some work to do anyway," his dad said. The table was set the way it always was. Two pairs of chopsticks, two bowls with that same floral pattern he had grown up with. A glass of milk each. His dad's work took up the other half of the table, a secure FBI laptop resting on papers and black-and-white photos. "How was the flight from LA?"

"Not bad."

"Good. Are you ready for your interview tomorrow?"

Daniel had considered not applying to Stanford Med. He was a good applicant, he knew, with his perfect GPA and 520 MCAT score and those years of extracurriculars, plus the kind of story about medicine that, told correctly, could bring an interviewer to tears. And yet for all the kids who had grown up in the Bay Area, in the shadow of Stanford's influence, this was the kind of school that felt equal parts too far away and too close to home. "I think so."

His dad nodded. "Good."

Daniel took a bite of bok choy, the crunch of it loud in the silence. Change ought to be measured like this. The house, the furniture, the scrolls of Chinese characters were all the same, and yet if this had been high school, his dad would have spent the next several hours going over interview questions with him, asking follow-up questions in stiff, serious English until he was satisfied with his son's answers. The past had never felt so far away.

Remember this: the sharp slope of his mother's decline, lives transplanted from Beijing to this foreign country for the sake of experimental treatments and Stanford doctors, everything that China could not give. *A new beginning,* his father had called it, and as they packed up their Beijing apartment, as his father spun his mother around in that newly empty living room, both of them giddy with laughter and with hope, Daniel had let himself believe. And then—his mother's last breaths, thousands of miles from home, Daniel and his father in a too-big house, everything familiar vanishing into the air like smoke.

This: the years after, his father's grief and his disappointment, Daniel the only one left to bear the weight of their family legacy, whatever that was, whatever that meant. His father had his new citizenship, his new job, and—what was left? Grief was another foreign country, and Daniel was alone. Recklessness for the sake of recklessness, to chase away the despair of not being enough, a tattoo that burned like the Beijing sun and his father's palm across his cheek, skin blooming red with broken capillaries.

This: senior year of high school and the Asian Art Museum of San Francisco, Will calling heads and Daniel slipping a stolen bronze coin in his pocket because what was one more failure? Nothing could be worse than the way things were. His father the next day, expressionless, as he picked up the coin from Daniel's nightstand and turned to leave, though Daniel had braced himself for something worse. And then, at the door, a bowing of the shoulders, a slow, trembling exhale. *Where did I go wrong?* his father had asked. His voice had held only grief.

Daniel finished his rice, took his bowl to the sink to wash. He had not had an answer then, but now he might have recorded this like a history, marked each year since they had come to America with a new hurt. Better to leave the past behind, to let it wash over him like water.

"I can do the dishes," his dad said. "You should prepare for your interview."

"It's okay," Daniel said, setting his chopsticks in the dishwasher to dry. There were, as usual, very few dishes. "I'll do it."

"Okay." His dad paused. "I'll drive you tomorrow."

"Okay." For a little bit, there was just the sound of the running tap, the feel of sponge and soapy water, and Daniel ran over interview questions in his head, all that he knew about Stanford and its medical school. There was nothing but this, this interview and his future and the ways in which he might find healing.

He wiped his hands on the kitchen towel, the dishes done. His dad was still at the dinner table, his laptop open and a manila folder spread out before him, his fingers running over glossy images. "Headed to bed?" he asked.

It would have been easy to say yes. He had told himself he would not let himself think about *this* here—the heist to come, all the preparation they had already done. "Just about," Daniel said. "What are you working on?"

Surprise crossed his dad's face. There were things that were off-limits, a list that grew over the years: Ma, art, Beijing, anything that required one or both of them to reveal anything vulnerable, anything true. And yet there had been a time when his dad had taken him around Beijing for work, taught his son to look at a museum with a detective's careful gaze. It was not so different from a thief's. "Do you want to see?"

"Sure," Daniel said. He supposed he ought to feel guilty. But in one week they would be touching down in another country, and to pull this off they would need all the help they could get. This was just research, nothing more. The past, the future—neither could hurt if he didn't let it.

Later that evening, as he switched off his lights one by one, he thought once more of the coming week, a museum in the dark and the sound of breaking glass. If all went well, they would be long gone before the police arrived. Daniel settled into bed, exhaustion from a day of flying and interview prep washing over him in a wave. Beneath his door was just a sliver of light, his dad up working even now. For a moment he thought of his dad examining images of Drottningholm Palace, whether he would recognize his son by sight alone, by intuition, and then sleep pulled him under with strange, flickering dreams.

Daniel crossed his ankle over his knee, the crisp lines of his suit shifting with the motion. "A time I worked on a team," he echoed, and for a moment he wasn't at Stanford but in a Beijing penthouse, the setting sun scoring across floor-to-ceiling windows, gilding the edges of priceless stolen art with evening gold. The five of them, spread out on leather couches and the cool marble floor, had faced a whiteboard full of reasons to walk away. They had all chosen to stay. These past three weeks—it had been late nights over Zoom and excuses made to friends, an ever-expanding text document on Alex's encrypted, remote-access laptop.

And so it had gone like this: researching museum security systems and interior design, heists pulled from history, taking notes from books and movies. Sometimes, if he did not think about Beijing and its promises, his father's certain grief, it was almost easy.

In that white, empty interview room, Daniel smiled, let himself pretend. This was the story he told: a research lab, an experiment that was bold and ambitious and almost certain to fail, students who were still almost strangers to each other. Long nights beneath the lab's fluorescent lights, a bench that grew more and more crowded with notes and new ideas. And yet, still, the lingering uncertainty, the fear of failure. All the important parts were true.

When he finished, his interviewer leaned forward. "So?" she asked, and her eyes were bright. "Did it work?"

This time, his smile was real, quick and true and just a little unsure. In one week, they would break into a palace. An experiment, he had called it, and what else was it but the five of them trying to control every variable they could and live with the outcome? "I don't know yet," he said, and it felt like a confession. For all their planning, things could go wrong in so many ways. "But I'm hoping for the best."

Overhead, the timer buzzed. The interview was over. Daniel rose, shook her hand one more time. "Daniel Liang," she said, and because it was the Bay, because it was Stanford, of course she pronounced his last name right, crisp and perfect. "It's been a privilege."

16

ALEX

California, when the light was right, could look like something out of a dream—palm trees against a clear blue sky and slow, unhurried clouds, sunlight lending something like grace to strip mall parking lots, the distant roar of the highway.

It was the last week of October, and Alex Huang was ready to leave this place behind.

She turned from the expanse of windows back to her dual monitors, her cursor blinking at her, and let out a long, slow sigh. It was not quite four in the afternoon, and her desk was already cluttered with empty bottles of cold brew. On her screen was some obscure, complicated task that would determine whether she would get promoted this cycle. A few months ago, it would have felt like her whole world.

Today, though, her mind was elsewhere. Next week, she would be in Sweden.

After that—

Alex thought of Interpol, of the FBI, of Irene Chen and her certainty that Alex could not be a hacker. She laced her hands together, watching the shadows shift over her desk. There was so much left to do and never enough time to do it, and tonight she would go home and lie awake in the dark, in her empty apartment, trying to figure out how to be better than she was. If they got caught—she could not let herself think about it. She would not let it happen.

Around her, her coworkers were already beginning to pack up. It was an early Friday afternoon, and the rest of them—all older than she, all with lives and identities outside of *software engineer*—would soon scatter to the places and people waiting for them. Alex wondered what it felt like.

"Another long night, Alex?" one of them called on the way out.

"The usual," Alex said, lifting her hand in a wave. And in truth, every Friday went the same way. Maybe this was the postgrad life for everyone, these aimless afternoons, the weight of the workweek pressing down on you, these long stretches of all-consuming loneliness. Maybe she would get used to it, after another year or two. And yet Alex was so *tired*. Of this, of everything.

In the corner of her screen, a notification popped up. She moved to dismiss it—another task for tonight, she suspected—before realizing it was a message from Daniel Liang. *Just got out of my interview*, he said. *We still on for boba after work?*

Alex rubbed her eyes, reread the message. She remembered, vaguely, Daniel mentioning that he would be in the area, her saying something noncommittal about doing something together. There were plenty of excuses she could have made—they had never really talked about anything besides art theft, they might not have anything else to talk about, she had *so much to do*—but even as Alex thought them through, she was sweeping her things into her backpack, pulling out her phone to respond.

The prospect of being at work any longer, as her coworkers continued to trickle out, as the sun set and the days and the years kept passing—

How about sooner?

Across from her, Daniel Liang slipped off his suit jacket, draped it across the back of his chair. The bubble tea shop, in late afternoon, had a line that went out the door, but they were seated already, drinks melting slowly on the table as they talked.

"How was the interview?" Alex asked.

"Oh, you know," he said lightly. "Somehow the least interesting part of my life."

Alex laughed. She understood that feeling exactly. "One week left."

He took a long, slow sip from his taro milk tea. "Yeah. You ready?"

Alex thought of museum alarms waiting to be set off and surveillance cameras that swept across empty halls, burner phones and police radio frequencies in a language staticky and foreign. She did not let herself think of Irene, her cool disdain, all the doubts that Alex shared. "I will be," she said. "You?"

The corner of Daniel's mouth lifted into a wry smile. "I have the easy part," he said. "I just have to trust you to get me out."

"Right," she said. She thought of the wail of alarms, Stockholm ablaze with light and sound. "In and out. What else is there?"

"Nothing at all," Daniel said, and it was easy to pretend, though both of them knew no part of this was easy. It'd been three weeks of not enough sleep and new complications every day, reminders of how much they didn't know. But in seven days, they would be in Sweden, all these moving parts set in place at last. Each of them knew their job. Each of them had to do it perfectly.

Outside the window, the sun was low in the sky, light slanting sideways and into their eyes. Alex glanced at her phone, the score of unread notifications. It was just past five p.m., but work had always been this way, bleeding into weekends and evenings. It hadn't mattered, before. There had been nothing else to do.

"My dad's leaving work. He wants to know if I'll be home for dinner," Daniel said, and Alex looked up, was about to offer to give him a ride when she saw the set of his mouth, the tension of his shoulders.

"You okay?" Alex had looked up Daniel's father the evening after she got back from Beijing, wanting to learn more about this investigator they might end up running from. It had been very easy to find out about his wife's death. It was harder to look at Daniel now and pretend she didn't know it. It would be ten years this spring.

"Yeah," he said, his voice too casual. "Just—we aren't on great terms, you know? Ever since my mom died he would always, like 拔苗助长."

Alex blinked. "I don't know that idiom," she said. And then, "Shit. I mean sorry. About your mom. I'm sorry."

He shrugged. "I'm sure Will's mentioned it. Besides, it's not like it's a secret."

"He didn't tell me," Alex said. She hesitated, worrying her straw with her fingertips. She could have left it like that, and yet in one week they would be in Sweden. Daniel had talked about *trust*. "I, uh, ran a search on your dad. Nothing too in depth, I just wanted to be prepared. I— shouldn't have."

Daniel was silent for a brief moment. His hands were pressed together, and Alex could see the veins there, blue and branching beneath his skin. "It's fine," he said. His gaze was at a point outside the window, where the horizon met gray highway. "I'm fine."

"Daniel," she said, "I'm sorry. Really, I am." They were just barely friends yet. Coworkers, mostly. And Alex had never been good at this, this emotions thing. This grief thing. "I don't want to fuck this up."

He met her gaze, gave her a faint smile. "Thanks," he said. "And I get it. Seriously. We have to control for all variables, right?"

It was true. "Still," Alex said. "I should have asked. We're a team, right?"

"We are." Daniel reached for her hand, turned it over. "Bá—miáo—zhù—zhǎng," he spelled in her palm, the characters quick and graceful. It felt like forgiveness, almost.

"What does that mean?"

He paused for a moment, thinking. "It's a metaphor. Something about raising kids, something about gardening. Imagine pulling up a plant by its shoots to try and force it to grow."

Her parents had a garden on their balcony, small and almost inconsequential. That was what she thought of now—how carefully her father tended to the herbs there, how her mother wrapped each plant in plastic when the weather threatened snow. There had been pride in their eyes when she left for MIT, and though she had known they were disappointed when she dropped out, they did not say it. She would have been the first in her family with a college degree.

"I'm sorry," she said. It did not feel like enough.

He shrugged. "It's gotten better," he said. He glanced down, turning his wrist so his watch caught the sun. "Want to come over for dinner?"

"Will that be weird?"

"Probably," Daniel said, but he was smiling a little. "But less weird than when it's just him and me. He might even be excited."

Forgiveness, Alex thought. She did not know Daniel's dad, but she knew family, how they were always hurting each other in new ways, always trying to figure out how to put themselves back together. "Okay," she said.

Daniel rose, swung his suit jacket over his shoulders. "Don't hack my dad's stuff," he said, and tossed her her car keys. Alex blinked. She didn't remember giving them to him.

"Thief," she called.

Daniel turned around, gave her a broad, glittering smile. With the sun at his back, he looked like he belonged in a foreign palace, surrounded by gold and priceless art, that same smile as he looked around, claimed it as his. "You know it."

"I don't think he's home," Alex observed dryly.

"San Francisco traffic," Daniel said. He knelt at the door, pulled pins out from his pocket with the careless elegance of one who had done so many times before. "Give me a sec."

The suburb was quiet, the light soft and pink as it fell over the two of them. Alex leaned back, slipped her hands into the pockets of her jeans. Fall was kinder here than on the East Coast, where the change in seasons stripped trees bare, turned sidewalks wet with rain. "I don't mind waiting."

He slid a second pin in the lock. There was no one else around, but still Alex faced away from the door, her gaze on the green, sprawling trees, the changing sky. "Tell me something about you, Alex. Since you know everything about me."

She didn't bother denying it. "What do you want to know?"

"Something true."

If she hadn't left MIT, she would have been a senior now. There was a way to tell this story that made sense—a full-time offer her junior fall, the kind of money that you couldn't walk away from—and then there was the truth.

When Alex had gotten Google's offer, she had not planned on taking it. Not then and maybe not ever. She had bigger dreams than that, and at MIT she could dream them. Already, there was a collaboration with

Harvard's Tech for Social Good club, partnerships with community organizations, classes about the ethics of big tech. She'd known, even then,
that it was not the same kind of stability as a job at Google or Facebook,
but there was no shortage of money in tech, and after so many years of
waiting to be here—it felt like she had finally arrived. There was so much
she was going to do.

That year, her parents' rent doubled.

And so—quietly, efficiently, Alex packed up her dreams. She accepted
the offer without telling her family, called them two weeks later from her
new apartment, her first Google paycheck already on its way. It had felt
worth it, then. It had felt like the best thing she had ever done.

When had things started to change? Alex couldn't remember, only
that by the time Will called her that September evening, all she wanted
to do was leave. In Beijing, Irene's voice had been like a warning shot.
Why are you here? she said, and Alex told herself she didn't owe this girl
an answer. It was true enough. And yet Alex had also known that she
didn't want to think of it herself.

It had been ten months since Alex had dropped out. Anyone else
might have felt relief. Silicon Valley glittered like California's gold mines
once had, full of vast, infinite possibility, promising a trajectory that
could only go *up*. Still, in Alex's perfect job, in her perfect life—she was
overcome with this impossible, aching grief. Once, she had wanted so
much more than this, had thought it was all within reach.

"Sometimes," she said softly, "I feel like I will never be more than
this."

On the locked door, Daniel's hands stilled. "What do you mean?"

The pink of the sky had deepened to sunset purples, a blue like a
bruise. Alex thought of the past year, of everything she had left behind.
How lonely California felt, even now. Her ambitions, her family's needs,
all of it in conflict, all of it so far away. "When I moved here," she said, "I

thought I could make it a beginning. But it's been less than a year, and already I want a way out."

The lock clicked. At last, Daniel looked up. "Well," he said, "ten million dollars is a hell of a way."

Alex's first language was Cantonese, not Mandarin, and the unfamiliarity of the tones lent the evening a sense of unreality, like moving through a dream. Daniel and his dad chopping up pork for dumplings, Alex rolling out the dough like she had so many times at home. A table set for three, steam curling up and into the air, Mr. Liang telling stories about art and art theft, his voice quick and certain and very much like his son's.

He's good? Alex texted Daniel under the table.

The best.

She glanced at Daniel. For all the tension between him and his father, there was a glint in his eyes that hinted of pride. His father, the sole expert on Chinese art theft in the Western world, asked to consult on cases that spanned countries and continents. What must it have been like to grow up like this, with a father who caught thieves for a living? What must it be like for Daniel now, to know that he was going to become one of them?

Alex excused herself to the bathroom, splashed cold water on her face. She met her gaze in the mirror, noting the circles beneath her eyes, the raised lines of her shoulders, and forced herself to take a long, slow breath. This evening was not supposed to mean anything, and yet she could not help but think about one week from now, a Swedish palace and the five of them piecing together a heist from nothing but books and movies and blind ambition. And then—Mr. Liang going over security tapes of that same heist, searching the museum for fingerprints, footprints, anything they might have left behind.

On her way back to the dining room, Alex took a wrong turn. The room she entered could only have been Mr. Liang's study—scrolls of Chinese calligraphy hung on the walls, and a bookcase filled with art textbooks lined one side. The room was lit only by the glow of a computer screen, still on.

Without meaning to, Alex stepped inside.

The desk was messy. She examined the stacks of papers, the framed photo of a young Daniel and his father by the Golden Gate Bridge, the miniature bronze zodiac head that served as a paperweight. Daniel, like her, was the year of the dragon, born at the turn of the millennium, and the paperweight was of a dragon too, mid-roar.

And then, at last, she came to the computer. She ran her fingers over the keyboard, taking in the locked screen, the FBI logo glowing blue. *ENTER PASSWORD HERE*, it said. The cursor blinked at her, slow and tempting.

"Alex?" Daniel called. "You good?"

Don't hack my dad's stuff.

"Coming," she said, and left the room.

Later that evening, Daniel walked Alex out. It was true night now, and all the light was silver: a thin crescent moon and the distant, glimmering stars, streetlights that glinted against the pavement. Alex reached for her car keys, the headlights flashing once, twice in the darkness.

"Hey," Daniel said. Like this, his face was all shadow, but there was a softness to his voice that she wasn't quite familiar with. "Thanks for tonight."

Alex thought of Daniel and his father moving around each other like faraway planets, their orbits never quite touching, how different this house was, with its silence and its grief, from her family's apartment, loud and messy and full of love. She would not have said she had an easy childhood, but it had not been like this. Yi Hua Lou, her grandparents had named their restaurant, and in English it was something of harmony, something of home. "Anytime," she said.

"Well," he said, "see you next week, Huang."

She wondered if he could see her smile in the dark. "See you, Liang."

Still, as she drove away into the vast, vast dark, Alex's mind drifted back to that empty study. She was not thinking about the computer, with its password and its possibilities, but that carefully framed photo and the paperweight that marked Daniel's zodiac year, all the ways father and son reached for each other without the other one knowing.

There were so many ways this could end in grief.

17

WILL

Will Chen rested his cheekbone against the back of his wrist, listening to the airplane's steady background roar. The plane might have been done in chiaroscuro, shadows stretching long across empty aisles, the sleeping figures of the other passengers, and he thought of the past few weeks and a Harvard studio, sculpting as the days grew colder, as this heist drew closer. When he closed his eyes, he could see the bared fangs of a snake's mouth, the flash of bronze off false light, all that he wanted almost within reach.

"Can't sleep?" Lily's voice was soft as she leaned over her armrest.

He smiled, just barely. "You too?"

Between them, Irene opened one eye slowly, catlike. "*I* am sleeping."

Lily caught his eye, winked. "Sorry," she said. "Switch with me? I want to watch a movie."

"You'll regret this."

"Oh, probably," Lily said cheerfully, but already she was sliding into Irene's empty seat, her knees pulled close. He could see her lashes as they brushed against her skin, the hollow of her throat as she tilted her head up to examine him, and he thought of a Rembrandt painting, everything in darkness save for this. "So," she said. "How's your sculpture?"

Will was quiet for a moment. He still had the rest of his final portfolio to finish, job applications to museums in New York and LA, all the cities that were big enough to swallow him whole. In a few months, he would graduate. He did not know if he was ready to leave it all behind.

"Out of my hands," he said at last.

Lily's voice was thoughtful. "You never told me. Why art history and not art?"

He almost smiled. That was always the question, wasn't it? "I'm good at art," he said, "but not good enough."

Lily waited, the light falling silver on her face, and he remembered Durham when the moon was high, the two of them still strangers to each other. *Tell me how it started*, he had said, and she had. When he spoke again, he was still thinking about the island Lily had grown up on and the breaking of the sea, how it must have felt to leave it all behind.

"I was never going to pursue art," he said. In the quiet dark, the words felt like a confession. He could have deflected—should have, maybe—but she had given him truth, weeks ago. He would do the same. "I think a part of me always knew that. Maybe if I had started earlier, if I had given it everything I had. But—" He stopped. What else was there to say besides this? All these years and he was not an artist.

"The risk was too great," Lily said softly.

He was not surprised she understood. They were all children of immigrants. They were all searching for something to hold on to. "Art history was the closest I could get," he said. "And besides—the classes aren't too different. I will have had these four years."

"Is it enough?"

Four years of falling light and watercolor skies, the slow, tentative tracing of a shoulder, a wrist, the curve of a spine. There was history to be made and found like this. "It has to be," he said, because there was nothing else left. He would graduate so soon.

Lily was quiet for a long moment. He was afraid she would press further, expose all the raw, ugly parts of him, his love of art eclipsed only by his fear of failure, but when she spoke, her voice was gentle. "How do you know?" she said. "That you aren't good enough?"

In the blue light of the airplane, Will examined her. The shadow of her collarbone, the dusting of freckles across the bridge of her nose. Her eyes the color of the sky beyond the window of the plane, dark and infinite. Had anyone ever asked him this? He wasn't sure. "Because," he said, "what I draw is never as lovely as what I see."

Her smile was quick, and he felt the conversation change shape, turn lighter and easier. It was a gift, he suspected, one that he was not sure he deserved. "Are you flirting with me, Will?" she asked.

"I wouldn't dare," he said, but he was smiling too.

"Good," she said. "I know your type."

Will raised a brow. "And what is that?"

"Temporary," she said. There was no judgment in her voice, just careful observation, and he thought of the past four years, Harvard as the seasons changed. Everything that was beautiful—painting in a studio washed with light, a stranger who might smile at him as twilight fell—could not last. How many times had girls wanted more from him? How many times had his relationships fallen apart because he could not bring himself to say *forever*? It had always gone like this, the late nights and the laughter and the fall of light on bare skin, everything going well until, inevitably, came talk of the *future* and *where is this going* and Will wondering, again, why the most he could offer was still not enough.

"And yours?" he asked.

He expected her to say something about permanence, about what might last. He was used to this, to never quite living up to what others expected of him. But Lily's smile was easy, effortless, and he remembered that this girl raced cars when night fell, had grown up on an island where every summer meant a storm. "The same," she said. Her gaze was steady on his. "But that doesn't matter, does it?"

Four years, and every relationship ended the same way. Once, one of his suitemates had asked him what he was looking for that no one seemed able to give. He hadn't had an answer then. How could he explain how it felt to know, with a terrible and unflinching certainty, that you were not enough for your dreams? There was so much he wanted, so much that would always be out of reach.

And yet—in a few hours, they would touch down in Stockholm. Will could see the lights in the distance, how they reflected against the waves of Lily's hair, the shine of her eyes in the dark. If this had been Harvard, it would have been a relief to hear her say it, that she was not looking for anything besides *temporary*. If she had let him—and he thought she might—he would have reached out, his thumb tracing the bow of her mouth as he tipped her head to his. He had never slept well alone. But Lily was not a stranger, not anymore, and they had bigger things ahead. This heist—it was worth more than just a moment. It was worth everything.

"No," Will said. "It doesn't."

Still, after they watched their movie, Lily leaned her head on his shoulder, her eyes drifting shut. "I didn't know you liked rom-coms," she said.

"They're unrealistic," Will said. It wasn't a denial. "But there's something about them, all the same."

There was a smile in her voice. "We're about to Ocean's Eleven our way through the Western world. I don't know if we can talk about *realism*."

"Fair." And this might have been out of a movie too, this girl's head on his shoulder, the plane as it cut through a sky as deep and dark as the sea, every moment bringing them closer to this impossible heist. "Besides, this could be a love story yet."

Lily laughed lightly. Her voice was soft, half asleep already. "Keep this up, Will, and I might do something I'll regret."

Another time, another place, he would have taken it as a dare. "Go to sleep, Lily," he said. They would land in just a few hours.

When Lily fell asleep, her breathing turning steady and even, he was still awake, his mind on foreign countries and faraway art. This weekend, however it went, would change everything.

How do you know that you aren't good enough?

Careful not to jostle her, Will reached for his sketchbook. He drew the plane first—long, reaching shadows and a window opening to the distant sky. And then, after a moment of hesitation, he drew Lily too, her hair spilling against her shoulders and the curved, crescent moons of her closed eyes.

The rest was a blur. He remembered the noise of the Stockholm airport, brightly lit signs, and the winding line through customs, leaning against a cool plastic trolley as he waited for Irene to make her declarations. Daniel disappearing momentarily into an airport gift shop, reemerging to toss Lily a pocketknife and a conspiratorial smile. The fierce blue of the midday sky. The five of them crowding into a too-small cab, Alex distributing new flip phones to the upbeat, unfamiliar chords of Swedish pop music. When they reached their hotel, Will checked them in, handed passports to the receptionist, waited. Everything seemed to be moving too quickly.

And then, at last, the two adjoining hotel rooms, with their neutral colors and low, low light. Will shut the door, collapsed on the bed. Next to him, Daniel turned off the lone bedside lamp, set an alarm on his phone. It was Friday afternoon. They had thirty-six hours until it was time to rob Drottningholm Palace.

Will slept, and did not dream.

When he woke, the room was empty. The curtains were still drawn, and he pulled them open to see Sweden in sunset, the sun low and red in the evening sky. The hotel room smelled of something light, sweet, and Will took his time brushing his teeth, changing into clean clothes. The evening stretched long and luxurious before him, full of possibility, and when he opened the door to the other room, he saw everyone else was already up. There was a box of pastries between them, and Irene held out a cinnamon bun.

"Dessert first?" he asked, raising a brow. Still, he pulled the bun apart in his hands, let sugar and cinnamon dissolve on his tongue. He could not remember the last thing he'd eaten. It had to have been something on the plane, hours ago.

"We were waiting for you," Lily said, a smile in her voice. "But I figured we should have dinner by the water, see some of Stockholm while we can."

Will checked his watch. He knew there was more to be done, and yet the sun was setting, the hotel room shot through with light, and the prospect of dinner by the open water, this city spread out before them—

"Let's go," he said.

⸻

They didn't talk about the heist. Instead they cracked open a bottle of cheap red wine, watched the sun disappear beneath Lake Mälaren. There were restaurants along the boardwalk, lights swinging low over uneven water, but somehow it was better like this, feet dangling off the edge of the pier, the world reduced to water and sky and a salt-laced wind. Dinner was an assortment of Swedish open-faced sandwiches, and there was dark bread and slivers of sharp cheese, salmon that glistened in the falling light.

Will leaned back, the cobblestone cool against his palms, his gaze not on his crew but on this unfamiliar city, its changing light. A month had passed so quickly. "What will you do with your ten million dollars?" he asked.

Next to him, Daniel skipped a rock off the pier, the stone flashing four, five, six times before sinking beneath the water. "Start us off," he suggested.

Will thought of his college years coming to a close, how it might feel to leave Harvard for the last time. If they pulled this off, what would come after? Without the weight of his student debt, without the pressure of searching for a stable job or health insurance—he did not know what he would do, what shape his future would take. "Something beautiful," he said at last, and that was the only truth he knew.

"A museum of diaspora art," Alex suggested.

"A takeover of China Poly." There was a glint in Irene's eye as she said this, and Will wouldn't have been surprised if that was his sister's own plan. He did not doubt that she could do it. "You could redo the Poly Art Museum, at least."

"Or," Lily said, her gaze searching, "you could make something of your own."

The water was a mirror to the darkening sky. "Any of those," Will said. "All of those."

As the moon rose, once in the sky and once in the mouth of the sea, they talked of dreams. Paying off student loans, traveling the world, sending money to parents and grandparents and distant relatives. *I've always wanted a building named after me,* Irene mused out loud, only half joking, and no one disagreed. Ten million dollars—here, it felt infinite.

When Will checked his watch again, it was just past midnight. They had twenty-four hours left before the break-in. His gaze swept over his crew, over the moon reflected in water, to the distant horizon. Lights studded the space where black water met black sky. If he squinted, he could almost see the shape of Drottningholm Palace across the water, outlined in the waiting dark.

18

IRENE

rene Chen stood at the steps of Drottningholm Palace, her head tilted up toward the clear blue sky. To anyone else, she might have been taking in the splendor of the palace exterior, the rows of windows that reflected the light of the morning sun. Overhead, the Swedish flag whipped gold and blue against the cloudless sky.

"Well?" Alex Huang said in her ear. "What are you waiting for?"

Irene didn't respond for a moment, her gaze lingering on the Royal Guards with their rifles and sharp-tipped hats, the cameras tucked discreetly at each entrance. If Irene had been her brother, Alex wouldn't have asked. Drottningholm was lovely in the morning light, and the two of them were friends in a way that she and Alex weren't. But Irene didn't need Alex to like her. She just needed Alex to do her job.

"Six guards that I can see," she said. "More that I can't. Two cameras at the main door." Before Alex could respond, Irene strode up the steps, past guards and cameras and into a museum flung open and waiting.

She knew the cameras caught her—dark hair and a tapered camel coat, boots that clicked against the marble floor.

Let them, she thought.

"Make a right," Alex said.

Irene, if she closed her eyes, could see the map of Drottningholm that they all knew so well. The main palace, the opera house, the gardens with their Baroque statues, stolen from Prague after a different war. And, of course, the Chinese Pavilion in gold and green and deep red, the zodiac head that waited for them within its walls. This was not the path that they would take tonight, but it would get her there regardless.

Irene, following Alex's instructions, turned toward the northern wing of the palace. She could have been any other tourist, taking photos of the painted ceilings, the marble busts of long-dead kings. And if her phone also caught a security camera tucked in one corner, or a guard with his back turned? It was chance, nothing more.

"Now left," Alex said. Irene was outside of the main palace now, and the gardens were spread out before her. They were green even in late October, with shrubs cut in precise geometric shapes, and though Irene knew the way forward as well as Alex did, she stopped at the fountain at the edge of the garden, reached for a map she didn't have. There was a guard at the fountain, and when he looked up she smiled at him, lifted a hand.

"Excuse me," Irene said, tilting her head so her hair fell over the wireless earbud tucked in one ear. Their burner phones had Bluetooth connectivity, but barely. "I'm a little lost. Can you point me to the Chinese Pavilion?"

"Irene," Alex said slowly. Irene imagined her in their shared hotel room, laptop open and blue light casting shadows over her face, two sharp brows drawn together. "What are you doing?"

"Straight through the park," the guard said, pointing southeast. "And then left into the forest, and then another left, well, somewhat—ah, I should have a few extra maps."

Irene twisted her hands together. "That would help *so much*," she said. "I'm supposed to be meeting my professor at the pavilion for a class and I'm already late—"

The guard patted his uniform again, searching. Up close, it was almost a Duke blue. "I'm sorry. I must have given them all away already." He paused, taking in Irene's expression. It was early enough that there was no one else in the gardens. "Do you want me to take you there?"

"*Leave.*" Alex's voice was an order. "You're drawing attention."

"Please," Irene said, her face breaking into a relieved smile. "If you don't mind."

They took the gardens at a brisk walk, almost a jog, the fall air crisp with possibility. "Thank you so much," Irene said. "This is my first time visiting Drottningholm, and I expected—well, I expected it to be easier to navigate."

"Happy to help," he said. "We're going to make a left here, cut through some of the gardens. Many visitors get lost on the palace grounds. That's why we're here. You are here on exchange, right? From China?"

"America, actually," Irene said pleasantly. "My accent didn't give it away? Everyone has been telling me that I drag my vowels."

The guard nodded. "You do," he said, and Irene laughed. "I'm just used to Chinese visitors to the pavilion. They tend to have a particular interest in our bronze snake head."

"Shit," Alex said.

"How fascinating," Irene said easily. "I don't actually know anything about the art at the Chinese Pavilion. My architecture professor just wanted us to visit because the pavilion exemplifies the merging of Western and Eastern design."

"That it does," he said. "Drottningholm Palace has many wonders, but the Chinese Pavilion is special. Do you want to hear about some of its art?"

"Please," Irene said. In the distance, she could see the curved roof of the Chinese Pavilion, gold in the morning light. "Tell me more."

◦━━━◦

"What the hell was that?" Alex demanded once the guard had left. "You could have just taken a map. Or listened to his directions. Or listened to *me*. You *knew* how to get here."

There were no cameras outside the Chinese Pavilion, no guards, just this summer palace, surrounded by trees and red, falling leaves. "Maybe I forgot," Irene said, walking up the pavilion steps. "Besides, he was out of maps."

"You were flirting."

"I wasn't." Her mind was not on this conversation but on the path the guard had cut through the gardens, the turns they had made through green shrubs and carefully maintained grass. "Not that it matters."

Alex was still talking, but Irene wasn't paying attention anymore. She pulled the door open, walked in, the click of her heels loud against the polished wooden floors. There were guards inside, cameras that flashed in the quiet light, and Irene took her time as she moved through the rooms of the pavilion. Each one was a different color, tinting silk wallpaper and porcelain vases in jade green or decadent red, a yellow that gleamed like the sun. Rococo, Irene remembered. Will was the artist in the family, but she knew enough to recognize the extravagance here. Art could be beauty, but it was also power. *Look*, it demanded, *and don't turn away.*

And then, in a room lined in blue and gold, Irene saw the bronze snake head. She was not foolish enough to linger on it, though she knew no one would think anything of it if she did. It was the room's centerpiece, after all, and the bronze flashed like a beckoning hand. Instead she examined the other pieces in the glass showcases that lined the room, caught a glimpse of a camera in a reflection as she turned away.

In her ear, Alex's voice was a low, angry murmur, less than background noise. Irene continued through the Chinese Pavilion, taking care to visit every room, to spend the same amount of time in each, building this palace in her head. This was how the rooms opened into each other; these were the hallways and the windows and the high, reaching archways, lined in gold and stolen history.

At last, Irene left the pavilion, crossing the threshold into sunlight and the slight October chill, a sky cracked open. As she walked down the steps, she removed a handful of palace maps from the inside pocket of her coat, dropped them into the waiting trash can. It had been so easy to brush against the guard, to lift these maps from the outer pocket of his uniform and pretend she did not know the way to go. In Drottningholm Palace's four hundred years of history, it had never been robbed.

That would change soon enough.

19

ALEX

Alex Huang could not remember the last time she had been angry. Growing up, she had watched her parents spend late nights balancing checkbooks, early mornings with customers who spoke in loud, overenunciated English. In high school, she had seen for the first time the stark contrast between her life and that of other Asian Americans in New York City, classmates who talked about Chinatown as a place for cheap eats, who always had money to spend on private tutors and SAT prep courses. At MIT, it had been the same way. Friends who called themselves upper middle class, who assumed Alex was the same way, who spoke of the Chinese American experience of science fairs and summer trips to Beijing or Shanghai as if it were universal. What was the point in calling it unjust? What was the point in calling it anything at all? When a classmate found out that she had gotten a return offer from Google, he had looked at her and said, so softly she could have convinced herself she'd imagined it, *a diversity hire*. She hadn't been angry then either. She would do the work. She would do it better. That was all there was.

From her hotel room, Alex Huang looked out at the Stockholm sky-line, her gaze tracing the line of buildings against the water, the bright, flashing light of the morning sun. She was slow to anger. Of course she was. She had been so many things before. A first-generation college student, a college dropout, a daughter and granddaughter of immigrants. A woman in tech, surrounded by software engineers who never quite saw her as one of them. If she let herself be angry, her anger would spill over. It would burn her alive.

The door to the hotel room opened. Alex turned, met Irene's gaze. Her whole life, she'd always had something to prove. And then there was Irene, who belonged everywhere she went, who did not need this job or anything else, who had never known what it was like to fight so hard to be seen as equal, as enough. Irene had never wanted for anything in her life, and yet Alex had thought—well, she had thought that Irene would do this right anyway. What had Will said about his sister? She had never failed at anything.

Alex took a step forward. Drottningholm in gold and sprawling green, Irene and a guard walking side by side. She could see it, even now. "What were you *thinking?*"

In the morning light, Irene's face might have been carved by a sculptor's hand, high cheekbones and a lovely, bored mouth. "Are you still on this?" she said.

"Am *I* still on this?" Alex asked. "You literally asked a guard for *directions to the place we're going to rob tonight.*" Saying it aloud—it might have been funny if it hadn't been so reckless.

Irene slipped off her coat, her shoes, the motions slow and unhurried, and set her tote on the desk that Alex was leaning against. She brushed close enough that Alex had to shift out of the way, just slightly. Somehow it felt like a concession.

"I did my job," Irene said.

Irene moved through the world like it was meant to give way before her. Alex crossed her arms. "Your job was to *listen to me*," she said, because she was angry, because it was true. "But instead—what? You decided you knew better? That you didn't need help? All you had to do was *walk through a museum* and *not draw attention*. Everything else is *done*."

Irene laughed. "Right."

"What's that supposed to mean?"

Irene raised a brow. "One month," she said slowly. "One month and you couldn't figure out how to hack into museum security. You couldn't figure out how to shut off the Drottningholm alarms. Tonight, three of us will rob a museum, and you'll watch as the alarms go off. Tell me again how *I* didn't do my job."

The hotel room was silent. Morning light cut a solitary square on the carpeted floor, and dust motes spun in slow, lazy circles above it. Out of the corner of her eye, Alex saw the door linking this room and the adjacent one crack open. Will, maybe, or Daniel, looking to play mediator. She strode to the door, slammed it shut before turning to face Irene. It had been one month already. One month of Irene acting like this heist was not Alex's too, like Alex was the one who was failing them. Irene, who got along with everybody, who Will claimed had once talked a Chinese museum curator into gifting her something from his personal collection, had never looked at Alex and seen anything worth keeping.

"Fuck you," Alex said.

Irene's smile was cold, mocking.

Alex couldn't look at her anymore. Instead she crossed the room to the open window, the balcony beyond it. In the sunlight, Stockholm was something out of a postcard, blue skies and distant, white-capped water, a palace rising from the waves. "I got in," Alex said, gaze still on the horizon, Drottningholm Palace outlined in light. "Not that it matters, but I got in."

They had all thought she couldn't. *Alex* had thought she couldn't. For all that Will liked to claim she was a hacker, she wasn't, and this was strange, uncrossed territory. But she had spent her whole life doing the impossible, and one late night, her room cast in blue light, Alex had watched Drottningholm Palace unfold on her screen, security feeds and alarm networks and a flickering mesh of possibility at her fingertips.

Then she had slammed her computer shut.

Irene's voice was a question. "But you won't turn off the alarms."

"I'm good at my job," Alex said. The sky was a pure, uninterrupted blue. Far below, streets and cars and pedestrians were small, make-believe. "But I'm not FBI. If I shut down Drottningholm, they'll be able to trace it back to us. We care about getting *out*. The alarms won't keep you from making it in. But you knew that already, didn't you?"

Irene crossed the room, came to stand by her side. It was just the two of them, faces turned toward Stockholm, toward Drottningholm, toward all the danger their future held. "I talked to the guard," Irene said, her voice low, "because tonight, when the alarms go off, we'll need to know the route the guards will take. The path he showed me, the fastest path to the Chinese Pavilion—that's the path we'll have to avoid."

Alex let out a long, slow breath. It wasn't an apology. "You could have told me."

"Would you have said yes?"

"You didn't give me a choice."

"I know." Irene reached out, caught a strand of Alex's hair between her thumb and forefinger. Alex did not flinch, not even when Irene's knuckles brushed the edge of her jaw. What were they? Tied together in this, no matter how much they didn't want to be. Just a few months, and they would have everything they ever wanted. Alex thought of when all this began, Beijing as the night fell. She thought of these past few weeks, Irene and her carefully constructed smiles, her words like the edge of a blade. It was better like this, maybe. To have all of it peeled back. To know that it wasn't in her imagination.

Alex caught Irene's wrist. For a brief, terrible moment, she was tempted to press, to see what would happen if she did. Instead she let go. What good did anger do? Ten million dollars. Her life and how it changed. She could survive this. She could survive anything. "Do your job, Irene," she said. "And let me do mine."

We're a team, Irene could have said. *Our jobs are one and the same.* But Irene had never liked her, and so instead she smiled. It didn't quite reach her eyes. "Stay out of my way, Alex."

Alex would not let it hurt.

20

DANIEL

Daniel Liang leaned against the railing of the hotel balcony, the iron cool against his skin. When he turned his phone over in his hand, clock face glowing blue in the darkness, he named flexors, extensors, branching vessels, anatomy pared down, stripped clean. This was what he knew. This was what stayed the same.

Tonight, after they had robbed Drottningholm Palace, he would not be the same person he was. But skin and tendon and bone would remain. He could hold on to this if nothing else.

Before he could change his mind, he pressed *dial*. The sound of the phone ringing, signal traveling across continents, was loud in the tentative dark.

"Hello?"

"Ba," Daniel said. His dad had picked up on the first ring. It was not enough time for him to figure out what to say.

"Son," he said. Silence stretched between them, and Daniel heard the shuffling of papers, the sound of a folder closing. "Have you been getting enough sleep?"

"Yes, Ba."

"How are your classes?"

This was easy. The questions, the answers. Daniel thought of a week ago, Alex in his childhood home, the three of them making dumplings together. He could not remember the last time he had cooked with his dad. He could not remember the last time he had called his dad like this. He was searching for something, he knew. He would not call it forgiveness.

"Fine," he said. *Hard*, he wanted to add, because they were. For all the time he spent on this job, he spent just as much on classes, on interview prep, on everything that went into making him the person he wanted so desperately to become. It was worth it. It didn't mean he wasn't tired.

His dad was silent. "Anything else?" he asked.

Change always felt like too much, like not enough. He didn't know what else to say. Before him, Stockholm was nothing but pinpricks of light in the darkness, distant and insignificant. "Will we go back to China this year?" Daniel didn't know where the question came from. In this hotel room, on the cusp of change, he was missing home.

"Of course," his dad said. Beijing and its sharp, lovely sounds, gray skies and harsh light, art museums and his mother's curved tomb. Whatever else changed, there was this. "Every year."

"Okay," Daniel said. When summer came, when they flew back to Beijing, these five thefts would be done. He dug his thumb into the palm of his hand, thought of capillaries breaking, blood that rose red and dark. "Nothing else," he said.

"Okay."

"Okay."

Daniel expected his dad to hang up first, but instead his father said, almost gently, "Son?"

What else was there? "Yes?"

A pause, soft and staticky. "Thanks for calling."

Daniel was the one who hung up, in the end. He tilted his head up toward the sky, the stars. He could have been anywhere. He wished he were.

Behind him, the balcony door slid open with a soft whoosh. "Come on," Will said. His hand against Daniel's shoulder was gentle. They had known each other for long enough that he would know what Daniel was doing out here, would have recognized his bowed shoulders, the curl of his hands against the iron rail. "Let's go inside."

Daniel bowed his head. "I'm afraid," he said. It was the kind of confession he wouldn't have made to anyone else, not now, when it was too late to turn back, when everyone else was jittery with excitement. It would be just the three of them this evening, running through a darkened museum, and he could not show fear.

Will moved to stand next to him, and for a moment it was just the two of them watching a foreign skyline, the darkness of a distant sea.

Daniel thought of another time, years ago, standing next to Will before the Pacific Ocean. It had been the summer before their freshman year of college and they had decided to hike part of the Pacific Crest Trail, just the two of them, one final adventure before the rest of their lives began. When they had made it to Oregon, bruised and exhausted, they had stumbled to the ocean. The water had stung their cuts, but the air it had tasted of salt, of sea, of things reborn.

"Me too," Will said.

Daniel took a long, slow breath. If he concentrated, he could still taste the ocean. "If this goes wrong—" he said.

"Then we'll face it together," Will said. "Like we always have."

It had been ten years since they'd met, since Daniel had seen California unfold before him like an unfulfilled promise. "I hate you sometimes, you know."

Will's gaze didn't leave the skyline. "I know." His voice was soft. "Sometimes I hate me too."

He had always thought Will had it all figured out. Will, who was at Harvard, whose Instagram was always pale colors and girls who looked like art, the edge of a museum skylight. But he remembered, too, the end of that long hike the summer before they had both left for college, how Will's voice had been very soft and very sad. *I am afraid*, he said, *Harvard will eat me alive.*

Don't lie, Daniel had said. Will had never been afraid of that.

Will had tilted his head up, to a sky strewn with stars, the Oregon trees stretching high and unforgiving above them. *I am afraid I will get everything I ever wanted.*

Why does that scare you?

Because what I want is not what my parents want. Because this is not the American Dream I was told I should chase.

"Will," Daniel said.

"There's still time to change your mind," he said, and Daniel didn't know if it was for him or for Will himself.

They had just hours left. "No," Daniel said. "There's not."

"Be honest," Will said. "If it hadn't been us—if you didn't know us— would you still have said yes?"

Daniel pressed his palms together. The evening air was cool against his skin. This might have been four years ago, the Pacific still a distant dream. *And you?* Will had asked. *What do you dream of?*

After all these years, and Daniel was still searching for a way home. *Healing*, he'd said.

That's it?

The past still felt like a wound. *That's all there is.*

"Will?" It was Lily this time, dressed in dark colors. A leather jacket was slung over her shoulders. "It's time to go."

Will's smile was sad. "If this goes wrong," he said, "I hope you'll be able to forgive me."

"And if this goes right?" He didn't want to walk into a heist like this, fractured open, uncertainty lingering in all the spaces between his ribs. Still, he thought of his dad, that ever-elusive promotion, how far away China felt.

Will pushed himself away from the railing. "I hope you'll forgive me still."

21

LILY

A month had passed like this. Lily Wu remembered wind, sharp and stinging, steering a speedboat through unsteady waves. Even now, on the cusp of their first theft, everything that felt like a beginning, she remembered late September and Myrtle Beach, the telltale shine of the Atlantic Ocean. She and Irene had driven down a week or so after Beijing, traded a handful of crumpled bills for a few hours on a boat that cut through choppy water. When the rental office had asked why they were here, on a nondescript weekend in early fall, Lily had spun the speedboat's keys in her hand, let it flash quick and silver in the gray light.

Something new, she said.

On the open water, she had looked at Irene, silhouetted against a dark expanse of ocean. None of this had felt real. China and a palace in ruins, the morning light breaking over stone. Missing art and foreign museums, a crew of college students just reckless enough to believe this could be done. Irene's knuckles were white against the dash, but when she met Lily's gaze, her smile was wide. *You're not afraid?* Irene asked. She had to shout to be heard.

The salt air stung Lily's face, her hair, all the exposed parts of her skin. *Not of this.*

Then what?

It had been the kind of weekend where she could feel the approach of colder days, a chill that bit into her skin. Lily's gaze lingered on the horizon, thin and wavering in the distance, the Atlantic rising to meet a tumultuous gray sky. Her parents had come to America with nothing, had staked their future on an island by an unfamiliar sea. And now— what was this if not the American Dream? She was at Duke, far from the hurricanes of home, from all that her parents had left behind, and yet she could never tell if she was running toward something or just away.

Still, there was this. An overcast morning, light that flashed off dark water. A heist to come and her hands on the wheel. Lily looked at Irene, smiled. What did she have to be afraid of?

Nothing at all, she had said, and the wind carried her words away, into the salt air and the expanse of the sea, an unbroken line of possibility.

<hr />

That night, Lily and Will were the first ones to leave. Night had fallen already, and Stockholm was all darkness and distant, wavering light. She had a pocketknife in her leather jacket, and she ran her fingers over its edge, thinking of how things opened, how things began.

Next to her, Will reached for her hand, caught it. His voice held a smile. "In case anyone wonders what we're doing out so late."

Before them, streetlights cast warm light over cobblestone, the occasional glint of a car. It was just past one, and the city was quiet at this hour, subdued in its promise. They could have been on a date, leaving a theater for a stroll by the water, neither willing to say goodbye just yet. Will, despite the heist to come, was dressed as cleanly as always—a wool coat and a carefully styled button-down, shoes that clicked as he walked. Over one shoulder, a leather messenger bag held the soft black clothes he would change into, everything that would be discarded later this evening.

Lily laughed. "Does that line usually work?"

Will raised a brow. "Who says it's a line?"

Lily laughed again. Across the street, a group of young Swedish college students tumbled out of a bar, their voices carrying in the stillness. She cast a deliberate look at them and then brought her free hand up, curled it around the fabric of Will's collar to pull him closer. Through his shirt, his skin was warm, and the low light glanced off his high cheekbones, those eyes the exact color of a Galveston night. He was the kind of beautiful that might pull her under, if she let him. "Then tell me it's not," she said.

His gaze lingered on hers. For a moment, she thought he might lean forward, call her bluff. What was college for, if not this? Fast cars and strangers with soft mouths. He would taste like salt, like evening air, and for a moment she might not feel so lost. But then he smiled, quick and lovely, and released her hand. "Fine," he said. "You win this round."

Lily untangled her hand from his shirt, smoothed out his collar. The group was gone by now, and even if it wasn't, it was dark enough that the two of them wouldn't be noticed or remembered. They both knew it. "No distractions," she said, because that was all this was. "We have a job to do."

The crosswalk light changed color, and Will smiled at her. A real smile this time, full of anticipation for the night to come. "That we do."

This late, the pier was empty. Wind whistled over the water, and Lily ran her gaze over the rows of waiting boats. They had been here last night, had dinner in full view of this pier, and Will's laugh was swept away by the October wind. "Convenient," he said.

Lily strode forward. "You're not the only one who plans ahead."

The boat—*her* boat, for tonight—was small and fast, the name painted on its side the Swedish word for *flight*. It belonged to one of Stockholm's wealthy, was used just enough that it would have fuel for the night, not enough that anyone would notice the damage until they were long gone. Lily examined the raised deck, the railing just out of reach from where she stood. Next to her, Will knelt, laced his hands together on his knee. "Come on," he said, "I'll prop you up."

Lily slipped on her gloves. "Thanks," she said easily. They had been flirting earlier—for fun, for no real reason other than that they could—but now the night pressed down on them, soft and serious. Stockholm, in the low light, was a beginning. What would happen if they pulled this off?

In one smooth motion, Lily was in the air. She caught the rail and swung herself over, landing with a soft sound on the empty boat. Her phone flashlight cast long, searching shadows in the darkness as she ran her fingers over the control panel, flipped her pocketknife open.

"How long do I have?" she asked.

Will leaned against the side of the boat, his stance deliberately casual. Still, his gaze was alert as he looked over the pier, the distant lights. "Thirty minutes until showtime."

She pried open the control panel. The wires were tangled, all the same color in the darkness, and she adjusted the light of her phone, began the slow, careful work of hot-wiring this boat.

"How did you learn to do this?" he asked.

She kept her gaze on the panel, her hands pulling wires apart, thinking of long summer days, the soft whir of the A/C at her neighbor's auto shop. Evenings spent beneath a wide Galveston sky, with a flashlight and the hood of her car propped up, music playing tinnily from a converted radio. No matter how late she stayed up, she could never make it until her parents came home. "Cars, boats, they all work the same way," she said. She shrugged lightly. "I had a lot of free time growing up."

Will's gaze touched hers, just for a moment, before he looked back at the water. "Do you like it?" he asked. His voice was light. "It's a little less glamorous than the street-racing part."

Lily laughed. It was true enough. "I do," she said, and meant it. Even when it was hard—and it so often was—there was something about working through a problem with a known solution, the certainty that she could find here if nowhere else. Sometimes it felt like these moments were the only times the world stood still.

Beneath her palms, the boat came to life. Lily smiled, fierce and pleased, and looked up at Will. There was something like awe in the soft part of his mouth, those wide eyes, and she couldn't help but laugh. She liked him more like this, when neither of them had to pretend. "Humanities majors," she said. "They're always impressed by concrete skills."

To her great pleasure, Will laughed too. "You wound me."

They had fifteen minutes until the heist. Lily untied the ropes that kept them docked as Will changed in the small cabin, and then they were flying through the water, dark waves breaking white against the speedboat. They were close enough to the Baltic Sea that it felt like the ocean, salt air and a cold, unforgiving wind. Lily cut one wide circle around the water before dropping Will off. Daniel and Irene were at Drottningholm already, and as she slipped in one earbud, she heard their voices, the last few moments of this plan taking shape.

"Five seconds," Will said.

A breath in, a breath out. Here on the water, idling, the only light was her phone. It threw long shadows over the boat, the darkness of Lake Mälaren at night. Clouds, low and fast-moving, covered the sliver of moon, the scattering of faraway stars. Tonight they would do the impossible. If Lily closed her eyes, she could almost see the arc of a Molotov cocktail in the air, fire blooming red against the heavy dark.

What are you afraid of?

Nothing at all.

In the distance, sirens began to wail.

ACT TWO

Win as though you're used to it and lose as if you like it.

—ISABELLA STEWART GARDNER

22

DANIEL

Darkness pressed down on the Chinese Pavilion. Daniel Liang could hear the sirens getting closer, see the flash of blue, fluorescent lights. Next to him, Will and Irene were still as statues, frozen in place next to Drottningholm Palace. It would be so easy to get caught right now. They were dressed in all black, ski masks obscuring everything but a slash of skin, the glint of irises and sclera in the dark. It might have happened without them even noticing. The tripping of a silent alarm, a guard passing by and hesitating, just for a moment, turning his gaze to the trees.

And then—in the distance, the police cars turned, the sound of sirens fading as they sped toward the other side of the city and the smell of fire and distant smoke.

"Go," Alex said.

Beneath his gloved hands, Daniel lifted his bat on his shoulder, found his footing on the stone steps. He didn't quite feel ready. It didn't matter.

He swung.

The glass doors of the Chinese Pavilion shattered.

Daniel stood there for a moment, waiting for the wail of alarms, a guard's distant shouts, the sound of glass falling like rain on the palace's steps. But the night guard had passed already and Drottningholm used silent alarms, and even the clear, distinct sound of breaking glass was carried away by the night wind.

They had six minutes.

Inside the pavilion, the only sound was their footsteps, the unevenness of their breath in the dark. Daniel followed Irene, each room a blur of silk and priceless art, thinking of palace guards running toward them, police officers turning their cars around. They had timed this already, traced out paths, Irene calculating how quickly the guards had to run from the main palace to here, Lily renting a car and driving it from one end of Stockholm to another, stopwatch running and foot on the gas, but there were so many things they still did not know, so many ways this could still go wrong. Six minutes could pass in the blink of an eye.

At last, Irene stopped.

This room was almost identical to the others, all the colors washed out in the darkness, but in the center, surrounded by the soft glow of a single emergency light, were three glass showcases. The snake zodiac head—mouth open, bronze gleaming—was in the center, illuminated beneath a solitary spotlight.

If this had been a movie, a TV show, any of those stories all of them knew so well, it would have happened quietly, effortlessly. They would have unlocked glass cases in swift, practiced motions, moved through rooms with their backs pressed against the wall, the security cameras looping an old feed. All of them knew the way these things were supposed to go. But they were college students, not thieves, and in the end they were never going to make it in without being heard.

They would've always had to do this differently.

This time, the sound of breaking glass was loud, violent in the stillness. Daniel smashed open each showcase—not elegantly, not beautifully, but efficiently enough, glass littering the ground like crushed gems.

"Three minutes," Alex said.

They each took a case, unzipping nondescript black backpacks to hold millions of dollars of Chinese art. Daniel lifted the bronze snake head off its pedestal, let it rest in his hands for just a moment. Three hundred years of Chinese history, lost and now found. Time was moving so quickly.

"One minute."

He set the bronze in his backpack, zipped it shut in one fluid motion. Out of the corner of his eye, he saw the slow, steady blink of the overhead camera.

Getting in had always been the easy part.

Now they had to get out.

"Time's up," Alex said in his ear, and they were running, across a floor that glinted with broken glass, past those same entryways and beautiful, untouched rooms, through the same entrance and then out into the waiting night air. In the trees surrounding the Chinese Pavilion, Daniel turned on his moped, felt it rumble beneath him. He saw Will and Irene do the same with theirs, and then the three of them were cutting through the trees and past the pavilion, past all the crimes they had committed tonight, counting on this one, impossible way out.

Four paths. One deeper into the palace, one to the forest, one to the water. One to the road. A month ago, it had seemed so obvious.

Was it still?

The road was blocked off already, the guards waiting for them. In the dark, Daniel could see the glint of spikes tossed onto the ground, the guards with their helmets, their rifles, everything that weighed them down. For a moment, he felt very small. It was just the three of them on their mopeds, flying toward an escape route they were never going to make.

Then he turned, suddenly and sharply, and Will and Irene followed. He could still hear the shouts of the guards, growing louder, Alex's voice urging them to "go, go, *go,*" the whine of his moped as he pushed it faster down the unpaved path. The lake in the distance drew closer and closer, until there was nothing but darkness ahead, an unbroken expanse of black water.

And then—there was Lily at the helm of her speedboat, the engine already roaring, and Daniel was running, Irene and Will at his side, mopeds discarded at the shore, and the boat was pulling away, they were pulling away, Drottningholm Palace behind them and millions of dollars of stolen art in his backpack.

⌒

It was a quarter till three, and they were back at the hotel. They had all changed clothes on the speedboat, and if anyone had seen them now, they would have looked like any other group of college students after a night out, all bright eyes and rumpled hair, cheeks flushed from the night air, from being twenty-one and feeling too much. Daniel pulled the curtains shut, Stockholm vanishing beneath his palms. Lamplight, soft and subdued, threw long shadows over the room. It was just the five of them now, made of nothing but skin and bone and bated breath.

Daniel unzipped his backpack, a new pair of gloves drawn over his hands, and pulled the sculpture out. It was carved in the shape of a snake, the sixth of the twelve animals of the Chinese zodiac, and in the low light its bronze mouth yawned open. It could have swallowed them all whole.

"Holy shit," he breathed.

"Holy shit," Will echoed.

Daniel passed it around, each of them pulling on gloves to touch it, to test its heft, to confirm that it was real. Irene laughed, suddenly and unexpectedly. "We did it," she said, and there was wonder in her voice.

"We did it," Lily said.

It had almost been easy. Just the three of them and the shattering of glass, time moving too fast around them. Even now, it didn't feel real. Was this all? He knew it wasn't. Tomorrow there would be police officers and a call to the FBI, his father stepping on a flight. A consult and then more as his father pulled the pieces together, found all the things they could not hide. But tonight it was just the five of them and a hotel room, and already it felt like victory.

"Fifty million dollars," Alex said, "here we come."

They put the sculpture back and ordered room service. Champagne, of course, because here they were all of drinking age, chocolate-dipped strawberries, anything on the menu they happened to want. Will paid with China Poly's cash, untraceable, and Daniel was grateful that Will was budgeting this, that the rest of them did not have to think. They could have gone to a nightclub, but it was better here, just the five of them, drunk off adrenaline and cheap champagne, the night stretching long and endless and full of possibility.

"Never have I ever," Will said, looking around the room, "done something quite like this."

Had anyone? Just a couple hours ago, Daniel had stood in this same hotel room, had called his father and thought of home. Somehow, impossibly, they had made it back.

Remember this, he told himself. The sputter of the A/C in the background, the scratchiness of hotel carpet against his palms. Irene, next to him, close enough that their shoulders touched. Will on his other side, face flushed and high color in his cheeks. Alex, who a month ago had been a stranger to him. Lily and her certainty that she could get them out. This was real, even when it did not feel like it.

Irene's voice held easy good humor. "I'm not sure you understand how this game works."

"Fine," Will said. He thought for a moment. "Never have I ever broken the law before today."

Daniel drank. So did everyone else. If this had been anywhere else—a party at UCLA, a dorm room with the same low light—he would have found it implausible. They were college students, or close enough, with careers and futures that cut bright, perfect, unwavering lines. But this hotel room held millions of dollars' worth of Chinese art, and all things considered he figured this was more likely than not.

"Well," Daniel said, "I guess that explains why we all agreed to this job."

Alex laughed. "What was your crime?"

He leaned back, stretching his legs out on the carpet. Three bottles of champagne were almost empty, glass and gold and scattered light. "Slipped an artifact out of a museum," he said, remembering that bronze coin, Will's look like a question. It didn't hurt as much, like this. The night was soft around the edges. "You?"

"Deleted footage of Will at Sackler," Alex said, and turned to Will. "Have you forgotten your theft so quickly? It's what got us into this whole mess."

"Shit," Will said, but he was laughing. He tipped his glass back, drained it, and Daniel remembered a jade tiger and a decision not yet made, how close he had been to walking away. Somehow, impossibly, they were here. "Thanks for deleting that, Alex. I didn't know."

"You didn't need to," Alex said easily. "Lily?"

Lily's smile was quick. "I don't think speeding should count."

"The way you speed?" Irene asked. "It absolutely does."

"Fine, fine," Lily said, but she was still smiling. "And yours? How have I never heard this story before?"

Irene spun the stem of her glass between two fingers. Daniel knew what she was going to say already. Still, it was lovely to watch the curve of her smile, those eyes that always held something like a secret. "Unjust laws shouldn't be laws. There's nothing wrong with breaking those."

"That's not an answer," Alex observed.

Irene raised a brow. "I was arrested at a Black Lives Matter protest a few years ago. You can ask Will or Daniel, we were all there."

Alex examined Irene for a long moment. Daniel could have spoken up, could have said something to ease the tension that had fallen like a blade over the room, but—the protests had been his freshman year of college. It would have been Alex's too. They had all been home, the year strange and tumultuous and full of grief, and none of them had emerged unchanged. They had lived through a pandemic, through all that had come with it. What could they not survive?

Healing, Daniel had said to Will once. He thought of wounds now, how they bled.

"The cops called it a riot?" Alex asked. Her voice was soft.

Irene had been bracing herself for an argument. Daniel had felt it in the tension of her shoulders, the edge to her voice. Now she loosened, just a little. "Of course."

"It was the same in New York," Alex said, and for a moment they might have all been there again, reliving those months when the country felt on the verge of collapse, on the verge of change. They had survived it, but there was privilege in that too. "For all that people in power claim to care about looting, it doesn't seem to matter when it's museums doing it. But"—Alex's smile was slow, edged with cruel humor—"that's why we're here, isn't it?"

Daniel thought of museums and shattered glass, of holding history in his hands. He thought of San Francisco during the protests, tear gas burning his eyes, the police dressed for violence. This was how things changed. "I'll drink to that," he said.

Will popped open another bottle of champagne, poured for all of them. "To taking back what's ours," he said, raising his glass. Once more, they all drank, glasses clinking against each other, the sound of their voices, of champagne spilling over, filling this small hotel room. Technically, Daniel knew, they were all criminals. They had broken laws before this, would break more in the days to come. Still, the light was soft, the room filled with warmth and laughter and possibility, and somehow—it didn't feel like they had done anything wrong at all.

⌒

The quality of the night changed, grew softer, blurred with alcohol and victory. They finished one drinking game, started another, conversations changing shape as the night did. Daniel leaned against Irene, his head on her shoulder. "Tell me something I don't know," he said.

She laughed. "You're drunk."

He wanted to touch her. "You're beautiful."

"I know," Irene said. The rest of their crew were somewhere in the background, Will in the other room, Alex and Lily caught up in their own conversation. It was just the two of them.

"Irene," he began. He did not know what came next. What was there, besides this moment?

"Yes?"

This time he did touch her, his hand light against a strand of her hair. It slipped between his fingers. *Break my heart*, he wanted to say. He knew she would.

Irene's gaze met his. He could not read the expression in her eyes. "I—" she said. Slowly, carefully, she reached her hand out. "I just want to see," she said. Her fingertips tilted his head up, and he closed his eyes, felt the lightest brush of her lips against his. She tasted like night air, like lipstick, like new rain.

"So?" Daniel asked. This might have been a dream.

Irene traced his collarbone, following the ink that spread across skin. Her smile was soft, almost sad. "Daniel Liang," she said, "don't spend your whole life chasing the impossible."

What was impossible? Irene, these crimes, his future. He had known her for ten years now, had met her gaze over dinner tables and high school classrooms and San Francisco piers, had known that she could never want him. He had loved her all the same. How could he not?

And now he was in Stockholm, breaking everything he had been taught not to, and the future could change with a rising moon. Tomorrow they would leave Sweden. He did not know if they could make it out. He caught her hand, brushed his mouth against the pulse point at her wrist. Once, she had told him she was tired of men looking at her like she could be more than she was.

"Irene," he said. He didn't know if he would remember this tomorrow. He hoped he would. Even when they were kids, he had thought she was the most beautiful person he had ever seen.

"Yes?"

"I'm going to let you go," he said. Impossible things, part of him thought. But they were in Sweden, and if he could break into a museum, if he could leave the past behind, then he ought to be able to do this.

Her smile was soft, almost sad. "Go to sleep, Danli," she said, and when she said his name in Chinese, he might have fallen in love with her all over again. "We have more left to do."

23

WILL

Will Chen had always known change came like this: on the wings of a sharp wind. He could still remember four years ago, the December evening that college decisions came out. He had checked his email in his high school parking lot, trees casting long, skeletal shadows across the pavement. His hands had been shaking when he opened the email, had still been shaking when he called his parents and when he hung up the phone, too overwhelmed to do anything else. He hadn't been able to drive home for a long time after. Instead he had sat in the driver's seat, pressed trembling hands to the wheel, read and reread the line that said *Congratulations*, the line that said his name.

Will Chen was many things, but in the end he was his parents' son, and all he had ever wanted was to make them proud. Worth should not have been measured like this, in the weight of Ivy League syllables and tuition paid like an offering, but this, always, had been the American Dream. It had been the best moment of his life.

And now, somehow—it was his senior year. He did not know what he dreamed of, just that until now it had always felt out of reach. Change was a Harvard acceptance, was a flight to Beijing, was *this*. Stockholm, the curve of the moon, a museum glittering with broken glass. If they pulled this off, no one would ever know they were here.

Still, he remembered a late night and a fast-food joint, Lily Wu against the hood of a car. *I don't make history*, he had told her.

He had tonight.

The rest of his crew was asleep. Will, hands gloved, pulled each art piece out of the backpack it was kept in, held it up to the light of a single bedside lamp. His notebook was open beside him, and carefully, meticulously, he recorded a description of each piece on the lined paper. He had always known they would have to take more than just the zodiac head, that their thefts could not look as targeted as they were. So—three cases cracked open in a Stockholm night, stolen art to be stolen back. He had transferred these pieces himself, set jade and bronze and soapstone into his backpack with all the care they deserved.

And yet—something was not quite right. He should have known all these pieces. He had spent hours on the Drottningholm Palace website, ensuring that they would take only objects from the Old Summer Palace, that they were not *stealing* but *returning*. But there were pieces here that were not listed on the website, recent acquisitions that somehow, impossibly, did not look recent at all. He lifted a sculpture that, in the darkness, he had mistaken for jade. Up close, it was a green soapstone, threaded with darker colors, a mountain scene carved by a swift, sure hand.

Qin dynasty, he guessed, and opened his laptop. Weeks ago, he'd purchased a book cataloging the stolen art from the Old Summer Palace, then spent a particularly boring lecture livestream scanning each page. He scrolled through it, searching, but even this was not complete. Will let out a long, slow sigh. So much had been lost to time, to history, to the shadowy world of art museums and private collectors.

"What is it?" Daniel asked.

Will looked up. He had thought Daniel was asleep, but now Daniel rolled over in his bed, squinting against the light of the lamp. From here, Will could see the tattoo of the dragon that wrapped around his torso, stark and black. They had gone to the tattoo parlor together, on an afternoon when the fog made San Francisco feel like something out of a dream, wavering and uncertain.

A bad idea, Will had said about the tattoo.

I know, Daniel had replied.

Will set the sculpture down. "History repeats itself," he said. How much of China's art was hidden like this, in museums that purchased it carefully, discreetly, in a way where it might never be found? "No matter what we take back, there will always be more missing."

Daniel was silent for a moment, and Will thought he might have fallen back asleep. But instead he propped himself up on an elbow, gaze skimming the art surrounding Will before resting on Will himself. "Let it go," he said, but his voice was gentle. They had always been there for each other's bad decisions.

Low light, stolen art, a city asleep. Will thought of the Old Masters, of scenes in sfumato, smoke and uncertain focus. In the other room, the rest of their crew was still sleeping too. "It's not that easy," he said. It was always like this, art changing hands when it shouldn't, cultures searching for what had been lost. How could they find their lost art—how could they ever get it back—when museums were not willing to speak of where their pieces came from?

"I know," Daniel said. "But think of tonight. Think of what we've done. We haven't been arrested. I can still go to medical school."

They had done the impossible. Everything else—what did it matter? Will shut his notebook, wrapped up the remaining pieces of art, and set them in suitcases heavier than they should have been. Tomorrow Daniel would return to UCLA. Will would go back to Harvard. It would be like they had never left, like nothing had changed at all. "I won't get expelled," Will said. And then, because he couldn't help himself—"yet."

Daniel reached over, switched off the light. "That's the spirit."

24

IRENE

The sun was rising in Stockholm. The news of the robbery had broken with the morning light, and already headlines showed a shattered Chinese Pavilion, photos of the stolen art. Irene Chen leaned over the bathroom sink, taking her time as she drew the black wings of her eyeliner, traced her lips in a matte red. In the background, a Swedish morning show played from her phone speaker.

Break my heart, Daniel had said last night, so softly that he might not even have realized it. She remembered tracing her fingers along his jaw, his collarbone, the heat of his skin. If she let herself, she could pretend it had never happened. She could've dreamed the night before, save for the headlines, save for the art waiting to go home.

She swept her makeup bag into her carry-on, opened the bathroom door. The cab was already downstairs. Irene had called for it half an hour ago, as Will was waking up the rest of the crew. Now the hotel room was clean, empty, art packed away in suitcases and hidden beneath clothes and other assorted souvenirs.

All they had to do was make it out.

Irene reached for her suitcase. Alex and Lily were downstairs, loading the cab, and Will was in the other room, doing one final sweep. For a moment, it was just her and Daniel. "Hey," she said.

He was dressed as he always was for flights, in a UCLA hoodie and black Adidas joggers. The angles of his face were more pronounced in the early-morning light. "Yeah?"

She hesitated. *Break my heart*, he had said, and she had.

"You're going to have to say it, Irene." Still, his voice was gentle. There was no cruelty, no anger. They had known each other for long enough that this was familiar too. Irene tilted her head up, let out a long, slow breath. Of all the things she was good at, she had never been able to get this right.

When she spoke, it was as soft as an exhale. "I'm sorry."

"For?"

The ceiling was a pale cream, lined with false, uncertain gold. Lies had always come easier to her than the truth, but both of them knew that already. "For kissing you when you were drunk," she whispered.

"And?"

"For kissing you when I knew you would say yes. It wasn't—it wasn't fair of me."

"It wasn't," he agreed, and at last she looked at him. His voice was low, serious, his dark eyes unflinching as they met hers. "I'm not stupid, Irene. We've been to Pride together. I've met your ex-girlfriends. But this isn't some game to me."

"I know," Irene said, very soft. "It's not for me either."

He fell silent. Sunlight, pale and tentative, reached through the curtains, touched carpet and empty space. "I forgive you," he said at last. "Of course I forgive you. And—I hope you'll forgive me too."

"For what?"

His smile was soft. "Don't make me say it, Irene."

He loves you, Will had told her once. Even though she had never asked him to, even though she could not love him the way he might want.

"I won't," she said. It had been ten years. She would not hurt him any more than she had to.

Daniel held the door open for her, let her step through and into the waiting light. They still had a country to escape, millions of dollars of Chinese art to clear through customs.

"Oh—and Irene?"

"Yeah?"

Daniel leaned in close. His lashes brushed against his cheekbones, cast shadows against the warmth of his skin. His smile was slow. "If you kiss me again, you'd better mean it."

Irene had always liked airports. It was easy to become anonymous here, to disappear into the rise and fall of unfamiliar languages or get swept up in the tide of movement. Now, though, she was motionless, hands clasped tightly together as she waited for her suitcase. The rest of them had made it through security already, were waiting for her on the other side. If she turned her head, she knew she would see them.

She didn't.

Her suitcase was just a few feet away. She had packed it hours ago, set the bronze snake head over folded clothes and extra newspaper, careful to keep her fingerprints off it. And of course it would be her. If anything went wrong, Irene was the only one who might be able to talk herself out of it.

The conveyor belt stopped. Her suitcase was still in the X-ray machine, and she didn't look, didn't even breathe, just pretended to check her phone. She might have been any other traveler, impatient to catch her flight.

What's wrong? Will texted her.

Nothing, she texted back.

The security agent pulled her suitcase aside. "Is this yours?" he asked in English. His voice was clipped, professional, though he couldn't have been much older than she was.

"Is there a problem?" Irene asked carefully. She had thought this might happen, but now that it had she felt her heart rate speed up.

"We need to take it for some additional screening," he said. He stepped past the partition, gestured toward her. "Follow me."

He wheeled the suitcase ahead of her, and Irene lengthened her stride, her boots clicking against the tiled floor. Her phone was vibrating frantically, and she silenced it in one swift motion.

This isn't some game to me, Daniel had said. That was the thing, wasn't it? None of this could ever be a game. There was too much at stake.

The room he brought her to was not meant to intimidate, with its bland, neutral colors and beige walls, and yet Irene's gaze went to the metal examination table in its center, the monitor that displayed a blown-up Technicolor version of her suitcase. Another agent, older, stood before the computer screen, examining the strange, fluorescent oranges of the suitcase edges, the deep, dark blue that yawned like a mouth at its center.

Behind her, the door clicked shut.

The two agents had a brief conversation in Swedish, too quickly for her to understand. Then the second agent snapped on gloves, ran his fingers along the edge of the suitcase. "This will be quick," he said. "Airport regulations, you understand."

"Of course," Irene said, lacing her hands together behind her back. She knew the regulations. She had translated them, read them, searched for all the ways around them. And yet she was here, surrounded by security and the blinking light of a video camera. Even if she had wanted to, there was no way out.

Time slowed down, turned malleable, as the security agent unzipped her suitcase, the two halves parting neatly on the cool metal table. Irene saw her clothes, stacked carefully, the folder she had slipped on top of them two days ago, and—at the center of her suitcase, exactly where it was supposed to be, the polished bronze of their stolen zodiac head. In the harsh glow of the fluorescent light, the snake head looked like something out of another time, another place.

Irene looked from the bronze to the two security agents, holding herself very still. The younger agent stepped closer to the bronze, bent his head to get a better look. "This is—"

Priceless, he might have said. *Stolen. Sacred.* There were so many words for the piece in her suitcase, so many ways for the future to fracture.

"Unnecessary," the other agent said, cutting him off. In his hand was the folder from Irene's suitcase, and he pulled out the first document, passed it to his coworker. In Swedish, he said something that Irene couldn't catch. It sounded like an admonishment.

"Is there a problem?" Irene asked. "I could have sworn I declared this at customs when I landed." She leaned over, pointed at the stamp and signature at the bottom of the page, the black-and-white photo of a bronze snake head taken in a room very similar to this one. As she did, she shifted farther into the video camera's line of sight. Anyone watching would see her, of course, but they would not see the zodiac head.

"You did," the older agent said, decisive. The first agent looked as though he wanted to protest, but let go of the paper in his hand, passed it back. "Apologies for my colleague. Next time he will be sure to check your documents *first*."

"It's no trouble," Irene said. She smiled at the younger man, wondered if he was the kind of person who listened to the news on the commute to work, if he had heard of Drottningholm's break-in already. But it was still so early, and this sculpture—which meant so much to China, to its people—was just another beautiful foreign thing, easily forgotten. "I'm in no rush."

The younger agent smiled back, relieved. He gestured at the bronze. "A lovely piece," he said. "Is it valuable?"

Irene thought of last night, the wail of sirens as they sped away from Drottningholm Palace, and smiled wider. "If you're interested, I'll sell it to you for thirty euros."

Both agents laughed. "Unfortunately, we must decline," the older man said. He set the sculpture back in her suitcase, zipped it up. He glanced at the customs papers one more time before handing them to her. "Safe travels, Ms. Chen."

"Thank you," she said, her voice very pleasant. She took her papers, her suitcase, waited as one of the agents hurried to open the door for her. And then Irene was walking out, past security, to where the rest of her crew waited, ten million dollars safely in her suitcase.

25

WILL

It had taken Will a month. Two weeks in the studio, all his quiet, half-way hours spent with cool limestone, the sharp, clear strike of a chisel. Another two weeks to learn how to dip stone in molten bronze, gloved and masked and so far from the art he was used to, paint that swept over empty canvas. The machinery had only been possible through an art department grant, an application where he made up more than he should and also used the words *performance art*. It wasn't quite a lie.

Next had been a flight to Stockholm, a heavy suitcase. Lily had smiled as she asked him about his sculpture, and though he knew the bronze was flawed, less a forgery than a passing imitation, he had smiled back. At customs, Irene had taken his suitcase, let security examine the bronze in all its imperfections. It was always easier to bring things in than to take them out.

And then, at last, a lake in the darkness, a rising moon. For the final time, Will had run his hands over the snake's bared fangs, the smooth, slippery bronze. The waves were choppy beneath the speedboat, but when he leaned over the railing, he felt no fear. The air tasted of salt, of possibility.

He let go. The sculpture slipped easily through his outstretched hands, and for a moment he saw white spray, waves cresting up to meet the bronze, and then—nothing at all.

The rest—well, it had happened already. An hour later he had held the true bronze in his hands, had packed it in Irene's suitcase next to those same customs declarations. The rest of the art—a gilded teapot, a soapstone sculpture, all those smaller, less obvious pieces—he had distributed in suitcases and carry-ons, wrapped in newspaper and plastic bags from souvenir shops. And today, when dawn had come, they had caught a cab to the airport, walked through security easily, effortlessly— except for one.

Will lifted his gaze, caught his sister's as she emerged from security. "How did it go?" he asked, though he knew the answer already. In all the years they had spent growing up together, he had never seen Irene do anything less than perfectly. Sometimes it was hard to look at his sister, to know that, if she wanted to, she could be everything he was and more. But in this moment her smile was quick, victorious, and he felt nothing but pride. She rolled her suitcase toward him, and he caught the handle. Its weight was unchanged.

"Let's go home," she said.

⸻

The flight back was nine hours. Will tapped his pencil against his jaw, thought for a moment before bringing it back to his sketchbook. "Hold still," he said.

"The *airplane* is moving," Lily said, but she kept her head tilted up. Her skin was almost gold in the morning sun, her profile all delicate lines and a soft mouth.

Will laughed. "Point taken."

He traced the curve of her cheek with his pencil, going over it a second time in darker, more definitive strokes. The plane was light and shadow, nothing more, and he remembered another flight, Lily's quick smile. *Temporary*, she had said, and she had been right. Will had always known that anything he loved would not last. Still, he didn't need more than this—her head lifted to the light, the sweep of pencil against paper. Art, beauty, all of it fast and fleeting. "So," he said. "Why engineering?"

"Haven't I answered that already?" she asked.

He added shadows, trying to capture the spill of her hair against her shoulders, the angle of her jaw. This was always the hardest part, getting the light exactly right. "You asked me why art history. I figure it's only fair."

A pause, soft and thoughtful. Will drew the brush of her eyelashes against her skin, the dusting of freckles like constellations. "There aren't easy answers in engineering," Lily said. "But there are always *answers*. Even if you get lost along the way, you can still find your way back."

He thought back to a month ago, Lily as the sun rose over Beijing. They might have been searching for the same thing. "And when this is over?" he asked. "If we pull this off, you don't have an impossible dream to chase?"

"Do you?"

He let himself look at her. Graduation, the future, it all felt too close. "I think you know the answer to that."

Lily was no longer posing, but it didn't matter. The portrait had only ever been an excuse. "I'm not sure," she said. "There are the obvious answers, aren't there? Paying off student loans, graduating college debt-free. Seeing the world. But after that—" She stopped, shook her head, and Will remembered the story she had told beneath a Durham sky, of an island and how it felt to run away. The vastness of the world beyond. "It's going to sound ridiculous."

"I don't think it will."

Lily was quiet for a moment. "There's an auto shop my neighbor owns," she said. "I worked there in the summers. And it's been in his family for three generations, and when I was in high school, I would sometimes see his children and grandchildren there, and I would think that this was it, you know? This was *home*, for all of them. And I'm not sure where I want to be, but I know I want something like that. I'm not like you or Irene. I don't need to change the world. I just—I want to live, and to know that it's enough."

And Will—even in this moving airplane, the morning light filtered through the reinforced glass of the window—he could see it. Lily, making something that was all her own. The sun as it bent over a distant horizon, over the gleam of a polished car, over the five of them around a single table, laughing about something that did not have to matter. She had made it seem like a small thing, but Will didn't think it was. To live without the weight of everything you were not—how could it ever be?

He tried to imagine it for himself. What would it be like to be surrounded by beauty, to no longer feel the hunger of his want? He didn't know the person he was without it. But here, now—he thought maybe he would like to.

"My family—" he began. He didn't know how to tell the rest of it. "I'm the oldest son. And I know that that doesn't have to mean anything, but I'm the oldest son, and so is my father, and the rest of our family is in China but we're the Americans, the ones who made it, and sometimes— sometimes I feel like I'll break under that weight."

When had he said those words before?

He didn't know if he ever had. This was the story he knew, the story he had grown up hearing. A village in southern China, the heat of the midday sun, nights that stretched long and hungry. His parents, the first ones to go to college, the first ones to leave. They had come to America with nothing but their educations, and they had built a life here, of dreams and hope and determination.

He could not be anything less than exceptional.

As the light changed, as the plane hurtled over the deep, dark expanse of the Atlantic Ocean, they talked not of the future but of the past. Immigration stories and unfamiliar history, what it was like to grow up knowing you had more than all your ancestors combined. Privilege, responsibility, all those words that sometimes had a weight too heavy to bear. In the end, that was what this heist was: a way out. If they could do this, it might be enough.

26

ALEX

The night of the heist, the Stockholm streets had been empty. Fog swept in from the distant Baltic Sea, carrying a swift ocean wind, a chill that hung over the dark like anticipation. Alex Huang flicked her lighter on, brought the flame to a cloth wick. The bottle was cool beneath her gloved hands. She should have been afraid. It was just past one, and this was the first of tonight's crimes. But leaders of Sweden's white power movement lived on this street, and it had been so, so easy to find.

She watched the wick burn down, thought of four years ago and New York City as night fell, as streets and cop cars caught fire. The air had smelled of smoke, of change. Once, Alex might have been bothered by property damage. She knew better now.

Sometimes, if you wanted change, you had to make it.

Alex flung the bottle, saw it shatter against a distant car. Two, three, four more times, until a row of cars was burning, fire and smoke and fog mixing together, until the sound of sirens drew closer and closer.

It didn't matter. She had done what she came here to do. Alex strode to the pier, the water illuminated by a distant sliver of moon. There, Lily was idling on a stolen speedboat, her smile widening as she met Alex's gaze. The police were on their way, rushing toward Stockholm's wealthiest district, but the speedboat was already pulling away, the blaze fading into the distant, heavy dark. Alex pulled out her laptop, balancing it on her knees, and adjusted the frequencies of her makeshift radio. On her screen, she could see the pinprick locations of her crew, waiting for her signal at the Chinese Pavilion. Wind whipped her hair against her face, whistled sharp and joyous against her headphones. Alex smiled.

Go, she said.

Across the lake, their heist began.

⁓

This was what Alex Huang returned to: a clean, empty apartment, windows thrown open to the California sky. She set her suitcase down, slipped off her shoes at the door. It was that halfway hour just after sunset, the light blue and pensive as it fell over polished wooden floors and stainless steel appliances, all the pieces of this life she had left behind.

The past weekend felt like something out of a dream, all bright colors and impossible motion. A plane touching down in an unfamiliar country, the sun as it sank below the water. Everything—this crew, this city—had been cast in a new red. Drottningholm Palace from afar, the slight, soft hum of her laptop, Irene Chen's hand as it brushed her jaw. Evening and an empty street, the parabola of a Molotov cocktail and the unfurling of fire in the waiting dark.

Alex pulled her laptop out of her backpack, set it on the smooth, polished wood of her dinner table. Tomorrow she would go back to work. She would take the same bus she always took, with its tinted windows and cool, constant A/C, lean her head against the glass and watch as they wound their way through gentrifying neighborhoods. She would sit at her desk and drink free, expensive cold brew, write code that would disappear into the mouth of an ever-expanding corporate giant.

Was this her life? She didn't know what she would do when these thefts were over, couldn't imagine a future where they might walk away with ten million dollars each. She hadn't been afraid in Stockholm—not when the first car had caught fire, not when the sound of sirens drew closer—but she was afraid now. That kind of money—it could change lives, break things open. Her parents' restaurant, her grandmother's medical bills, her siblings' college educations. Her own dreams, whatever those might be.

Alex opened her personal laptop, waited for the screen to light up. There was a flash drive sitting next to her laptop, untouched, and she looked at it for a long moment before turning away. Her heart was beating too fast, and she remembered the blue wash of Mr. Liang's study, the slow, steady blink of the cursor. Her hands as she slipped this same flash drive into the computer case, as she waited, listening to the sound of her breath, the whir of the computer as it processed this new information. Alex was not a hacker, not FBI. She was just a software engineer, trained to write code, to pull it apart.

When Daniel called her name, she had pulled the flash drive out, left before she could see what she had done. But here, in the soft violet light, California as lovely as it always was, time stretched long and luminous before her.

She picked up her phone, pressed *dial*.

Lily picked up on the first ring, and Alex thought of the past few weeks, a software engineer and a mechanical engineer, how they had fumbled their way through this. A bit of code, almost as a thought exercise, a flash drive that she got into the habit of carrying around. She had never expected anything to come of it, not really. "What if it doesn't work?" Alex asked.

Lily's voice was all confidence. "It will," she said.

A day ago, they had been in Stockholm. She could remember the feel of the speedboat beneath her feet, the steady motion of the waves, how the whole world had been cast in black and white. The way forward had seemed so obvious then. "You don't know that."

Lily was quiet for a moment. It would be late afternoon on the East Coast, and Alex could almost see the blue of the sky, Lily leaning against her desk as she took this call. In the background, she heard the soft murmur of someone else's voice, and she wondered if Irene was there too, what Irene would be doing right now. They had not told anyone else about this. Why would they, when it might not even work? "I don't," Lily agreed. "But sometimes you have to pretend, you know? The certainty comes later."

Alex let out a slow breath. It shouldn't have surprised her that Lily understood how this felt, the lingering fear that everything you were, everything you had, could slip away too quickly. Of everyone in this crew, the two of them were here for the same reasons. Not out of a love for art, like Will, and not loyalty, like Daniel and Irene. Not even as a test of their skill. They were here because they couldn't not be, because it was a chance to be more than they were. Sometimes this heist was the only thing that made Alex feel like she existed at all.

"I'm nervous," Alex said, and almost laughed. She was in an empty apartment, far from all the crimes they had committed over the weekend, and yet it was true. Her hands trembled, just a little, and she curled her fingers tighter around the phone. Before her, the flash drive was a cool, ordinary gray, not quite bright enough to catch the dying light. It did not look like very much at all.

"It may not work," Lily said. And then, very gently, "But Alex, what if it does?"

Alex did not know what she was more afraid of. She took a long, slow breath. Her living room was washed in the blue of early evening, of the glow of her computer screen, everything that was waiting for her. "I'm going to go," Alex said.

"Go," Lily said. There was a smile in her voice. "Can you believe this is our life?"

"Never," Alex said.

The call ended, and Alex was alone once more. She picked up the flash drive, the metal cold against her burning skin, slipped it into a USB-C converter and then her laptop's waiting port.

For a moment, nothing happened.

And then her laptop gave a soft sigh, and lines of code began to unfurl on the screen. Alex rested her hands on the keyboard for just a moment, let her gaze sweep over her apartment with its clean lines and open windows. Outside, beyond the street and the strip mall restaurants, she could see the mountains, limned in gold and possibility. In three weeks, they would do this all over again.

ENTER PASSWORD HERE, the screen read.

She did.

27

IRENE

They were talking about her in her public policy class. Not by name, of course, but they talked about the heist, read and underlined articles speculating who could be behind it. *Brazen*, her classmates called it. *Daring. Unbelievable.* If Irene Chen had been someone else, she would have kept quiet, but instead she leaned forward. It had been less than a week since she had been at Drottningholm Palace, listening to the distant wail of sirens.

"I think," she said, "it was a long time coming."

The class fell silent. It was not quite five p.m., but the shorter days meant that the trees cast long, reaching shadows into the classroom. Outside, she could see Gothic spires and pointed arches, a sliver of uncertain light. Irene laced her fingers together. "China is a rising global power," she said, and she thought of a penthouse in Beijing, the sun rising on the capital city. "What is art but another way of exerting power? It was inevitable."

Silence, brief and triumphant. And then—

"I disagree."

Irene smiled wide. If it had been one of the many white boys in her class, she would have asked what they knew about things that were lost, things that were *taken*. But she and James Reyes had been in the same classes since freshman year, and they seldom disagreed when it came to issues of colonialism. After all this time, she knew his story as well as he knew hers, both of them children of immigrants, his parents from the Dominican Republic and hers from mainland China. "Tell me more," she said.

James folded his hands together, the motion slow, deliberate. "Look at the style of the theft—it's bold, reckless, not at all characteristic of the long game China seems to have been playing for the past few decades. It seems too—obvious."

Irene wanted to laugh. *Reckless*, he said, when they hadn't been caught, when they had spent over a month planning for it. And yet she thought of the weeks prior, of video chats and heist movies and their casual, easy confidence. They were college students, young and brilliant and destined for greatness, and they did not fail.

Reckless, she thought, *might be right.*

Still, that was not the direction she wanted this conversation to take. "Let's say you're right," she said. "Who else could it be? What incentive would anyone else have to do this? The thieves only took art looted from the Old Summer Palace. They left behind many more valuable items."

A long, thoughtful pause. Irene remembered the past weekend, running through Drottningholm in the dark. "What if," James said, "it's not the Chinese government that's stealing the art? What if it's private entities within China vying for power?"

China's not a capitalist country, Irene could have said, but even she wouldn't have been able to keep a straight face. This was how China was in the twenty-first century, a ship slicing forward in a vast, infinite ocean, unencumbered by bureaucracy, democracy, any of the other things that pulled America forward, that pushed it back. "You're saying there's competition," Irene said.

His voice was steady. "Isn't there always?"

Wang Yuling, certain in the righteousness of her mission. A penthouse filled with stolen art. To Irene, China Poly and the Chinese government could've been one and the same, different puppeteers pulling the same strings. But China was changing in the twenty-first century, and someday this country might be more than the heavy hand of the Communist Party. It might be more already.

Her professor spoke, brought the class back on track. They had readings they needed to discuss, a paper due after Thanksgiving break. Irene took notes on her laptop, let her mind drift to thoughts of France, of a new country and another museum. The next four zodiac heads, the millions of dollars—it felt almost inevitable.

Still, she would keep an eye out.

"Irene, do you have a second?"

Irene looked up from her phone. James was leaning against the Allen Building, waiting for her. The setting sun was warm against his skin. "Yeah, what's up?"

He ran a hand over his waves, his smile quick and confident. "I was wondering if you wanted to grab coffee sometime."

Irene raised a brow. "Are you asking me out?"

His smile widened. "Are you interested?"

Irene laughed. "Not at all."

"That's what I thought," James said. They went to the same parties, after all. He knew her type. "I found your comments about the theft interesting, that's all. It'd be nice to talk more about policy stuff at some point. Everyone else is so"—he shrugged lightly—"you know, *white.*"

She would have liked to say yes. She recognized his easy confidence, those smiles that made it clear he was used to getting his way. *Arrogant,* she imagined Will saying. She had always liked people who reminded her of herself. But Thanksgiving break was in less than three weeks, and they had another museum to rob. "Another time," she said. Her smile matched his. "We can talk about it after the next theft."

Surprise crossed his face. "There hasn't been another theft."

In the distance, the chapel bells tolled. The sunset washed the world in gold, made the campus look like something out of a painting. She imagined stretching a hand out, her fingers wrapping around its frame. "There will be," she said, and it was a promise.

That night, Irene called Alex. She hadn't meant to. But over Zoom they had all been planning their second theft, and when Will asked Alex about what she had found from the Sweden investigation, Daniel had flinched. It had been so quick no one else had noticed it, but Irene had been watching him. Mr. Liang had spent the past two weeks in Stockholm, working with Interpol on this case. Irene had tracked his flight when Daniel wouldn't.

"Irene?" Alex said, and it was a question.

"Tell me instead," Irene said. The call was on Telegram, voice only, encrypted from end-to-end. It was the kind of thing Irene had never thought about until recently. "About the investigation."

Alex's voice was flat. "I thought we were going to stay out of each other's way."

Irene leaned against the chapel stone, the chill seeping into her skin. The sun had almost set in North Carolina, but California right now would be shot through with light. "We are," Irene said. She hesitated. She didn't want to tell Alex about Daniel and his grief, reveal this thing that he held on to so tightly. Irene had always been able to understand that, at least. How to carry the weight of something, alone. "I suppose that means you didn't find anything."

"You're baiting me," Alex said.

Irene waited.

Alex sighed. "I got into the FBI," she said. "Don't ask me how."

Irene blinked. Of all the things she was expecting Alex to say, it wasn't *this*. "How?"

"I *just said*—ugh, whatever. Some conversations with Lily. A bit of clever code. And a few minutes alone with Daniel's dad's computer."

Irene didn't know what to say. There were so many ways this could go wrong. She thought of Daniel's father and the job he loved so much, all the times she had gone over to their house. "You shouldn't have done that," she said.

"Listen, I'll just call Will—"

"Tell me what you found," she said. The rest—did it matter? For all that she wanted to keep family out of this, for all of Daniel's grief, they were just college students. *Reckless*, Irene thought. They needed all the advantage they could get. "And tell me they won't trace this back to us."

"You're not the only one with something to lose, Irene." Alex's voice had an edge to it—hurt, or maybe just anger—and Irene thought back to a week ago, a fight and a Stockholm hotel room. It might always be like this, the two of them facing each other with their knives drawn.

"Alex," Irene said, and it was a sigh. She was tired of coders who thought the world spun around Silicon Valley, tired of this girl who looked at her as though she knew everything there was to know already. "Can we work together this one time?"

Alex sighed through the phone. "I'll send you the images. Make *sure* you delete them."

Irene bit back a retort. Alex thought too little of her if she thought Irene was stupid enough to save incriminating files. But there were more important things than this. When the images came up, she read quickly, gaze skimming the fine text, the black-and-white photos. It wasn't much. No fingerprints, no DNA, nothing left behind but footprints washed away by the forest and the tide. Three figures, a speedboat that had vanished into thin air. It was the stuff of stories.

"Well?" Alex asked.

Irene thought back to all the evenings she had spent with the Liangs. She had always paid attention when Mr. Liang spoke of work. What thieves might leave behind, the ways they could be caught. Interpol, the FBI, they were all searching for them. So what? Irene had seen this coming. Only a fool wouldn't have. "Their job is to look for us," she said evenly. "Our job is to not get found."

"Do you really think that's possible?"

Irene thought of the files she had looked at, the notes scribbled in the margins. The words *Sackler connection?* written in Mr. Liang's hand, all these pieces that came together and apart. "You and I both know this isn't enough to implicate anybody. If you're looking for more reassurance than that, go to Will." Irene could have hung up then. Should have, maybe. Instead she tipped her head back, took in the vanishing light. She thought of Alex and an FBI server, a computer and its blinking, expectant cursor. "Was it hard?" she asked.

Alex was quiet, the silence stretching between them. Irene could almost see her in an empty apartment, saturated with California light, all cheekbones and sharp angles and anger. Not art, like Will had seen in her, but something else. She thought of Stockholm, the fierceness in Alex's gaze. Somehow Alex had broken into Drottningholm's security system. She had broken into the FBI. It did not seem possible.

"Not too bad," Alex said at last. "I can call Will next time. I know— this isn't what either of us want."

It was true enough. Still, Irene lingered on the chapel steps. The bus stop, the quad, the buildings with their familiar Gothic architecture—

all of Duke was spread out before her. It was easier now that she and Will were both in college, their edges no longer scraping against each other the way they did in childhood, in high school, in all the ways the world weighed them against each other. He was her older brother, her best friend, and yet sometimes she looked at him and saw everything that she could never be.

Irene pushed herself off the steps, strode toward the setting sun, the promises found in the rising dark. The FBI, the thefts to come. Between her and Will, they had never failed before. "It doesn't matter to me," she said, and she almost believed it.

28

LILY

It was an early morning in November, and the sky was a cool, slate gray. In Galveston, they would have heard the storm warning days ago, boarded up windows and checked their generator. Hurricane season, even so close to its end, always meant caution. Growing up, Lily Wu had had nightmares about these kinds of storms—the lash of tree branches against trembling windows, darkness that was plunging and absolute. Things were different here, at Duke, but Lily could read the sky well enough.

A storm was on its way.

Lily pulled the windows of her dorm room shut, turned the lock on the door. Irene was already on her laptop, setting up Zoom on a monitor big enough that both of them could see. The room smelled like Dame's Chicken and Waffles. They had driven downtown early, before the rest of campus had woken up, some routines maintained even when everything else was changing.

In two weeks, they would be in France.

Alex's voice cut through the quiet of their dorm room. "The police finally spoke to the press," she said, her video crisp. As usual, she was in an empty apartment, her surroundings still edged in darkness. Lily did the math quickly. It was not yet daybreak in California. "They're saying this is an ordered job."

On another screen, Will laced his hands together. He was in a Harvard art studio, early-morning light glancing off his glasses. "They're not wrong."

Lily remembered Beijing in the evening sun, the CEO of China Poly as she laid her expectations out. Even then, Lily had known this was not something she could ever walk away from. "Their next question," she said, thoughtful, "will be *who* is doing the ordering."

"Exactly," Alex said. "The local police have already passed this higher up. Interpol, the FBI, you know how it goes. But—if they think it's China, they won't think it's *us*."

"I'll see what my dad says," Daniel said. He was sitting in an airport waiting area, on the way to another med school interview, the only still point in a blur of motion and light. "He told me he was getting pulled on a special joint task force for his Chinese art expertise. It had to have been for this."

"I don't like the amount of attention this is getting," Irene mused. "If this becomes a political issue, it will only end badly."

"It always was," Will said quietly. In the studio light, he was all lean lines and expressive hands, and Lily remembered the sun as it rose over the Old Summer Palace, Will's hands as they ran over an inscription she couldn't read. *Reclamation.* Everything lost, now found. She wondered what it would feel like.

Next to her, Irene nodded. "You're not wrong," she said. "But they don't know that yet. We have to make sure they don't find out."

Lily leaned back against her chair, watching the changing sky and thinking of storms. The FBI on the hunt, Daniel and conversations with his dad. Alex and Irene, the tension that ran between them like a wire. There were so many ways the lightning could come.

But there was still this: Will, almost done with his forgery, spinning the laptop so they could see a sculpture of a rooster resting on a studio bench. Stone, not bronze, but it would be soon enough. Irene taking over the screen share, pulling up blueprints for their next museum, Daniel pointing out where the cameras would be. Finally, Lily traced the path from the museum to the streets of Paris, thinking of what kind of car she would need. Whatever else was on the horizon, the air tasted of change.

When their call ended, Lily and Irene looked at each other, exchanged quick, conspiratorial smiles. "The news called us *experts*," Lily said, thinking of the news article Alex had referenced. She pulled out a textbook from her bookshelf. "If only they could see us now."

"International art theft," Irene said, laughing, "let me just add that to my résumé."

The dorm room still smelled of waffles. It was hard to believe that this was her life—junior year and weekends in foreign countries, schoolwork that still felt the same. It was strange and impossible and true.

The rest of the day might have gone like this. Clouds that gathered low and gray in the distance, a Spotify playlist of chill study music. The two of them sat at their desks, side by side, Irene typing up a paper and Lily working on her weekly fluid mechanics problem set. Out of the corner of her eye, her phone lit up. Lily set her pencil down, opened Will's text. They did this often enough that it wasn't a surprise.

Forgot to send this to you, he said.

It was a photo, taken in the same studio he had called in from an hour ago, of a sketchbook flipped open. She pressed her fingers to her phone screen, her breath catching as she recognized herself. One week ago, they had been on a flight, voices low and subdued as they talked about family and the weight of expectation, all the history they didn't know. Lily had almost forgotten how their conversation had started—his hand tilting her head up to the plane's blue light, the quiet scratch of his pencil against paper. She'd known, of course, that he was flirting with her, that he had done this a thousand times before, but she wouldn't have expected any less from him. Besides—they had just pulled off a heist. What was a little more recklessness?

"What is it?" Irene asked, slipping off her headphones.

Lily shook her head, trying not to smile. Even though she shouldn't have been, she was just a little flattered. He had drawn her portrait in quick, elegant pencil lines that caught the hint of a smile on her lips, eyes that were dark and luminous. It looked like *art*. "Your brother's showing off."

"He does tend to do that," Irene said dryly. "Please don't tell me you're impressed."

"Absolutely not," she said.

Irene examined her, long enough that Lily looked away. When this began, she had been sure it was privilege that let Will talk about running a con so easily, the certainty that all he touched would turn to gold. She could see it, sometimes—in the lazy tilt of his smile, how when he ran his hand through his hair he made sure someone was watching—and it had fit with everything Irene had ever said about him. Will Chen, who had spent his whole life getting exactly what he wanted.

And yet—there was this too. Plane flights and talk of dreams, how soft Will's voice went when he spoke of art. After she told him about growing up in Galveston, how it never felt like home, he had started texting her with Zillow ads in different parts of the country, always captioned with something new. *For an auto shop*, he would say, or sometimes, *For an art studio*, and then it would be two a.m. and Lily would be lying in bed, trying to decipher the knot within her chest. There was a melancholy to Will that she hadn't expected, that she didn't quite know what to do with.

"Are you sure?" Irene asked. "Will—well, you know what he's like. Girls break themselves trying to change him."

Lily thought of ships against dark water, rocks that flashed like knives on a distant shore. She had grown up by the sea. She knew well enough what it meant to throw yourself against immovable things. "Please," she said. She smiled at her roommate, quick and sure. Even if she had wanted more—nothing with Will could ever last. He had told her as much himself. "I know better than *that*."

She hoped it was true.

29

LILY

From a distance, France was nothing more than the jut of the Alps against an eggshell-blue sky, the mountains outlined in snow and jagged edges. Lily pressed her palm against the window, watching Paris draw closer, the glint of distant light. If she closed her eyes, she could imagine the weight of bronze in her open hands, the flash of headlights against slick cobblestone.

Another country, another theft. The plane landed, the rumble loud enough that she felt it in her bones, and then they were in the glittering Charles de Gaulle Airport. Customs, baggage claim, an airport bakery for five pains au chocolat, and then, finally, a rental car kiosk. Irene exchanged words in rapid French with the representative, and then Lily had a set of keys in her palm, the paperwork already signed and dated. She spun the keys once, pressed *unlock*. The garage was all concrete and dark colors, and she scanned the empty parking spaces for something sleek and fast and nondescript.

A yellow Kia Soul flashed its lights.

"*Excuse* me?" Lily asked.

Another time, another place, it might have been funny. She walked around the car, taking in its boxy edges, the bright, sunshine yellow of its paint. She tried to imagine driving it through Paris in the low light, the spin of police lights behind her, and began to laugh.

"So," Will said, dragging the word out, "does this mean it'll work?" There was a note of amusement in his voice. There was discreet, and then there was this.

"I can *drive* it," Lily said. She had built her Mustang, after all, from old parts and a used frame, made it fast enough that she never saw taillights unless she wanted to. "But every surveillance camera in Paris is going to see us coming."

They returned to the kiosk. Irene had another conversation in French, gesturing elegantly, but the man just shrugged.

"There must be *something* you can do," Irene said, switching to English.

"I am very sorry," he said. He sounded like he meant it. "This is the last car we have. Paris is a very popular tourist destination. I know it isn't very fashionable, but perhaps I can give you a discount—"

This early, every other rental car company was closed. Lily leaned against the counter, thinking about what she wanted, what she had thought this would be. A car with tinted windows and stripped-off plates, the labyrinth of Paris streets.

What other choices did they have?

"Will," she said. He was on his phone, looking up other car services, but at his name he looked up. She kept her voice low. "How much cash do we have for the weekend?"

"A couple thousand euros," he said. "Including our hotel, food—"

"How much can you spare? Including the rental."

He didn't question her, just opened his calculator app, did some quick arithmetic. "Six hundred euros, if you need it."

She could make that work.

Lily placed a hand on Irene's wrist. Regardless of discounts, of waived fees, of whatever else they might offer, this could not be their getaway car. "I'd like to make a return," she said, and pushed the keys across the counter.

Six hundred euros.

It would have to be enough.

First: a used car dealership. It was just Lily and Irene, the rest of the crew deposited at the hotel to prep or more likely sleep off the jet lag, and as they walked through the glass doors, Irene asked, voice pitched low, "Any car preferences?"

Lily looked around. "Anything under four hundred euros."

Irene let out a slow breath, her eyes fluttering shut for just a moment, and Lily knew she was visualizing this the same way Lily did before a race, everything that needed to go exactly right. "It's not going to be a good car," she warned.

"As long as it moves," Lily said. The rest—she would take care of it later.

And then they were inside. There was one Asian sales rep, and he rose to greet them, said something in Chinese. Irene responded in French, and so it went—Irene could charm anyone she ever met. They looked at cars, and Lily browsed through auto shops on Google Maps— it must be nice, she thought wistfully, to know another language—and then an hour later he was handing them some paperwork and Irene was handing him their fake IDs. That had been Lily's doing, of course, because it seemed that the people who liked to bet on those Durham street races were the same people who knew where to get a perfectly made fake. She was afraid they wouldn't hold up, that there would be more paperwork required of them, but at some point the sales rep said something and Irene gestured and said, in English, "It's four hundred euros, does it matter?" and he laughed at that too.

And so they walked out with a car.

Next was the auto repair shop. Lily dropped Irene off at the hotel, picked Daniel up. She could have done this part alone, but Daniel—with the harsh line of his mouth, the shifting ink of his tattoo—*looked* like a street racer. And it was easier, too, to have him next to her as she walked inside the shop, felt the lingering gazes of the other customers here. The entire place felt like a well-kept secret—despite its nondescript exterior, inside the garage there were cars that gleamed in the afternoon light, the steady pulse of French Algerian rap as racers leaned against the hoods of their cars, compared engines and exhaust systems.

It was easier than Lily had expected. Even in another country, some things stayed the same. She talked down the price of a nitrous oxide system—at some point Daniel crossed his arms menacingly, and Lily had to try to keep a straight face—and when the shop owner asked her what it was for, she raised a brow. "Isn't it obvious?" she said.

And so that was how they found out there would be a race tonight. Lily wasn't surprised—in a city like Paris, where everything felt quick and humming and alive, every night could bring something new. Daniel helped her carry their tools outside, and she popped open the hood of the car in the parking lot.

"This might take a while," Lily said.

Daniel leaned against the car, head tilted back to the November sky, the clouds that were so fluffy they looked almost false. "I don't have any-where else to be. Besides," he said, and he gave her an easy smile, "I'd be more concerned if it didn't."

Lily laughed. "Pass me that wrench, will you?"

He did. They were close enough to the highway system that circled

Paris that Lily could see the cars flashing silver in the distance, feel the highway's roar in her ears and where her feet met the ground. If anyone had told her, one year ago, that this would be her life—she never would have believed it. They had pulled off one heist, and soon it would be two, and Lily could not remember the last time she had felt like this, like she was exactly where she was supposed to be.

"You know," Daniel said, and she looked up, "this almost reminds me of China. The smell of exhaust, the sound of the highway. Everything in motion."

Lily thought back to those few days in the Beijing summer, the rumble of a motorcycle beneath her. Everything had been unfamiliar—the streets, the signs, all these people who looked like her. She still didn't know how she felt about it. Will, Irene, they both spoke of China with so much longing. "What was it like?" she asked. "Growing up there?"

Daniel paused. "I don't remember all of it," he said.

"Then the best part."

Daniel gave her a rare smile. "New Year's in Beijing, then. We lived in an apartment on the fourth floor, and it was always so miserably cold in the winter that we wore our coats inside, but on New Year's there were enough people over it didn't matter. Everyone else in China would watch the fireworks on TV, but we were in Beijing, in what felt like the center of the world, and it would be my mom cooking fish in the kitchen because 鱼 is *fish* but sounds like *plenty*, and all my relatives playing mah-jong, and my dad and me on the balcony, in that terrible, cold February night, watching the fireworks and laughing because everyone was so *loud* and we were so lucky, you know? To have everyone we loved, all there." Daniel looked away. In the distance, the highway was all concrete and industrial noise. "I think that was the year before her diagnosis. And then we left for America, and—I don't know. China, those years before everything went wrong—it's the only place that's ever felt like home."

Lily didn't know what to say. She couldn't imagine what it felt like, to have so many people who loved you, to lose it all so quickly. "I'm sorry," she said.

He shrugged. "It was a long time ago," he said. "What about you? What was Texas like?"

She wiped her hands on a towel, watched it darken with soot. For so long, Galveston—its beaches, its piers, the hum of the mosquitoes in the summer—was the only place she had ever known. Lily did not know how to describe it in a way that made sense. She never had. "Lonely," she said at last.

He waited.

"Growing up," Lily said, "it felt like I was the only person who didn't know where I came from. So many of the other families had been there for generations, and my parents—even when I saw them, we never talked about this kind of thing."

Her parents had come from so far, had given up so much—for what? Her dad worked at an oil company in Houston and her mom was a nurse at UTMB, and if she let herself, she could imagine that they had never been anything else. Lily continued, "There's so much I don't know about them. And what I do know—they left China, and they never looked back, and sometimes I wonder if I'm just doing the same thing they did. So many of my classmates never leave Texas, and here I am." She gestured at their surroundings, at the distant, roaring highway, the brightness of the Paris air. But it was more than that too—it was Duke in the fall, the leaves changing color, how the first time she had driven down I-85 she had thought that the evergreens were the biggest trees she had ever seen. It was her junior year, and the world felt so much larger and more terrifying than she had known to expect.

Daniel looked over at her. "And is it still what you want?" he asked. "To leave?"

"Most of the time," she said. "But sometimes—I'm not so sure. It feels like home shouldn't have to be this complicated."

Daniel laughed. "That's how I feel too. About my dad, about med school apps and the Bay Area. You want to go and you want to stay and how can both those things exist at once?"

And it was exactly that. She supposed she shouldn't be surprised that Daniel—who had moved across an ocean when he was a child, who knew better than she did how much it cost to leave—understood how it felt. Still, she couldn't remember the last time she had put these feelings in words. If you were missing something, but you could not even name what it was—did it count? Did it *matter*?

That might have been the end of their conversation. The nitrous oxide system was fully set up, and Lily shut the hood of the car, went over to the driver's side to make sure the engine would start. Daniel unfolded himself from the other side of the car, opened the passenger door just wide enough to duck his head in. "Hey," he said.

"Yeah?" Lily said.

"Come back with me."

She blinked. "What?"

"To China," he said. "My dad and I go every summer. I can show you around Beijing, and we can do all the tourist stuff—the Great Wall, the Forbidden City, everything. You can see it for real, not just for a couple of days. I'd bet money that the rest of the crew would be down too."

"I don't speak Chinese," she said.

Daniel raised a brow. "I do."

Was it this easy? Lily tried to imagine it, couldn't. Her whole life— China had always felt distant, unreachable as a dream. Even now, thinking back on that weekend in Beijing, she was not fully convinced it had actually happened.

"Come on," Daniel said. "It doesn't have to be Beijing. It doesn't even have to be with us. It's just—you should get to see where your parents grew up."

Lily looked down. "I don't know where that is."

"Ask," Daniel said. His voice was gentle. "We have time, don't we?"

On this fall afternoon, summer could have been years away. By then, they would be done with all five heists. If all went well, she would have ten million dollars. Lily thought of her parents, of Galveston in just a handful of days, the porch light that they always left on. She thought of all those late nights alone, the money her parents had scraped together for her Duke tuition, how even after all these years she did not know what she was searching for. Maybe just this: a place that felt like hers.

What was she so afraid of?

"Okay," Lily said. "I'll ask."

His smile was wide. It was a bright, cold November day, and it felt like nothing could go wrong in the world. Lily slid into the driver's seat, waited for Daniel on the other side. "Oh, and Daniel?" she said.

"Yeah?"

Lily thought about how he spoke about China, as if all the years since had only brought grief. Daniel and his dad, the space between them like an ocean too. "Maybe you could talk to your dad too."

"About what?"

"Anything," Lily said. "We have the rest of our lives ahead of us. There are still things we can change."

Daniel was quiet for a long moment. Both of them, wishing their lives had gone just a little differently. Maybe this was how it could. She thought he would say no—she wouldn't have blamed him if he did—but at last he smiled. "Damn," he said. "I hate personal growth."

"Me too," Lily said, but she was smiling too. "Come on, we should go back."

Daniel leaned back in his seat, put his feet up on the dash with a lazy insouciance. "Make it fast."

Lily laughed. There had never been any question of *that*. "You know I will."

She stepped hard on the gas, pulling them out of the parking lot and onto the waiting road. And then they were flying through Paris, in this car she would race tonight, and even with the afternoon traffic, the rattle of this car's broken A/C—Lily rolled down the windows, breathed in the crisp fall air and the promise of Beijing in the summer, thought to herself, *It doesn't get better than this.*

⸺

The rest of the day passed quickly. There was dinner in a Parisian restaurant, a walk along the Seine, plans finalized for tomorrow and all the preparation they had left to do. Lily had told the rest of her crew there was no need to come to the races—if they went well, they would be over soon enough—but of course everyone had wanted to, and so evening found the five of them just outside Paris, surrounded by cool night air and the glint of unfamiliar headlights.

Lily pulled up to the starting line, her car humming softly beneath her. This was not a Durham street race, with its cheap beer and loud, pulsing music, college students made reckless with their parents' money, but it was familiar enough—fluorescent lights and the feel of her foot on the pedal, the smell of smoke and gasoline and possibility. Lily let her gaze run over the car next to her. In the darkness, it was a slash of red, quick and hungry.

She would take it next.

And then she would take *more.*

⸺

The night in fragments:

Lily and an outstretched hand, car keys smooth and silver in her palm. Her used car, with its nitrous oxide system and burst of sudden, temporary speed, traded for a sports car that would have been enough if she didn't have her eye on something else. Her crew, lost in the crowd and then reappearing each time she crossed the finish line, an evening that seemed to change color and shape out of the corner of her eye. Silver engines and adrenaline, everything she ever wanted concentrated in these few moments.

And then, finally, the race she had been waiting for.

The outside world fell away as Lily pulled up in a yellow Lamborghini, her smile wide and waiting. She had never driven one of these before, and it hummed beneath her palms, all grace and predatory speed. It was the second-best car at the races tonight. The best one—

Next to her, a matte black Bugatti pulled up to the starting line. Europe, it seemed, did races differently. The car was as dark as the Paris night, without plates, and as the evening deepened, Lily had watched its driver win every race he had competed in. She hadn't seen his face—just a glimpse of dark hair as he stepped into the driver's seat, a hand that dangled carelessly out an open window, but it didn't matter. This would be their getaway car.

She just had to win it.

The other driver rolled his window down. Lily glanced over, curious, and he met her gaze, surprise crossing his face. He was Asian too, the first Asian street racer she'd seen tonight, and couldn't have been older than her by more than a couple years.

"中国人?" he asked. He had to shout to be heard.

She shook her head.

He switched languages. "Êtes-vous français?"

She shook her head again.

He threw up his hands. "Allez, aidez-moi!"

Lily's smile was quick. She didn't understand his words, but his meaning was clear enough. *Come on*, he might have said. *Help me out here.* She knew she shouldn't have answered—they were here for the zodiac head, nothing more—but in all these years of racing, of long roads and changing lights, she had never met someone who looked like her, who might *understand*. She could win and win and win, and each year at the races strangers would look at her as though this were not her world to take.

"American," Lily shouted back.

"American," he echoed. In English he had just the trace of an accent, though she couldn't quite place what kind. "And what are you doing here?"

The starting flag came down.

Lily winked at him. "Taking your car," she called, and stepped hard on the gas.

He was a good driver. She could see it in the way his car accelerated, the ease with which he took his turns. He drove like he had spent his whole life doing it. In another car, one without this silver supercharger, without three separate systems for exhaust flow, she wouldn't have stood a chance. Even with all of this—their cars almost perfectly matched—it would be close.

Lily could see the end of the race approaching, lights that drew closer and closer, and they were a hundred feet away, fifty feet, ten, and he pulled just barely ahead and she pressed down hard on the throttle, held her breath. *Come on, just a little more—*

They flew across the finish line, her car just a breath before his.

It was the last race of the night. The crowd was yelling in French, rapturous, but all she could hear was her pounding heart. She rested her hands on her steering wheel, bringing the car slowly to a stop, and turned off the ignition. The air smelled like burning rubber.

She had won.

She had *won*.

She didn't know what to do with the information, what she felt. Her heart was still beating too fast. She knew it had been too close, that she had almost lost their getaway car for her arrogance, for her certainty, and yet—Lily let herself smile, let herself almost laugh. It had been so long since she had raced like this, without knowing the outcome. She wanted to do it again and again.

A tap on the glass. Lily rolled her window down, the night air washing over her. This might have been a dream—Paris, distant and glittering, the roar of the crowd, this other driver bent down before her, his palm open. "Yours," he said, his keys glinting silver in his hand. "And well earned."

Lily took it. There was a slip of paper there too, folded around the keys, and she opened it to reveal a phone number, done in a sharp, sure hand. "And this?"

"A rematch," he said, his gaze never leaving hers. There was a hint of a smile on his lips. "If you're interested."

She should have said no. "I'm not in town for long."

His smile was quick. He hadn't given her his name, she realized. "Neither am I."

30

WILL

The Château de Fontainebleau was an artist's dream. The sun rose, splintered red and gold against dramatic Italian frescoes and richly sculpted stucco, vaulted ceilings painted in the style of the French Renaissance. Napoleon had called the Fontainebleau *the true residence of kings.*

Will could see why. Once, this had been home to da Vinci's *Mona Lisa*, and Michelangelo's *Hercules* was raised on a plinth in the Cour de la Fontaine. All the Renaissance art he had discussed in classes and read about in glossy textbook pages surrounded him now, saturated in color and morning light. In front of him, the tour guide gave the history of the Fontainebleau in rapid, flawless Chinese.

"I can't believe you signed us up for a tour," Irene muttered. The gallery was filled with Chinese families, a sea of sun umbrellas and visors and the click of expensive cameras. The tour bus had picked them up from the hotel at six in the morning. "I am *so tired.*"

"You wanted to blend in," Will said. He gave her a quick smile. He hadn't slept much either—how could he, after watching Lily race?—and yet he had never felt more awake. "And we've never been here before."

"I wasn't expecting *this*." Her gaze skimmed the room, lingering not on the art but on the velvet partitions, the lone guard at the doorway. Earlier, she had called the Francis I Gallery *a fancy hallway*. "How much longer?" she asked.

The Château de Fontainebleau had over a thousand rooms. "Four hours."

Irene gave him an incredulous look. "All of these rooms look exactly the same. I'll meet you at the Chinese Museum." She slid the map out of his hands, looked over it with dangerous interest.

He thought of Stockholm, one month ago, Alex and Irene arguing in the other hotel room. He trusted his sister, but still—someday, he feared she would find herself in a situation she could not talk her way out of. "What will you do until then?"

Irene shrugged lightly. "Chat up a guard. Steal some art. The usual."

Will laughed. He might be wrong. Irene had always walked through life like it was meant to part before her, and it had. She had been high school valedictorian, class president, debate captain. She had done everything he had and better, gone to Duke on a full-ride scholarship. He looked at her and felt nothing but pride, absolute and overwhelming, and yet sometimes he couldn't help but wonder if things were switched—if she had been the one who pursued art, instead of him—whether she would have given up so easily.

Somehow he doubted it.

"No stealing," he said, and then lowered his voice, smiled at his sister, "yet."

Irene laughed, quick and bright, before vanishing into the crowd of Chinese tourists.

The tour guide led them through the rest of the grands apartments. There were throne rooms with chandeliers that dripped gold, salons draped in velvet and precious silk, galleries that were all light against intricately carved woodwork. If this had been his freshman year, he would have stood beneath these painted ceilings and felt nothing but awe.

Instead, as they drew closer to the Chinese Museum, the two stone lions that stood guard at its doors, Will thought of Beijing, of how the pale morning light had fallen on the ruins of the Old Summer Palace. He had only ever seen it as stone columns and empty space, but once, it had looked something like this. There had been Western influences too, a sweeping staircase just like the one at the front of the Fontainebleau, rooms of gold and gilded frames.

All of it had burned.

Inside the Chinese Museum, for the first time, Will saw all that had been taken from the Old Summer Palace. He looked around and he could almost believe he was there, three hundred years ago, surrounded by lacquered panels of black and gold, Chinese washing over him as if this were an imperial court.

Will had always known history was told by the conquerors. And yet it was another thing entirely to be here, surrounded by all that had been taken years ago, as the tour guide spoke of diplomatic gifts and priceless treasures as if this country had not promised China a truce and then burned the Old Summer Palace to the ground. The Second Opium War had only ended in 1860. Once, he had thought it very far away. It did not feel that way now.

He raised his hand.

"Yes?" the tour guide asked in Chinese. At the start of the tour, he had mistaken her for another tourist, a college student like him or Irene. But she walked through the palace like it belonged to her, and when she spoke to the other guides, her French was flawless.

"You said some of this art was a gift from the ambassador of Siam,"

Will said, as if he was not sure he heard her correctly. His Chinese was not as good as Irene's, but he could do *this*. "What about the rest of it?"

The other tourists fell silent. They were all Chinese here. They knew what he meant. Still, her expression was smooth, unbothered. How many times had she been asked this question before? "The rest was taken during the destruction of the Old Summer Palace," she said, "though I think you know that already."

"And you don't think there's anything wrong with that?"

"The Château has seen the rise and fall of Napoleon," she said, her high ponytail swishing as she gestured toward the windows, the light that poured in. "We have walked through the same rooms as Marie Antoinette, who was guillotined by the French public. France has a long, bloody history. Our role is not to pass modern-day judgment, but to remember, to preserve. To serve as record keepers for the next generation."

It was a very art-historian answer. He had heard the same thing from Harvard professors, from museum experts, all those who viewed objectivity as the highest ideal to aspire toward. Once, he had even believed it. But history was retold as civilizations rose, and museums had always been part of that retelling. He thought of Drottningholm Palace, of Chinese art that had been bought and displayed without any indication of its history. "History is an ongoing process, though, isn't it?" Will asked. "And what we remember has always been determined by what museums choose to display."

"Is that a question?" she asked, her voice cool. "Or may we proceed?"

Will hesitated. He wanted to say more—he had spent so many years learning about how the West shaped history into its image—but he suspected it wouldn't have mattered. There was no truth to be found here. "Please," he said at last. "Proceed."

She did, so seamlessly it was as if he had never spoken at all. He knew he shouldn't have said anything in the first place—he imagined a security guard winding back the tape, Interpol searching facial recognition for a match—and yet he thought of the Old Summer Palace burning, of all the ways history was retold, made easier and softer and less true. So much had been taken that museums would not even acknowledge.

Tonight they would take something back.

Still, as the group continued through the Chinese Museum, Will couldn't help but notice the tour guide's eyes following him, her gaze narrow and probing.

⁓

Paris, in the evening light, did not feel real. They had spent the rest of the day being tourists, posing by the Eiffel Tower with scarves wrapped tight, coats buttoned up against the November wind. Will had gone to the Louvre alone, took in paintings hung in great, gilded frames, and thought, *Someday.* He didn't know if he was thinking about thefts, things stolen and returned, or just his name on a placard, something of his on these walls. When he returned, the rest of his crew didn't ask him where he'd been. Instead they walked along the Champs-Élysées, took in fall colors and the curving Arc de Triomphe, Paris as the sun set.

Will didn't want it to end.

They sat at a table by the restaurant entrance, candlelight flickering over the dark red tablecloth and a basket of fresh bread, the glass of the window separating them from the glittering Paris streets. Irene had ordered already, her French perfect despite the years since high school. When the waiter arrived, it was with carefully plated dishes that Will didn't know the names of, sauces and herbs arranged to look like art. It was the kind of dinner they could only have had because of China Poly.

"The French are so pretentious," Irene said when the waiter left, but she was smiling. At some point, the waiter had looked at the rest of them—who clearly did not understand a word he was saying—and then continued in French. Irene pointed to each dish. "Soupe à l'oignon, coq au vin, tartare aller-retour—"

"That's still not English," Daniel said.

Will laughed. Paris was not always a welcoming city, and yet he didn't mind. It existed just as it was. "We should come back when this is all over. We could be tourists for real."

"A senior trip," Daniel suggested.

Lily raised a brow. "Have you forgotten about our China plans so quickly?"

"Absolutely not," Daniel said, leaning back against his chair. Will had the strange, sudden sensation that something was slipping through his fingertips, but then Daniel said, easily, "It's an open invitation, if anyone wants to come. We're going to do the tourist trip that Lily never got growing up."

And somehow it was easier for Will to breathe.

"Please, not the Great Wall," Irene said. "The tourists will *eat* you."

"You know it," Daniel said. "What is the Chinese American experience, if not white people gawking at you when you speak English?"

Alex laughed. "You can get that in Chinatown."

"Anyway," Lily said, but she was laughing too. "Paris in the summer."

"Paris in the summer," Will echoed. "Alex?"

"I have a full-time job," Alex said. A moment later, she smiled. "With paid time off, thank *god*."

Will smiled too. "Irene?"

His sister smiled wide. "I'd call this trip Eurocentric, but we're about to take a great deal from the Europeans. We could give them this. Although—I think Lily and I both have plans until late July."

Will looked at Lily. He knew Irene's plans, of course—consulting in New York City, the kind of thing she was good at without even trying—but a month ago, Lily had still been applying for internships. Lily smiled.

"Got an offer a few days ago from Microsoft. I figured I'd wait until we were together to share the news."

Will couldn't say he was surprised. He had seen her race on these Paris streets, hot-wire a speedboat with nothing but a pocketknife and the light of her phone. He had never met anyone who could be so many things so easily. "Congrats," he said, and meant it. "They're lucky to have you."

"As are we," Irene said, and lifted her glass. For a moment, there was just the sound of glass clinking, and Will thought of museums in the low light, how China had felt two months ago, everything he wanted within reach for the first time.

"So there we have it," Daniel said. "When summer comes, we'll do our reunion here."

May in Paris. Will let himself imagine it. The flowers in bloom and spring on the Seine, the softness of the colors like a Renoir. This crew of his, everything stolen now returned. The year after, it might be Stockholm, or London, any of the other cities they would rob. It might be somewhere new entirely. They would have fifty million dollars between them. Anything was possible.

"Daniel," Alex said, and there was easy good humor in her voice. Somehow being here made friendships easier. "Did you just admit that you want to hang out with us?"

"I would never," Daniel said, but he was smiling.

This was what Will knew: They had all come here for different reasons. They had all chosen to stay. He had spent so many years thinking that nothing good could ever last, but—maybe this could. His crew was here, had chosen this and him and a future that felt out of a dream.

Next to him, Irene leaned over. "When did those two become friends?" she asked, tilting her head toward Alex and Daniel.

"When did we all become friends?" he asked. "Like this." It had been two months. He remembered Beijing and a rising sun, plane flights and

Lily's smile in the blue light. Stockholm, hotel rooms, champagne. Paris, pale and glittering, all these moments in camera obscura. Temporary, perhaps, but lovely all the same.

The candlelight was low, flickering. Will looked between the members of his crew, laughing in this restaurant as they planned for a summer still months away. He would graduate in May, walk across a stage and leave Harvard behind. He still did not know what it meant. But here, surrounded by friends, on the eve of another heist—

For the first time, Will was not afraid of what his future held.

31

ALEX

In these early-morning hours, nothing felt quite real. Alex Huang spun in her chair, the hotel room lit only by a solitary lamp, the tentative blue glow of her computer screen. The curtains were drawn open, the wrought-iron balcony opening up to the distant Paris lights. The Château de Fontainebleau was forty miles from the heart of the city, and the silence felt like a held breath.

Alex adjusted the police dial on her radio, waiting for the static to resolve. In her mind, she saw a palace cast in moonlight, her crew slipping through gates and gardens and the changing of the guard. For a moment, she wished she had tried to access the palace security. Never mind the hours it would have taken, the risks that came with it—it would have been worth it to be there for this moment, to see the swing of Daniel's bat or the glint in Irene's eyes, her careful, practiced movements in the dark. Will might have looked up at the security camera, smiled like he had a secret.

In the end, though, it wouldn't have mattered.

Alex already knew how this would go.

Bells, slow and heavy, began to toll. It was the turn of the hour, and Alex brought her hands to her keyboard, took in one slow, deliberate breath. She had played piano, years ago, and somehow tonight felt like the rising of a curtain, that first press of an ivory key. This was not a concert hall, her hands on the smooth, flawless surface of a grand piano, but it was a performance regardless.

"Go," Alex said.

A beat, and then she heard the sharp, bright sound of breaking glass.

Their second heist had begun.

She turned back to the police radio, adjusting the dials until the static cleared. She had been expecting silence—the alarms would take a few seconds to go off, to send signals through looping wires and circuits across the city—but already there was conversation, the background noise of sirens. Everything was in French, brisk and urgent, incomprehensible.

"Shit," she said, almost to herself. They had planned for seven minutes. This would have to be less. She switched tabs, tapping her fingers impatiently against the keyboard. It might not have meant anything. But she had done her research on the Château de Fontainebleau's alarm system, on police response times, on all these tiny details that, in a heist like this, *mattered*.

Her screen loaded. It was a mirror of the police station's own vehicle tracker, with blinking red pinpricks for each car and its coordinates, and Alex went cold. Police cars were moving, moving, moving, tracking fast toward the Château de Fontainebleau. She counted a handful of streets, maybe less, before they would arrive at the Chinese Museum.

"What is it?" Lily's voice was low, clear through Alex's headphones. She would be idling outside the palace, waiting for the rest of their crew to emerge, victorious. They had all been so certain that this would go just like the last theft: perfectly. Even now, Alex didn't know what had gone wrong, where they had fucked up. All she knew was that they had been counting on her, and now she could hear the sound of sirens outside the hotel room, slicing open the hollow peace of the night.

"Something's wrong," Alex said. She had to press her hands against the desk to keep them from trembling. Every second, the police drew closer. "You have to get out."

32

DANIEL

aniel Liang flexed his hands in his gloves, brought his bat up to rest on his shoulder. He thought of one month ago, this same motion on the steps of the Chinese Pavilion. The air was colder now, the country different. He didn't know if he was changed. This month had been interviews on different coasts, calls with his crew in empty hotel rooms, and airports he wouldn't remember. Alex had found a way into the FBI server, and though he could have been upset, he wasn't. There was too much at stake. So this month, too, had been spent reviewing the evidence, calling his father and waiting, wondering, if he would mention the investigation. He nearly always did. It was the most they had spoken in years. Daniel knew he should have felt guilty.

He swung, glass falling around him like stars. He had college debt to pay off, a med school education within reach. And, stepping into the Chinese Pavilion, he couldn't help but feel that this was *his*.

Last year, he had given up his Chinese citizenship. It had been about time, his father had said, who had applied for US citizenship when they first arrived, but Daniel had held on to his passport, the red of it dark as blood. But he was about to apply to med school, and international applicants always had it harder, and so on a bright clear day in November, he had gone to answer questions about presidents and amendments and to call this country his. He had waved a mini American flag, posed for a photo, thought of China.

Some days the loss was harder than others. It had been ten years since his mom had died, ten years since they had left all this behind. But that passport, his citizenship—it felt like saying goodbye. So many of his friends were Chinese American, but he had always thought of himself as Chinese. China, its history and its grief, lingered in his bones and his blood.

All this to say: This museum, its art, it was his by right.

He would bring it home.

At the heart of the Chinese Museum, Daniel stopped moving. Alex was speaking in his ear, her voice a warning, but they didn't need it anymore. In this room that was meant to hold the bronze rooster head, porcelain vases, all that was taken from the Old Summer Palace so many years ago—

It was gone.

Daniel stepped forward, looked down at the sound of glass crunching beneath his feet. For a moment, he thought he had missed something. It was as if they had come and gone already, time catching in a strange loop. Shattered glass, empty cases, a theft that had somehow, impossibly, occurred already.

"The police are already on their way," Alex said. "You have a minute, maybe less."

"Lily?" Will said, his voice very quiet. In this empty room, they might have been playing pretend, not thieves but just ordinary college students, lost and uncertain. Daniel cast a glance at the cameras, still blinking red.

"Ready when you are," Lily said. Her voice was steady, and he imagined her car cutting through the darkness like a knife. If they left now—they might still have a way out.

Will didn't move.

Daniel grasped his wrist. "Come on," he said. He spoke in Chinese, just in case, his voice low and urgent. "We have to go."

"We don't have anything."

Daniel looked around the room. In the moonlight, there was just the glint of broken glass, cabinets thrown open. "What's left?" he asked. Even the walls were stripped of their lacquered panels.

Will shook his head. "But—"

Irene wrapped her fingers around Will's other wrist. "We're leaving," she said, and her voice left no room for argument. "Before we can't."

Outside, the wind was cold, the sky dark and threatening. Lily was idling by the side gates, and when they slid into the car, she stepped hard on the gas, the door slamming shut before they could close it. Behind them, he could hear the sound of sirens, see the flash of blue police lights against wet cobblestone.

Daniel closed his eyes and thought of loss.

<hr />

"What was that?" Will's voice cut through the silence of the room. They were back at the hotel, doors locked and curtains drawn, fluorescent light casting harsh shadows over everyone's faces.

For several heartbeats, no one spoke. Daniel thought of the museum, its missing art, tried to think of it like his father might. Somehow, impossibly, someone else had gotten there first, had taken everything they were looking for.

Irene's voice was thoughtful. "Our competition."

Will let out a long, slow breath. "How could this happen?" he asked, and Daniel didn't know if he was talking to himself or the rest of them.

They might have still been at the Château de Fontainebleau, those first few moments when everything felt like a dream. "How do you *know*?"

"It's obvious, when you think about it," Irene said. She ticked it off on her fingers, her voice cool and almost unconcerned. "There are more people than Wang Yuling who want this art. Our heist last month was all over the news. These morning hours are when security is the lightest."

"You couldn't have said something before this happened?" Will said. His voice was low, not quite an accusation, but Daniel recognized the emotion there. Grief, anger, layered over each other, searching for some place to go.

Irene raised a brow. "There was a classmate speculating in my public policy class, Will, it wasn't exactly hard evidence. What did you expect me to do?"

Daniel could feel the tension in the room shift, take shape. So much had gone wrong tonight. So much could go wrong still. Will crossed his arms. "We just lost *fifty million dollars*, Irene. Just because it doesn't matter to you—"

"That's not fair," Daniel said, but neither of them was listening.

"You're so quick to blame anyone but yourself," Irene said. "But you and I both know it wouldn't have changed anything. It's not like we could have chosen another museum, or an earlier weekend. Just because someone else got there first—" She didn't finish her sentence. Daniel couldn't imagine how she would. What was left, after this?

"What?" Will demanded.

Irene held his gaze. "Who *cares*?" she asked, and even after all these years—Daniel could not tell if she was lying. Her voice was cold. "We did everything we could, and someone else got there first. It *happens*."

"Not to you," Will snapped. Daniel thought it had to be true, but—so briefly that he might have imagined it—Irene's face opened with something like surprise, something like hurt. "We could've talked about it! We could've had a backup plan. But you're so set on this *failing*—"

"*Will*," Daniel said, and his voice was sharper now. He jerked his head toward the balcony. "Let's talk outside."

Will might have said no. He was on edge, and so was Irene, both of them angling for a fight. This night had never been meant to end like this. Will held Daniel's gaze for a long, terrible moment, and then he pushed himself off the edge of the desk he had been leaning against, strode to the balcony door.

Daniel shut the glass door behind them.

"Talk," Will said.

Like this, Paris looked so far away. It was cold outside, the wind cruel and biting. "Get it together," Daniel said.

"That isn't fair," Will said, wounded. "Irene—"

"This isn't about her."

"It always is."

Daniel pressed his palms against the metal railing. He knew the two of them, how they always looked at each other and saw everything they couldn't be. "It's not," he said. *I'm going to let you go*, Daniel had said. He was trying. "Don't you remember how this began? You were *there* when the Sackler got robbed. We always knew there were more players in this game."

"So you're saying it's my fault." Will's voice was flat.

"No," Daniel said. "I'm saying that—" He tilted his head up, took in stars and the distant sickle moon. He had broken into a museum today and felt no fear. "This heist isn't just *yours*, Will."

"I know."

"Do you?" Daniel asked, meeting Will's gaze. "I know what this means to you. But it means something to all of us. It's a chance for—for something new. For healing. For a future. And right now we're all waiting for *you* to tell us what to do."

"I know," Will said again, softer. He hesitated for a moment, his hands laced together. His gaze was on the lightening sky, the distant Paris skyline. "I'm afraid."

"Of?"

This conversation had happened before. "What if I fuck up?" Will said. "I don't know what I'm doing either."

Daniel remembered Stockholm in the darkness, the two of them on a different balcony. They had only ever been making this up as they went along, hoping that it might work anyway. "We all know that," Daniel said. "We're trusting you to figure it out."

Will's laugh was just a little shaky. "You sure you want to do that?"

Daniel slid open the balcony door. It had been ten years of trusting Will, of trusting Irene, of knowing that if he could not have family, he could at least have them. Suddenly, unexpectedly, he thought back to an afternoon from years ago, the three of them sprawled out on a San Francisco pier. They had just finished a midday showing of some movie or another, and beneath the endless blue sky, the faint chill from the Pacific Ocean, Daniel had looked over at these two siblings and realized, with a startling and absolute clarity, *There is nothing I would not do for them.* Somehow they had made it here. Even on this evening, with everything that had gone wrong—he could be glad for that, at least.

"You're our leader," Daniel said. "Lead."

Will stepped inside. The room was the same as they had left it. Irene and Lily, shoulder to shoulder against the hotel bed; Alex at the desk with her laptop open. There was no evidence of all that had happened tonight.

Will looked at Daniel, nodded just slightly before turning to address their crew. "I'm sorry," he said, his voice low. "Irene, this isn't your fault. This isn't anyone's. We just—" He closed his eyes, opened them again. "We need to find a way forward from here. There's footage of us talking in the museum. We have to get rid of it."

Daniel nodded. It was what he would have done too. "What about the other thieves?"

"We take care of ourselves first," Will said. "If we can find out who they are, all the better. But it's more important that we make sure we aren't held responsible for something we didn't do."

"We *did* break in," Irene said.

"They don't need to know that," Will said. "Alex?"

Alex's silence was long, excruciating. Daniel remembered a month ago, planning for their first theft. Already they had asked her for so many impossible things. "I—" she began. "I'll go by the palace. See what I can do from there."

Daniel began to get up. They all knew she couldn't go alone, not when the police would be there already, when Paris watched them in the careful, early-morning light. Will caught his gaze, shook his head. "Irene," he said. "Go with her."

The rest of the crew looked at him, incredulous. The two of them— well, it had been this way since the beginning, Alex and Irene moving around each other as if neither of them could bear to get too close. "I don't care if you don't get along," Will said. "Irene, make sure nothing stands in Alex's way. And *get that footage.*"

They left.

And then it was just Will, Daniel, and Lily.

"What now?" Lily asked, her voice soft. She hadn't spoken since the car ride. Her knuckles had been white against the wheel, but the car had cut a fast, unwavering path through back alleys and around the watchful gaze of surveillance cameras, hidden in the heavy dark. He didn't know what she had done with the car after, but he trusted her, trusted that the police wouldn't be able to find it.

Daniel and Will looked at each other. They knew how this part went. "We wait," Daniel said.

So they did. The sun rose, reaching long fingers over the trembling horizon, and they didn't move from the hotel room as red light washed over them, as a new day dawned.

33

ALEX

Alex Huang was not a hacker. She had never been more aware of it than at this moment. They stood just a few streets away from the palace, the night air pressing down on them like a vise. It was cold, the street empty and cast in long, forbidding shadows. "What next?" Irene asked.

Alex fiddled with the strap of her backpack. She knew why Will had sent Irene with her, though he shouldn't have bothered. Irene, no matter how persuasive she was, couldn't help them now. "I need access to their internal server," she said, more for herself than Irene. She paced along the alleyway, going through the steps she had gone through to get into Drottningholm, the Poly Art Museum. She had done this before.

You shouldn't be here, Irene had said once.

Alex was beginning to think she was right. To do this, before morning came, to get in and out before the FBI or Interpol or even the palace security forces noticed she was there—it was impossible. "I need access to their internal server, and then their security system, and I need it before anyone else gets to it, and—"

"Breathe," Irene said.

Alex was hyperventilating, just a little. She pressed her palms against the brick wall, forced herself to slow her breathing. "Don't tell me what to do," she said. She knew, intellectually, that this wasn't Irene's fault. But Irene was standing there, perfectly composed, and Alex felt on the verge of falling apart.

"Fine," Irene said. She crossed her arms, leaned against the wall. In the darkness, she could have been made of marble, all shadows and the curve of a cheek, the pale column of her throat. Without makeup, for once, and yet her features were no less beautiful, no less cold. "An internal server. How are we going to get that?"

"We can't," Alex said. She resumed pacing. Maybe, maybe, she thought. If she could get in, somehow, if the Château de Fontainebleau's security system was the same as Drottningholm's, all contracted to the same third party. Museum security had been easier than she'd expected that time, hadn't it? Simple, almost appallingly straightforward. A relic of the past, she had joked to herself. But she had done that for fun, just to see, without the hours counting down, without the distant sound of sirens or the weight of everything that had gone wrong this night. She couldn't do this in a few hours. She didn't know if she could do this at all.

"You have to," Irene said.

"Why?" Alex snapped. "Because your voice was caught on tape? Because you're afraid of getting caught? Because for once you won't get exactly what you want?"

Irene crossed her arms. "You don't know me."

"You don't know *me*. You've never thought of me as part of this team. You should be pleased—you're right. I don't know what I'm doing."

"I don't think that."

Since the beginning, Irene had looked at her like she had no right to be here. Alex was suddenly thankful they were in a side street, that no one else was there to see this. "Don't lie to me."

"Fine," Irene said, emotion bleeding through her voice at last. *Finally,*

Alex thought. "You're here because Will likes beautiful things, and I've only ever thought you were a software engineer wasting our time."

Irene had always chosen her words like she was wielding a weapon. Still, Alex felt a terrible, vicious pleasure to hear her say it, to have proof of what she really thought. "Great," she said. "So what now? You *win*, Irene."

"I don't," Irene shot back. "This whole time, you've been so fucking intent on proving me wrong. So *prove me wrong*."

"I can't do this!" Alex yelled back. She was so tired, and so afraid, and Irene couldn't understand. She never had. "I don't even have their wi-fi!"

Irene stopped moving.

"What?"

"Is that all you need?"

Alex laughed, sharp and biting. "Do you have any idea about what my job is?" she asked. "Of course not! But it'd be a place to *start*, and right now I have nothing."

Irene ignored her. She took a few steps forward, checked the street signs, before beginning to walk. Her boots clicked against the pavement.

Alex hated that she had to follow her. She was in a foreign city, before dawn, and Irene was as insufferable as she always was. "Can you *say* something? I'm trying to have an argument with you—"

Irene stopped in front of a coffee shop. "Set up your laptop," she said, and it was a command. The place was closed, of course, but they had chairs and tables set up on the street, and Irene pulled one out, sat down. The iron must have been cold, but she didn't flinch. With her foot, she nudged the other chair. "I'll give you the password."

Alex sat. "This is a coffee shop."

"They use the museum wi-fi. I was here yesterday."

"They didn't give you the guest wi-fi?"

"I asked for the other one," Irene said.

"And they gave it to you?"

"Of course," Irene said, as if that was what was supposed to happen, as if asking was enough. And maybe it was, for her. Alex could imagine Irene walking into an artisanal coffee shop, leaning over the counter, and purchasing an eclair in her perfect, lilting French. Had anyone ever said no to her? "I said I was a visiting art student and the internet wasn't fast enough for me to load my lectures. They were very happy to help."

"Why did you do it?"

Irene shrugged. "Will was on a tour. I was bored. I thought it might be useful." She raised a brow. "Don't we have a job to do?"

Alex opened her laptop. She was exhausted. But Irene was sitting across from her, now silent, her fingertips pressed together and her gaze never leaving Alex's. Alex wouldn't give Irene the satisfaction of watching her fail.

She began to type.

Before the sun rose, Alex had finished. She downloaded the footage, deleted it off the museum server and every backup she could find, her IP address set to a province in China. If they thought China was behind this, she would let them. It was messy, imperfect, but—if they were caught, it would not be through this.

McDonald's at five in the morning always felt like a liminal space. Irene set their order down in front of Alex, the smell of salt and fast food permeating the air.

Alex took a fry, dipped it in ketchup. She didn't want to say anything, but Irene was sitting across from her, hands laced together, waiting.

"Well?" Alex said.

"What?" Irene said.

Alex shook her head. She didn't know what she had expected. "Do you think this is the end?" she asked instead.

Irene examined her hands. "I don't know," she said. A pause. "I don't think so."

"Why?" Alex asked.

"Because my brother wants it," Irene said, as if that was all there was.

"And you?" Alex said. "What do you want?"

Another pause, longer this time. "I don't know," she said again, and Alex was not used to this, Irene and her uncertainty, her honesty. "I know that China has a right to this art, and that the fact that museums haven't given it back already is because of lingering colonialist mentalities. Art is power, just like everything else. And yet—"

Alex waited.

Irene sighed. "Sometimes wanting isn't enough," she said. "And when it comes down to it, if it's between our futures and this art, what it means for China, I'm not going to choose art."

For a moment, they both ate in silence. Alex thought of power, of China, of all the relatives there she had never known. Her parents, her grandparents—they had all grown up in America, their history tied to New York City, to the shops and restaurants and parks in Chinatown. She didn't know if it made her feel closer to China or further away. And she thought, too, of her future, of New York and Silicon Valley and all the dreams that rested on her shoulders.

"Why did you say yes?" Irene asked. "You didn't know any of us."

It would have been easy for Alex to dismiss her. *I don't owe you my truth*, she could have said, and it would be true. Two months ago, in a Beijing airport, she had not answered this same question. But Irene had stayed with her for all these hours, had bought her fries and told her something of herself. Alex thought back to that first day, the Sackler lit up from within. "I dropped out of MIT," she said, though she was sure Irene already knew. "I wasn't planning on it, at first, but I got offered more money than I'd ever seen, and my parents—well, it would mean something to them. So I left, and I started working, and even though I wasn't happy, I tried to tell myself I was. This job—it felt like a second chance."

"I didn't know you felt that way."

Why would she? "You never asked."

"I know." Irene examined Alex for a long moment. "You don't like me."

"You don't like *me*."

Irene's smile was quick. "True enough." She reached for a fry, ate it. "To be fair, I never like Will's exes. It's nothing personal."

Alex sighed. "I'm not his ex, Irene. It was two dates. And even if I were—that isn't everything. That's barely *anything*."

Irene was silent for a long moment, examining her. "You're right," she said at last, and she looked almost surprised to hear herself say it. She hesitated, and Alex wondered if this would be how things changed, if they might be friends after all. But then Irene looked away, her gaze going to the McDonald's window, the rest of the world waiting for them.

Outside, the sky was beginning to lighten. Pale light touched Irene's hair, the brush of her lashes against her skin. "Does everyone like you?" Alex asked, because she could not bear the silence any longer. Irene would never apologize to her, she realized. Why would she?

"Yes," Irene said easily.

"Why?"

Irene took another fry, the motion quick and elegant. "I give them something to like."

"You haven't done that for me."

"Should I?" Irene asked. She lifted her gaze, her smile slow and deliberate. If Alex hadn't spent so long learning all of Irene's expressions, she might not have caught the trace of mockery in it. "I can, if you'd like. We can start over."

Alex looked away. The thing was, she believed Irene. But this felt *honest*. Irene was all sharp edges and a quick tongue, and Alex did not want to pretend. She rose, swept the remains of their tray into the trash can. They didn't have to be friends. Perhaps it was better that they weren't. "No," she said. And then, because it was true, because she couldn't help herself, "I'll have you exactly as you are."

34

LILY

It was strange, watching the heist that should have been theirs. Lily leaned over Alex's shoulder, the five of them clustered around a single laptop. It was quick, efficient, almost exactly what they would have done. Smashed glass, dark backpacks, gloved hands. She could have sworn one of the thieves winked at the camera as he was leaving, his backpack heavy with the bronze rooster head. Her crew had only planned to rob one of the Fontainebleau's many rooms, but the other thieves had been more ambitious. They had missed each other by just seconds.

"Anything?" Alex asked.

Will shook his head. None of them had slept while they waited for Alex and Irene. Instead Will had reached for his notebook, gone through his list of the Fontainebleau's art. "The other thieves only took items from the Old Summer Palace," he said. "They took *everything* from the Old Summer Palace. It feels very—purposeful. Like us."

Lily thought of a few weeks ago, talking about *an ordered job*. The question had always been who was doing the ordering. "What now?" she asked. On the screen, Will, Irene, and Daniel appeared. If Lily hadn't known who they were, she might have mistaken them for members of the other crew. "What happens without this zodiac head?"

Will turned his phone over in his hand. "I'll call China Poly when we're back," he said. His smile was quick, false. "Maybe it won't matter."

"It's Wang Yuling," Irene said. "It'll matter."

"What else can we do?" Will asked, his voice low. "Even if this other crew is Chinese, even if their intentions are the same as ours—it's not like we can find them."

The video was still playing. The angle switched, the camera moving over the Fontainebleau's courtyard, the side gates with their cut locks. Lily leaned forward, waiting, wondering. She had been fast, but she didn't know if she had been fast enough to avoid the cameras. The time-stamp was just moments before she had pulled up when she caught a glimpse of color.

"Wait," Lily said.

They all fell silent. On the screen, the video kept playing. She saw her car in shadow, Will and Daniel and Irene as three dark figures in motion. She had been afraid, waiting for them outside, hearing the sirens draw closer, but when they got to the car, all that fear had vanished. She could outrun the cops. She could outrun anybody.

"Rewind it," she said, and Alex did.

The mood in the hotel room was somber, serious. They had lost the zodiac head, and the future was heavy with uncertainty. But Alex re-wound the tape, and Lily drew in a shallow breath. The car on the screen wasn't theirs.

A yellow Lamborghini, almost too fast for the camera to catch, sped off into the waiting dark.

She thought of the night before, Paris and the smell of smoke and gasoline. A stranger in an unknown car, the phone number he had pressed into her hand.

A rematch, he had said.

Lily looked up, let herself smile. "I know how we can find the thieves."

35

IRENE

The courtyard of the Louvre Museum was pale, imposing in the morning light. Irene Chen stood next to the pyramid, with its iconic glass panes, her gaze skimming the pedestrians who walked past them, the cameras that flashed brief and bright in an attempt to capture how Paris felt in the rising sun, all light and heady promise. The pyramids in front of the Louvre had been designed by a Chinese American architect, and the choice of location felt deliberate—a place where history could be remembered, where it could be made. Irene checked her phone, making sure her connection still held. Alex was on the line, ready to look up any information they found today, and Daniel stood at the other end of the courtyard, his stance deliberately casual as he leaned against the classic French Renaissance facade. It was just Will, Irene, and Lily, waiting to meet the other crew.

"There they are," Lily said.

It felt, strangely, like looking into a mirror. Though there had been at least five people in the video, there were just two of them here, crossing the courtyard with an easy confidence. Irene recognized one as the driver Lily had raced against, the glint of his smile in the Paris light. These thieves had just robbed the Château de Fontainebleau, walked off with millions of dollars of stolen art, but they moved through Paris as if it were *theirs*.

"你," Will said, and Irene recognized the other thief. *You*, her brother had said, catching what she hadn't. She hadn't been paying attention at the time, too occupied with the guards, the security, all that was obvious, to wonder about anything else.

"好久不见," their tour guide said, her smile quick and pleased. *It's nice to see you again*. Here, now, it was easy to notice that she was beautiful. She was dressed in the clean lines so typical of Parisian fashion, and her dark hair was pulled back in a bun, revealing high cheekbones and eyes that flashed in the pale light.

The other driver raised a brow. "I think introductions are in order." He spoke in English, inclining his head toward Lily. "My name is Zhao Min."

Irene had not been expecting his real name. Through her earbud—covered by the brush of her hair—she heard Alex typing, searching for aliases. If she could've, she would've told Alex not to bother. Anyone who studied China—anyone who had spent time in Beijing—knew the Chinese socialite scene, the nouveau riche who spent their time gambling and traveling and spending careless sums at art auctions.

This had just gotten a lot more interesting.

"Liu Siqi," their tour guide said, and Irene knew that name too. She was the heir to another Chinese empire, something with fashion, culture, *art*. Anything they had been planning, anything they had expected from this meeting—it had all changed.

"An honor," Irene said, and already she was making new plans, shifting pieces around in her mind. "I never would have expected Beijing's fuerdai to spend their time here."

"You know of us."

"Doesn't everyone?" Irene asked. They were already rich. They wanted to be adored. "I'm Irene Chen, and this is Will Chen. You raced Lily Wu."

"What are you *doing*?" Alex demanded in her ear.

Perhaps they would never get along. It didn't matter. These thieves had given their names. Irene wouldn't bother trying to lie.

"Americans," Min observed.

"College students," Siqi said, and when she tilted her head, Irene caught a glimpse of an earbud. They had someone on the line, too, searching them up as they spoke. "What are you doing here?"

"You robbed the Fontainebleau," Will said. It wasn't an accusation, just a statement.

"Yes," Min said. He looked at Lily, his smile quick. "You took my getaway car."

Lily smiled like she couldn't help herself, spread her hands out. "And you took our heist."

He raised a brow. "Did I? We didn't mean to."

Before coming here, they had drawn up a plan. Alex had transferred a copy of the stolen museum footage to a flash drive, pressed it in Irene's palm. The zodiac head for the evidence of their theft. Irene pulled it out now, held it up to catch the morning light.

"We have the security footage," she said. She knew what she was supposed to say next, the terms of this agreement, but looking at the two of them—

Irene dropped the flash drive onto the gray stone of the courtyard, crushed it beneath the heel of her boot. "We're here to make a deal."

Irene heard Alex sigh in her ear. She could practically see it—Alex and the falling shadow of her hair along her jaw, her brows drawn together in the blue light. "Why are you like this?" Alex demanded. "What have I ever done to you?"

Irene almost smiled.

"And what kind of deal would that be?" Siqi asked. "You can tell your lookout to join us, by the way. He looks terribly out of place."

Irene caught Daniel's eye, waved him over. Siqi wasn't wrong. Daniel, with his arms crossed, his perfect stillness as he leaned against the facade, looked nothing at all like a tourist in the City of Light.

"Did I see you crush our bargaining chip?" Daniel asked, coming to stand next to her.

They were improvising now. "Yes," Irene said. She turned back to Min, to Siqi. "This is Daniel Liang. He's from Beijing too."

"A pleasure," Siqi said, her smile wide. "Now, where were we?"

Irene turned to Will. For all their differences, when it mattered, he always knew what she was thinking. "You didn't come for the zodiac head," Will said, slow and very careful. "But we did. Wang Yuling hired us to steal back the missing zodiac heads from the Old Summer Palace."

Min smiled. "I knew Yuling was planning something." And of course they knew each other. Beijing was a big place, but when it came to the dazzlingly wealthy—it could be small when it wanted to be. "We wouldn't want to interfere with her plans. But you'll understand we can't give up the rooster head without something in exchange."

Will examined Min for a long moment. Irene did not say anything, waited. This was her brother. He would know exactly what to do. "One month ago," Will said, his voice thoughtful, "Sweden's Drottningholm Palace was robbed."

Min raised a brow. "That was you?"

"It was," Will said, and he looked so at ease like this, talking about art and how it was taken. How it was returned, perhaps. "We took the bronze snake head, but we also took more. All items stolen from the Old Summer Palace. We'll give you those in exchange for the rooster bronze."

They looked at each other.

"Why are you doing this?" Siqi asked. Her gaze swept over the four of them, curious. "You're Americans. You have nothing to gain from this."

"I'm not," Daniel said. Irene knew it wasn't quite true. He had given up his Chinese citizenship last year. Still, he was Chinese, more than the rest of them, more than anything else. He switched to Mandarin, that lovely Beijing accent of his crisp and perfect.

"I'm doing this for the same reason you are," he said, and despite the months Irene had spent in China, she knew she could never speak like this, like this language was home. "Because the Old Summer Palace means something to me. Because I know what was taken, and what is owed. China remembers, and so do I."

Siqi touched his shoulder, and for a moment, it was just the two of them, dark heads bowed together, a grief that Irene could never understand. "And the rest of you?" Siqi asked.

Will looked at Min. *He's an artist,* Irene wanted to tell him, like that might help, like that might give Will the right words to say. But perhaps her brother knew that already, could tell in the way Min's hands moved, in the care in his voice. Like might recognize like. "Art belongs to the creator," Will said, his voice soft, "not the conqueror. No matter what the law says, or what treaties are signed. For too long, museums have held on to art that isn't theirs to keep, bought more because they know they can."

"That's an accusation," Siqi said.

"It is," Will said. He looked at Min. "Am I wrong?"

In another life, Irene thought, they could have been friends. Maybe in this one too. Min leaned against the base of the pyramid, swept his gaze over their crew. "If we could buy this art back, we would," he said. "But museums see it as theirs by right, by conquest or colonialism."

"Would we?" Siqi asked. "Why should we be spending our money to buy back what was once ours? These pieces—they were stolen from us *first.*"

In the daylight, this place was all open air and reflected glass. Irene thought about art, about power, about all the ways it might change hands. And she thought, too, of museums that didn't care about where an object came from, only that it could be theirs. "We're on the same side," Irene said. "But I think you knew that from the start."

Min and Siqi exchanged glances, and then Min turned back to them, inclined his head. "We are," he said.

Irene waited.

Min's gaze swept over them, rested on Lily. His smile was quick. "You took my car, and I took your heist. We could call it even. But if we do this for your crew—"

Lily's smile mirrored his. "A rematch," she said.

"A rematch," Min said. "If you win, you get the zodiac head in exchange for Drottningholm's other art."

"And if I lose?" Lily asked.

"I thought you said you never lose."

If it had been Irene, she would have said no. She never would have wagered their future on a race in the dark, no matter how certain Lily was. But Lily did not hesitate as she stretched out her hand, as Zhao Min clasped it. "I don't."

36

Lily

In the darkness, the lights of Paris glittered like an unfamiliar sea. Lily rolled down her window, met Min's eye. He was smiling. "Still sure about your win?" he asked.

"Always."

He laughed. "Don't get too confident," he said. "Last time, we were in different cars." It was true. Lily ran her hands over her Bugatti, all clean lines and darkness. Still, she couldn't imagine losing. On the other side of the car, she could see the rest of her crew, mingling. Daniel and Siqi were talking, and Irene and Alex were in different conversations with two members of Siqi's crew who Lily didn't know. Only Will was alone. He met her gaze, smiled at her, and she remembered Durham at night, the two of them against the hood of her car. Had she known then how her life would change? She must have. Beijing awash in red light, the Old Summer Palace in the morning sun. This language, this country, that she might someday call hers. What it might feel like to run toward something instead of away. These weeks, planning and dreaming and having all of it made real. She was so close to everything she could ever want.

Lily turned back to her steering wheel, to her car, to all the possibilities of this Paris night. Next to her, Min's Lamborghini rumbled.

She smiled. In this moment, nothing else mattered. There was just this: the feel of the night air on her skin, the sound of her car beneath her palms. The smell of smoke and gasoline and possibility. They might pull this off yet.

"Ready?" Min called.

"Of course," Lily said. Whatever else happened, she would have this.

And then the light changed, and they were off.

⌐——୨

If Lily were asked how it began, her answers might have changed with the tides. Will Chen and an August evening, the chance to choose her future. A plane touching down in China for the first time; the way the sun rose, shattered, against the Beijing skyline. This country that she had never known.

When Lily thought of her past, she thought of Galveston, the waves that broke against the rocks, sunsets that bled red and heavy gold. A house by the Gulf of Mexico, those long summer days spent in her neighbor's auto shop as she learned how to take a car apart and put it back together. She thought of those years she had spent trying to leave it behind. Hers was the story of every small town, every immigrant family trying to hold on to the American Dream. She had spent her whole life getting asked where she was from and trying to make sense of the answer. She did not know what was true. She only knew that, growing up, neither China nor America felt like it was hers.

Lily's hands did not tremble as she turned the steering wheel, as Zhao Min took the turn at the same time. In these cars, in any cars, they

might be as evenly matched as anything, and she remembered the beginning, the true beginning, how her life had changed. Galveston in the
rising dark, a high school parking lot, and cars that gleamed silver as the
moon against water. She had looked around at a race that had not yet
begun and thought, for the first time in her life, *This doesn't look too hard.*

Lily didn't know what her future would be, how she could be the
daughter her parents needed. She didn't know how to be Chinese and
American both, how to leave Galveston behind. But she knew the feel of
a steering wheel beneath her palms and the press of her foot against the
gas, how streetlights and highway rails blurred as she pushed this car
faster and faster, the impossible drawing closer with every passing
breath.

37

WILL

Will Chen leaned over the Pont des Arts, the wind whistling over the steel beams. This late, Paris was all darkness and wavering lamplight, and he took in the darkness of the Seine below, the distant glow of the Eiffel Tower. Had it been just this morning when they had broken into the Fontainebleau?

"Chen Jiatao," a voice said, and Will looked up at this name he seldom used. Zhao Min, in his tailored suit, his wristwatch glinting in the evening light, looked like he had stepped out of a Parisian party. Maybe he had. If anyone walked past, they would see two young men facing opposite directions on a familiar bridge. Strangers, nothing more.

"Zhao Min," Will said, inclining his head. Locks dangled off the bridge railing, carved with names and inscriptions. For all that Will did not think of himself as a romantic, this meeting location had felt appropriate. A place for promises to be made.

"My end of our deal," Min said. He rolled a small black suitcase toward Will, and Will caught it. He didn't need to open it to know that the zodiac head would be there, the bronze smooth and perfect.

"Thank you," Will said. From his bag, he took out a folder. Photos, descriptions, all the information on the art they had stolen from Stockholm. He passed it to Min. "I'll get the art to you when I'm back in Boston."

"I know," Min said. He looked through the papers, his gaze sharp and discerning. Will had looked him up when he got back to the hotel. Min had gone to art school with Yuling, might have pursued a career in art if it hadn't been for his family name. "I don't recognize some of these."

"Neither did I," Will said.

"False provenance?" Min asked.

"It has to be," Will said. He sighed, thinking of that Stockholm hotel room, searching for where these pieces were from. He had spent all of Harvard studying provenance—the history of objects, how easily they changed hands. Fifty years ago, the UN had passed a treaty barring the sale of cultural property. It didn't matter. "Theft is theft, whatever they call it."

Min slid the papers into his coat. "Then we'll steal it back," he said.

"You're not worried about getting caught?" Tonight Will and his crew would leave, but Min, Siqi, and their crew were staying in Paris. They were suited to it, Will could admit. Paris and its decadence would be familiar to those who had grown up in the heart of Beijing, and there was more left to take. Still, it didn't seem wise to linger.

Min shrugged. "They'll suspect us, sure. But they don't have the power to make any real accusations, and they can't stop us from leaving on our own plane. Once we're in China, well, no one will dare touch us there. Besides," Min said, and his smile was wide, unbothered, "why would we steal art when we could just buy it?"

Like that, Will could almost believe him. "Is that what you tell the authorities?"

"You'll be amazed at what you can get away with when you're unbe-lievably wealthy," Min said, tilting his head up to take in the Paris night, and Will wondered what it felt like to rob museums just because you could, because you knew that even if you were caught, there would not be the same consequences. "How will you leave? The authorities will be watching us, but if you need a ride—"

Will set his backpack down, took out his own rooster sculpture. It was just the two of them here, the rest of Paris caught up in their own revelries, and the bronze gleamed dully in the evening light. Even if he hadn't been meeting Min here, he would have come anyway to tip this sculpture into the water. "A forgery," Min said, and Will wasn't surprised he caught on instantly. "How long did it take?"

Will ran his hands over the bronze. Imperfect, still, but—getting better. "A couple weeks."

"You won't be sad to lose it?"

Even if he was, it wouldn't have mattered. "It's temporary," he said. "As is everything."

"Art is never temporary," Min said. He leaned against the bridge, lacing his hands together. "And neither is this, no matter how fleeting it seems."

Will leaned over the railing. A breath, and he let go of the zodiac head, of these weeks spent working on it. The wind carried away the sound of the impact, but Will could see the rise of white foam, the van-ishing of bronze into dark water. It felt like an ending. Tomorrow they would leave Paris. They had their documents prepared, but he suspected they wouldn't need them. This city—it was large enough to disappear in. "Where will you go next?" he asked.

Min shrugged. "We haven't decided yet. And you?"

"There are three more zodiac heads left. Maybe the UK."

It was strange, to be standing in Paris on a cold night, talking to an-other thief. Min's smile said he knew it. "I'm glad we were able to come to a compromise. This could have ended differently."

Will thought of hours ago, the Louvre in the morning light. At first, he had been in shock. Irene, her boot against the pavement, the sound of their flash drive shattering. But she had always been one step ahead of him and everyone else.

"No," Will said. "I don't think it would have." It would have always come to this. Part of him thought this might be the last of it, that he might never see Min again. The rest of him thought of Siqi's clever gaze, Min and Lily racing in the dark. It might not be the worst thing in the world to know there were others out there, playing this same game.

"Send Yuling my best," Min said. He looked at Will, thoughtful. "I told her she was foolish, you know. When we robbed the Sackler and she left you her card."

Will blinked. For a moment, he was at the Sackler again, watching the thieves smash open glass, fill backpacks with Chinese art. The wail of the museum alarms, the detective and his questions. "It was you?"

"Yuling, Siqi, and I," Min said. "And some professionals, of course. I always wondered what Yuling would do next. I will admit, though—I am surprised that she chose your crew for the zodiac heads. I thought she would want those who knew the loss of the Old Summer Palace."

Will thought of China. He thought of Stockholm. The five of them—they were searching for a way home. He didn't know if Min would understand. The Old Summer Palace, to him, might have just been flames and righteous anger. But Will had looked at the ruins, thought of what was left behind.

Why had Yuling chosen them?

He hadn't had an answer then, but he might have now. "We're children of the diaspora," Will said. He had grown up in the US, knew that no matter how much he wanted it to be, China would never be home to him. "All we've ever known is loss."

"Perhaps you're right," Min said. He reached out a hand, and Will took it. In a different life, this could have been an oil painting, the two of them and the heavy dark, wind that swept over the Seine. "Best of luck, Chen Jiatao. I hope—" He hesitated, thought for a moment. "I hope you find what you're looking for."

And then Will was alone on the bridge. Tomorrow he would go home. Back to California, to sunshine, to the start of Thanksgiving break at last. It felt so far removed from this Paris night. He lingered, taking in the faraway lights, the feel of the wind on his skin, and thought of all that his parents had left behind when they came to America, all the dreams they had built on a foreign land. With this job, he might have been doing the same. In this strange, impossible year, there was so much to be lost, so much to be found.

38

DANIEL

Daniel Liang was dreaming of China. This past weekend had been one impossibility after another—races in the Paris night, a museum broken open, a crew of Chinese thieves. He leaned against the uncomfortable back of the airport seat, watching planes take off and land in the distance. He still remembered the grief he had felt when they had broken into the Château de Fontainebleau and found it empty. He had joined this crew because Irene had called, because Will had asked, because he couldn't bear for his friends to do this alone. He had joined because, however unlikely this was, ten million dollars was too much to turn down.

At some point, that had changed. Daniel had grown up hearing stories of the Old Summer Palace, how it burned. During that first theft, as he held the zodiac head in his gloved hands, he hadn't been thinking of museum security or distant sirens, but of all the years Beijing had been waiting. Outside the Louvre, facing Zhao Min and Liu Siqi, he had realized—at last—what the return of this lost art meant to China. What

it meant for him. Even Will, who loved art so fiercely, might not understand this. No matter how many years Daniel spent away from Beijing,
when he closed his eyes, he still dreamed in Chinese, saw red turrets and
crowded streets, the squares and palaces and skyscrapers that made up
his city. How could he ever leave it behind?

They had fifteen minutes until their flight boarded. Daniel checked
his phone, the clock face glowing pale and blue. It was morning in Paris,
almost evening in California. He had one unread text, and he opened it.

Safe travels.

Who is this? he asked.

I thought you were smarter than that.

He thought to the past few days, tracing his movements back to the
Louvre and an unfamiliar crew. *Liu Siqi*, he said. *I never gave you my
phone number.*

You didn't have to.

Daniel wasn't sure if he should be amused or concerned. In that moment, though, a call from his dad came through, the screen lighting up.
Daniel sent the call to voicemail. He did not want to talk to his father
now, to be reminded of all the ways he was failing him still. He opened
his phone again, the message Liu Siqi had sent him. A penthouse in Beijing, the knife of Wang Yuling's smile. These people—they were China
and its power, and no matter how much he loved China, he was not foolish enough to get comfortable. *What do you want?*

Just saying hello.

Three dots typing.

Next time you're in Beijing, let me know.

A voicemail appeared on his phone. Daniel examined Siqi's text one
last time, considering, before rising from his seat.

"Where are you going?" Will asked.

Will would have understood. Daniel knew he would, and yet he still
shrugged, tilting his head at the rest of the airport, bright lights and an

unfamiliar language. "Just getting a snack," he said. He hesitated, just for a moment, before pressing voicemail, held his phone up to his ear as he walked through the airport.

"Son," his dad said. The background was loud. He may have been at an airport too. "I won't be home for Thanksgiving. I just got the call, I'm needed in Europe for the next few days. Another investigation."

Daniel purchased a croissant from a kiosk, handed the cashier five euros. Airport food was always overpriced. He supposed he shouldn't be surprised his father was coming. They had brought this upon themselves.

"They're officially appointing me the lead of these Chinese thefts now. I suppose I should be happy—if we can figure out who's behind this, I'll get promoted. Your old dad could rest a little easier."

Daniel had never thought about his dad as old. He broke apart the croissant, listening. It was easier like this, when he didn't have to talk. "Anyway," his dad said. "Enough of this." In Chinese, the phrase was 滔滔不绝. Something of a river, unending. Perhaps his dad felt the same way, that it was easier to talk when it was just to empty air. He used to never listen to his dad's voicemails anyway. "I know you're at an interview, Danli. I'm sorry I won't be home for Thanksgiving, but the Chens have invited us over as usual. I won't take up any more of your time."

Daniel threw away the wax paper the croissant had been wrapped in. Outside, planes were still coming and going, the world moving too fast. It would be another Thanksgiving at Will and Irene's house. He was used to it by now. The first year he and his father had been invited—before either of them knew how to celebrate Thanksgiving—they had spent hours on Thanksgiving morning scouring Santa Clara's Chinese supermarkets for a turkey, convinced somehow that they were supposed to provide it. It had burned spectacularly in their new oven. He could still remember the smoke detector going off, the two of them with no idea where that sound was coming from, Will and Irene's parents running across the street.

Every year after that, they had brought a bottle of baijiu instead. The adults got drunk, the three kids watched a movie upstairs, and—even the years his dad came late, he was always there, softened by the holiday, the easy love between the Chen family. Daniel leaned against the window, thought of the wind as it moved over the bay, the empty house he would come back to. It didn't matter so much. He had interviews to prepare for, this next heist to plan.

Daniel checked his phone. It was silent now, but his dad hadn't hung up, and for a second he thought his dad had set his phone down, forgotten, but then he heard a soft, careful sigh. "For many years, I thought I had to be strict on you. That that was the only way you could grow up strong with only one parent. But after your senior year of high school, and seeing how hard you worked in college, even those months it was online . . . it was as if I blinked, and you had grown up. And at some point I realized that I did not know how to talk to you anymore."

The glass was cool against his cheek. He could see Will, Irene, the rest of his crew getting ready to board. They were waiting for him. He didn't move.

"I'm glad we're talking again," his dad said. Through the phone, Daniel could hear the sound of another loudspeaker, calling for a boarding flight. His dad was going to Paris, and he was leaving. Wasn't it always like this?

Still, it was a relief that this was a voicemail, that he wasn't expected to respond. "Son," his dad said. A long, shuddering pause. "I hope you'll forgive me for these years. I'm proud of you. I love you. Good luck on your interview. I'll be home soon."

A click.

Daniel's flight was boarding. He forced himself to listen to his breathing. The expansion of his lungs, alveoli and bronchi opening against pressure. Ribs, diaphragm, empty space. He would not cry. It had been ten years in America, but they were still a Chinese household. They did not speak of love. There were dinners together, his father's hands steady as he set more food on Daniel's plate, bowls of cut fruit when evening fell and both of them were still up working, though always in separate rooms.

He didn't need his dad to be home for Thanksgiving. He didn't need any of this. He must have known it already. But when the voicemail ended, when the system read him his options, he pressed *save*.

He got on the flight, slept almost the whole way through, went through a handful of Anki flashcards, talked with Alex about something or another. Security had been easy, effortless, Paris's Charles de Gaulle Airport busy enough that no one looked too closely at their luggage. When they landed, Alex and Lily transferred flights, and the Chens picked up Will, Irene, and Daniel from the airport. He made small talk in the car, chatted about college and med school interviews and all those things that felt very far away.

And then Daniel was unlocking the door to his house, stepping inside. The lights were off. He flicked one on, and then another, until the whole house was flooded with light, and then he sat at the kitchen table. There was his father's chair. There was his ma's, in those first few days in America, before things went from bad to worse. He rested his palms on the wooden table, took out his phone. In that empty house, he listened to his dad's voicemail again and cried until he felt empty, until it felt like someone had reached a hand inside him and taken everything out.

Morning dawned clear and cold. Daniel rose, got dressed, came downstairs to find Irene in his kitchen, a cup of tea in her hands. A box from 85°C Bakery was open next to her, and the kitchen smelled like Chinese breads, light and faintly sweet. He had a sudden, strange sense of déjà vu. They had done this so many times before.

He sat down across from her, and she poured him a cup of tea.

"Want to talk about it?"

"No," he said. He didn't bother asking how she knew something was wrong. It had been ten years, and some things did not change. Irene knew him as well as he knew himself.

Daniel took a taro bun from the box, took a bite. His chewing was loud in the silence. "Is it my fault?" he asked. "For so long, I made him a villain. And then, when all this began—I don't know. I should have felt guilty, but I also felt like I was getting back at him."

"For what?"

"I don't know."

Irene pressed her palms together, waiting.

"For leaving?" he said. "For moving us here?"

She lifted her gaze. "Is that really what you're angry about?"

"No," he said. He kept his gaze on the wall, the scrolls of calligraphy that hung on either side of the table. Poems, about silver water and the fall of light, all that was beautiful and forgotten about China. He took a slow, careful breath. "When she died, I thought at least we had each other. In this foreign country, I wasn't alone. But it always felt that way, you know? We used to have so much to talk about and then—nothing."

Irene poured him another cup of tea, her hands steady. "And now?"

"He's been trying," Daniel said. "And he thinks I have too. And—" He thought of making dumplings in this house, Alex laughing with his dad. "I don't know. He's trying, and I don't know what to do."

"Can you forgive him?" she asked.

"I don't know," he said again. All this time, he had been searching for healing. But all of this still felt like an open wound. "Should I?"

Irene was silent for several heartbeats. "All my life, I've always suspected my parents favored Will. They've never said it, of course. But no matter what I do, I'm always just the younger sibling, the daughter, the one who isn't at Harvard."

He looked at her. He remembered conversations with Will, about parents and family and all the ways failure might feel, but never with Irene. She was not the kind of person who failed. "I didn't know you felt that way."

Her smile was quick, a little sad. "I've realized lately that I'm not as honest as I should be."

He raised a brow. Irene had always been guarded, all hard edges and infallibility. "You only just now realized?"

She narrowed her eyes. "Be gentle with me."

"I always am," he said.

"I know." She sighed. "All parents leave their own scars. We're the ones who have to heal from them."

Daniel looked at his cup, his clasped hands. Ten years, of him and his father and this solemn, empty house. His dad had moved on and Daniel had not. He did not know how to, how he could ever leave China behind. "It's hard."

"It is. But we're in college. We don't have to have it all figured out yet. We have the rest of our lives ahead of us."

Daniel thought of the future. In a few months, they would be done with this job, the five missing zodiac heads returned to China at last. He would graduate from UCLA in May, begin med school come fall. It felt like a beginning, an ending, a long-awaited change.

There were so many ways for it to go wrong.

39

WILL

Will Chen spent the first few days of Thanksgiving break avoiding his responsibilities. There were apple orchards beneath golden sunlight, the San Francisco pier as the fog rolled in, evening strolls with his parents and their dog through these suburbs he knew so well. On early mornings, he sketched outside, surrounded by cool fall air and skies like Chinese watercolors, all pale light and tentative lines. He spent his time with his sister, with Daniel, texted Lily and Alex about everything besides museum break-ins and stolen art.

And then, when he figured he should avoid it no longer, Will called Wang Yuling. It was late afternoon, and he took the call outside, the trees rustling in the breeze as he walked around the cul-de-sac. It could have been any other year, any other time.

She picked up on the first ring.

"Will Chen," she said. "I was wondering when I'd hear from you. How was France?"

Will wondered if she watched the news, if she had seen the reports of

Min and Siqi's theft. Three rooms cleared of priceless art, a fire extinguisher emptied to mask fingerprints, security footage wiped clean. He knew she had. "I think you know," he said. He thought back to two months ago, the Sackler broken open. It had been that crew that brushed past him, that started all of this. He hadn't known. "Zhao Min sends his best."

"Ah, yes," she said, and he could have sworn he heard her smile. "I thought you might see him sometime."

He bit back something harsher. "A warning might have been nice."

"What's the fun in that?" she asked.

He imagined her draped over a white leather couch, light gleaming off the marble penthouse floors. It was easy enough for Yuling to treat this lightly. Min had been right. Their crew—all Chinese, all billionaires—were protected by their government, by the ease of wealth, by their names and their legacies. But the five of them—

If Yuling changed her mind, there were so many more Chinese American college students just like them, hungry for wealth, for fame, for the chance to be part of something more, who she could hire for this same job. And if they failed, well—they would be the only ones to take the fall.

"We're headed to the UK next," he said. He began another circle around the cul-de-sac, stepped on a particularly crunchy leaf. "The plan is for late December."

It was in three weeks.

"Not the US?"

There were three museums left. The British Museum, the KODE in Norway, and—the Met. Will had seen the zodiac head in the Met before, a bronze dragon gleaming beneath a glass case, light that pooled like water. "Not yet," he said. He didn't know if he was ready for that. He didn't know if he'd ever be. "What happens," he said slowly, "if we don't get them all?"

"Are you worried about this other crew?" she asked.

He could have said yes. Zhao Min and Liu Siqi were better thieves than they were, and he could not imagine a world where that crew did not get everything they wanted. But he thought, too, of Daniel's dad searching for them, of the articles that came up each day. He had set up a Google alert weeks ago. *Chinese zodiac thefts, stolen bronzes, Old Summer Palace art.* When would museums begin to realize what they were after?

When would the FBI?

"Not just them," Will said.

A pause. "China has been waiting almost two hundred years for our zodiac heads to come home," she said. "It has been long enough, don't you think?"

He thought of the bronze rooster head in his suitcase, the bronze snake head tucked under his bed frame in his dorm. He didn't doubt that if Yuling wanted to, she could take them away, leave them with nothing. But—she had been there when the Sackler was robbed, had stolen the art he had written about in the *Crimson* all those weeks ago. She had seen something in him worth taking a chance on. Wang Yuling was China, and China was this missing art, its history of conquest and loss and the fierceness of its want.

He would not let her down.

"It has," he said. "We'll make it work."

40

ALEX

When she was away from home, Alex Huang remembered it only in the abstract: the stairs winding from Yi Hua Lou to their apartment upstairs, her bedroom window that opened to the Chinatown streets below. When she was back, though, it all felt real, immediate, as if she had never left. In her room, even with the door closed, she could hear the sharp, musical sounds of Cantonese from the kitchen, smell rice and sizzling, fatty pork, the fragrance of garlic with green vegetables.

She opened her laptop, pulled up Zoom. Everyone else was already on, their backgrounds a study in character, in place. Will, in his childhood bedroom, was surrounded by easels and art prints, while Irene's room was all clean white walls and empty, negative space. Daniel was in the kitchen, familiar from her visit to his house, textbooks spread out across the table. Lily, in Galveston, had a window open to the sea.

Alex pulled up her notes. Originally, they had been planning to take their time: another museum, maybe two, before year's end, a final theft come spring break. France had changed things. "There are three more zodiac heads," she said. "The KODE 1, the British Museum, and the Met. We need to get to all of them before the end of the year."

"Is that enough time?" Lily asked.

"It has to be. We can't afford to wait, not when there are other thieves out there."

"Min and Siqi won't get in our way," Will said.

"Regardless," Alex said. Even if Zhao Min and Liu Siqi were friends with Wang Yuling, even if they had given their word—there was too much to lose. "These thefts are getting a lot of press. There are other wealthy Chinese art collectors who view art theft as a way of displaying their patriotism, and soon enough museums are going to realize that they need to up their security. When we get to the third missing zodiac head, the pattern will be clear."

"Three thefts, back-to-back," Will said, lacing his hands together. "It'll be hard." He didn't say impossible. "How will we do it?"

Alex had spent the past few days thinking about this, turning it over while washing dishes in the kitchen or scooping rice into perfect, round bowls for customers, pulling open the storefront's metal shutters on all those early mornings. She could almost convince herself she had never left, that her whole life was this place. Her siblings were still in high school, but her sister would apply to college next year. This job—it was not just for her. "It'll have to be winter break. Europe first, and then we can come back to New York. I'm already looking into their security systems."

They spent the rest of the call making plans. Despite the break, it felt like time was pressing down on them, an urgency to all of this. There were other thieves, and the authorities were drawing closer, and they had to be careful enough to avoid attention but fast enough to make it out with everything they wanted.

They would call again tomorrow. One by one, people began to hang up.

"Alex," Irene said. "Stay on a moment, will you?"

And then it was just the two of them. For a strange moment, Alex remembered the end of her freshman year of college, when the pandemic had brought everyone home. It had felt like this, calling friends over Zoom, the silence soft and tentative. The whole world was used to video calls by now, all these years later, but in this room with Irene, it could have been the first time all over again.

"What is it?"

Irene swept her hair over her shoulder. The light was warm against her skin, tracing the angles of her collarbones, the high, haughty planes of her face. "You and Daniel have been keeping track of the France investigation," she said. It wasn't a question.

"We have." It had made the most sense. She pulled information from the FBI's servers; Daniel read it and called his dad when they thought it might help. It had been easy, almost pleasant, to work with Daniel on this. Sometimes it felt like this crew was split in half, Irene claiming Lily and Daniel as hers, Will taking Alex's side when he could, but when she and Daniel were working together, Alex could almost dismiss it as her imagination.

"I'll do it instead."

Alex pressed her palms together. Irene was so used to getting exactly what she wanted. "You'll write code to get into the FBI?" she asked, raising a brow. "Go for it."

"You and I both know that's not what I mean," Irene said. "I want Daniel out of this. You and I can work on this together."

"*You* want to work with *me*."

"Is that so surprising?"

Yes, Alex wanted to say. "He's not yours, you know. You don't get to keep me from being friends with him."

Irene blinked. "What?"

"What?" Alex asked.

"I'm not that petty," Irene said. "And you consistently overestimate how much time I spend thinking about you."

It was probably true. Still, Alex sighed. "Then why? We've been doing perfectly fine."

Irene's gaze flickered down. "I don't care that you and Daniel are friends. I'm glad for it. But he and his dad are still figuring out how to exist together. It's not fair to ask this of him."

Alex didn't know how to respond to that. She remembered weeks ago, Irene calling her to ask about the FBI investigation. She hadn't mentioned anything about Daniel then, and yet—now Alex knew it had been out of kindness. Irene could be kind, to everyone except her.

Alex crossed her arms. "You were the one who brought him into this," she said. And maybe it wasn't fair of her to say. But if she closed her eyes, she could still see Irene on that first day, draped over a couch in a Beijing penthouse, the smile she gave a boy Alex did not know.

"I know. I don't need your criticism, Alex. Just—please. I'm asking as—" Irene hesitated.

Alex raised a brow. "As what?"

Neither of them would call each other friends. If Alex hadn't known better, she could have sworn Irene smiled. "Colleagues?" Irene asked.

Alex thought, maybe, she could have made Irene say it. But Irene would have looked her in the eye and said *friends*, and somehow it still would have felt like Alex was the one who lost.

"Fine," she said.

"Thanks," Irene said. "I'll text you."

And then it was just Alex in her room, thinking about how she had never heard Irene use the word *please* with her before. She dropped her head in her hands, thinking about how this heist might break her open, and then she got up and went downstairs, to the kitchen and the restaurant and all its sounds.

Alex knew her history. It was the difference between her and Will, who was always searching, why she and Daniel saw something familiar in each other. Home was Chinatown, the sounds of Cantonese shouted from balconies and storefronts, this city that her parents had lived in almost their whole lives. Her grandparents had come to New York in the sixties, opened Yi Hua Lou when Chinatown was still recovering from the Chinese Exclusion Act. She had always known that this city, this place, was hers, but she wouldn't forget how hard it'd been to come by, how fiercely her family had fought to make it so.

She made her way through the din of the kitchen. Her sister was upstairs, studying, but her younger brother was here, taking orders and running them back. "Alex," Henry called, "it took you long enough. We have a long day ahead of us."

"Don't we always?" she asked, but she was smiling. This was home. For all the distance she traveled, coming back was always a relief. She took over the cash register, sending the employee to wait tables, and as guests came in, she called out a rapid "歡迎光臨," directed them to open tables. Some things had changed over the years. She no longer recognized most of their customers, though when she did, they looked at her twice, said her name as if testing out the syllables.

Then neighbors began to poke their head in, make conversation. Questions about when she was last home, about California, about applying to college or working in tech, all the dreams they had for their children. Alex didn't mind. She leaned over the counter, rang up receipts, let everything that was familiar wash over her once more. "California is beautiful," she said, and when she described it, she could believe it too. She promised help on college applications, tours around Silicon Valley, more. She had grown up here, at the front of this restaurant. These people had helped her all her life.

When they had all left, Alex opened her laptop again, began to work on these next thefts. Museum security, police systems, all the intricacies of the technology meant to keep them out. It felt almost familiar. The sounds of Cantonese, the clatter of wooden chopsticks against bowls and plates, the ringing of the bell as new customers arrived. Even after all these years, some things stayed the same.

This was what Alex knew: the journey her grandparents had made, the years her parents had put into this restaurant. Her family had survived in New York for two generations, despite gentrification and rising rent prices and a healthcare system that was never kind to the self-employed. And now—she was the oldest of three, the one who had made it first to one of New York's most competitive public schools and then to MIT and Silicon Valley, all the ways California gleamed in the light.

She pulled up security for the British Museum. In two weeks, they would be in the UK. From there, it would be a flight to Norway and the KODE 1, and then to the US. From here, the Met was less than half an hour away. Uptown on the 6 train, just a few avenues' walk from 86th. She knew this city, its history, all that it meant to her and her family.

And so: Alex carried history with her. Where her family had come from, where there was left to go. Sometimes she felt only pride. Other times she looked around this restaurant and wondered how she could ever leave it behind. Silicon Valley, her job, the people who counted on her—sometimes it felt like an anchor, reminding her who she was, who she was meant to be.

Other times she only felt the weight of it, threatening to drag her under.

41

IRENE

A week slipped away like this. Santa Clara in the changing light, evening skies in neon colors, making plans for final papers, for this third theft, for all that her future held. At her desk, Irene Chen watched the sun set, her mind on China, on power, on those who would claim it as theirs. Before her, she had printouts of transcripts, interviews between Zhao Min and those who would accuse him of theft, photos of Liu Siqi's room. They had not found any art, of course, just bottles of expensive champagne, several thousands' worth of Siqi's glittering jewelry.

She should have felt relief. But there had been two crews there that night, and Irene couldn't help but wonder when the authorities would figure that out. It was only a matter of time.

Her phone was ringing. "Yes?" she asked.

"You're in their security footage," Alex said.

It was strangely familiar. Irene remembered an evening in Durham, Alex's voice on the phone. They had spent the past week like this, splitting the work of keeping up with the FBI and Interpol. "You're going to have to tell me more than that," Irene said. "I thought you deleted their footage."

"I did. But they have the footage from the day *before*. You and Will are both in it."

Alex could have called Will about this. Irene rose from her chair, moving to stand by her open window. They would see this other crew again; she was sure of it. The world was too small for anything else. "So?" she asked. "We were two of many visitors. Besides, we didn't actually rob the Fontainebleau." She only said the last part to bother Alex.

"They don't know that. And breaking and entering is still a crime."

"Your point?"

Alex hesitated. "There's also footage of you at Drottningholm the day before. That's two museums robbed, and you in both."

Outside, the sky was a heavy red. "Have they put it together yet?"

"No," Alex said. "And they're still trying to figure out if and how the zodiac heads are getting out of the country. Thank god for the massive bureaucracy that is airport customs. But for our next heist—"

Irene let out a slow, controlled breath, thought of the FBI at her dorm room, the ways this might unravel as they moved forward. "We'll have to do things differently," she finished, and it was something she had known from the beginning. She was always going to be in the FBI's footage. Once meant nothing. Twice could be a coincidence. But three was a *pattern*. Irene pulled up their plans for their third theft. The UK in December, the British Museum with its high columns and winding stairways. "Anything else?" she asked.

Alex was silent for a beat. Irene thought of the FBI closing in, the zodiac heads still waiting for them, Min and Siqi chasing China's missing art. But when Alex spoke, it was about none of these. "Daniel's dad booked a flight home. He should be back tomorrow."

Irene hadn't known that. Daniel wouldn't have either. She pressed her hands together, thinking of all the pieces of this job, coming together at last. "Okay," she said.

"Irene?"

"Yes?"

Alex's voice was soft. "You aren't worried about what the authorities will find on you?"

They were all counting on Alex. Alex and her code, her deleted footage. She would get them out. If this had been another time, months ago, Irene would have been doubtful. She had only ever counted on herself—her ability to plan, to prepare, to anticipate the words other people would say. But she thought of Alex on the streets of France, early-morning light skimming her face, her fingers moving over the keys of her laptop in perfect concentration, how she had looked up when it was all done. Alex was all certainty and sharp, surprising confidence, the kind of girl who would not shatter against Will, against her, against anyone.

"No," Irene said, and somehow it was true. "I'm not."

Still, that evening, Irene could not sleep. She sat in bed, knees pulled up and her mind elsewhere, as moonlight fell soft and contemplative through her open window, into this bedroom that always made her think of childhood.

It went like this: Irene had spent her whole life being measured against her brother. It hadn't mattered at first, because why would it? She had done everything he had and more, felt a fierce, certain pride in doing so. Even after he had gone to Harvard, Irene had not been worried. She would be there too, someday. But in college, the closest to real life he had ever been, he had chosen *art*—chosen a future of uncertainty, of beauty, turning his gaze from the damage he might inflict on anyone else. Maybe she shouldn't have been surprised, and yet she was. Even though she knew how much he loved art, a part of her had always been waiting for him to realize that his responsibilities were worth more than his dreams. He was the eldest, after all. But if he would not do it—if he would not think of the expectations placed on him by their parents, their grandparents, all those in China who saw them as the American Dream—Irene would. She would do what he wouldn't, and while she was at it, she would make sure she did it better.

Irene Chen had never failed.

She could not afford to.

She got out of bed, turned her lamp on. In that childhood bedroom of hers, as the night stretched before her, Irene sat at her desk and began to plan. All of this—the FBI drawing closer, this other crew, Daniel's dad and his return flight—it might mean nothing. It might mean too much. But when it came, she would be prepared.

42

DANIEL

The early-morning sun rose over the Dish, set the trail ablaze. Daniel Liang stretched, turned to Will. The last time they had run together like this—it would have been sophomore year of college. All their classes had been virtual, and each morning they'd driven to Stanford campus, the trail along it, let themselves pretend they were in college together, that these months in quarantine were like any other.

He didn't know when his dad would be home. He didn't know what to say. Daniel hadn't called him back, hadn't said anything to show he'd heard the voicemail. Instead he had cooked on his own, studied for the finals that would come right after break, planned for those last three thefts.

Soon this would be over.

"Are you ready?" Will asked. Of the two of them, Will was the runner, had run varsity in high school and then club in college. Daniel had picked up boxing when he got to UCLA, kept it up even now. Either way, this wasn't a race. Just a way for them to clear their minds, to remember what it felt like to just *be*.

"Let's go," Daniel said.

The trail was easy: familiar sloping ground and clean, bright morning air. Even now, out of habit, they stayed six feet away from other runners. "What do you think?" Will asked. "Would you come back?"

Daniel's interview had been two months ago. He would hear back before the end of December. He had interviewed at more schools, of course. UCSF, UCLA, all the schools on the West Coast. On the East Coast, he had gone to Harvard, Yale, Duke, a handful more. "I don't know," he said, thinking of a few days ago, talking with Lily about this same unanswered question. *Home shouldn't have to be this complicated,* she had said, and yet it always was. "I used to think I would never. But there are things I would miss about California."

Will looked at him sideways. "Like?"

When he thought of home, he thought of Beijing. But the Beijing of his childhood didn't exist anymore. Healing was not always looking back. Sometimes it was looking forward. "Like knowing the names of all these streets," Daniel said. "Taking Caltrain to San Francisco, getting egg tarts at that bakery with its unpredictable hours. The Pacific Ocean. Sunrise, on these early-morning runs. How when you go up Palm Drive, it feels like an unfolding."

Will smiled. "It always does, doesn't it?"

So many of his memories here had been with Will and Irene. Summer days at Lands End, the Pacific Ocean shrouded with fog and the waves against their feet. Will's track meets in San Francisco, Daniel and Irene ducking out to bring back boba from Plentea when the sun was high and unyielding. All the times they had walked around Stanford campus, the three of them dreaming of what the future could be.

Still, there had been some with his father too. As Daniel kept pace with Will, the morning air burning his lungs, he let himself think back on it, Daniel and his father and the Bay Area before he knew what to call it. Those first few years had been hard, near impossible, but he remembered the two of them driving over the Golden Gate Bridge for the first time. It had been one of those rare days when there was no fog, and the bridge had looked like it might hold up the world. They had parked the car, walked along the rocks and the crashing waves, and his dad had taken Daniel's hand. There was a picture of that moment somewhere, taken by a stranger and likely lost long ago, of Daniel and his father side by side in front of the Pacific, squinting against the midday sun. He could still remember how it had felt. The roar of the sea, the steady warmth of his father's hand in his. Someday, he had thought, America might not feel so unfamiliar.

All these years later—Daniel looked out across this trail he had run so many times before, at the trees and the golden foothills and the distant radio telescope that gave the Dish its name, and knew it to be true.

They finished their run, went back to the bike racks. Daniel unlocked his bike, put on his helmet, and soon enough they were back in their neighborhood, the morning air still cold enough that Daniel could see his breath curling up.

His dad's car was in the driveway.

Will looked at him. "I thought he wasn't going to be home for the break."

"Me too," Daniel said. His gaze touched the frame of the house, the lines of the roof against the sky, the curving driveway. In this moment, none of it looked quite real.

"You want to come over for a bit?" Will offered.

It was not yet eight in the morning. Daniel could have gone to Will's house, pretended that this was just another day. But he needed to face his father.

He didn't know what he would say.

"You go ahead," Daniel told Will. "I'll meet you in a bit."

Still, after Will left, Daniel lingered at the door, thinking about Beijing, about home, about all the journeys he and his dad had been on since then. They had traveled so far from each other.

His dad was in his office, the door closed. Daniel walked past it, quietly, and took a shower first, tilting his head up to the steam, the water that sluiced against his skin. As he scrubbed, he named veins and arteries, mapped out the blood that traveled from vena cava to atria to ventricles, to lungs and limbs and curving spine.

When he came out, he dried his hair, changed into sweats and a UCLA hoodie, slippers that kept away the cold of the tiled floor.

His dad was waiting for him in the kitchen.

Daniel hadn't known what to expect. His dad was home early, home for Thanksgiving, and Daniel should have felt glad. This might have been healing, after all these years. But his dad raised his head, and Daniel recognized something in the shadows beneath his eyes, the way his hand moved over his jaw. He thought of ten years ago, a hospital waiting room. He thought of his senior year of high school, the day his dad had found that stolen bronze coin on his nightstand. This could have been any of those moments. This could have been all of them.

"Danli," his dad said. "Take a seat."

Daniel sat. His dad's work was with him, but his laptop was shut, powered off, his folders closed and stacked neatly on top of each other.

"Ba," Daniel began.

"Tell me," he said. "What do you know about museum security?"

Daniel knew the body's stress response, the physiology behind the jump in his heart rate, the sudden tension to his muscles. He knew that it would pass, if he let it. Still, he shivered once, violently, the motion a betrayal. "Not much," he said, and it was true.

His dad's voice was soft, almost sad. "Do you want me to tell you what I know?" he asked.

Daniel didn't look at him.

"Museums have backups. Automatically, on external servers. They added them years ago, when technology meant that hackers could go in and change footage, delete it. They would keep them stored somewhere else, accessed on the slight improbability that something happened they needed to verify."

One week ago. If he closed his eyes, he could see it again. The sun rising over Paris, a palace shattered in the early-morning light.

"That was the first place we went when we found that the Château de Fontainebleau's footage was deleted. It wasn't particularly useful, to be honest. Black-and-white, very fast, a little confusing. My team thought there might have been a glitch. How else could the thieves leave and come back? Even the audio was difficult to make out. All in Chinese, soft, very low. Impossible to match using voice recognition, any of the other tools that we have."

This should have been good news.

So why couldn't he look up?

"Liang Danli," his dad said, and Daniel was a child again, in this same vast, unfamiliar country, bowing his head before his father. But he didn't feel the strike of a hand against his cheek, the wrench of his jaw tilted up. "Did you think I wouldn't recognize Will's voice? Did you think I wouldn't recognize *yours*?"

And there it was.

He had spent all these years trying to leave his father behind. To be someone else, to be someone *more*, to prove that he did not have to be the person his dad thought he was.

He did not know what to say.

I hope you'll forgive me, his dad had said. *I'm proud of you. I love you.* In Chinese, the words had been almost too much to bear. All those terrible, impossible things he didn't know how to believe. And now this.

Daniel had never thought of his dad as old. But he saw it now, in the gray that threaded through his hair, the lines that had carved themselves into his face. "Ba," Daniel said. What else was there? He could not deny this. "I'm sorry," he said. "I'm so sorry." He thought of a Chinese saying about falling flowers, about the water that carried them away. He felt like that now.

There was nowhere to go from here.

His dad met his gaze. There was a heavy grief there, and Daniel knew, with a sudden, painful certainty, how this would end. It had always been this way, after all. His father leaving him behind. They had been in America for ten years, and they did not talk of the past. Daniel pressed his palms against the wooden table, thought stupidly, foolishly, of how badly he had wanted to be a doctor. How he hoped his dad would not be too lonely when this house was just him once more.

His dad rose.

The future, the past. What difference did it make? This had only ever been an ending. "You are my son," he said, slowly and carefully, as if making sure the words were true. "I—" He stopped, bowed his head. "You are my son," he said again. "I would forgive you for anything."

Daniel could not move. He could not breathe. Ten years in America and his father had never spoken of forgiveness. He had never spoken of family. For a moment, his dad looked like he might rest his hand on Daniel's shoulder.

Instead he turned away, back to his office, his work, all the things that Daniel had broken. "But Danli, there are some things I can't save you from."

And then Daniel was alone in the kitchen, his future in pieces before him, all the proof of his failure across the table, in folders that he couldn't bear to open. Still, he thought of his father, the pain in his voice. Forgiveness. He had not expected it to hurt so much.

On the Chens' back patio, he went through the folders, the evidence of their failures. Irene in Stockholm, caught by a security camera, the image meaningless on its own. But—again, in France. Their shadows in a deleted recording. Facial recognition from the days before. Daniel spread it out before Will, before Irene, the air heavy with everything he could not say. He knew they should have called the rest of their crew, and yet somehow he couldn't bring himself to. It would always come down to this: the three of them and this house they had all grown up in, the weight of the world pressing down on all their shoulders the same way.

"My dad knows," Daniel said, though the evidence was enough. They had known each other for long enough that no one asked questions. There was just silence as Will and Irene waited, as Daniel tried to put himself back together. He dug his nails into his palms, hard, the pain of it grounding him. Blood and breaking capillaries. There were some things that he knew.

He told the story from the beginning.

"So this is it, then," Irene said.

He looked between Irene and Will. Will, who had wanted this so badly from the start, who had given him the choice to stay or to go. "What do you want?" Will asked, his voice soft.

Daniel did not know what to say. Even if there were a way out, he didn't know if he would take it. Not when his father was in that house, alone, when he knew all the ways Daniel had disappointed him. "I want this to be over," he said at last, and it was a relief. "I don't care about the money, or the sculptures. I—I can't do this anymore."

It was the first true thing he had said in a long time.

Will didn't say anything. Instead he rose, went back inside the house for a moment before returning to the backyard with a lighter. He flipped open the grill, handed the lighter and the folder to Daniel. It shouldn't have mattered. There were electronic copies, evidence, more. He did not know if he could go to med school, who his father would tell. If he would follow the rules, as he always did. Still, Daniel brought the lighter to the first paper, watched smoke curl into the air. It burned rapidly, hungrily, flaring up for a moment before vanishing. He knew it didn't mean anything. But they stayed there, watching the paper burn into a clear blue sky, let themselves pretend that this was an ending.

43

WILL

Will Chen had always known the shape his future was meant to take. His parents had grown up in rural China, in a time when there was never quite enough to go around. They had come to the US for graduate school, built this life and this American Dream from the ground up. Two doctorates, two young children now grown up. Art had never been for those like him, the children of immigrants, who knew dreams were measured by more practical metrics. Income, prestige, everything that meant certainty when you had left all that you knew behind.

The first time he had thought a future in art might be possible, it had been because of Daniel's father. Will had grown up in a house of scientists, but the Liangs—they had scrolls of Chinese calligraphy in every hallway, paintings in watercolor, flowers sewn and framed in gold. When he had taken AP Art History, he had brought his homework across the street, asked Mr. Liang all the questions his textbooks didn't have the answers to. If Daniel had found sanctuary in Will's house, Will had found possibility in Daniel's.

Will hesitated, just for a moment, before knocking on Mr. Liang's door.

"请进," Daniel's father called. *Please enter.* His tone was neutral, unreadable.

Will pushed open the door. Mr. Liang was at his desk, his blinds drawn open to let the light in. It was achingly familiar—the books on Chinese art, the handsome cherrywood desk. Mr. Liang himself, unchanged. Like this, he looked very much like Daniel, all straight, severe lines, eyes that spoke of grief.

"Uncle," Will said. He spoke in Chinese. "I think you know why I'm here."

Mr. Liang's voice was a sigh. "Sit, Jiatao."

Will sat, lacing his hands together. Daniel was still at his house, with Irene, the two of them trying to figure out where to go from here. His sister, who could talk her way out of anything, was likely the better choice for this. But Will couldn't help but feel like this was his responsibility. He had gotten them into this impossible situation. He would have to get them out.

Mr. Liang pressed his fingertips together. "Well, go ahead. Speak."

In the end, he was not his sister. He did not have any solutions. "I won't deny what we did," he said. Maybe he should have. And yet he did not know what else to do, what else he could give besides the truth. "But you and I both know we wouldn't be sitting here if you hadn't been the one assigned to this case, if you didn't know us all so well."

"What's your point, Jiatao?" Mr. Liang looked very tired.

Will took a slow, careful breath, let himself believe that this was not too much to ask, that Daniel's father was family first and everything else second. "Don't arrest us," he said. "Not yet. If anyone else discovers anything, if new evidence emerges, then I'll take the fall for the rest of them. But—"

"You want me to let you get away with this."

"I want you to give us a chance for a future."

Mr. Liang sighed. "Haven't I done that already?" he asked, and Will thought back to four years ago, a San Francisco museum and a stolen bronze coin. Anything that happened in this house, Mr. Liang knew about it.

"Please," Will said. The first time Will had heard the story of the Old Summer Palace, it had been in this house. So much of what he had learned in school had been stories of the West. Its conquests, its glory. "You're Chinese. Doesn't the Old Summer Palace mean something to you? Don't you understand why we did it?"

Mr. Liang met his gaze for a long moment, searching. "It has been almost two hundred years since the palace burned," he said.

"And yet I learned that story from you."

Mr. Liang turned his gaze to his computer, adjusted his glasses. Will sat there as he clicked through his files, the silence of the room weighing down on him. At last, Mr. Liang spoke. "Does it matter?" he asked. "Evidence is evidence. The zodiac heads, your role in these thefts— eventually it will all be found out."

"I know," Will said, and it could have been true. There were so many ways they could get caught. And yet—he did not want it to be like this. "We just—we just need a little more time."

Mr. Liang didn't ask for what. Will didn't know what answer he would have given. The FBI was closing in, and yet all Will could think of was the grief on Daniel's face, how this might be what tore a family apart.

Mr. Liang pressed his hands to his temples. Daniel and his dad had always been cut of the same stone, hard and uncompromising. Will dug his nails into his palms, forced himself to remain still.

At last, Mr. Liang looked up. "Very well," he said. "For now, you have my silence."

"Thank you, Uncle," Will said, fervently. It was all they could ask for. Even then, it might not be enough.

Mr. Liang sighed. "Be careful, Jiatao. And know this—if you do this again, I *will* catch you."

What do you want?

I want this to be over.

Outside the window, it was a perfect California day, clear and cloudless. Will thought of dreams, how they might slip through your fingertips. "It—" He stopped, swallowed hard. "It won't happen again."

44

ALEX

It was late in California, later in New York. The rest of her family was asleep, and Alex Huang kept her voice down. In the end, she knew this was her fault. She pressed her palms to her face, her breathing shallow and fast.

"Alex," Irene said. Her voice was clear, unwavering, even now. "I'm in Mr. Liang's study. I need you to tell me how to do this."

It had all happened very fast. "His computer," Alex said. "That's where we need to go." In the darkness of her room, the only light was her computer screen. Even just past three in the morning, she could hear the sounds of New York City outside her window, cars honking and the distant wail of an ambulance. Midnight in California, then, everyone asleep besides this girl on the phone with her.

"I'm in," Irene said.

"I didn't give you a password."

"It was Daniel's birthday," she said. "Everything is."

Alex closed her eyes, imagined the room as the last time she had seen it. Irene leaning over Mr. Liang's monitor, the light as it touched the planes of her face. The scattered papers, the framed photo, the dragon paperweight. She should have known then that this was the only way things could end.

"What next?" Alex said, and she wasn't sure if she was asking about this moment, Irene at Mr. Liang's computer, or something else. Daniel's father knew what they had done, and Alex could not see a way out. Even if they could find the evidence on his computer, even if they deleted it, he would *know*. All these months, and they had only ever been making their way through the dark.

Irene was typing. Alex could hear the sound of her fingers across the keyboard. On her mirrored screen, new windows opened, closed. "This is where I need your help," she said.

Once, Alex would have given so much to hear her say it. "I don't understand," she said. "What are we doing here?"

Irene hesitated, just for a moment. "We need to find your code," she said. "Or however you managed to access his system the first time."

Alex was awake, awake, awake, her skin thrumming, heart beating too fast. So why couldn't she keep up? "What for?" she said.

"Isn't it obvious?" Irene asked. "We can't *do* this anymore, Alex. Even if Mr. Liang doesn't report us, he or anyone could discover your code here."

"It's not that easy."

"I've told you already," Irene said, her voice cool, "I don't understand what you do. But I know the FBI can do it better."

It was three a.m. and the shadows in the periphery of her vision kept changing shape. If Alex closed her eyes, maybe this could be a dream, a nightmare. She knew Irene was right. And yet—against her better judgment, against all her fears, she could not quite let go of this. It had taken her so long to write that code, to figure out how to do this one impossible thing. She had *hacked the FBI*. There was so much they still needed to do.

The screen was still changing, flickering. If she lost access to the FBI, if Irene removed her code—

"I know you have a plan," Alex said. She thought of France, less than a week ago, the sun rising over the Château de Fontainebleau and Irene reading off a wi-fi password. "You always have a plan."

"You expect too much of me, Alex."

That was the thing. She didn't. Irene was infuriating, arrogant, more confident than she had a right to be. But—she had always managed to pull off the impossible.

"Tell me," Alex said, "how was this supposed to end?"

The two of them on different coasts, washed in the same blue light. Irene's voice was soft. "Like this," she said. "We don't have any more loopholes, Alex. Even if it's not this time, it'd be the next. And even if we could do this—Daniel would never forgive us."

Alex thought of these past months, of late nights and this crew, all that had seemed possible. She thought of Daniel, his father, what might break if she could not let go.

"Walk me through this," Irene said.

Alex did.

The next thing she knew, there was a soft click, a door closing. Irene would be outside now. It had all happened so quickly. In the end, maybe she shouldn't have been surprised. Irene always knew exactly what she was doing. If she had seen this coming, then it would come.

Alex tried, one final time, to access the FBI server. She was not a hacker. She had been one, for a little bit. It did not let her in. "Does Will know?" she asked. "That we did this?"

"Does it matter?"

Either way, this was the end. Alex was silent. She thought of her empty apartment in California, the job that waited for her there. Every day would be the same. "I can't go back to the way things were," she said.

"Then don't," Irene said. Her voice was almost gentle. "Make something new."

They had spoken of dreams, that night in Stockholm. Of what would happen if they pulled this off. Alex opened their encrypted folder. At the start of this job, she had purchased a new, unregistered computer, set up remote access for the rest of the crew. She'd shown them how to SSH in, edit text files without ever sharing anything over the internet. Now, one by one, files were starting to vanish. She knew this had to be Irene too. *Make us a plan*, Will had said months ago, *for when the FBI comes calling.* Irene had.

"Someday," Alex said, watching these past two months slip through her fingertips, "things aren't going to go your way."

Irene's voice was soft. "I hope you're right," she said. She was silent for a moment. "Goodbye, Alex," she said. It felt like an ending.

Alex rose. Moonlight, cold and unforgiving, fell through the window. She stayed there for a long time, her gaze on the city, its changing lights, thinking of all that had been lost.

Then she called Will.

45

WILL

Will Chen was thinking about beginnings. Two months ago, the Sackler and its bright alarms, the museum showcases cracked open one by one. In his dorm room, the last of the autumn sun had been gold against his bed, his desk, his steady hands.

When China Poly's card had fluttered to the ground, when he had picked it up—he had not hesitated. Maybe he should have. But really, what had he expected when he had slipped that tiger into his pocket, run his fingertips over the edges of its spine with something like possession? That evening could have been a Salvador Dalí painting he had first seen in high school, clocks melting in a scene by the sea. It had felt like he had walked into a surrealist landscape, that to question the impossibility of it all was to let the illusion slip through his fingertips.

This, he realized, was waking up.

Will leaned against his windowsill. It was the turn of the seasons again, fall deepening to winter, and moonlight stretched over Santa Clara, its suburbs and distant mountains, touched all the things he had thought might someday be his. It had been just hours ago when Daniel had shown them what his father had found out, since Will had spoken with Mr. Liang. He did not know what came next. He thought of his call with Yuling, of conversations with Min, of all that was left to do.

It won't happen again, he had promised. Even without Mr. Liang, the authorities were closing in. He tried to imagine another interview, the feel of handcuffs around his wrist. They might still be released. If things went right, if their alibis held, if Irene did what she always did. They could get together in a year or two, talk about the time they had pulled off a heist. It would not be Paris in the summer, or Lily's dreams of an unending horizon, but they would still have clean enough records, college degrees and the certainty of a career, all those things that their parents had dreamed of when they had come to America for the first time.

Alex was calling him.

He hesitated for just a moment. He had not told her yet. He didn't know how he could, what words he could use. From the start, he had known what this job would mean to Alex. Alex, who had left Boston behind, who had chosen responsibility over any dreams of her own. Her grief, the weight of it—they had always recognized in each other something of themselves.

Will closed his eyes and thought of Beijing, of the Old Summer Palace, of the moments when his future seemed close enough to touch. After all that had happened, all they had done—how could anything else be enough?

He let himself imagine, for a moment. Talking with his sister, finding a way out. Working with Min, with Siqi, with Yuling. What it might feel like to do this without Daniel. There was still London, Norway, New York. It was a foolish thought, reckless. Daniel's dad had caught them once already, and they were running out of time.

Still—he could not quite let it go.

"Alex," he said, picking up the phone at last. It might have been two months ago. She might have been in California, and he might have been in Boston, and this could be a beginning. They could start over, perhaps. They could do this better. He had to believe it.

If he didn't—what was left?

"Will." Her voice was low. "You need to talk to your sister."

It had been years ago. Will and Irene had been arguing over something he couldn't remember, and his dad had gone to the kitchen, set a knife in each of their hands. *If you want to hurt each other*, he had said, *then do it*.

Will had met his sister's gaze, and, as one, they had put the knives down.

On this November evening, years later, Will opened the front door, faced his sister again. Once, he had thought they would always be on the same side.

"What have you done?" he asked.

She met his gaze, as steady as she always was. In childhood, looking at her had felt like looking into a mirror. He could not remember when that had changed. "I deleted the evidence."

"What evidence?" he asked.

Irene moved to brush past him, but he didn't let her. She raised a brow. "You talked to Alex."

"You don't get to look upset."

"Oh, I'm not."

Will crossed his arms. The November air was cool, the streetlamps throwing soft light over the empty sidewalks. "You deleted *everything*. Alex's access to the FBI, all our research, everything we've fucking done for the past two months—"

"All the evidence of our crimes," Irene snapped back. "You think someone else won't figure it out? You think Daniel's dad will just let us go, because—what? Because family just gets a free pass on international art theft? Because you want us to keep *going*?"

If this had been another time, he might have agreed with her. He could feel his pulse roaring in his ears, the wind cold as it scored across his skin. But his sister had done this without saying a word, had assumed she knew better than he did. What else was new? "You had no right—"

Irene shook her head. "Tell me that you weren't making plans already. You are so *arrogant*, Will. You think that we can pull anything off—"

"I already talked to Daniel's dad," Will said. "He already agreed not to say anything. We could've—"

"Should I be impressed?" Irene asked, her voice scathing. "What does it matter? I could have done the same thing. I did that and *more*, as always."

"You're supposed to be our con artist," Will snapped. "You're supposed to have our way out. And the one time—"

"The one time? Every fucking time, I've gotten us out of this. Customs in Sweden. After the Fontainebleau went wrong. I've been doing everything for this and what have you done?"

"Then what now?" he asked. He swept his hand across the street, these suburbs, everything they knew. "Claim the credit. It doesn't matter to me. But where was your plan for when this went wrong?"

Irene said nothing. Her arms were crossed. They were in the middle of the street now. This could have been any other fight, but they hadn't fought this way in years. Even when this had begun, when he had thought she would say no, that she would argue with him—

Will almost laughed. While he had been talking with Mr. Liang, trying to find them a future, Irene had been planning this. "*This* was your way out," he said, the realization coming to him slowly. He shook his head. "You were never expecting this to work, were you?" He had accused her of the same thing in Paris, had felt *guilt* about it afterward. He was only realizing now—she had never denied it.

Irene's gaze was steady. "Were you?"

"Yes," Will said. "Of course. I thought you and I—"

"That we could rob five museums and get away with it? That Daniel's dad, who is in the *FBI*, who is *leading this investigation*, wouldn't catch his *son*? If you wanted to keep doing this, you're more selfish than I thought."

He could not look at her. His skin felt hot, feverish. "You should have said something," he said, because he knew it to be true. "You should have asked. You always think you know exactly the right thing to do—"

"Because I *do*."

"Because you don't ever fucking *talk* to anyone! You are closed off and selfish and you have ruined this for all of us—"

Irene cut him off, her voice acerbic with anger. "Are we calling each other names? Because I have *plenty*."

"You just called me selfish—" Will began, incredulous.

"You are!" Irene snapped, and now they were both yelling, their voices echoing down the empty street. Will couldn't bring himself to care. "You are selfish and arrogant and you would jeopardize everyone's future just for a chance to be a part of the history you love so *fucking much*—"

Will cut her off. "Why did you say yes? If you thought this was so stupid from the beginning, if you've been planning for our fucking failure all this time?"

"Because you asked! Because I've spent my whole life trying to fix your mistakes!"

These stolen zodiac heads had meant everything to him. They had been a way out. A future. Something that could be his. He looked at his sister and did not recognize her. "You shouldn't have," he said, his voice low.

She pushed past him. "Well, it doesn't matter anymore," she said.

"Are we done?" he called. He didn't feel done. He was still alight with anger, with frustration, with all the words he had never said to his sister until today.

Irene was already heading up the stairs. She didn't bother looking at him. "We were done a long time ago."

And then Will was alone.

46

LILY

ily Wu had spent her whole life dreaming. She had grown up in Galveston, close enough to the Gulf of Mexico that wherever she was, she could hear the crash of its waves. When the summer storms swept through, they boarded up the windows, watched the lights flicker out, and Lily would look at her parents in the wavering candlelight and think of how seldom she saw them like this, standing still. She was so used to them only in passing, a whirlwind of work calls and late-night shifts, the days and the years blurring together. Her childhood—it had been long, lonely nights, summer days, the rumble of a car's engine beneath her palms. It had been races in the dark, all those risks that her classmates would not take, because Lily had known it even then: There had to be more to life than this.

She applied to Duke early decision. She had been eighteen years old, unsure even then if she could find Durham on a map, and North Carolina had seemed like the farthest she could ever go. They did not give her financial aid. It didn't matter. She had always known she was going, whatever the cost. That spring, when COVID came, when her parents were afraid of going outside because of the virus, because of the names they were called—she would not repeat them, she would not let them hurt—she had stayed home, spun dreams of Duke and its possibilities.

Her parents had started over in America.

She could do the same.

On a Galveston beach, Lily slipped off her shoes, breathed in the harshness of the salt air. In the distance, a foghorn blew, loud and mournful. The sand was dark, wet, and waves broke white against the gray shore. Tomorrow she would fly back to Duke.

"Lily?" Irene asked through the phone. "Are you still there?"

For several seconds, Lily couldn't answer. Irene, Will, both of them were so full of burning, righteous anger. But all Lily could feel was grief like an ocean, rising and rising. This had felt like a future, a chance for her to make something of herself, and while she was at home, so far from the rest of her crew, it had all vanished like smoke. Racing, everything else. It might have only ever been a dream. "Yes," she said. "I am."

Irene's voice was soft. "Did I fuck up?" she asked. "Is this my fault?"

"No," Lily said, and she even believed it. "You didn't. But . . ."

"What?"

"Why did you say yes, Irene?" Lily asked. She walked along the shore, the water cold against her bare feet, her exposed ankles. Winter in Galveston did not often fall below freezing. Still, now, it might strip her raw. "When Will asked you to join this crew, why did you?"

Irene was silent. "Because he asked," she said. "He's my older brother, and he asked. And I knew he would do it anyway. Why?"

Lily thought of two months ago, Will Chen with a smile and an impossible job. She could've said no to him. The China of her parents' past was cold, unfamiliar, full of unspeakable loss. What did she care for the glory of China, its right to reclaim what had once been theirs?

And yet—

Beijing, the first time she saw it, was not what she expected. In the evening smog, it had been all skyscrapers and neon lights, something out of a fever dream. She had raced through its streets, a motorcycle humming beneath her, seen the sun rise on the ruins of the Old Summer Palace. Her parents, when they spoke of China, always spoke of loss. But standing there, Beijing unfolding before her, she had thought for the first time they might have been speaking of longing.

Lily could feel the first few drops of rain. Wasn't this how it always happened? "I think," she said, her voice very soft, "this has never mattered as much to you as it did to the rest of us."

Irene was silent for a long moment. "It *did* matter," she said.

Lily thought back to a stolen speedboat, Paris and races in the glittering dark. There was so much she would never do again. "I know," Lily said. It wasn't enough, not now. "I have to go. I'll—I'll see you back at school."

It was raining harder by now. Lily knew she should go back inside, but instead she lingered, looking out at the trembling horizon. She had spent so long dreaming of elsewhere, of a way out of this town, its expectations and its fears, everything her parents would never say. If she wanted to, she thought she could find her way out of this too. The five of them had fake passports, the remains of China Poly's cash. They could do these next three thefts, disappear to a foreign country, somewhere with sunlight and no extradition. It was the ending of every heist movie. A long road, a setting sun, cars that shone in the falling light. Everything you knew, left behind.

She might have said yes, if any of them had asked. What was left for her here? She wasn't sure. She would graduate next year, slot neatly into the workforce, not extraordinary like Irene or brilliant like Alex, and if it hadn't been for these past few months, she might have thought it was enough. But now—Lily thought of these years as they passed, how long she had been running without knowing where or why. These heists had been the first time she had ever felt like she belonged, not just one part of her but *everything*.

By the time the lightning came, the wind howling over the flat gray sheet of the Gulf of Mexico and the thunder rattling the stilts of their house, Lily was inside. This could have been every storm from her childhood, every dark, lonely night dreaming of something more. If things had gone differently—there would have been Beijing in the summer, cities that she did not know the names of, her parents and all the history they had left behind. But after all these years, she thought maybe she should have seen this coming. Diaspora had always been an unmooring, a boat cast free.

She did not know how to find her way back.

She never had.

ACT THREE

The role of the artist is to make the revolution irresistible.

—*TONI CADE BAMBARA*

47

WILL

Outside, snow drifted over the Charles River. It was an early morning in December, and the sky was the pale gray of a knife tilted to the light. Somehow, while he hadn't been paying attention, fall had turned to winter. He was halfway through his senior year.

Will Chen pulled on his coat, his scarf, his heavy boots, before stepping out into the cold. Harvard was quiet on these wintry Sundays, and he walked through the Yard, his footsteps leaving marks in the fresh snow. This was not how he had expected the semester to end. Two bronze zodiac heads were gathering dust beneath his bed, waiting for their return to Beijing. He should have shipped them already, but he could not bear to let them go, this last memory of what they had done, what they could have been. It should have ended with a private jet, champagne, summer air. Beijing, red and rising. One year and five heists, ten million dollars to make his future his own.

He had lost it all so quickly.

He pulled the door to the art studio open, the lights overhead flickering on with the motion. The studio, as ever, was all clean lines and open space, the windows high and soaring.

Will hung up his coat, wiped down his glasses with the hem of his sweater, breathed new warmth into his hands. He was not here to paint. Instead he walked over to the station he had called his own all these years at Harvard, began to clear it out. He was not taking an art class next semester. This place was not his anymore.

"Will?"

He looked up. For a moment, he could have mistaken her for Lily—tumbling brown hair, a half smile curled on her lips. But he hadn't talked to anyone in his crew since Thanksgiving, and the girl standing before him was just another classmate. It took a moment for her name to come to him. Rachel Tang, he remembered. She was a junior, an art history student like him. Lately, the days passed like a dream. "Hey," he said. "What are you doing here?"

"I could ask you the same thing," she said, tilting her head toward his station. They had never talked outside of class before, but they had crossed paths often enough this semester, on late nights or early mornings when they were both in the studio. "Cleaning out?"

"Yeah," he said. "My last art class."

She was quiet for a moment. "I'm sorry," she said, and he believed her. She, too, might have known the shape of this loss.

He shrugged, reaching for his coat. He wasn't done clearing out his work, but—he wasn't sure he could do this with other people around. "It's fine," he said. "Not everyone gets to be an artist."

"I know," she said. If it had been another time, months ago, he would have asked to paint her, done the same thing he always did with beautiful girls. She looked at him like she might have said yes. "But—I thought you might be."

He had spent so many hours in this studio. Will took it in one last time—snow falling over exposed skylights, pale morning sun as it touched easels and paints and unfinished sculptures—and put on his coat. He was halfway through his senior year, and there were some dreams he had to let go of. "Good luck," he said, and pushed the door open, stepped into the waiting cold.

Back in his dorm room, he opened his laptop, began the terrible, tedious work of applying for jobs once more. Weekends now were always like this. There were dozens of unread emails, rejections left unopened during finals, writing papers and creating art that felt empty. He opened his Excel sheet, began to update it. The spreadsheet had been Irene's template, something she had created for him when he first began applying for jobs.

It felt like so long since he had spoken to his sister.

Outside his window, the snow was falling harder, stripping Harvard of everything but winter wind and hungry trees. He had painted this once, in quick brushstrokes and heavy colors, the first snowfall he had ever seen. It had been his freshman year, and he had still thought he might be an artist.

Will did not know where to go from here. When he had first started applying for jobs, he had thought he could get anything he wanted, that a Harvard degree and the sheer force of his want might be enough. But he would graduate in just a few months, and he did not know what his future held.

The last email was from the Met.

Will took a deep, shuddering breath. He had applied for this early on, too, with the same sort of recklessness that had led him to say yes to Wang Yuling, that had brought about all of this that felt like an ending.

Dear Mr. Chen, it read. *The Metropolitan Museum of Art was impressed by your application and would like to invite you to interview for the position of assistant curator of Asian art . . .*

His hands were trembling. His whole body was trembling. He read the email a second time, a third, just to make sure it was real.

The interview was in a week and a half.

If he and his sister were still speaking to each other, he would have called her. Irene had always been better at this kind of thing. She could have mock interviewed him, given him the words that would get him this job. Her whole life, she had gotten everything she ever wanted. But he thought of this past semester, all the ways they had hurt each other. He didn't know how they could come back from that.

In that Harvard dorm room, surrounded by stolen art and falling snow, Will felt very alone. He read the email one more time, marked the date in his calendar. He would book his flights tonight. And then, because he didn't know what else to do, because he wanted someone to *know*, he took out his phone. He had gotten so used to talking to his crew every day. Now—what was left?

The phone rang once, twice, three times.

"Hello?" Lily said.

"Hey," he said, and was glad that this was over the phone, that she couldn't see him smile. He could have called Daniel or Alex, but after all this time, Lily knew his dreams, how scared he was to speak them out loud. *How do you know you aren't good enough?* she had asked him once, and in that moment he thought maybe he could be. He wanted to hold on to that feeling now. "How are you?"

"I just finished my last final," she said. There was a brief exchange in the background—he thought he heard his sister's voice—and then the sound of a door clicking shut. If he closed his eyes, he could almost see Lily walking through Duke's campus, the wind swirling around her. "Heading back to Galveston in a few days. You?"

"I have a couple more papers to finish," he said, and it was so easy, so normal to be having this conversation. They could have been any two friends at the end of the semester, waiting for the break to come. "And— I got an interview at the Met. Assistant curator."

"Oh my god, you couldn't have led with that?" Lily asked, laughing. "Will, *congrats*."

Will leaned back in his chair, smiled wide. For a moment, it felt like they were back in a restaurant in Paris, the world unfolding before them both. "Nothing is certain yet," he said, and it was true. "I still have to make it through the interview. But—I don't know. It was the first good thing that's happened in a long time."

"Yeah," she said, and he knew she was thinking of the same thing he was. France, the FBI, how it had all fallen apart. It might have been inevitable. It still hurt. When she spoke again, her voice was deliberately light. "It's a good thing we didn't see this to its end, then."

The last museum they had planned to rob was the Met. "If they hire me," Will said, "maybe I'll just *tell* them to return the last zodiac head. Take them down from the inside."

"The long con," Lily said, and he could hear the smile in her voice. "Thanks for calling, Will. I'm glad to hear you're doing well."

"Lily . . ." he began. He didn't know what else to say. *How are you?* he wanted to ask. *How have you been?* It had been so long since they'd talked. "Take care," he said instead, and hung up the phone. In the end, she had been Irene's friend first. He set his phone down, looked outside at the falling snow. This was not the future he had wanted. But he would interview at the Met, would be as close to art as he could get.

Maybe, someday, it would be enough.

48

IRENE

This was how the weeks passed. This was how the semester passed. Irene Chen finished her classes, turned in final papers, sang a clear, perfect solo for her a cappella group's winter showcase. For her public policy class, she wrote about the thefts, analyzing China's rise, the thieves' motivations, received the A she knew she would. She got coffee with James Reyes, at last, and the two of them made plans to run for student government together, all the things at Duke they might change. *This is an institution built on white supremacy*, he had said, and Irene had known they were going to work well together.

She should have been happy. She had known how this would end, planned for it, and now it was the last day of the semester. Her classes were done, her finals over. Her flight home left tomorrow. Will wouldn't be back for another few days. She didn't know how to talk to him anymore.

Someday things aren't going to go your way, Alex had said.

Irene almost wanted it to be true. She had spent her whole life doing everything right, and she was miserable for it.

The door opened. "It's freezing outside," Lily said. Snow was melting in her hair, and she took off her boots, unwound her scarf.

"How was fluid mechanics?" Irene asked.

Lily laughed. "Done with, thankfully. Are you packing?"

They were halfway through their junior year. How had time passed so quickly? "I should be," Irene said, though it was clear that she wasn't. She glanced around the room, and Lily's phone caught her eye, the screen lighting up. "Someone's calling you."

Irene hadn't meant to look at it, but she saw her brother's name.

Lily, halfway through reaching for her phone, went still.

This was how their crew had split. Will would not speak to Irene. She would not speak to him. Alex and Daniel, in California, had both vanished into their work, but Irene knew that Alex was on Will's side, that Daniel would take hers. And Lily—Lily had said so little since all this had ended. They were still friends, still roommates, but there was a distance to her that Irene had never felt before.

"Take it," Irene said.

Lily picked up. "Hello?" she said.

"I can leave—" Irene began, but Lily was already shaking her head, pulling her coat back on.

I'll be back soon, she mouthed, and then she was closing the door, and Irene was alone.

⸺

Irene had always known how this was going to end. She thought back to those days in California after the Fontainebleau had gone wrong, Daniel's voice breaking beneath a cold November sky. Will had left first, and then it had been just the two of them and the ashes of their evidence.

It wasn't enough.

I'm sorry, she had said, very quietly. She had been the one to call Daniel first, had asked him to go to China and known he would say yes.

In the pale morning light, his tattoo curled around his throat like an outstretched hand. *I'm so tired*, Daniel had said. *Of this uncertainty, this fear. Where do we go from here?*

He looked at her like she had an answer. Irene wrapped her arms around her knees. The sky was a harsh, unforgiving blue, the bricks they were leaning against still a lingering cold. She could feel the warmth of his shoulder against hers.

Neither of them could afford to fail. Not when Daniel had a career in medicine ahead of him, when he would hear back from schools before the year's end. Not when they had families here and in China, so many people who were counting on them to be more than they were.

He won't report us, Irene said, and tried to sound more certain than she was. She knew her brother. He would be at Mr. Liang's door now. No one could say no to Will. *And you and I both know that no one else at the FBI is as good as your father. We can still make it out of this.*

There are still files on the FBI database, Daniel said. *Eventually someone will put it together. And once we're subpoenaed—*

They had been so careful. Fake IDs, burner phones, nothing that would leave a paper trail. And yet—there were still those shared files, hidden on an encrypted computer, several months' worth of incriminating Telegram messages.

I know, she said. From the beginning, they had been reckless, overconfident, careless. There had been times when even she had thought they could pull this off. An airport security office in Stockholm, a stolen zodiac head taken and kept. The days after, following the news, waiting for an accusation that never came. A month later and Paris in the cold morning light, Alex across from her with her laptop open. The only sound had been Alex's hands over the keys, their breathing almost in time.

Irene would not be so foolish again.

She rose, held her hand out for Daniel. *You've never doubted me before,* she said, and smiled a smile that did not waver. *Don't start now.*

⁕

Even now, after all that had gone wrong, Irene did not know what she could have done differently. They were just college students, after all, trying to pull off the impossible, and sometimes she thought Will must have known it too. He was her brother, and once she had believed they knew each other as well as they knew themselves.

When Lily came back, Irene had still not started packing. Instead she sat at her desk, watching the wind pull leaves from the dying trees, the buses that came and went outside her window.

"How is he?" Irene asked.

"Do you really want to know?" Lily asked.

Irene sighed. Her whole life, she had measured herself against her brother. Without him—she was not sure this was relief. "He has no right to be upset with me," she said. "If we had kept going, we would have gotten caught."

"Do you think that's why he's upset?" Lily asked, raising a brow. She leaned against her bed, crossed her arms. "Irene, you're smarter than that. We all knew that this would be the end."

Irene fell silent. She had always been good at this—at unraveling people's motivations, at figuring out what they *wanted.* This time, though, she hadn't wanted to. Will was her older brother, and she was tired of bearing his responsibilities.

You were never expecting this to work, he had said, and his voice had held only grief.

Irene could count their faults, hers and her brother's, the ways they had hurt each other in these weeks. He had wanted to keep going when he knew this could only end in expulsion, in arrest, in all the conse-quences that he had never faced. She had decided, without him, how this would end instead. That fight, midnight and an empty street, the knives of their accusations in the dark.

I've spent my whole life trying to fix your mistakes, Irene had said, and meant it. She was still angry at him. But even through that anger, she could see how much he had wanted this, how much of himself he had poured into this impossible job.

He had thought she believed in it too. And even if she didn't—he had thought she would believe in *him*. Never mind how ridiculous this was, how reckless.

Irene closed her eyes. "I fucked up," she said.

She felt Lily move to her side. "If it's any consolation, we all did."

Irene laughed. She couldn't help it. They had committed so many crimes in the past few months. The fact that the two of them could be here, talking about it—it was a miracle in itself.

"Okay," Lily said. "So what do we do now?"

Irene was silent for a moment. *Nothing,* she could have said. Tomor-row Irene was supposed to fly back to California. Lily was supposed to go home to Galveston. But all of this—it still felt unfinished. "How do you feel," she said, "about a trip to Boston?"

They packed quickly, haphazardly, before sliding into Lily's Mustang, tossing suitcases in the backseat. As Lily drove through Durham, Irene changed flight reservations, calling airlines and spinning stories. And then they were on a long flat stretch of road, those North Carolina ever-greens rising on either side of them into a clear, midday sky, and it felt like starting over.

They took turns choosing the music, rolled the windows down just enough that the air was crisp and alive around them, and when Irene looked over at Lily, she felt only relief. Even without these thefts, without their promises, they could still have this. "Thanks," she said, her voice soft, "for coming with me."

"Always," Lily said. "Besides, our junior year is halfway over. Days like these won't come again." Her voice was filled with some quiet, unnamed grief.

Irene examined her. In a few months, it would be spring. It should have felt like something opening up. They would be seniors soon, and then—the rest of their lives. It was both too close and too far away. She could hear the soft *whoosh* of the winter air, the song playing in the background, something of Carolina pines and a southbound train, how to leave the past behind. "Are you looking forward to Microsoft?" she asked.

"Are you looking forward to consulting?" Lily said.

"That's not an answer," Irene said.

Lily's gaze was on the road, those great trees, the perfect blue of the sky. One exit passed, and then another. "I don't know," she said at last. "I thought I was. But the world of Microsoft—the world that I'm supposed to be in—it feels so separate from racing, or museum break-ins, or everything we've done in the dark. I don't know how I'm supposed to put it back together. What about you?"

New York in the summer would be all reaching skyscrapers, glass that reflected the light. Irene imagined taking an elevator to the top floor, evenings spent ordering delivery from a downtown office, solving problems for companies that her professors always liked to call *too big to fail*. She should have said yes. And yet—"It's the next step," she said.

"Is that it?"

"What else is there?" Irene said.

Lily glanced over at her. "And if we had pulled this off? What would you have done?"

Irene had never thought about it, not seriously. She had never expected them to see this through the end. But in this car, flying toward Boston and colder days, toward everything she needed to repair with her brother, she let herself imagine. They would have gone to the UK first. They might even have been there now, walking through the British Museum and observing the spoils of empire. Irene had never cared much for art, but she did know power, how those with it always took from those without. Next would have been the KODE Art Museums in Norway, and then, finally, the Met.

What would she do when it was all over?

Irene had spent her whole life knowing that she could not fail. She wouldn't let herself. Her future—it was Wall Street, or law school, any of these things that promised certainty. But she had always been the most comfortable at grassroots organizations, politics that started small and became something bigger. But politics, political office—these things were not won by the best candidate, by the most capable. Irene had always gotten her way, but in this she was not sure if she could. Senate seats could be bought and sold, and white men had decided the fate of this country for hundreds of years.

What was the use in dreaming?

Lily was waiting for her answer. Irene turned her gaze to the window, watched this place she knew so well pass in a blur of blue and green and winter gray. After all that had happened, she owed Lily honesty. "I'd do something of my own," she said.

Lily was quiet for a long moment. Irene thought that she might not have heard her, but then Lily said, very softly, "That's what Will said too."

49

LILY

The motel smelled of chlorine and winter cold. Lily turned the heater on, its rumble as loud as any engine, drew the curtains shut in one swift motion. It was dark in Philadelphia, the city's lights distant and bright. "Remind me," she said, "why are we doing this again?"

Irene smiled. "Because we're halfway done with junior year," she said, "and there isn't anything a road trip can't heal."

"I'm not sure I believe that," Lily said, but she was smiling too. She let herself fall on one of the twin beds, the covers cool against her skin. There were other answers Irene could have given, about Will or racing or all the things that Lily could not have, but this was as true as the rest. She looked up at the ceiling. White paint curled at its edges, made patterns like the cresting of waves.

When Irene had asked her to road-trip to Boston, she hadn't hesitated. She missed driving, but—it had been more than that. It might have been Will, just a little, how the shape of his longing had always resembled her own, but it wasn't just for him. Lily had spent her whole life searching for something to call her own, and these years, the change they brought with them, had felt like a start. College was races in the Durham dark, late nights and the spill of cheap beer, this time where she could live without having it all figured out.

Lily looked over at Irene lying on the other bed. These four years— soon they would be over. She didn't know the person she would be when they were. But in this motel room, Boston still a distant destination, she could almost convince herself it didn't matter.

It was snowing in Boston. Lily drove slowly, carefully, grateful for the snow chains they had bought in New York, for all the years she'd had to learn how to control this car. It was afternoon, the sky a pale, unbroken gray, and she thought not of storms but of the moments after, a quiet that felt like forgiveness. She parked, turned the car off, looked at Irene.

"What do I *say*?" Irene asked. "It's really not completely my fault."

"It's not," Lily agreed. Whatever else there was, this much was true. Irene had only done what they all ought. "But maybe don't say that."

"You're right," Irene said. She let out a long, slow sigh, then straightened as if bracing herself. "Okay, let's go." Any of her earlier uncertainty, her fear, had been smoothed over, and Irene looked as composed as ever. It had been almost three years, and Lily knew Irene, the standards she held herself to, the pressure she felt—the pressure they all felt—to be enough for her parents and their dreams.

What are you afraid of? Irene had asked her once, before this all began.

Nothing at all, Lily had lied. There was so much that she feared. Not racing, but the moments after, when the world stilled. How to be the daughter she was supposed to be, her parents' American Dream. How to untangle the parts of her that were Chinese and the parts of her that were American, how *both* so often felt like *neither*.

But she had gone to China for the first time, had seen it and wanted more. She had raced on foreign roads, had been part of a crew to bring something lost back home. She had watched it all come apart.

In the end, this job had demanded truth from them. It would do so one last time.

"Should I come in?" Lily asked. Part of her wondered if this was between Will and Irene. If it had always been.

"Please," Irene said.

They left the suitcases in the car. A Harvard student, a stranger, held the door to Eliot House open for Irene, and Lily smiled. Some things would always stay the same.

And then they were in front of Will's dorm room.

Irene knocked, the motion crisp and expectant.

A moment later, the door opened. Will looked like the quintessential Harvard student, standing there in his glasses and dark, messy hair, a crimson hoodie with the words *HARVARD ATHLETICS* across his chest. He was wearing slippers, white and fluffy. "Lily," he said, and he had the grace to only look surprised for a moment. "Irene. I guess you should come in."

⌒⟋

Within the suite, it was easy to tell which room was Will's. There were prints on the wall, a sketchbook tucked in a bookshelf filled with art history textbooks. When Will's suitemates began to appear, to introduce themselves to Irene with broad, winning smiles, Will suggested the three of them talk elsewhere, but Lily had chosen to stay behind. It was a bitterly cold day, and she suspected that this conversation was between

Will and Irene alone. Even after all these months of seeing the two of them together—she still could not imagine what it was like to have siblings, did not know if fights like these were the kind that bent a relationship or the kind that broke it.

She took a seat on the couch, pulled out her phone. From here, she could see Harvard before her, pale and glistening in the snow.

When Lily had left for college, it had been her first time out of Texas. She thought of that now—how big the world had seemed beyond Galveston, how Duke, with its Gothic spires, its evergreen trees, had been so different from anything she had ever known. In this year, they had been to Beijing, to Stockholm, to Paris. A month ago, she had felt only grief. There was so much she still wanted to do. Even now, it hurt to think about, but every day it was a little less. There would not be ten million dollars, a future wide-open, but they had had those few months.

Someday it might be enough.

She had a text from a number she knew. Lily opened it, curious. She and Zhao Min did not talk often, and when they did, it was mostly about cars.

Your turn, his message read, and nothing more.

Lily stared at her phone for a long moment. Then, for no reason she could put her finger on, she opened her phone browser, switched to incognito mode.

Chinese art theft, she typed.

This morning, Norway's KODE Art Museums had been robbed. She read through the news article, heart racing. She was an ocean away, and yet she could see it unfold before her. The wind as it whistled over the fjords, sweeping away the sound of glass breaking, backpacks full of stolen art. Every item in the Chinese Collection gone except one.

Zhao Min and Liu Siqi had kept their word. They had left the zodiac head behind, and every newspaper in the world was asking why.

Lily knew that this could only end badly. Already, the FBI was searching for them. But Min's text had felt like a challenge, and when she swept her gaze over Will's room, she saw, tucked beneath his bed, the glint of two familiar zodiac heads. For all that they had left behind, some things still remained. She did not know if she should bring this up to the rest of her crew, how she could. They had lost so much already.

Still, in the winter light, the bronze shone like possibility.

50

WILL

I t was too cold to walk along the Charles River, but they did anyway. It was almost completely frozen over, stark and silver in the gray light. Later the snow would become slush, but right now Boston was lovely, delicate, something out of a dream.

"How was the drive?" Will asked.

"Fast," Irene said. "Listen, Will—"

He cut her off. In these weeks, he'd had nothing but time. "I owe you an apology," he said. He kept his gaze on the river, ice and careful light. "More than one."

Irene's voice was careful too. "For?"

It might have started with this job. It might have started earlier. "Do you remember," Will said, "when you left for China?"

She had spent a semester in Beijing. He could still remember how he had felt when she had come back, when she could speak to their parents, their relatives, in so many ways he couldn't. "Of course," she said.

"I felt—I felt like you were leaving me behind." And perhaps a part of him had always felt like that. When he had chosen art history and she had chosen public policy, when she had taken a full ride to Duke over her own Harvard acceptance. His parents had never made this a competition, but he had still felt like it was. All the choices she had made, as if his own were not good enough, as if she could not bear to be like him. "And then we started this job together, and I couldn't help but think that you would have done it better."

When he exhaled, his breath rose white into the winter air. They had stopped walking, and Will brought his gloved hands to curl over the iron railing separating them from the river below. Pale afternoon sunlight glanced off the ice.

This heist isn't just yours, Daniel had said.

He had wanted it to be. He had wanted this thing that could just be his, that he could pull off on his own. He was the oldest child, the only son, all the things that meant something to their family in China, and though he had accepted he would never make history, he had wanted to anyway. He'd always felt like he had so much to prove.

Irene drew in a slow, careful breath. "Growing up," she said, "I always measured myself against you. And somehow—I always came up short."

He glanced sideways. His sister was leaning against the railing too, and in the light they were almost mirror images of each other. They wore grief the same way. How could it have been so many years of the two of them weighing themselves against the other?

"That day I got into Harvard," Will said softly. "I'm afraid it was the first and last time I'll make our parents proud." The words felt like a confession. For all that he and Irene were close, as siblings went—they did not share this kind of thing with each other.

Irene's gaze was on the river, that thin layer of ice. "Your art is in their offices," she said. "Did you know that? Every time you gift them a painting, they have it framed."

He hadn't known that. Irene had always been the good child, the one who made time to have lunch with their parents at work, who asked questions about their days and remembered the answers. He had thought—for all that his parents loved him, they were both scientists. He had never been able to imagine them wanting the same future for him that he did.

Her voice was soft. "I shouldn't have expected this job to go wrong. I just—everything goes your way. This seemed like the first time it might not."

He had asked Irene to do this with him, had been so sure she would say yes. *Are you certain?* she had asked, and he hadn't read the hesitation in her voice. He hadn't wanted to. "You were right," he said. "You always are. I just—I wanted this so badly I couldn't see it."

A museum in Beijing, the feel of bronze in his open palms. *What's wrong with wanting everything?* he had asked her once.

Nothing, as long as you know how to get it, she had said.

In the gray light, his sister looked at him at last. Perhaps they had always been like this, reaching for each other without knowing it. This job had only ever been temporary: an unfinished painting, an unmade dream. Still, Irene smiled. "Maybe next time," she said, "we'll get it right."

That evening, beneath the high, arched ceilings of Harvard's dining hall, Will pretended he was at the Met. Irene and Lily interviewed him, asking him questions about Asian art, about history, about all these things he had spent four years studying. In exchange, he gave them stories. Some he had told them before. Others were new. He talked about the Old Summer Palace, seeing it for the first time, how he had spent all of high school studying the Old Masters. How after so long, Chinese art had felt like coming home. There were art historians who believed their role was preservation. Will knew it was *change*.

"What would you do differently?" Lily asked. "If you got the job, what would you change about the Met?"

It was an interview question. Still, there was something in her eyes that made him think that there was truth in this too. Long ago, they had talked of dreams. What would he make of this future he had been given? When everything else was temporary, what parts of him stayed the same?

"Art's purpose is to create bridges, not to burn them," he said. "We have a responsibility to look to our own collections, examine what belongs to us and how it was obtained. Like every museum, the Met ought to make its decisions based on not just the law but on moral grounds."

"Careful," Irene said. "Museums never like to grapple with their history of colonialism. If you remove everything that was looted, then what's left?"

"What should remain," Will said easily. "Look at the Benin Bronzes. Look at the return of Nazi art. It's happening already."

"It's happening because of public pressure," Irene said. "Nothing more. Don't confuse that with the good intentions of museums."

Will sighed. "I'll change my answer," he said. "Maybe I'll say something about the lighting, or more pre–Qin dynasty art."

"Be just boring enough that they'll hire you," Lily said, and smiled quick. "And then when they do, take them apart from the inside."

Will laughed. Like this, he could pretend they were sitting here, planning another heist, that this was not the rest of his life that stretched out before him, confined within museums that saw their stolen art as something owed.

⌒

He hadn't been following the news. There hadn't been a point, after they had decided that this was the end. But he woke to an email from the Met, a joint statement released by the vast majority of Western museums.

We condemn the recent thefts of Chinese art, it began, and went on to talk of everything Will, Irene, and Lily had spoken of the night before. There were words like *spoils of war*, like *the preservation of history*, all the excuses conquerors always gave when asked to return what was not theirs. Even if he had believed them once, he didn't anymore. Not when the five of them had robbed Drottningholm and found that stolen art was still being purchased, when no one had cared about the zodiac heads until they had started going missing.

This was how it always went. Museums overlooked colonialism, conquest, a history of blood, until it was laid in front of them, until violence was met with violence.

He set his phone down. He didn't finish reading the email. What was the point? He had an interview to prepare for, the rest of his life to live. If he got this job—change might come slowly, in the end. The choices he made, the art he purchased or returned, it could mean something.

He could only hope.

Will rose from the couch, folded his blanket. It was not yet morning, but he couldn't imagine going back to sleep. The last of his suitemates had left for winter break by now, and Lily and Irene would still be asleep in his room. He changed, carefully and quietly, pulled on his heavy coat. He would finish clearing out his studio space this morning, come back in time to take them to breakfast in the dining hall. The waffle maker produced fluffy golden waffles that said *VERITAS* and was the most pretentious thing in this entire place.

There was so much he'd miss when he was gone.

"You're up early."

Will turned. Lily might have just woken up too, but her eyes were bright when they met his. She was in an oversize Duke basketball shirt, her hair falling in waves just past her shoulders. The moonlight pooled at her feet, silver and searching, and he remembered the drawing he had finished of her. It had not quite captured this—her smile like a question, the slight arch of her brow. He would have to do it again.

"So are you," he said. "Couldn't sleep?"

The motions of this were familiar. Texts, plane rides, all the times they had kept each other company in the dark. It had been temporary, he knew. He almost wished it weren't.

"Where are you going?" she asked.

He thought of the studio, empty in this early morning. Last time, he had thought he needed to be alone, but it might be better like this, Lily next to him as he left this place behind.

Her gaze was steady against his. He tilted his head toward the door, let himself almost smile. "Want to come?"

They walked across a silent courtyard, the snow still falling over them both, talked of things that meant nothing. The rest of her semester at Duke. His weeks here at Harvard. Weather and how it changed. It should have been terribly boring, and yet—he looked at her out of the corner of his eye, smiled anyway. He was not used to missing people, but he had missed her.

"Tell me again," she said, "what are we doing here?"

As he'd expected, the studio was empty this early. Will walked over to his table. There were easels still there, canvases leaning against them, paint tubes still half full. He'd left here unfinished. He hadn't realized just how unfinished it'd been.

"Cleaning it out," he said.

Lily walked around the table, her fingers light against the wood.

"I made the first zodiac head there," he said. He didn't know why he was speaking, only that Lily was here and she wasn't saying anything, and somehow—it was harder to let this go. He walked over to another table, pulled out a tray of chisels. "And the second. Neither of them was anything special, but I thought maybe with the third—"

Lily stopped in front of an easel, did not move for several heartbeats. "Will," she said. Her voice was soft. "Can you come here?"

He walked over. It was a painting he had done months ago, oil against canvas. Will touched the edges of it, the memory coming to him easily. He had painted it on an early morning like this, not long after the Drottningholm job. He had come home from Stockholm and felt like the whole world was open before him. For days afterward, he had closed his eyes and imagined the glint of moonlight against glass, the slow, leisurely movement of dark waves. To anyone else, it would have looked like nothing but slashes of silver—the moon in the sky, reflected against the water and the glass—against a dark, tremulous background.

"Our first heist," Lily said softly.

The studio was quiet. Will could hear his breath, hers, the distant fall of snow. "How did you know?" he asked.

Her fingertip almost brushed the edge of the canvas, and he shivered. "That night—the light hit the water exactly like that. I didn't think anyone else would notice."

If he had nothing else, at least there was this.

"Keep it," he said, on impulse. "I was going to throw it away anyway."

"I don't believe that for a moment," she said, and it was true. These heists—they meant the same thing to both of them, too much. Her gaze was still on the painting as she said, carefully, "Zhao Min texted me yesterday."

He blinked, trying to follow the transition. "Does he—does he do that often?"

Lily laughed. "You haven't read the news, then."

"I got an email from the Met this morning," he said. "I figured it was—" He stopped. He hadn't read the rest of it. He reached for his phone, pulled it out. "I'll finish reading it."

Yesterday, while he and Irene had walked along the Charles River and spoken of healing, a third museum had been robbed. In Norway, thieves had rappelled through a glass ceiling, cleaned out the KODE Museums' Chinese Collection. They had taken everything but the bronze zodiac head.

Will lifted his gaze. He looked at Lily, surrounded by light, at this painting of their first theft. "What did he say?" Will asked.

Lily passed her phone to him.

Your turn.

It didn't have to mean anything. But they were surrounded by art and high, soaring windows, the pale morning light turning this space into something sacred, and Will thought of the statement the Met had released, of Zhao Min and Liu Siqi leaving the zodiac head like a challenge. This could have been history, lost and found.

What did he *want*? Not empty studios and forgotten art, museums that only cared about what was theirs when it went missing.

Lily looked at him for a long moment, studying him as if she might find something new in the space between them. "You want to rob the Met," she said. Her voice was wondering.

He met her gaze, held it. He wanted to rob them *all*. But the Met—it would do for now. "Don't you?"

When she smiled, it was Beijing in the rising sun.

51

DANIEL

Daniel Liang was at home when it happened. He got the text from Siqi first. They weren't friends, not quite, but in the days after everything had gone wrong, when he could not talk to anyone else, she had sent him photos of Beijing. The Forbidden City in the morning light, the cats that wandered its halls. The hutongs, with their cobbled streets and open-air vendors, the alleyways crowded as they always were. He had not bothered to ask her why. It had felt like finding something lost. And so, when she texted him again, he opened the message.

Where are you? she asked.

San Francisco.

Do you have an alibi?

It had been right before his interview. His last one, at UCSF. *Yes*, he replied, and adjusted his tie, walked into his interview room.

He hadn't asked his dad to pick him up from the interview, but he recognized the car waiting outside, the steady blink of its emergency lights. Daniel didn't bother asking why. The news had already broken.

"You know I didn't do it," Daniel said. He slid in the passenger seat, clicked his seat belt in. The sound was loud in the stillness. "I've been here the whole time."

His dad's hands tapped against the wheel as he drove. Daniel did the same thing when he didn't know what to say. "Do you know who did?" he asked at last.

Daniel was silent.

"Son," his dad said, and it was a sigh. In Chinese, the word was two syllables, the first quick and expectant, the second one almost an exhale.

"It wasn't us," Daniel said. He didn't know what else he could say without incriminating himself, Siqi, anyone else. "Will, Irene, they weren't involved."

"I hope you're right," his dad said. "I'm going to Norway tomorrow. Will you be okay at home alone?"

Once, Daniel had thought this could be healing. It wasn't. Daniel laced his hands together, his gaze on the window, San Francisco in the dying light. "I always am," he said.

"Danli," his dad said, and it was a command. Daniel looked at his father. "I don't have to go."

"Don't you?" Daniel asked.

His dad didn't look at him. "There are some things more important."

"Go," Daniel said. The traffic moved slowly through the city at this hour. All these weeks later, and he still didn't know how they could come back from this. He had failed his father so many times over.

The car inched forward. "Why did you do it?"

He didn't want to talk about this. "Do what?"

They were speaking in Chinese. Still, Daniel's dad reached over, shut down his phone. Daniel did the same thing. One could never be too careful. "Danli, please," his dad said. "I'm not angry. I just want to understand."

It was hard to reconcile his father with this man. Daniel remembered his dad's voicemail, how he had spoken of regret. Daniel didn't know how to explain this, what words might make this better. "I know it was foolish," Daniel said. He kept his gaze on his lap, his laced hands. "But Beijing, its art—how can we forget what has been lost?"

His dad fell silent. Daniel thought of that early morning in Paris, Liu Siqi asking him the same thing. All of them who called China home— they knew what had been taken, what was still owed. Two hundred years, almost, and the Old Summer Palace was still an open wound. His dad knew it as well as he did.

"I brought us to America with the hopes of a better life," he said at last. "For it, I will do what's expected of me." His dad's gaze was on the road, the hills that were lined with gold. A better life. Daniel wasn't sure this was.

Either way, though, it wasn't an answer. Daniel thought of those first few years here, an unfamiliar school and an unfamiliar tongue, the two of them learning English in that great, empty house. TV shows that played into the night, a dictionary open between them. His dad, bent over the kitchen table, sounding out vowels with slow, careful precision. And even after all of that, his English might still be called *broken*, as if he didn't know every word in two languages, as if they hadn't spent all these years trying to put themselves back together.

Daniel kept his gaze on the hills, the changing sky. "Does America want us?" he said. He did not know how he could ever call this place home, when his mother was not here, when so often it felt like his father wasn't either.

"Does it matter?" his dad said. "We are here. This country is ours too. And my job will always be to catch these thieves."

It was all true.

At last, the traffic cleared. Daniel's dad pulled onto the highway. California, in the setting sun, was beautiful as it always was. Palm trees and gold light, the mountains as they reached for the sky. "But if they're good enough," his dad said, and he didn't look at Daniel, didn't change his expression at all, "they won't get caught."

⁓

It began the way it always did: Irene Chen called, and he picked up.

Daniel took the call outside, the December air cool but not yet cold. It was evening, fog sweeping over the bay, and Daniel sat on an empty sidewalk, stretched his legs out. "Irene," he said. "It's been a while."

"It has," she said. Her laugh was bright. "We've done this before, haven't we?"

Her voice on the phone, a flight to Beijing. That penthouse apartment, everything that looked new in the light. "A thousand times," he said. "What are you planning?"

She didn't ask how he knew. She didn't need to. "Nothing that you need to be involved in," she said, and there was rare honesty in her voice. "But . . ."

This could only end badly. "What?" he said, because he knew she was waiting for him to ask. Part of him wanted to know. He had never tired of watching Irene pull off the impossible.

"We're going to New York," she said. "This is an invitation, if you want it."

Daniel could have said no. He was supposed to be in the Bay for the rest of the year, and even without his father at home, he had work to do, research to analyze, a senior thesis to write. When the new year came, he would go back to UCLA, begin the last few months of his senior year, wait to hear back from med schools. It was what he had wanted. He had planned it all out. "What will you be doing there?" he asked.

"Do you want to know?"

"No," he said.

"Then how about this," she said. "We'll pay too much for ice skating at Rockefeller Center, or get Chinese food in Flushing, or go to Korea-town for late-night karaoke."

"Is that the truth?"

"It's part of it."

Daniel closed his eyes. *If they're good enough,* his dad had said, *they won't get caught.* Tomorrow his dad would board a flight for Norway, investigate a crime that, for once, the five of them did not commit. It might have been permission.

"I won't help you," he said. He rose, thinking of glass, of bones, of all the things that broke. It felt like so long since he'd seen this crew. "But I'll come."

52

ALEX

Winter fell quickly, viciously, turning the air biting and cold. Alex Huang took her last meeting of the day from her childhood bedroom, noise-canceling headphones on to prevent the sounds of the city from seeping in.

This was how the weeks had passed. Silicon Valley as the days grew shorter, shadows stretching across her empty apartment, work a continuous, unending line of code, meetings that she entered and left without ever knowing what they were about. A call from the hospital while she was half asleep, her grandma's stroke in those early morning hours. *Come home,* her mom had said, *before you don't need to anymore.*

Alex, for a brief, terrible moment, had felt relief.

She had flown to New York the next day, asked to work from home for the rest of the year. They had said yes, of course. How could they not?

Alex thought back to late November, Irene on the other end of the line. Alex had been in this same house, had closed her eyes when she said, voice breaking, *I can't go back to the way things were.* It had flayed her open like only the truth could.

Then don't, Irene had said.

Alex wished she had told her it wasn't that easy. The world did not yield for her the way it did for Irene. But she was in New York, not Silicon Valley, and she was searching for a way out.

Her laptop lit up.

Irene was video calling her.

Alex rested her head in her hands, just for a moment. She didn't know if she could do this again. She was coming apart at the edges, and Irene had always demanded more.

She took a deep breath and accepted the call.

All these weeks, and she had almost forgotten the contemptuous red of Irene's mouth, the perfect sweep of her black eyeliner. Alex swallowed hard. "What is it?"

Irene raised a brow. In the background, Alex saw the Boston skyline, the silver of the Charles River. And of course Irene would be there, a reminder of everything Alex might want and never have. "Did you miss me?"

"*Please,*" Alex said. Her life was easier without Irene in it. Still, she almost felt relieved to see her again. Irene, whatever else she brought with her, always promised change. "Why are you calling?" she asked.

Irene's gaze swept over Alex, deliberate enough that, even through the video, Alex found it hard to meet her eyes. "What would you say," she said, "if I told you we were going to rob the Met?"

"You're joking."

If Alex didn't know better, she would've sworn a smile flickered over Irene's face. "I think you know that I'm not."

"Why?"

A brief pause, almost imperceptible. "Will's interviewing there next week."

"That's not enough time."

"We've done this before."

"We've gotten caught before."

"No," Irene said, "we haven't."

There was truth in both their statements. Daniel's father had found them out. Daniel's father had kept his silence. And Irene and Alex—they had deleted anything that might incriminate them.

"We don't have any of our files," Alex said.

Irene raised a brow. "You don't need to lie to me, Alex."

"What are you talking about?"

Irene laced her hands together, expectant. "You don't have a saved copy somewhere?"

Alex thought back to that November evening. Irene's call had woken her up in the middle of the night. She had gotten out of bed, opened her computer, the light washing her bedroom in blue. Everything had felt like a dream. Walking Irene through the steps of breaking into Mr. Liang's computer, watching everything they'd done vanish on her open laptop. Of course she had saved their work. How could she not?

Today marked one year since she had left MIT for a job in tech. This crew, these thefts—it had been the first time she had felt like she could be something better, something more.

A few clicks, and there they were. All their files, their notes, the research they had spent two months collecting. Heist movies, art history books, security system manuals. Alex skimmed her hands over her laptop keyboard, thinking of piano keys, of performances, of what it might feel like to do this one last time.

"How did you know?" Alex asked.

"Maybe I know you better than you think," Irene said, her gaze never leaving Alex's. And then she shrugged, quick and effortless. "Or maybe it was just what I would do."

"We aren't the same," Alex said. Still, she couldn't bring herself to look away from Irene. Once, they had talked of power. That was Irene, now and always, so certain in who she would become. Alex had hated her for it. She might hate her still.

"I know," Irene said easily. This time, her smile was softer, more true. It could have stripped Alex to the bone. "I'll see you soon."

⁓

It all happened very quickly. Years ago, Alex might have been embarrassed to bring friends over, to have them in the small apartment over Yi Hua Lou, the sounds of Chinatown loud and demanding behind their flimsy wooden door. She didn't mind now. She shepherded her siblings into her own room, arranged for Irene and Lily to share her sister's room while Will and Daniel took her brother's, and through a series of elaborate promises—no, she couldn't *guarantee* Instagram verification, but yes, she would talk to her friend there; it just didn't seem right that she had to do that and help with this AP Computer Science project, but *fine*, just sleep on the couch—no one complained. In the mornings, when the restaurant opened, her friends went to the kitchen, helped set tables and welcome guests, and when evening fell, they planned this final heist.

And then, somehow, there were three days left.

Alex was up before the sun rose, the noise of the restaurant soft and muted this early. She had planned on setting up, but her mom was leaning against the wall, arms crossed. "Go see your grandmother," she said. "It's been long enough."

Alex knew it was true. She had been home for almost two weeks now, and she had avoided the hospital. Her childhood had been this restaurant her grandparents had opened, the knowledge that no matter what changed, wherever she went, she could always come back here. Slowly, carefully, she filled up two tote bags. One with Chinese food, still warm, the other with fruit from the vendors outside. She would not go empty-handed.

Irene was waiting for her at the door. Alex hesitated. "What are you doing here?"

"Your mom asked me to go with you," Irene said easily. Alex turned, and her mom was standing at the entrance to the kitchen, gesturing at them to go. "I figured I was awake anyway."

"You don't have to do this."

Irene examined her. "My grandparents are in China. It's a privilege to be able to see them so often." It should have sounded critical. Still, Irene's face was open, searching, and whatever else there was, Alex didn't want to go alone.

"Fine," she said. "Let's go."

They took the 6 train up, from Canal all the way to 96th, and it was almost easy to talk to Irene about a childhood in the city, all the history that was hers. Diaspora meant something different to all of them, but for Alex it was Chinatown and the places that surrounded it, her parents and grandparents and this life they had built.

At Mount Sinai Hospital, Alex pressed a hand to the door of the hospital room. Her grandmother was inside, her eyes closed, surrounded by machines that Alex didn't know. Alex could see her hands folded together over the hospital sheet, the sweep of her hair against the white pillow, the steady rise and fall of her chest.

"Alex," Irene said softly.

Alex looked away. She had thought she had gotten used to these hospitalizations after the first time, and yet it was always a new hurt to see her grandma here instead of in the restaurant she had built, that she had named for harmony and for home.

"I can't go inside," Alex said. Her voice was a whisper. She had in the past. And yet—how to explain this? Growing up, she had known some things to be true. History was her grandparents' journey to America, the years spent creating a piece of home within Yi Hua Lou's carefully painted walls. It was her parents working in the kitchen when her grandpa died, when her grandma's hands had trembled too much to cook. It was Alex, the oldest, her own journey to MIT, to everything after, all that she had made possible. They had all come so far.

If she pulled this off—if this last, impossible heist actually *worked*—this weight might not be hers alone to bear. She could quit her job, find something new, some place where her code might matter at last. She could go back to school.

But if this went wrong, she would bring her whole family down with her.

"Alex," Irene said again, and Alex looked up. Her voice—it was almost gentle. "You don't have to go in yet. Go for a walk. Get some water. She'll be here when you get back."

Alex nodded.

When she came back, she hesitated at the door. It was cracked open, just a little, and Irene was already inside. And so it was like this: Alex's popo and her trembling hands, the unyielding, insistent glare of the fluorescent lights, the low-level murmur of the machines keeping her alive. And Irene, her head bowed, singing Communist songs in her clear voice, though Alex didn't know how she could have ever known them. Irene sang of the red east, of Mao rising, of all the things she didn't believe in, as Alex's grandma drifted into sleep.

Alex pushed the door open.

Irene looked up.

It was easier now that her grandma was asleep, now that Alex did not have to face all the ways she might fail her family. She knelt at her grandma's side, took one of her hands. "Popo," she said, softly, "I'm sorry I didn't come earlier."

The rest—if this had been another time, Alex would have cared that Irene was here, that she was listening to her spill all her hurt. But Alex traced the veins of her grandma's hands, told her all the things she hadn't been able to while her grandma was awake. Her fears, her grief, how it felt like she might collapse beneath the weight of everything she could not be. "I'm afraid," she said. "Afraid of how this will go wrong, of all the ways I might fail our family. But it's not just that." She closed her eyes, took a long, shuddering breath. It had been so long since she had been happy. With her job, with her life, with the choices she'd made. "I don't know," she said. "I'm afraid that even if this succeeds, it won't be enough. I don't remember how to live anymore."

And then, when there was nothing left to say, nothing left to confess, Irene's hand touched Alex's shoulder. "Come on," she said. "Let's get something to eat."

"We have work to do," Alex said. They had just three days left. It did not feel like long enough.

"It can wait," Irene said.

They took the train back down, got off at Canal. They walked through Chinatown, and at some point Irene slipped her hand in Alex's. The sky was a flat, slate gray, the gray of smoothed-over asphalt, of grief, and Alex shivered, just a little, through her coat. A lifetime in the city, and she had never grown accustomed to the weather, how the winters here could strip you to the bone. Still, it was better like this, her insides turned out, any sadness left dissipating among the smoke and the snow and the sky.

They went to a dumpling place on Grand Street, the kind that only took cash, and Irene paid for them both. The tables were pressed up against the glass, and the restaurant was crowded enough that her shoulder touched Irene's, that she could feel the other girl's warmth through her coat. They didn't speak as they ate, just broke apart chopsticks and passed sauces, the silence almost easy. It was a relief not to be talking about the hospital, about the heist, about all the things that might go wrong in Alex's life. For now, there was just this.

"Thank you," Alex said softly. Their plates were empty. They had no reason left to stay.

"Don't," Irene said. She was quiet for a moment, her gaze on the frosted glass. Outside, New York City was quick, alive, waiting for them. "We don't have to be this way, Alex."

Three months of this, of late nights and arguments and never being on the same side. Sometimes Alex was certain she hated Irene. Other times she thought of Irene across from her on a Paris morning, her features softer without the makeup she wore like armor, the practiced knife of her smile. For a moment, Alex had had the urge to brush her thumb against the curve of the other girl's cheek, press her fingers to the hollow of her throat.

She swallowed hard. This had to be hatred. She would not allow it to be anything else. Not when they still had this last impossible job to pull off, when Irene had always looked at her with ice in her gaze and a voice meant to cut her open.

"What else could we be?" she asked. Somehow it was hard to speak.

Irene caught her gaze, held it. "Anything you want."

53

WILL

I t was a clear, perfect morning, and Will Chen stood at the steps of the Met, took in high stone columns and curved glass windows, those iconic red banners. For years, he had dreamed of this place. Every great artist, wherever they came from, always ended up at the Met.

He adjusted his tie, checked his leather portfolio for his résumé one final time. There were moments that, even as they happened, you knew would *matter*. This was one of them, standing on the museum steps, his future waiting inside. Months ago, this would have been all he ever wanted.

Will took a deep, steadying breath and walked inside.

⸻

The interview went like any other. He talked about working at the Sackler Museum, research in Harvard's East Asian art program, the graduate-level coursework he had completed. He talked about his admiration of the Met's collections, the Chinese brushwork he had seen for the first time when he visited the Met. It was all true. There was so much that was lovely about this place, this art. The interview was only supposed to go on for an hour, but it went longer. It would have been easy to forget why he was here, to think only about art and what it meant, how this museum was history unto itself.

And then, at the end of his interview, Will stood, smiled at his interviewer. "Thank you so much," he said, and meant it. He hesitated. "If possible—would you mind giving me a tour of the restoration rooms? I feel like there's so much of the Met I haven't seen before."

They didn't typically give tours. But Will was smiling, clear and guileless, and he had come all this way for an interview and an opportunity.

Of course she said yes.

His interviewer badged in, the light flashing green and temporary as the door unlocked. "Can you tell me more about how the Met's collection of Chinese art began?" he asked. He had practiced these questions before, run through them with Irene and Lily to ensure that nothing he asked was too targeted.

"Of course," she said. "We try to choose art that will accurately capture the history of the Chinese empire, vast as it is . . ."

He held the door open for her as she talked, kept it open as someone else fumbled for their badge, and then they were inside. He was no longer paying attention. They walked through rooms where conservators were bent over Chinese calligraphy, their motions slow and deliberate, the overhead lighting soft against the brushstrokes. There were sculptures, jade and stone and bronze, and Will's gaze lingered on those. The dragon zodiac head wasn't here, of course, but there was other art that might have belonged to the Old Summer Palace too.

Tomorrow they would take it back.

Lily was waiting for him at the entrance to the Chinese art gallery. She was reading a placard, her face in profile, and if this had been three months ago, he would have held this image in his head, painted it with cool colors and the slash of morning light, thought it was enough. What else was there besides beautiful girls and moments that could never last?

Now he cleared his throat, waited for her to look up. This wasn't a date. Still, he felt almost—nervous. "Hey," he said.

Her smile was quick. "Hey."

"How was your tour of the museum?"

"I was mostly looking at the security cameras," Lily said, and he couldn't quite tell if she was joking. "How was the interview?"

"Done with," he said. His interviewer had liked him, but it didn't matter. Regardless of whether they pulled off this heist, he didn't think he'd get the job. He didn't think he wanted it. He held an arm out. "Walk with me?"

It might have been that they were cast in the low light of a museum gallery, that this place felt like it was out of another time. It might have been that they were in New York, and tomorrow they would rob the place they were standing in. Whatever the reason, Lily looped her arm through his. The glass reflected them: Will in his gray suit, light glinting off the frames of his glasses; Lily in a cream blouse and the slightest touch of makeup on her bare face. They were both dressed a little nicer than usual.

"Are you going to tell me about the Met's history?" she asked, her voice teasing.

Will had asked his interviewer almost that same question. He smiled quick. "Only if you want."

They didn't end up walking through the Chinese art gallery. There was no reason to, not when they would be back tomorrow. Instead they walked slowly, leisurely, through the rest of the museum, until they arrived at the Temple of Dendur. The Egyptian temple was the most iconic location in the Met, the place that appeared in photos and postcards, and he had saved it for last. He knew its history, of course. It was one of the rare items that had come to the US not by theft or conquest, but by gift. But looking at it now, he saw only the sandstone as it caught the winter light, a piece of the past brought close enough to touch. This hall, with its floor-to-ceiling windows, its wide, empty space around the temple, was large enough that even now, at midday, it felt like they were the only two people there.

"What do you think?" he asked. Lily had told him, back in Boston, that she had never been to the Met. This felt like a promise fulfilled.

Her smile was wide. "I'm going to walk around," she said, and this was how art should be appreciated, up close, nothing but truth and open air. "Want to come?"

He shook his head. This exhibit always gave him a sense of quiet, of peace, and so while Lily explored the temple, he sat at one of the benches near the windows, took out his portfolio, and flipped to a blank page. He sketched the temple first, in quick, certain lines, and then built the rest of the exhibit out. The fall of pale light, the wavering edges of the reflecting pool. Lily, as she walked around the temple, as she leaned forward to examine the reliefs carved on cool sandstone.

He had thought once that this was all he wanted. To hold beauty in his hands, to have four years where he could be careless with his time, his love. What did it matter when it would all end? But tomorrow they would rob the Met. No matter what came after, he did not want this to be an ending.

When Lily came back, he was done. He closed his sketchbook, tucked it beneath his arm. He'd shown her his art before. He had sent her a picture of the sketch of her he'd done on their flight, thought nothing of it when he did. He had spent all of college like this, tracing the curve of parted lips, the hollow of a throat tilted up.

This time, it felt different.

Lily's gaze flickered to his sketchbook, but she didn't say anything. "Should we head back?" she asked.

He rose. "Let's."

And so they left the Met, without sirens or alarms or any or the things that might come tomorrow, walked down Fifth Avenue on that bright, cold winter day. Will bought them both halal food from a cart near Central Park, and they ate at one of the benches beneath the trees, the chill seeping in through their coats, tried very hard not to spill on their nice clothes. When they took the train back, Lily leaned her head against his shoulder, and Will thought of months ago, a flight to Stockholm and the two of them side by side as the plane cut through a vast, dark sky.

This could be a love story yet, he had said. He hadn't meant it then.

Now Will looked at Lily, her features soft despite the unforgiving fluorescent light of the train, and did not think of art but of how she had smiled at him this morning at the Met, all the ways she made the impossible feel closer. When this heist was over, if they could pull this off—he brushed a strand of her hair from her face, thought of what this might become.

54

ALEX

And then, somehow, it was the night before the heist. Alex Huang had spent the whole day on her laptop, sifting through the Met's security, but now it was a Friday evening and Chinatown was humming with color and sound. Dinner had been in the apartment, Daniel cooking for the five of them, Alex's siblings banished downstairs as they planned out these last details.

"This might be your last night of freedom," Daniel observed. He set plates down on the table, laid out wooden chopsticks. They could have brought food upstairs from Yi Hua Lou, but Alex had known that would result in conversation, time lost that they couldn't afford. Daniel had cooked instead, and there were eggs with tomato, thinly shredded potato slivers, a whole steamed fish, all of it made with meticulous attention to detail. Daniel had been here this whole week, looked over their shoulders while they had planned for this job, made slight, careful adjustments, but when tomorrow came, he wouldn't walk through the Met's doors.

Alex would take his place.

Beneath the table, she pressed trembling hands against her thighs. For all that she had argued with Irene about this weeks ago, there was a difference between watching something unfold behind her computer screen and knowing that she would be there, in an empty museum, the bronze dragon head winking at her in the darkness.

"I hope you're wrong," Irene said. "But in case you aren't"—she smiled quick—"let's do something tonight."

And so, after dinner, they ended up in Koreatown, at a karaoke place that Alex knew, and when Irene smiled at the server, he brought them three bottles of soju with no charge. The lights were dim, flashing, and Alex sorted through the songs, added them to the queue. The night might have been out of a dream.

Later Alex would remember it only in pieces. The darkness of the room illuminated only by the glow of the karaoke screen, the multi-colored lights that spun around and around. Music sung loudly and off-key, soju that tasted of something sharp and sweet. And then—Irene, all angles and cheekbones in the low light, her lips brushing the mic as she sang, *Got a girl with California eyes / and I thought that she could really be the one this time / but I never got the chance to make her mine.*

The bass was a low, steady beat, the kind that Alex could feel in her bones. There was more to the song, but this was what Alex remembered: Irene's voice, clear and perfect, her gaze meeting Alex's for just a moment. Alex, as always, looked away first. She didn't want to see how the hazy light touched Irene's face like a promise, the curve of her eyeliner like wings. She had always found Irene beautiful. That was the worst part about it.

⁓

It was cold outside. Alex didn't care. The air smelled like cigarettes, like alcohol, and she leaned against the wall, tried to pull herself together.

Past midnight, K-Town was all flashing lights, karaoke bars and night-clubs, and late-night Korean food.

"Hey," Daniel said. He moved to stand next to her, and she shifted over. Neither of them was wearing their coat. "You good? You were gone a while."

Alex kept her gaze on the street, the incandescent red of the stop-lights and the traffic that, even at this hour, never quite died. "I don't know," she said. This night could have stripped her raw.

"Are you thinking about tomorrow?" he asked.

"No," she said. She should have been. For this to work, so much rested on her shoulders. And yet—Alex wrapped her arms around herself, her mind on a smoky karaoke room, everything that the darkness brought closer.

Quiet, brief, and tentative. "There's something about nights like these," Daniel said at last, "that always makes me want the impossible."

"Like what?"

He could have been talking about so many things. These heists, the future they promised. The five of them, different as they were, all knew what it meant to have greatness expected of them. Even then, they still might not be enough.

But Daniel's arms were crossed, the changing light casting shadows on his face, and she thought he might be thinking of something else too. When he spoke, his voice was soft. "When Irene sings," he said, "it's like I forget everything I've ever known."

Alex looked at him. If she had been paying attention, she would have noticed it before, how whenever he made a joke he looked first at her, the way his mouth softened when he said her name. "You love her," Alex said, and it was a realization a long time coming.

Daniel looked at her. She had never noticed before—the way the light cut across his jawline, the brush of his lashes in the artificial light. His gaze was searching. *You hate her*, he might have said. He had been there, after all, when they had fought in Beijing, in Stockholm, in Paris, all those weeks when Alex looked at Irene and saw everything that she wasn't.

"So do you," he said.

Alex looked away. She could have denied it. But it was late and cold and the two of them were outside a karaoke bar, in love with the same girl, and what was the point?

What else could we be?

Anything you want.

Alex closed her eyes, let out a shaky breath. "We have a heist tomorrow," Alex said. She didn't know what else to say. "There are more important things."

"We're twenty-one and in New York City," Daniel said. He tipped his head back. Above them were streetlights and flashing K-Town signs, the distant, forgotten stars. "What could be more important than this?"

And it was true. The whole world felt concentrated to this, winter air and the brush of cold light, the two of them shivering next to each other. Three months, and when Alex looked at Irene, she knew, with a terrible and startling clarity, how much she wanted and could never have.

Alex wrapped her arms tighter around herself. When she spoke, her breath curled up and into the night air. "Where do we go from here?"

Daniel glanced at her, his smile quick and almost easy. "Inside, probably."

Alex laughed. "Does this mean we're still friends?"

"When all this began," Daniel said, and his voice was softer, more serious, "I told Irene I would let go. All these years, and I'm still figuring out how."

"I'm sorry," Alex said.

"Don't be," he said. "Whatever happens tomorrow—I spent so long holding on to the past. It's time to move forward."

Alex thought of these past few months, of New York and Silicon

Valley and all that tied her to these places, all that this job might break clean. If Daniel could leave the past behind, she might be able to too. She took one more breath of cold, bright air. Tomorrow would come so soon.

It was not here yet.

"Come on," Alex said, and caught his wrist. His skin was warm against hers. "Let's go inside."

55

LILY

The night went like this. Low, changing light, songs that slipped effort-lessly into the next, lyrics set against nonsensical backdrops. Lily Wu leaned against the leather couch, listening to Will as he sang in Chinese, his voice low and lovely in the soft, dreamlike dark. It was the last song of the night, and the lyrics were familiar, a fairy tale.

He held out his hand. It might have been a challenge. She took it, and he spun her around, his hand guiding hers, until they were close enough that his arm was wrapped around her waist.

Lily lifted her head up, met his gaze. In the background, the piano was slow, tentative, lingering on those final notes, and Lily thought of stories and how they unfolded, how words always felt softer in this language like a forgotten country. "Do you think," she said, "you're the first guy to try and impress me?"

She had been expecting him to laugh, to brush it off. Instead he dipped her, his hand pressed against her back. This close, his eyes were dark, reflective, the shadows tracing his cheekbones, the curve of his mouth. She could feel the heat of his skin, the barest suggestion of space between them, and she shivered. Tomorrow they would rob the Met. There would be a museum in the dark, the gleam of a car against slick Manhattan streets, the future unraveling before them, but tonight there was just Will, his fingers spread along the small of her back and his gaze steady and certain in a way that she was not used to. He leaned close, his mouth brushing the shell of her ear. "Maybe," he said, soft enough that only she could hear, "I'd rather be the last."

It was a relief when the song came to a close, when the lights came on. Their time was up. Will released her, and Lily reached for her coat. It didn't mean anything, she knew.

For the first time, she wondered if she wanted it to.

Lily couldn't fall asleep. Moonlight, pale and silver, fell through the window, touched Irene's sleeping figure, the lines of the bed frame, the desk, everything that was made new in the careful dark. She was thinking about tomorrow, about this heist, about everything that could go wrong. And she was thinking, too, about Will, about a karaoke bar in the hazy light and all that she *wanted*.

Soon this would all be over.

She rose.

Warm light spilled through the crack beneath Will's door, and Lily knocked before she could change her mind.

A few seconds later, Will opened the door. "Lily," he said. He didn't sound surprised. "Come in."

They had done this so many times before. Plane flights, late-night text conversations, a Harvard studio beneath the early-morning light. Daniel wasn't in the room, and Will leaned against the desk, his gaze steady on hers.

"I've been thinking," Lily said.

"About?"

"Art." In the low light, he could have been a study in portraiture. She didn't know anything about art, but she knew him. The angles of his face, that slow, careful smile, all his fears and his wants.

"Really," he said, and it was a question.

She leaned against the opposite wall. Tomorrow, tomorrow, tomorrow. It had all come to this. "What were you drawing at the Met?" she asked.

His gaze flickered away. Lily thought back to that quiet morning, the two of them walking through the museum's halls. Will, his head bent over a sketchbook, the morning light crowning his dark hair. He looked at her now the same way, his gaze soft and searching. She was not sure what he was looking for. "Do you want to see?" he asked.

Lily nodded.

His motions were slow, careful, as he crossed the room, as he pulled a sketchbook from his backpack. He handed it to her, looked away as she flipped it open. A muscle moved beneath his jaw.

There she was, in profile, hand reaching out. Another of her, months ago. The lines captured the pale blue light of the plane, her lashes brushing against her cheeks as she slept on his shoulder. It would have been right before they had robbed Drottningholm Palace.

"Will," she said.

He looked up.

Lily stepped forward. Slowly, carefully, she traced his cheekbone with her fingertips, followed the line of his jaw up until her hand was in his hair. "Lily," he sighed.

"I think," she said, her voice soft, "it's been long enough." It was the night before their final heist, and she wanted to tangle her fingers through Will's dark hair, feel his breath against her skin. What else was there besides this?

"It has, hasn't it?" he said. He curved his hand around her waist, his skin warm through the thin fabric of her T-shirt. His face was so close to hers. "What do you want, Lily?"

"The same thing you do," she said. She thought of months ago, Stockholm and the two of them beneath the glow of a streetlight, how easily his hand had fit in hers. She had pulled him to her, had let go. All her excuses no longer mattered, not tonight. They were in New York City, and anything was possible. She took a step closer. "I don't care if this doesn't last."

"Lily," he said again. He was very still. "I *do*."

Lily hesitated. "What?"

"I mean," he said. He swallowed hard, and Lily could have sworn that was a blush rising to his cheeks. "This—" He swept his hand across the room, at the sketchbook on his bed. "This *means* something to me. You are—I don't want just—oh, *fuck this*—you *mean something to me*."

Lily blinked. *Girls break themselves trying to change him*, Irene had said once. Slowly, carefully, she thought of these past few months, plane flights and his voice in the quiet dark, the sketches he had made of her when she hadn't been paying attention. She had been so certain that this was pretend. If it wasn't—

It had been three months, and she had never let herself think about it. She knew Will, how easily he flirted, how little it meant. It hadn't *mattered* to her. They were in college, after all, and neither of them was looking for forever. But he was standing here, so close to her, and his ragged breath was the only sound in the stillness. Outside the apartment window, New York City spun on.

There were so many ways they could break each other's heart.

"Lily?" Will said. His voice was soft, hesitant.

Lily looked up at him, wondering. She could have stayed, she knew. Part of her even wanted to. But they had one last job to do, and she didn't know how it would end. Still, as she pushed open the door, she thought of just hours ago, how Will had dipped her in a dark room, spoken of what might last. His hands tracing these sketches of her, the light changing in each one. What would it feel like to get everything she ever wanted?

"Ask me again tomorrow," she said, "when this is over."

She didn't go back to her room. She was too awake for that, didn't want to lie in the dark and think about everything Will had said. If this had been home, she would have gone outside, stood before the sea and the depths of the sky. Everything else felt small when the Gulf of Mexico was spread before you, the waves vanishing into a dark, distant horizon. Instead she went to the kitchen to pour herself a glass of water, let the tap run for longer than it should. Her skin still felt too warm.

Daniel was sitting at the table, his laptop open and a notebook by his side. There was a stack of folders next to him.

"You're up late," she said.

With his foot, he pushed out a chair for her, slid her a folder. "So are you."

She flipped it open. It was a relief to be working again, even at this hour, to think about something other than Will, his mouth almost on hers, the heat of his hand against her back. She had thought she knew what she wanted, had convinced herself that it wasn't him.

They worked in silence for a while. Lily read through reports about the Met's security protocols, police response times in New York City, highlighted, swapped with Daniel. He was easy to work with. They had the same careful, meticulous approach.

Why cars? he'd asked her once.

Why people? she'd replied.

It was not quite the same thing. But he'd laughed, and everything after had been easy.

"What do you think?" he asked.

She looked it over. In less than twenty-four hours, Will, Irene, and Alex would be in the Met. It would be just her and Daniel left to pick up the pieces.

The light was harsh, fluorescent, as it fell on the two of them, this empty room. "They're going to get caught," she said.

Daniel's voice was soft. "I know."

56

DANIEL

Daniel Liang stayed at the kitchen table for a long time after that. One by one, the rest of the house went to bed, shut off lights, until it was just him and a window that opened to the city lights, the glow of his laptop screen. He thought of hours ago, karaoke and how the world had felt wide-open, waiting.

In a few months, he would graduate. There would be a stadium, open air in the LA summer, a diploma that bore his name. Beijing would come after, those streets that always felt like home, and then with the fall would be somewhere new. Medical school and the beginning of the rest of his life.

He thought of his conversation with Alex, how they had talked of letting go. Whichever way this heist went, he would lose something.

Daniel rested his head against his hand. Why did it always come to this? His father, his friends, his past, his future. He could not tell any of them apart.

Then he picked up his phone. It rang once, twice, three times, and he imagined signals running along wires like synapses, the fire of neurons in the heavy dark. In the end, this was all they were: bone and marrow and electricity. It would be early morning in Norway. He closed his eyes, imagined a pale lavender sky, the color of a new bruise, his father drawing the curtains open. Once, he had asked Lily how she was so sure her parents loved her if they were so rarely home, if they did not say it in as many words. She had looked at him, her gaze steady and searching. *Because*, she had said, *no matter how busy they are, they always pick up when I call.*

"Hello?" his dad said.

"Ba," Daniel said. He closed his eyes. He did not know how to say this, how to put it in a way that would not carve him open, spill blood and old hurt. *If they're good enough, they won't get caught.* The five of them—they had never been good enough to get away with this. Part of him had known it all along. "You need to come back."

57

WILL

The moon was silver as a coin. Will Chen stood at the intersection of 77th and Fifth, Lily's car parked in an alley, emergency lights blinking steadily. The forecast had promised snow, but an hour before dawn the air was only cold, the sky cloudless. He looked at his crew. Lily in the front seat, her gaze steady as it met his. Daniel next to her. Irene and Alex were on either side of Will, waiting for his signal.

"Ready?" he asked Alex.

"Wait," Daniel said. His window was rolled down, and he reached out, caught Will's wrist. "Exactly as we planned."

In the darkness, Will turned his hand until he was gripping Daniel's wrist too, the motion almost a handshake. Ten years, and Daniel was the closest to a brother he had ever had.

"I will," he said.

He looked past Daniel, caught Lily's eye. "Remember," he said, "if we pull this off, you owe me a date."

"I won't forget," she said.

"If I go to jail, you have to wait for me."

Lily laughed. "Don't go to jail, Will."

"I can't make any promises," he said, but he was smiling too. He rose, looked at Irene and Alex.

"Whenever you are," Alex said.

He nodded.

She didn't have a laptop with her. She didn't have anything except an empty backpack, a phone, her smartwatch. Like the rest of them, she was dressed like this was any other night. She turned her watch face to catch the light, tapped twice.

For a moment, nothing happened.

And then, like dominoes falling, the emergency lights of the Met shut off one by one. He didn't ask how she did it. He wasn't sure he wanted to know. He just knew that they strode up the empty steps of the Met, the security cameras shutting off around them, and pushed open the unlocked doors. It was the kind of risk that they never would have taken in a foreign country, but here, in New York City on a cold winter morning, anything felt possible. There was no smashing of glass, no sound at all, just the whistling of the winter wind, the soft *swoosh* of the doors beneath his hands.

Inside, the Met was all neoclassical architecture, columns that gleamed bone white in the moonlight. To anyone else, its corridors would have been a labyrinth, but Will led them through the galleries, eerily silent save for the sound of their footsteps, their path lit only by the swing of their phone flashlights in the dark.

And then they were in the Chinese art gallery, the carpet dampening any sound. Will lifted his phone, walked slowly and deliberately up to the dragon zodiac head. He was born in the year of the dragon. Their last heist was always going to be this one. He couldn't help but think it meant something.

He reached his hand out, brushed it against the glass. The dragon head was almost close enough to touch. This close, he could make out each of its bared teeth, the lines of its whiskers. He knew how these sculptures were made now, of stone and careful chisel and bronze that melted in high heat. It felt like a lesson. This was how you survived the flames. This was how you made it out.

He might have been there for seconds or minutes when a familiar voice said, *"Freeze."*

Suddenly, the exhibit was awash with light.

Will closed his eyes, let out a long, slow breath. When he opened his eyes again, they were surrounded, the light harsh and demanding. What had he expected? He didn't know.

He lifted his empty hands, held them up.

⁓

"State your name for the record, please."

This was how things came to an end: New York City and the falling snow, handcuffs that were cool and silver around Will's exposed wrists.

"Will Chen," he said, and it was an exhale.

"And what were you doing at the Metropolitan Museum of Art, Mr. Chen?"

This might have happened before. But this time, there was no excuse. It was just past dawn, the sky a pale, uncertain blue, the snow falling steadily as the sun rose. He could see it even here in this empty conference room, repurposed for Mr. Liang's investigation. "I was in the neighborhood," he said, "and the door was unlocked."

Mr. Liang leaned across the table, and Will remembered the last time he had seen Daniel's father. *If you do this again, I will catch you.* "Do you expect me to believe that?"

"If you look at my record, Agent Liang, you'll see that I have no criminal history, I've never been arrested, I've never even gotten a *speeding ticket*—"

"I know that," Mr. Liang said, because of course he did, because he was Daniel's father, because Will looked at this man and saw his childhood. Mr. Liang shut off the recorder, the red light blinking off.

"Jiatao," he said. He pressed his hands to his temples. "What do you expect me to do here?"

"Nothing," Will said, and it was the truth. There was nothing left for Mr. Liang to do. He laced his hands together, the motion pulling at his handcuffs. The sound they made was loud, jangling, and Mr. Liang winced.

"Breaking and entering," he said, counting off their crimes, "theft on multiple counts. This isn't a joke. This is the end of your *life*."

"There was technically no breaking," Will said softly. "Just the entering. And there was no theft either."

"Was there going to be?" Mr. Liang asked.

Will looked down. He thought of this museum in the cold winter light, all that the West had taken and displayed. Art and conquest. They had always been one and the same.

Mr. Liang shook his head. "Don't answer that. I don't want to know."

"I'm sorry," Will said. Of everything he had said, all the ways he had brushed this off, he meant it. He had never wanted Daniel's dad to be involved. They all knew what family meant, how hard it was to hold on to. "I didn't want it to be you."

"It was always going to be," Mr. Liang said. He sighed. "Explain this to me, Will. I'm afraid I still don't understand the *why* of it."

"You're Chinese," Will said. "Isn't it obvious?"

"But you aren't," Mr. Liang said, and it was a quiet, terrible grief to hear that, even though Will knew it was true. China's history was his parents' history, but it was not his. Not fully, not in the way that it was Mr. Liang's, that it was Daniel's. "It's not a bad thing, Jiatao."

"I know," Will said.

Mr. Liang laced his hands together, his expression pensive. "Let me tell you this," he said. "Ten years in this country, and when I speak to strangers, they will always ask me where I'm from."

"Does it bother you?"

"No," he said. "I'm proud to be from China. But you—you were born here. This place is yours. Why would you want to take from it?"

Will closed his eyes, leaned back in his chair. He thought of months ago, the Sackler in the fall, how this had all begun. He thought of a bridge in Paris, Zhao Min and an outstretched hand. *I hope you find what you're looking for*, he said.

"I've lived my whole life here," Will said softly, "and I get asked the same question. I want to think that I'm Chinese and American *both*, but depending on the country, I feel like I'm not enough of either. But then there was this, and it felt like these sculptures, this art—" He shrugged, lightly, his gaze on the window, the falling snow. "It might mean something, if I could bring them home."

Mr. Liang was silent for a long moment. "These sculptures have always belonged to China," he said. "Wherever they are, they will always be ours. We know it in our hearts."

"Is that enough?" Will asked.

Mr. Liang rose. He didn't meet Will's eyes. "I have more interviews to do," he said. "I'll be back soon."

58

IRENE

This seems like a lot to go through for trespassing," Irene said. She ran her finger along her wrist, the empty space where the handcuffs had been.

Mr. Liang sighed.

"Jiaqi," he said. "Please don't make this more difficult than it has to be."

She held out her wrists. "Fine," she said. "You can do it again."

He clasped the handcuffs on. "Can we begin?" he asked.

Irene leaned back, smiled wide for the security camera tucked in the corner of the room. "Yes," she said.

He pressed *record*, switched to English. "State your name for the record, please."

"Irene Chen."

"And what were you doing at the Metropolitan Museum of Art, Ms. Chen?"

Irene thought of Alex, in the other room, of weeks spent lying to themselves and to each other. *I'll have you exactly as you are.*

Pale winter light fell through the windows. What was left besides this?

"Trying to impress a girl," Irene said.

59

Alex

State your name for the record, please."

"Alex Huang."

Daniel's father took a long, slow breath. "And what were you doing at the Metropolitan Museum of Art, Ms. Huang?"

Alex thought of just hours ago, darkness washing over the museum. That was the thing about code. It was always easier to take something apart than to build something up. She had found a back route, rebooted the system. There were backups, of course, but they could be powered off too, one by one, until the Met was blacked out. It was supposed to give them ten minutes without cameras, without alarms, without anything standing in their way.

If she were Will or Irene, she might have had something clever to say. Instead she thought of all that they had risked for this last chance, of her parents waiting for her at Yi Hua Lou, of all the choices she had made to bring her here.

"I think you know," she said.

Mr. Liang's phone was vibrating.

He ignored it.

"You should get that," Alex said.

The sound was amplified in this empty room. They both looked at the phone as it moved across the table, the vibrations loud, demanding. He sighed, reached for it. "Hello?"

She could only hear one side of the conversation. Mr. Liang was silent for several moments, listening, and then he nodded, shut his recorder off. "Yes," he said into the phone, his brows drawing together. "Absolutely. I'll be right there."

"What is it?" Alex asked.

Daniel's father held her gaze. There was no accusation there, no anger. "I think you know," he said, and then he left the room.

60

WILL

Will Chen had spent all of college studying art history. He knew the artists of the Renaissance, the transition in technique from Romanticism to realism to art nouveau, all the ways art shifted form. But art history was museum history too, and he knew the stories of the Getty Museum, of the Met, of all the museums that had been accused of purchasing looted art, the museums that knew how to cover it up.

Stolen art always took the same path. A smuggler in a foreign country, art that was shipped across oceans. Forged papers, a curator who was willing to look the other way. *From a private collection in Europe*, the documents would say, and there would be no questions after that. He had seen it in the art at Drottningholm. History did not change. Thieves just got better at hiding.

When the news broke, he was still handcuffed. Mr. Liang came in, slid a *New York Times* printout across the table, and Will thought of three months ago, another detective doing the same thing with his article for the *Harvard Crimson*.

Museums Trafficking in Stolen Art, the headline read, and went on to list evidence. Email correspondence between the Met, its sister museums, all those great cultural strongholds of the Western world. Purchase records of art that had been illegally looted, not just from the Old Summer Palace but from all over the world.

That was not the new part.

The new part was that the museums *knew*. When they bought it, when they displayed it, they had known it had been smuggled out of Greece, Italy, China, an intricate network of smugglers and intermediaries and museum acquisitions teams, built over years and years. *What does it matter where it comes from*, one quote read, *as long as it's ours now?*

A history of colonialism laid bare, impossible to look away from.

"Is this your work?"

They might have come full circle. Will thought of that first article. *What is ours is not ours.* It was still true today. The detective had slid the papers across the table like an accusation.

"How could it be?" Will asked. "I've been *here*."

Mr. Liang looked at him. They both knew it was true. They also knew the facts: that the evidence this article drew from—emails, documents, more—had been stolen from this museum; that today the Met had been robbed, even if no art had been taken. That the whole time, Will, Irene, and Alex had been under the watch of the FBI.

Mr. Liang could have pressed him. There were other questions that Will did not know the answer to, that might peel back layers of his story like paint. But Mr. Liang looked at him, the corner of his mouth lifting into the slightest hint of a smile, before reaching out and unlocking the cuffs that kept him here. "Go home, Jiatao," he said. "Trespassing isn't a crime that warrants the FBI, and I suspect the Met has bigger issues to deal with right now than a few college kids running around after hours."

He rested his hand on Will's shoulder for just a moment before holding the door open.

Will walked through winding, empty halls, through the quiet of these early-morning hours, until at last he was outside. He tilted his head up to the falling snow, the clear blue sky.

61

LILY

ONE HOUR AGO

ily Wu dropped Will, Irene, and Alex at the steps of the Met. The night was clear, cold, and behind the wheel of the car, she turned to Daniel Liang, sitting by her side.

"Ready?" she asked.

His smile was quick. "Let's go," he said, and then she was pulling out of the alley, to one of the Met's many side entrances. The parking spot read *EMPLOYEES ONLY*. She ignored it.

Then they strode to the entrance. Lily pulled it open, the door turning easily beneath her gloved hands. The Met was dark, empty, though across the museum the rest of their crew would be making their way to the Chinese art gallery.

She did not think of that. Instead she followed the path that she had traced two days ago. At the end of Will's interview, he had asked for a tour. His interviewer had badged him in, and when he had stepped through that locked door, he had held it open for a second more. It had been so easy for Lily to slip through. She had been dressed like a curator, in a silky blouse and tapered pants, and she had moved through these restricted halls with an easy confidence that she had picked up from Irene. She had been there for only a few minutes, learning the layout of these halls, before leaving, and Alex had done what every hacker in a heist movie did, overriding the video feed with footage from the day before. To anyone else, she might never have been there at all.

Tonight, in the early dark, she and Daniel ran the same path, their footsteps soft in the stillness. The security guards were all on the way to the other end of the museum, where the FBI was waiting, and when they reached a locked door, Daniel knelt, drew out his lockpicks with easy confidence. He had done this before, she knew.

He angled his head toward the lock, adjusted the picks once, twice, three times, and then Lily heard the sound of pins falling, a soft click. They were not thieves, not really, but in this moment she could believe that they were.

Daniel opened the door.

The office was dark, silent. "Well?" Daniel asked. His voice was pitched low. Alex's power outage meant that the computer was shut off, the internet down. The Met's backup generator would turn on soon, but its priority would be to keep the HVAC running, to maintain the precious, temperature-controlled environment for the Met's art. Even if they had wanted to hack something, they couldn't have.

Lily tilted her head toward the desktop. "We're going to use that."

He raised a brow. "You want to take the *desktop*?"

"I'm a *mechanical* engineer," she said. "I know hardware, not software."

She knelt by the desktop, took out her pocketknife. Daniel held his phone light up, giving her something to work with, and she disassembled the computer case carefully, deliberately.

"Time?" she asked.

"Five minutes left," he said. "The FBI will have secured some Met offices to interrogate them by now."

"How do you know?" she asked.

"I know my dad," Daniel said. "He doesn't waste time."

And then she had the hard drive. She held it up to the light for just a moment, wondering—such a small thing, to hold so many secrets—and then she slipped a replacement into the computer case, set the real one safely in her pocket.

They had done what they came here to do.

By the time the Met's lights came back on, they were speeding down FDR Drive, the moon wavering over the water, a clean, straight shot toward Chinatown.

Back at the restaurant, Lily transferred the hard drive to her own computer, sent the data to Zhao Min and Liu Siqi on an encrypted browser. She wasn't Alex, but she knew technology well enough for *this*.

From there, it was easy. News organizations picked up when the new elite of Beijing called. Lily and Daniel stayed at the restaurant, helping Alex's parents serve food, ringing up customers, an alibi that could be corroborated by all of Chinatown, and at some point—neither of them could be sure when—the news broke.

Her phone was ringing. Will was calling her.

"Hello?" she said.

"Lily Wu," Will said, and she heard him smile, slow and confident, "how about that date?"

62

WILL

Will Chen leaned against the columns of the Met, breathed in the cold, bright December air. He was not ready to go back, not just yet. He still couldn't believe that he was here, that he had made it out. That they had pulled this off. There would be more later, he knew— follow-up questions from FBI agents who were not Daniel's father, questions about other museums and their missing art—but with so much happening, who would be surprised if that fell through the cracks? All these months, and they had never been caught.

Will thought back to that trip to Beijing, at the dawn of all that was to come, standing next to Lily before the Old Summer Palace. Everything had felt like art—the sun as it glanced off the ruins, the columns that might have been a part of a palace still. The girl standing next to him, lacquered in red light. Anything had seemed possible.

Wang Yuling was calling him.

He picked up, his mind still on Beijing, on the Old Summer Palace, on all the history that had brought him here. "Hello?"

"Congratulations," Yuling said. Her voice was crisp, certain, pleased. "All five zodiac heads are coming home. The Met, the KODE, and the British Museum have all reached out to us this morning with an apology and a public acknowledgment of our right to this art."

"That was fast," he said. He took in the Met and its red banners, the snow that fell over this museum, over New York City, over everything that felt like the world. The zodiac heads returned to China at last. It didn't feel quite real.

"Public pressure," she said. "They needed to do *something* to save face. And with two zodiac heads stolen already, they seemed to think it was only a matter of time. Safer to return them. Although—I suspect this was your plan all along."

The article had taken him hours. He had read it out loud to his sister, to Lily, sent it to Zhao Min and Liu Siqi for their edits. When the evidence from the Met arrived, while Will was still in handcuffs, Min and Siqi had added that in too—proof of what everyone knew but could never say before now. It was a story about the West, but it was also more than that. Art and empire, how those in power always took from those without. This was how things changed. With museums and shattered glass, history stolen back, but also the eyes of the world, the weight of expectation.

"Did you expect us to pull this off?" Will asked. "When it started, did you think it would work?"

Yuling was quiet for a long moment. "No," she said. She had switched to Chinese. It did not make this feel like any less of a dream. But the snow was still falling, and the wind was cold and bracing against his skin. What was real, if not this? "And never like this. But there are worse things than being wrong once in a while. Enjoy these fifty million dollars, Will. I hope you make something of it."

"It wasn't just us," Will said, because it was true, because he could still remember Zhao Min and Liu Siqi striding toward them on a Paris morning, the feeling that the world as he knew it was about to change shape yet again.

Yuling laughed. "I know," she said. "But I wouldn't dare offend Siqi and Min by offering them *money*. For them—for us—it has always been about more than that."

That Will could understand. Still, he tried to imagine it. Fifty million dollars. So much was about to change. "Yuling?" he said.

"Yes?"

These three months. Beijing in the sunrise, Stockholm and moonlight falling silver against water. Museums and shattered glass, Paris and street races in the glittering dark. It had all brought him here. "Thank you," he said. "For everything."

He could hear her smile over the phone. "Thank *you*. And if you ever need another job—"

Will laughed. "Goodbye, Yuling."

"Good luck, Will."

She hung up.

Will thought of the zodiac heads, of how this had all begun. *Why art?* he had been asked so many times. He thought of a studio at Harvard, of all that he still had to return to. Of what his life might look like after graduation. Art was many things, but in the end it was a question asked: *What do you want to be remembered for?*

At last, he had an answer.

63

DANIEL

Daniel Liang knocked on his father's hotel room door. The hallway was all muted colors, the flicker of electric lamps on steady, repetitive carpet patterns, and he shifted in place, nervous despite himself. He had one last thing to do before this was over.

The door opened.

"Ba," Daniel said.

His father was wearing glasses, the lines on his face more pronounced. "Come in," he said.

They sat at the table by the window. They were on the twentieth floor, and Daniel could see Manhattan covered in gauzy white clouds and falling snow, the skeletal, branching trees. A teapot rested between them, and Daniel poured jasmine tea first for his father, then for himself. The cups were already laid out, side by side.

"Did you know?" Daniel asked.

His dad took a slow sip, both his hands curling around the teacup. Wherever he went, he always brought his own set. "I knew enough," he said, and despite the precision of his Beijing accent, the words were soft. "And even if I didn't, my son called me to come home. I would always have come."

Daniel's gaze flickered down. "I'm sorry," he said.

"Don't be," his dad said. His dad was always surprising him. "What you've done—all of China will remember. The whole world will remember."

Already museums were starting to make changes. To return looted artifacts, but also to display the history of the art they had, to speak of conquest and war and all that had been taken by blood. After so long, it was a beginning. Still, Daniel looked up, met his dad's gaze.

"You aren't mad?" he asked.

His dad set his cup down. "You are my son. My only son, my closest family. My work is just my work. It is not my life."

Daniel could not look at him. "It always came first," he said, softly. "After—after Ma died. It was the job, and then it was me, and I felt like I had failed you."

"I know," he said, and Daniel remembered those first few years, how this country had been strange and inhospitable to them both. "It was my failure. I didn't know how to take care of you alone, how to speak of my own grief. And then, somehow, you were leaving for college, and we didn't know each other anymore."

Daniel didn't speak for a moment. All these years, both of them mourning, both of them alone. "I never wanted to hurt you," Daniel said, and the words were a confession. "Even when this began—it was with the story of the Old Summer Palace, of everything that you told me."

It was so hard to talk to each other after all this time. But Daniel's dad reached over, placed his hand over Daniel's. There were lines there, the veins blue and tracing beneath pale skin. His father had aged in these years.

They still had a long way to go. But neither of them moved for a long time, and when they did, it was to finish their tea, to brew another pot. They did not speak of the heists anymore. Everything else would come later. For now, it was just the two of them, the small, quiet moments in which they could find healing.

64

ALEX

They were released. It was a cold December morning, and Alex Huang ran her fingers along her wrist, feeling the space where her handcuffs had been just a few minutes ago. Irene stood next to her, her face tilted up toward the pale gray sky.

"We did it," Irene said. She turned to Alex, her smile quick. "Ten million dollars each."

"You don't know that yet," Alex said.

Irene arched a brow. "Bet you one million that the other museums will return their zodiac heads. How can they not, after all this?"

Irene had never been wrong before. Alex looked away, her gaze on the city and the falling snow. "What will you do next?" she asked.

"Anything," Irene said. "And you?"

Alex was silent for a moment, thinking. It had been a year since she had left MIT, a year since she had started working in Silicon Valley. "Start over," she said. Ten million dollars. Anything was possible.

"Tell me the truth," Irene said. "Did you think we were going to pull this off?"

"Yes," Alex said.

"From the beginning?"

The beginning had been an apartment in California, Will's voice on the phone. Or maybe it had been a Beijing penthouse, seeing Irene for the first time. "I needed something to hold on to," Alex said. All those months ago, it had been the only thing she was sure of. "Back then, I felt like I was drowning. If I didn't believe in this, I didn't have anything."

Now the future stretched out before her, bright and full of unexpected possibility. She looked at Irene, thought of those first few weeks, of Stockholm and an empty hotel room. "I hated you for a while," Alex said.

"I know," Irene said.

She was supposed to apologize for it, she knew. For all the ways they had hurt each other in these months. But Irene had hated her too. They had thought they knew each other from the very beginning, had been proven wrong every time.

Irene looked at her, held her gaze. "Do you still?"

Alex didn't know how to lie, how to tell the truth. She couldn't talk to Irene without feeling like she was preparing for a war she had already lost. "You're arrogant," she said, "and too used to getting your way. You act like—like the world is meant to bend to your will."

Irene was leaning against one of the Met's stone columns. The morning light touched her face—those high cheekbones, the curve of her red lips. The snow was still falling around them, and the FBI's black cars circled the building perimeter. *It is*, she might have said. When had Irene not gotten exactly what she wanted? Instead Irene lifted her gaze, looked at Alex. "That isn't an answer," she said.

Alex took a step closer. Slowly, deliberately, she brought her hand up, her fingers brushing against Irene's jaw. How many times had she dreamed of doing this? "I hate you," Alex whispered. From the beginning, Irene had been everything she could not be, everything she could not have.

Irene didn't flinch. Her skin was warm against Alex's hand. Her gaze was searching. "I don't think you do."

What else could we be?

Anything you want.

Alex moved her hand up, curled her fingers tight in Irene's dark hair. Alex should have been the one in control here, but Irene lifted her gaze, met Alex's like a challenge.

"I hate you," Alex repeated, as if this second time it might be true. Irene was beautiful, unattainable, and Alex had her hand in her hair, her back pressed against a stone column, and Irene did not look away, did not even flinch.

Her smile was sharp, pleased. "Then prove it."

Alex tightened her grip on Irene's hair, yanked her head forward. And then Alex was kissing her, and Irene was kissing her back, her hands tangling into Alex's hair, and the snow was falling and Irene was dragging her closer, her hips digging into Alex's, and she tasted like snow, like winter air, like this city that had always been hers.

Alex was wildly, joyously alive.

65

LILY

It went like this: Lily Wu at the start of summer, the Durham heat sticky against her skin. She ran her palm along the steering wheel, the glow of the stoplight red and fluorescent on her skin. It was the last race of the year. It didn't matter. There would be more to come.

So much had changed, and yet this was the same. The red Solo cups, the music steady as a pulse, the smell of night air and gasoline. She could have bought a new car, but there were some things she wanted to hold on to. Most of her ten million dollars had gone into an offshore bank account, set up by one of Yuling's assistants, with steady payments for her loans. And, of course, there was a trip to Paris this summer. Another one to Beijing.

The light changed, and Lily stepped on the gas. This was what she loved about racing. It was just her and the blur of her surroundings, the feel of the steering wheel beneath her palms, gas pedals and car systems and all these parts that might come together in a whole. Everything exactly where it was meant to be.

She won every race that night.

What came next: an internship at Microsoft, a new city to explore, and then, when August came, a flight to catch. Two weeks in China with her parents, in a city called Changsha, before onward to Beijing, to Paris, to her crew once more.

Lily remembered the first time she had seen China from the air. It had been vast, glittering, impossible. It had not felt like hers. How could it be when she knew so little about it, when she had never felt the pulse of its streets? But she had taken a Chinese class this semester, was learning what it was like to be proud of where she came from.

Galveston, China, all these places that were hers, by birth and by blood. They were not all she was, but they were a part of her. She would claim it at last.

When the night was over, when Lily was the last one left, she walked to her car. Will Chen was leaning against it, his profile all shadows and elegant light. When he saw her, his smile was slow, deliberate. "Lily Wu," he said. "It's been a while."

"You graduate in a week," she said. "I'm seeing you then."

"I wanted to see you earlier," he said.

She unlocked the car, slid into the driver's seat. Will took the passenger side, and she looked over at him, smiled. "Well?" she said. "Let's go."

The first time she had seen Will, it'd been her freshman year. It was strange to look at him now, to linger on the curve of his cheekbones, those eyes like a Galveston night. Her classes were done, her junior year over. The summer air tasted like a beginning, and she remembered Stockholm in the early fall, how it had felt something like that too.

In the car, the quiet dark, he took his hand, pressed his mouth to the inside of her wrist. So much had changed since the start of the school year.

The winter had passed quickly. The Met, that Chinatown apartment, the five of them scattering before Christmas came. They had families to get back to, lives to live. Still, there had been Zoom calls, weekend flights, ways to keep in touch. There would be no more heists. But there was Korean barbecue in LA to celebrate Daniel's first medical school acceptance, a Durham bar when Irene was elected student body president just days before her twenty-first birthday. There were road trips to Boston, music turned up and the windows rolled all the way down. There was Will painting in a Harvard studio, Lily working on a problem set as she waited for him to finish, the light falling soft and silver over them both. It had felt like home.

Cook Out was almost empty at this hour. Lily ordered two Cheerwine floats, fries that came out quick and hot. They ate on the hood of her car, and Lily looked over at Will.

"What are you thinking?" he asked her.

"How things change," she said, and it was true. She was thinking of Galveston and the darkness of its waves, how the moon looked when it was reflected against water. How it might feel to one day take Will there to see it too. After so long, she thought she might be done running away. "You?"

"The same," he said, and there was a smile in his voice. "Graduation. The summer. Everything before us."

"Are you afraid?" she asked. He had been once. She had been too. It meant so much to be the children of immigrants, to build on a legacy that spanned oceans, that had traveled lifetimes.

"Not anymore," he said.

Durham, that night, might have been just this. The two of them and a dark summer sky, the stars strewn above them. Fluorescent signs, the flash of distant cars, the world as it spun. Lily leaned her head on Will's shoulder. The future stretched before them, long and gleaming as an open road.

66

ALEX

The sun was setting in Silicon Valley. Alex Huang unwound packing tape, pulled it over a final cardboard box. She could have hired movers, but it was better like this, her windows open to the evening air, her apartment scored in red and gold. It was empty now, save for boxes labeled in stark black marker, a memory foam mattress pushed up against the wall. Alex leaned against the kitchen island, her elbows resting on cool marble.

Tomorrow she would leave this place behind. She would go home first. To New York, to Chinatown, the sticky heat of the city in summertime. There were restaurant renovations to do, family to visit. Her sister was applying to college this year, and Alex would have come home for that anyway, to walk her through the complicated process of going somewhere their parents had not been before.

After New York—

Her phone was ringing. It was Will, of course, because time was a circle, because beginnings and endings felt the same way. "If this is another heist," she said, picking up the phone, "I'm going to hang up on you."

"Alex," he said, his voice warm. "It's good to hear from you too."

Alex smiled. It had been almost a year since he had called her in this same apartment, with an offer he knew she wouldn't refuse. She had reached for her laptop, watched him on the black and white of the Sackler's security footage, seen the gleam of a jade tiger within his open palm. "Will," she said, "I would say it's been a while, but it hasn't."

He laughed. "Just making sure I'll still see you this weekend."

"For your graduation?" she asked. "I wouldn't miss it." It was true. She thought of Boston in the summer, the years she had spent at MIT. There were some things that were still unfinished.

"Good," he said. She could imagine him in his Harvard dorm room, his window open to the Charles River. "What will you do next? When summer ends and you're no longer needed at home?"

Once she wouldn't have been able to imagine it. Who was she if not her past, all these years of trying to bear its weight? Now she looked around this empty apartment, what she was leaving and what might remain. She thought of the days to come, a flight to New York and then another one to Boston. The Charles River, mirror bright; Quincy Market and all its sounds. She thought of the admissions office, the appointment she had made, what it might feel like to walk through MIT's doors once more. Alex knew she didn't need this—a diploma, a degree, all the things that society used to determine worth—but she wanted it anyway. She had traveled so far. She would finish this journey.

"Everything," she said. They had ten million dollars each. It was all possible.

Will laughed. "I believe it," he said, and she remembered a year ago, a smile in his voice as he said, *I didn't think there was anything you couldn't do.*

She walked to her room, did another sweep of the empty walls, the bare cabinets. After MIT, she might come back to Silicon Valley, figure out what her life could become. Start-ups, tech for good, something that *mattered.* "I started seeing a therapist," she said. This past year, alone in California, had almost broken her down. She was still in the process of building herself back up. "I figured—it might help."

Will didn't say anything for a long moment. And then, very softly, "Alex. I'm proud of you."

Tomorrow she would leave. This—working for a tech giant, writing code that meant nothing but more money for corporations that had too much already—had never been her dream. She had spent too long trying to shape herself to it anyway. Ahead of her was New York, Boston, all the ways her future might change. Alex thought of the sun rising in Chinatown, a girl and a love song, how, at long last, she would make this life her own.

"I'll see you soon," Alex said, and it was a promise.

67

DANIEL

Daniel Liang was boarding a flight. LAX was crowded, even on a Thursday night, the airport all fluorescent lights and faraway sounds. He scanned his boarding pass at the gate, walked through the tunnel and to the plane. He could have bought a first-class ticket, but old habits died hard, and he slid into a window seat near the back of the plane, pulled up the hood of his Stanford Med hoodie. He had a missed call from Irene, but he didn't call her back. He didn't need to. They would see each other soon enough.

Have you boarded? his dad texted him in Chinese. Will's parents and Daniel's dad would fly in tomorrow, all of them coming to Boston for Will's graduation.

Yes, Daniel replied.

Safe flight. I love you.

In Chinese, the characters were 我爱你. This language had always felt like truth.

Daniel hesitated, just for a moment. Then, before he could change his mind, he replied, 爱你. *Love you too.* It was the first time he had said it to his father.

His dad sent back a smiley face.

Daniel almost laughed.

Outside his window, fog hung low and heavy. This felt strikingly familiar—a plane flight, the distant sounds of conversation. Nearly a year ago, he had been on his way to Beijing, certain his life was about to change, not sure he wanted it to.

Now he was on another flight. Will would graduate this weekend, and Daniel would graduate in a few weeks more, when UCLA's spring quarter ended. Everything he knew, coming to an end.

He leaned his head against the window, the glass cool against his skin. This summer, he would go to Beijing again. He would see the Old Summer Palace, rising from the ruins, fulfill a promise he had made to Liu Siqi. He would sit around a table with family, his grandparents and his uncles and all those relatives who he seldom saw, and then, on a quiet, fog-wreathed morning, he and his father would make the trip to his mother's grave.

After all these years, he could recognize it as a gift. Beijing, this place of his childhood, had always had mountains and cityscapes, palaces and high, reaching skyscrapers. The past, the present, the future—it might have been a river, time tumbling over itself, stories that could be told and retold. Grief, healing, it was all possible.

When summer turned to fall, he would fly back. Back to California, to San Francisco, to the start of Stanford Med. For so long, the past had been a wound still open. Now he could run his finger along the mark those years had left. Scars were nothing but tissue, keratin, a reminder of what the body could endure.

The plane was taking off. Daniel looked out the window, at fog and smoke and summer night, and imagined his future unfolding.

68

IRENE

It was eleven in the morning, and Irene Chen was the first one to arrive. The dim sum place was in Boston Chinatown, and Irene leaned against its entrance, pulling out her phone to write an email. In a few weeks, she was supposed to be in New York City, surrounded by skyscrapers and other consulting interns, getting paid too much money to solve problems for wealthy corporations.

But she had ten million dollars in her bank account, and she was tired of doing things just because she could, because she knew she was supposed to. Irene had spent her whole life afraid to fail, afraid that any uncertainty might mean weakness.

She was not afraid anymore.

"I should've known you would be here before me," Daniel said. There was a smile in his voice.

Irene looked up. "Daniel," she said. In the morning light, his features were gentler than she was used to. Or perhaps it was just that he no longer held himself like he was prepared for hurt. "Right on time."

"What were you doing?" he asked.

She glanced at her phone, pressed *send*. "Quitting my internship."

He raised a brow. "What will you do instead?"

Alex would be in New York this summer. DC was not far at all—a train ride, nothing more. Enough time to answer emails, make calls, create this life she wanted. "Working for a political campaign," she said. Someday it would be her own. "You?"

"Going to Beijing," he said. "Want to come?"

Wang Yuling, Zhao Min, Liu Siqi, they were all there. Irene thought of power, how it might be inherited, how it might be held. Someday she might want to be there too, to know how it felt to hold your hand over the pulse of a country. But America was hers, just as much as China was, and she had things to do here still. "Another time," Irene said. She winked at him. "Give Siqi my best."

"You presume," Daniel said. He leaned against the wall next to her, face angled toward the sun. His profile was all sharp lines, ink that wound its way up his collarbone, just barely visible through the throat of his button-down.

"I do," Irene said. Still, she knew Daniel. She thought she might know Siqi too. "Am I wrong?"

Daniel's smile was quick. "Are you ever?"

⁓

The restaurant was loud, full of waitresses yelling in Cantonese, dim sum carts pushed precariously fast. It reminded Irene almost of Beijing, that semester she had spent there, how everyone always seemed like they had somewhere to go. Still, that morning they ate slowly, deliberately, savoring these last few hours before their parents landed, before Will had to start packing, before everything became real. Tomorrow her brother would graduate. The months, the years—had they always gone so fast?

Alex ordered for all of them, the table piled high with soup dumplings and fluffy white cha siu bao, egg tarts that glistened in the early-afternoon light. They drank pu'er tea, took turns pouring it for each other, talked loudly enough that the other patrons cast them glances. Irene, in another life, might have cared. Instead she flashed a brief, bright smile at the other tables before turning back to her own. Will made a toast, and then they were all making toasts, to things that got steadily more ridiculous, and if the FBI had been listening, they definitely would have been arrested for their talk of stolen art, of all that was right and good and moral in combating imperialism.

For the first time, Irene was not making plans for the future. Instead she laughed with them, made her toasts, caught her brother's eye. After all these years, the tension between them had finally been cut loose. It had been a lifetime of her measuring herself against him, of trying to be the one who did everything right. It was impossible, she knew. They were both going to fuck up. They were both going to survive it anyway.

And then, when they were finally kicked out of the restaurant, when the rest of their crew splintered off, it was just Irene and Alex. They walked along the Charles River, sat on a bench near the water. Irene looked at Alex. Alex's head was tilted up, toward the late-afternoon sun, and light slanted across her high cheekbones, the line of her throat and her jaw.

"What are you looking at?" Alex asked, her eyes closed.

Irene reached out, her fingers light against Alex's hair. She thought of an early morning in Stockholm, doing this same thing. This past year, these three heists, everything after and in between—she remembered the very beginning, how terrified she had been of change. How could she have seen this coming? There had been a time when she only knew who she was in comparison to her brother, when she had thought honesty could only be weakness. But Alex had always seen her exactly as she was.

"Let me tell you something true," Irene said, softly.

"What is it?"

Irene thought of seeing Alex for the first time, Beijing in the rising light. She had thought Alex was the kind of beautiful that felt dangerous, the exact right poison that made Irene want to tip her head back, drink her in. She would burn going down. "I never hated you."

"Really," Alex said.

"It's true," she said. Even then, that first day, Alex had felt more real than anything else in the world.

"You once called me a software engineer wasting your time," Alex said dryly.

Irene laughed. She could still remember it, that morning in Paris, the two of them in an empty alleyway. "I did," she conceded. For so long, she had thought it could have only been like that, the two of them with just their words as knives. Irene had always known how to wield them, how to hurt. There were so many ways this could have gone wrong, so many ways for this to go wrong still. In another time, she might have planned for it, left Alex before there was the possibility of hurt. *You have a mouth made for lies*, an ex-girlfriend had told her, and Irene had believed it.

Now she brushed her thumb against Alex's jaw, tipped her face to hers. "And yet," she said, softly, "my time is yours."

Alex smiled, then. They stayed there for a long time afterward, watching the sun move across the sky, the boats that traveled over the water. Irene thought of all that was to come. Senior year, everything after, a future that shone vast and infinite and full of possibility. In the summer air, it felt like truth.

69

WILL

Graduation was strange, dreamlike. Will didn't remember the graduation speaker, or the long, winding commencement address. He remembered only the heat of the Boston summer, how the air shimmered with it. He remembered early-morning graduation pictures with his college friends, throwing his cap up, and then more pictures with his crew, one arm slung over Irene and the other over Lily, looking at the photo after and thinking of how these, right here, were all the people he loved most in the world. He remembered walking across the stage at last, shaking his professor's hand, that brief moment when he looked out at the audience and thought, *This is it.* Four years, and he was leaving Harvard behind. Like this, it was not so terrifying.

And then, that afternoon, Will went to the Sackler. It was the first time he had been back since September, and as he stepped through the doors, he remembered the wail of alarms, the thieves who brushed past him. The card Wang Yuling had left behind. It felt like a lifetime ago.

He had asked his crew to come with him. They lingered at the entrance for a moment, and he turned to look at them. His sister, his con artist, who could solve every problem. Daniel, his best friend, headed to Stanford Med this fall. Alex, not quite a software engineer anymore, not quite a hacker, this girl who could pull off the impossible. She leaned over, said something to Irene, and his sister laughed. At last, he looked at Lily. She was looking at him, and he thought of street races and her smile in the fluorescent light, how he could draw her a thousand times and still find something new in the tilt of her head, the shine of her eyes. They had always dreamed of the same things. How to make this life their own, how to love a country that had never belonged to them.

"Why are we here?" Irene asked.

Will took a slow breath, let it out.

Why art history, Lily had asked him once, *and not art?*

It had been almost a year since Wang Yuling had broken into the Sackler, since his life had changed. He had graduated Harvard today, had left everything he knew behind. Some things were temporary. Art was not. Neither was this.

"Follow me," Will said, and he turned into the gallery. It was his first time at this newly opened exhibit, but the paintings on the clean white walls were familiar enough. Six months, four years, it had all brought him here, to a series framed in careful gold, the Old Masters redone. *Reclaiming History*, the description read. Below that was his name.

He had asked each of them to sit for him. He had not told them why. At the start, he was not sure he could pull it off, but now he walked around the room, took in the brushstrokes, the fall of pale violet light through the wide, wide windows. He had spent so many years studying Renaissance art, European styles that had never felt like his. He had claimed it here, had painted his friends, his family, in the style of Michelangelo, Raphael, Botticelli.

Once, he had thought diaspora was loss, longing, all the empty spaces in him filled with want. He could still remember standing before the Old Summer Palace, afraid of what it might mean to leave Harvard behind, who he would be without it. But diaspora was this, too: two cultures that could both be his, history that was waiting to be made.

Will waved a passing tour guide over, handed him his phone. Another college student, perhaps, dreaming of art. "Would you mind taking a picture of us?" Will asked. He smiled. He couldn't help it. "This is my exhibit."

They had taken so many pictures already. Still, his crew came together, in front of the description that bore his name, smiled wide for the camera in their lovely, formal clothes. His phone flashed once, blindingly bright, and it took a moment before the world came back. His friends, this art, this museum where it had all begun. There was more to come. A summer studio in New York City, artist residencies to apply for, all the dreams he still had to reach. But Will looked around, at this place he knew, his paintings and his crew and all they had done in the past year.

For the first time, it felt like enough.

ACKNOWLEDGMENTS

What a journey this has been. When I first started dreaming up this book, I was in my early twenties and living alone in New York City, and it felt so wildly, unrealistically self-indulgent to write an Asian American heist story, full of characters who could've been my college friends. Over the next several years, I moved cities, I started medical school, I thought back to the person I was at twenty-one. I visited family in China; I had plans to visit family in China fall through because of the pandemic. I finished writing this book. So much of me is within these pages—my love for art, my favorite *Fast & Furious* movies, my memories of China in the summer—and I feel deeply, deeply moved to be able to share this story with you. Thank you for reading, and thank you to all those who made this dream of mine possible.

To my agent, Hannah Fergesen: Thank you for being the first professional to believe in my words. It has been a long, tumultuous, wonderful road with you, and I'm grateful for every moment. You changed my life five years ago and you keep changing it now. To my editor, Amber Oliver: I knew from our very first conversation that you got the story I was trying to tell, and this book is sharper, brighter, and more honest because of you. Thank you for believing in this book and in me. Here's to many more stories together. To Phoebe Robinson and the entire Tiny

Reparations Books team: I don't know where to begin. It means so much to me that this book about identity, diaspora, and colonialism has a place on the Tiny Rep list. Publishing is a difficult industry and you all have made it feel easy. In particular, thank you to Christine Ball, John Parsley, Stephanie Cooper, Amanda Walker, Jamie Knapp, Isabel Dasilva, Lee Ann Pemberton, and Laura Corless for your work in bringing this story into the world. To Melissa Cox, my UK editor, and the entire team at Coronet: Thank you for giving this book about diaspora a home in the UK. Daphne Tonge and the Illumicrate team, what a gift it is to work with you. In addition, thanks to my film agent, Steve Fisher, and the wonderful Sugar23/Netflix team. I don't know what to say except that this entire journey has been beyond my wildest dreams. Ashley Zalta, Margaux Swerdloff, Camille Swersky, Tyler Erb, Tia Williams, Laura Delahaye, and Wendy Chuong, thank you for everything you have done so far to bring this book to TV.

My writer friends, near and far, and in particular all those of the Asian diaspora who have come on this journey with me. Marina Liu, you are the other half of my heart, my very first reader, and the only person to know the precise joy—and heartache—of balancing both publishing and medicine. Amélie Wen Zhao and Katie Zhao, thank you for lighting the way, for being my earliest and most enthusiastic readers, for writing the stories I wish I had growing up. Krystal Song, thank you for all the stories—and the desserts—we have shared together; it is my absolute joy to be debuting with you. Andrea Tang, I will read everything you ever write; you are a kind and generous reader, writer, and friend. Christina Li, here's to many more coffee dates on Stanford campus, and to all the stories to come. Roselle Lim, thank you for sharing your words with me and for believing in mine, and for that very first blurb. Jesse Sutanto, thank you for your guidance as I navigated the whirlwind that is Hollywood.

To Becca Mix, this book wouldn't exist without you and those weeks we spent swapping messy first drafts. Thank you for your wisdom, your sense of humor, your love. Sarah Underwood, the best thing Pitch Wars did was give me you. You are thoughtful, generous, and so very kind, and I am grateful for you every single day. Thank you both for being there for me every step of the way, for celebrating the highs and easing the lows. I can't wait to watch you two shine. To Alice Fanchiang, Morgan Al-Moor, Eunice Kim, Anna Bright, Chloe Gong, Daisy Hsu, Victoria Lee, Rebecca Kuang, and Jamie Pacton: Thank you for the gift of your friendship over these years. Ava Reid and Allison Saft: Palo Alto is a better place because the two of you are here. Ann Liang, thank you for seeing the heart of this book so clearly. Tigest Girma, thank you for loving this book from the start. And of course, to the Hannah client chat and the entire KT Lit family: Thank you for giving me a home in this industry.

A special thanks to my educators, professors, and mentors over the years, including Mrs. Connie Clark, Mr. George McKendree, Dr. Hunt Willard, Dr. Jenny Wood Crowley, Dr. Michael Gillespie, Dr. Katharine Dubois, and Dr. John Kugler. In addition, Dr. Christina Askounis taught me, gently and elegantly, how to write and revise short fiction, and Dr. Laurel Braitman has been a steady source of support and good humor as I navigate writing at Stanford and the publishing industry as a whole. Thank you also to the Angier B. Duke program at Duke University for the scholarship that changed the course of my life, and to the Stanford MedScholars Research Program for giving me the time and space to write, as well as believing that the humanities are a necessary component of a medical education. Thank you to the Cantor/Anderson Student Guides program for giving me a deeper insight into art and museums; I promise that despite this book I have no plans for art theft.

Writing this book involved a great deal of research; thank you to the many, many authors whose books I consulted on art crimes throughout history, and to all the Asian authors whose works taught me by example how to write about identity and diaspora. A special thanks to Weike

Wang, whose novel *Chemistry* was the very first time I saw myself in fiction; I am more myself because of your words. Thank you also to the heist movies and shows that have been so foundational to this book, including the *Ocean*'s movies, the *Fast & Furious* franchise, *Black Panther*, *CZ12*, *White Collar*, and *Leverage*. To the many reporters, journalists, and writers who have covered these real-life art thefts, and in particular Alex W. Palmer, from whom I also borrowed the title "The Great Chinese Art Heist," thank you for shining a light on the repatriation of looted Chinese art. And, of course, to the thieves behind all this: Let's chat.

My endless gratitude to my friends outside publishing, who have learned so much about this perplexing industry over the years. Sarah Nekoufar and Beylul Negassi, the very best teachers and the very best friends: I am thankful to Bronx Compass for many things, but most of all that it gave me the two of you. Brittany Wenger, we could spend every minute together and never grow tired of each other's company, and we have. Here's to New York, and all the memories we'll make there together. Emily Pang, you know all of me. Thank you for being the best roommate—and friend—that I could ask for. I can't imagine this medical journey without you. Alex Dao, thank you for giving me the ability to write about friends who feel like family. You were always going to be here.

Daniel Wu, I can write childhood best friends because of you. Brandon Choi, I still remember the evening we went to the Strand and you took me to the L section and said, *This is where you'll be*. Now it's your turn. To the Cameron Reasonables, thank you for making it possible for me to write about the Duke experience with so much honesty and so much happiness. In particular, thank you to Neil Patel, who was the first one to know that I had an offer of representation. Rishabh Jain and Kevin Shao, thank you for your friendship throughout those tumultuous high school years, and for all the growth we've shared since then. Thanks to my friends Jaleelah Abdulai, Santiago Sanchez, Antonia Chan,

Annabel Chen, Connor Phillips, and Katherine Yu. I am so grateful for our shared language of books. Thank you also to Sachi Chandiramani for all your graphic design expertise. And, always, thank you to Danny Oh for your steadfast support, your sense of humor, all the times you've stayed up to listen to me talk about stories. These are the moments that make up a life, and I am so glad to share them with you.

Finally, my family. My parents, Yi Li and Shixia Huang; my siblings, Sharon and Eric Li; my cousin Valerie Huang. What a joy it is to come home to you. Sharon, I am constantly learning from your bravery, your work ethic, your capacity for kindness. I'll admit it here, just once: You are the best kid. How lucky I am, that my sister is also my best friend. Eric, I never would have thought that my kid brother would grow up to be so wise, funny, and thoughtful. Thank you for designing my website, for fact-checking my Harvard references, and, most of all, for being my friend.

To my parents: I used to think because of how far you have traveled in this life, I had to do the same. But this is a story about growth, and I know now that all you have ever wanted was for me to live fully and happily. I promise to do my best. Thank you for your love, and for this perfect little piece of the American Dream. It is the greatest privilege of my life to be your daughter.

最后，我要感谢我在中国的亲人。爷爷李少清，奶奶陈素珍，大伯李林，大伯妈韩广平，小叔叔李勇，婶婶韦燕铭，姑姑李扬，姑父肖树，堂姐李楠，堂哥李柏，堂嫂韩梦雨，堂姐李雪微，表弟肖天翱和肖天翔。外公黄加谷（已去世），外婆李东秀（已去世），大舅舅黄益品，大舅妈周辉杰，大姨妈黄亮霞，大姨父任学高，二姨妈黄暑平，二姨父易国宁，小舅舅黄益武，小舅妈易群林，表姐黄慕云和任烨，表哥易律和易胜，表弟黄恒博。因为你们，我才能写出对中国文化的感情和认同。感谢你们让我回国有回家的感觉。

ABOUT THE AUTHOR

Grace D. Li is a medical student by day and writer by night. She grew up in Pearland, Texas, and is a graduate of Duke University, where she studied biology and creative writing. She currently attends Stanford University School of Medicine. *Portrait of a Thief* is her debut novel and is also in development at Netflix. Say hi on social media @gracedli or sign up for updates at www.gracedli.com.